Astral Fantasia

His Name Was Augustin
Book III

C.L. Carhart

ASTRAL FANTASIA

Book 3 of *His Name Was Augustin* series

ISBN: 978-1-954807-04-4 (paperback)

ISBN: 978-1-954807-05-1 (eBook)

https://www.clcarhart.com

Edited by Elizabeth Johnson

Cover Design © J. L. Wilson Designs | https://jlwilsondesigns.com

*For Liz
who told me years ago
that this series was worth publishing*

Other Books by C.L. Carhart

Arcane Gateway
His Name Was Augustin, Book I

Mystic Passage
His Name Was Augustin, Book II

Brief Pronunciation Guide

Augustin – Au-GUS-tin
Bayerisch – BEYE-rish (eye is pronounced like eyeball)
Bayern – BEYE-urn (eye is pronounced like eyeball)
Eihalbe – EYE-hahl-buh (eye is pronounced like eyeball)
Freia – FREYE-yuh (eye is pronounced like eyeball)
Isar – EE-zahr
Jarvis – YAR-viss
Muniche – MYOO-nih-khuh
None – Nohn
Swanhilde – Swan-HIL-duh
Thaden – TODD-n
Torstein – TOR-stein (stein is pronounced like a beer
    stein)
Toteheri – TOH-tuh-hare-ee
Wuotan – VOH-tahn

You can find a full pronunciation guide and translations at
the end of this book.

Table of Contents

Prologue

It took me a full week to pick up the pen again after I had finished with Book II of my story. The horrid memories of that wretched day descended upon me afresh as the words laid themselves out plain on paper. Part of me wished to cast the entire work into the fire, as if such a ridiculous emotional act could erase that indelible curse. But it remains with us still.

Eventually, I crept into the chamber once more in the dark of the night to return to the writing desk. I knew, as soon as I closed the wooden door behind me, that I was not alone in confronting the past again, although at first no light graced the walls save that of the intermittent flashes from the storm outside. But I could see Augustin's eyes glowing blue where he stood at the desk, bending over my work. The angles of his face appeared as though they had been chiseled from very dark granite, and his fists were clenched into tight balls.

I had somehow managed to avoid him that entire week, though such things are often difficult for me. I feared his reaction to where I had chosen to end Book II, for I suppose I could have ended it somewhere else, in some happy place. But happy places are hard to come by under the weight of the filial curse . . . so I steeled myself and came to his side, ready to speak some sort of defense, an apology.

A long moment passed in silence. As I stood centimeters from Augustin, trying to discern his mood in the darkness, lightning crashed outside the window and a nearby candlestick burst into blue flames in the same instant. He turned to glower at me, his black robes sweeping the floor, his jaw working in furious agony, his fiery blue eyes burning me to ash. I felt his anger churning in the air between us, along with his eternal betrayal. I stared back at him wordlessly, my mouth going completely dry. I saw tears welling in his eyes, trickling down his cheeks to splash upon the stone floor beneath us.

"I . . . I *had* to write it." My voice barely escaped my lips, a frigid whisper of wind, tears coming to my eyes at the sight of Augustin's pain. "It's . . . it . . . it happened." I could hardly speak. He glared at me as though I were one of Wuotan's sirens, risen up from the abyss to taunt him. "I couldn't ignore it." I gave him a pleading look, a request for mercy, for understanding, for forgiveness.

He said nothing, but his anger gradually evaporated. His posture relaxed and his eyes averted from mine to the storm outside the window. I drew in a shaky breath and stepped forward uncertainly to retrieve a new sheet of parchment and inkwell. I set them onto the desk in front of the stool, to the right of that vile stack of papers that comprised Book II. When I sat down upon the stool and reached for the pen, Augustin screamed suddenly, his cry echoing the thunder, seeming to rend the stones holding the room together from their mortar. The blue flames of the candlestick flared brightly at their master's anguish. He stomped harshly toward the door, away from me.

"This isn't the end," I reminded Augustin as he flounced from the room, but I doubt he heard me. And when I lowered my gaze to the blank paper before me, a pair of tears loosed themselves from my eyes as I considered the future . . . .

Chapter One:
Pulled from the Mire

I do not know how long I lay prone upon the decaying leaves and needles, the rain soaking me through, grime caking my fingers and staining my dress and hair. The full weight of what I had done had dragged me into dejection. As I wept icy tears, I knew that in spite of my efforts I would never see Augustin again. He was a Black Priest now, a Cursed One, an outcast, forever forbidden to enter Teuton lands. No city would welcome him; no one would offer him acceptance. He would never again walk the streets of Muniche in the mortal world or in spiritual form. He would be forced to crawl on his knees before Wuotan himself, facing the fate of eternal damnation, the very deal he had made for the sake of my life and Joel's. His name would be erased from all writings, burnt from the records, ignored in Teuton history, cursed for all of time.

And I would never stop loving him, for I had preserved our bond.

Many thoughts churned in my mind while I groaned in torment on that rainy afternoon, not giving a thought or care to the passing of time, to how drenched my body had become. For a while I wished that I had never come to the eleventh century in the first place. Everything I had planned to do in the past had gone completely haywire, from that first half hour when I had watched my cousin die before my eyes. I had arrived twenty years too early, lost the Torstein due to my own inattention, killed a Gypsy, befriended the most hated man in Muniche, ignored the potential of love with a decent man, forsaken him for a wretch, a demon-worshipper, a devil, a rapist, a sadist, a curse . . . .

At some point, a horrible realization hit me. Perhaps if I had *not* used the Torstein, perhaps if I had stayed in the twenty-first century where I belonged . . . maybe Augustin would never have been cursed. It had all come about because he had taught *me* forbidden secrets; it was all a result of my foolish curiosity. If I had not come, someone else could have stepped in and taught him a better way, someone from his time, someone with a pure and virtuous outlook. Perhaps his cruel heart could have softened and he could have forgiven the Prince one day. *And then . . . ? Maybe if Augustin had not been cursed, Muniche would not have fallen . . . .*

I wanted to die. I wanted to just lie there in the dirt until death sent me back where I belonged. I had written myself into history whether I liked it or not, since my inquisitiveness had cursed the one man in the Bayern family who seemed to have common sense, the one who undoubtedly could have held the Saxons back. I had ruined everything. I had corrupted my people's future . . . I had spoiled all hopes of their recovery . . . .

Suddenly, something yanked me from the ground with the intensity of fire, forcing me to confront reality again. I staggered for a moment, my eyes darting around the deepening shadows of the forest, seeing the rain pouring from the sky though I no longer felt it. Confusion took hold of me as I turned my gaze upon the River Isar. Its choppy currents lapped at my bare feet, which, I noticed, resembled sculptures of ice. Frowning, I looked down at myself and saw that I no longer wore my dirt-stained light pink dress. Now, dismal robes of grayish green enveloped my body, their dull hue matching the waters of the river. And when

I circled around to face the trees, my eyes widened at the sight of Augustin standing beneath a lowering birch, its branches sagging with wet leaves. He wore the vibrant cerulean of the spiritual realm, and he was glaring at me.

"If you continue to lie that way in the rain, you shall unquestionably make yourself sick, Swanhilde." His tone sounded coarse, and he jerked his head toward the forest behind him.

I was too busy having a heart attack at his unexpected appearance to notice anything but the magnificence of his spirit. "Oh . . . Augustin . . . ." I gasped, stretching my arms out toward him. I ran to where he stood—and found myself clutching the birch tree while he stepped gracefully aside.

"You cannot touch me here, Swanhilde," he reminded me as I backed away from the tree in consternation. "We are in the spiritual dream world, for you have wept yourself into an agitated slumber."

An instant later, I found myself standing before a crumpled woman curled into a ball on the forest floor, her dress in tatters, her hair muddy, her face a mere shadow of my own. Her eyes were squeezed shut, and she moaned plaintively in her slumber. I sensed Augustin's presence behind me as I stared blankly at my mortal body, disgusted by its revolting appearance. "You should not torment yourself over me, my darling," Augustin whispered in my ear, his concern flowing into my spirit. "You are going to become ill, and I cannot restore your health from a distance."

"But it's my fault this happened," I confessed to him, lifting my gaze to my lover's gorgeous spirit. "I was thinking about everything before I fell asleep. And I realized that the Prince may not have cursed you at all if it hadn't been for my idiocy at Joel's blood-transfer. I should never have come to the eleventh century, because if I hadn't . . . maybe you could have fought the Saxons in 1066 instead of being banished . . . and maybe our people wouldn't have fallen. It's all my fault." My sorrow burst out from my spirit, and I turned away from Augustin in shame. I trod down to the banks of the Isar and summoned its waters to merge with my feet, swirling my dull robes around me.

"My darling, I told you once before that you must not think in those terms," Augustin reproved me. He walked onto the river himself to eye me seriously as my tumultuous thoughts threatened to pull me deeper into depression. "What became of me today had nothing to do with you. The Prince would have discovered the particulars of the filial curse eventually. I have committed more than enough sins to warrant this awful punishment."

I shook my head at his words, my guilt infusing my spirit with weariness. Augustin sighed and stepped close to me, lifting his right hand to trace it slowly down my face, though his fingers passed through my form. "Come sit down with me and hear the truth. You must not blame yourself for this, and if you insist upon doing so, I shall force you to heed my advice." His mouth quirked into a sly smile. He slipped his right hand beneath his fiery robes to touch my heart with a degree of reproach, a wordless reminder of the power he held over me. Then he led me to the riverbank and gestured that I should sit upon him, though our spirits could not touch in our spiritual dream.

I obeyed him without speaking, my heart still steeped in melancholy. The fact that I appeared to crush his legs when my spirit sat down did not improve my mood. He requested that I meet his eyes, and when I did so he began to speak softly, his smoldering blue eyes gazing into mine with a depth that rivaled the ocean.

"Swanhilde, my love, for one who travels time, you have the tendency to view major events within the bounds of a small box. You must not make assumptions about your place in history, in the past or the future. Our paths are laid down by our Creator, and He knows every choice we shall make, right or wrong. I have become convinced that our destinies cannot be altered through the use of the Prince's song or the Torstein or through any other means. Seeing the future in your blood has persuaded me forever.

"You must not assign the faults of 1066 to your account, for they have already been inscribed upon the currents of time. What difference could it have made if I had not been cursed and could have fought alongside the Prince for the preservation of our people? The Saxons shall still have the song and shall still raise an invincible army, whether I am there to scorch them or not. It is not given to us to know the future, for although you have traveled to the past, you have no inkling of what may happen upon your return to the twenty-first century. Perhaps that is where the true change shall occur, for you shall return as one who has seen events not meant for your eyes. Perhaps you shall be the one to pull our people from the mire one thousand years in the future."

The possibilities of this proposition grabbed hold of me while I stared into Augustin's earnest eyes, bringing light into my thoughts afresh. "But what could one woman do to change the future?" I wondered, shaking my head at the enormity of such a suggestion. "I don't know what I *could* do to get the Teutons of my era to reclaim the glory they lost in the past. No one cares about that sort of thing in my time. Most people would rather just immerse themselves in mainstream culture." I frowned a bit as something else occurred to me. "What our people *should* have done was to rise up after the Saxon conquest and take Bavaria back. But I haven't read much on the centuries directly after our defeat. Few Teuton writings were set down in those days due to the scattering of our people."

"Then perhaps we should both resolve to do what we can, following the failure of 1066." Augustin's eyes glimmered and a wraith-like smile stretched across his face. "Perhaps with my new . . . position . . . I could bargain with Wuotan more freely and convince him to use me as a scourge against the Saxons. I do not know, for as yet I have no concept of the extent of this curse."

Augustin fell silent, his smile darkening into a grimace. He looked down at his right arm, its skin hidden beneath his sapphire robes. "I fear that I may be damned to hell, Swanie . . . but what can be done?" He drew his sleeve back and there, to my chagrin, I saw a jet-black scar about ten centimeters long upon the forearm of his spirit, the mark of the Cursed Priest.

I ordered myself not to back away, to remain seated upon his lap, to view the scar calmly, without fear. "It still means nothing to me. There is always hope, Augustin."

He unrolled his sleeve to hide the mark from both of us and eyed me scathingly. "You should stop calling me that."

I shook my head, smiling in spite of his fierce expression. "You will always be Augustin von Bayern to me."

He growled and slid himself out from under me, folding his arms as he brought his knees up to his chest. "And you once seemed so respectful of Teuton traditions. Now listen to your blasphemy, refusing to acknowledge the first Black Priest in nine centuries for what he is. It is no wonder you were destined for this misery, doomed to watch our people fall, to lose your mother at so young an age, to yearn for a fiery old man, to forever love a Cursed Priest, one who will ultimately come to despise your goodness. And I was fated to be cursed, yes . . . fated to lose my name, my family, my blood . . . fated to stand by and watch while my city falls, unable to help, unable to interfere. Fated to lose everything I ever had . . . everything I ever wanted."

"Everything but me," I finished quietly, unwilling to allow him to wallow in despondency himself.

He stared balefully at me, rising to his feet and reaching his right hand into his fiery robes to retrieve my beating heart from where it rested at his breast. I climbed to my feet as well, a hint of triumph rushing through me when I looked at my heart, held once more in its master's hands. "How could you have done such a thing?" Augustin whispered, his gaze riveted upon my heart. His right hand grasped it tightly, and he raised the index fingers of his left hand to stroke it in wonder.

I closed my eyes to concentrate on the security of our bond, the gentleness of his touch, the devotion that poured from his spirit into mine. "Because I love you," I whispered back, a contented smile gracing my lips. "I couldn't let you go . . . no matter what they did . . . no matter what *you* did. I love you too much . . . and I can't live without you."

"And that love shall become your torment." Augustin's expression twisted into anguish when he placed my heart beneath his robes. Lifting his eyes to mine, he said flatly, "I shall rip you to shreds, my darling, for Wuotan does not recognize love, only hatred. He shall cause me to forget, induce me to treat you as my slave, not as my beloved. And our destinies must part ways for twenty-one years, never to touch again, a permanent separation."

The truth of this clawed at my spirit, but I pushed it aside and asserted with a mad confidence, "But you will always be mine."

"That remains to be seen, Swanhilde." Augustin's face grew caustic, and he cast his gaze back toward the trees. "Now you must awaken, and I must continue my journey, an exile until someone grants me asylum."

I knew that he would force me to awaken; but before he could, I grabbed at his left arm, my fingers finding no purchase. "But we'll meet again here." My spirit trembled with silent longing.

Augustin smiled at me, a half-hearted curl of his lips. "I shall be the specter in your dreams, my swan princess." He leaned down to kiss my hair, and a moment later, I opened my eyes to the dirt and rain and leaves, my entire body soaked through and coated with mud. I heard Jarvis' voice calling in the distance, somewhere in the misty forest. So I lifted myself from the ground, brushing the strands of wet hair away from my face, and gathered all of my strength to face the broken shards of my destiny.

Chapter Two:
Gloom of Loss

Count von Meldorf's bailiff found me in the clearing soon afterward, his expression hued with distress at the sight of my haggard appearance. He wore a rather hefty overcoat complete with a hood that protected him from the rain. He swung it off of his body and flung it upon me without a word as he gathered me into his arms. Murmuring a few comforting phrases in my ear, he carried me through the trees to the place where he had tied his horse. He set me carefully atop the horse and leapt into the saddle, snapping the reins without further ado. I locked my arms around his waist as the sky above grew dark, the clouds occasionally rippling with lightning bolts that seemed to reflect themselves in Jarvis' eyes.

During the short trip home, I began to ponder what exactly I needed to say to Freia, how much I should tell her . . . how much I should tell the count . . . how much I should tell Joel. My entire world had fallen apart in that tempestuous day, and now I would have to pull myself together and accept the dull future that awaited me. I would have to marry Joel even though I did not love him, for I knew that my erotic night with Augustin may bring unwanted consequences. I had once marveled at the possibility of bearing Augustin's children, but now the mere concept scared me to death. He would not be there to protect me in childbirth, and any of his offspring would claim an extraordinarily high level of Teuton blood.

Weakness had descended upon my sopping body by the time we reached the manor, and I knew that I would end up ill before the next morning. Though I had hoped to avoid the archaic strictures of medieval medicine, I could not evade sickness indefinitely. The thought of leeches crawling on my skin made my stomach twist, but at least I could postpone my confessions until a later date. I hoped that my ridiculous panic connected with doctors would keep itself under wraps.

Jarvis carried me inside after giving the horse to the stable hand. Freia and Ulka met us at the threshold to the kitchen, and Jarvis summarily passed me off to them. They led me to a corner of the kitchen where a steaming bath had already been prepared, their kind hands helping me undress and climb into the tub. When I immersed my body beneath the hot water, resting my head against the edge of the tub, a wash of gratitude warmed my chest. I would not lose Freia's friendship, and the count's servants were all so helpful and understanding, never prying into my business. One day they would all be under my charge, if the count kept his word now that Joel had Teuton blood. Maybe this new destiny would not be so bad.

Late that night, as Freia pressed a damp cloth to my forehead to ease my fever, I related the entire story of what had taken place in the forest earlier that day. When I told her how empty I had felt after Augustin had severed our heart-bond, I began to cry softly, a weak, choking sound. Freia soothed me then, murmuring that I needed rest and should not think of such things now. She put a glass of wine to my lips and urged me to sleep. But before I heeded her wishes, I managed to tell her that I had restored the bond myself through the strength of my love; thus I would forever claim the privilege of meeting Augustin in my dreams. I ruminated on the triumph I had felt after that fateful moment as I drifted off to sleep. And I knew that no matter what hardships may come upon me in the next two decades, my love for Augustin would never fade, despite the filial curse.

When I awoke Monday morning, Freia brought me a tray of toast and milk and said that the count had called one of the city doctors on my behalf. That knowledge did little to improve my failing health, for I started seeing black insects starkly in my mind, creeping insidiously up my arms. *You have to keep your cool when the doctor shows up no matter what your panic tells you,* I ordered myself. *Just count silently in Latin or recite the Lord's Prayer while he's doing his dirty deeds. It's not like he can hook you up to any tubes.*

Once I had finished picking at the victuals on the tray, I gestured for my best friend to take the remnants back downstairs. The moment Freia left the room, I gathered what little strength I had within me and focused with difficulty on my ice, channeling it into my sickened veins to heal my burns from two nights prior and lower my body temperature. The effort rendered me almost breathless. The particles of ice seemed to stab the linings of my veins, their medicinal power hamstrung by the fever. When Freia returned to our bedroom, I calmed my ice once more, feeling slightly thankful for once that my element was not fire.

The doctor appeared at my bedside shortly after I had consumed a small bowl of soup for lunch. He was the same elderly hunchback who had attended Freia during her illness when we first arrived at the Meldorf estate the previous summer. He introduced himself politely as Dr. Greunke, his appearance reminding me of a bearded Dr. Jekyll. I said nothing while he took my pulse, felt my forehead, and looked into my eyes and ears. I spent that time concentrating on breathing steadily, my distrust of doctors shackled firmly within.

The elderly man eyed me in speculation when he concluded his assessment, asking me what I had eaten that day and whether I had slept well the night before. I replied as honestly as I could—leaving out the nightmares that had plagued me in my sleep, apparitions of a devilish Prince dragging my lover into hell. Then, to my consternation, Dr. Greunke announced that I ought to stop messing with my element while my body was in such a weakened state.

I blinked at his admonition, taken completely off guard. Freia said that she had not seen me do such things recently, but the doctor rejoined, "Oh, she has, my lady, for she is ice. Its blue tints her gray eyes even now, clinging to her veins. Lady Swanhilde, you must not push your body to such limits during your illness, for your element does not have the strength to cure you. It can relieve your fever for a short time only. Fighting physical ailments with supernatural gifts rarely meets with success." He glared at me while he spoke, his own eyes appearing slightly beige as he pawed around in his medical bag.

My opinion of Dr. Greunke went from bad to worse at his scathing advice. Apparently he could not care less that he was using his own element here and now, mixing herbs together in a jar. His taupe-tinted eyes suggested that he must be some type of earth; that had doubtless enhanced his talents with herbs and remedies over the years. He handed me some sort of thick concoction in a pewter cup while I stewed silently about his counsel, ordering me to drink it in full. It tasted awful and I could hardly choke it down, even though he had mixed it with honey.

After I had managed to swallow the potion, the doctor retrieved a sleek leech from his bag, saying that he needed to extract just a bit of my feverish blood. My anxiety shot through the roof, and I pressed my left hand upon my now sprinting heart. I cringed away from him when he took hold of my right arm and pushed up the sleeve of my nightgown. "Can't you just use a knife?" My voice sounded far too frail to suggest any sort of threat to his intentions. My chest had begun to tighten, but I forced my lungs to breathe deeply, beating against my panic.

Dr. Greunke frowned at me, and Freia came to his side. "Medical bleeding is traditionally done with leeches, Lady Swanhilde," he told me, "for the use of a knife would result in unnecessary wounds as well as tainted bed sheets. Just relax now, and you will feel no pain."

He held my arm firmly while I recoiled. Every fine hair upon my flesh stood as straight as a telephone pole. My disgust abruptly surmounted my weakness as I watched him bring the insect ever closer to my skin. "Use a knife, or I'll freeze my arm before that parasite can find purchase there." The order shot from my lips, and a veil of blue sharpened my vision. My blood exploded with ice, cooling my fever anew.

The doctor ogled me, his gray-bearded jaw working in frustration at the sight of my element's vitality. His elderly fingers transformed into solid earth where they gripped my forearm, and my skin took on a crystal sheen in response. Freia took a step back, her mouth agape. Dr. Greunke huffed in aggravation. "Can your element hold this madwoman still so I can finish my work?" he asked Freia, his stony fingers tightening on my arm.

Freia's green eyes widened. "I . . . I don't know . . . Doctor Greunke. I am light . . . I don't think I could . . . defeat her." Her frightened eyes averted from the doctor's face to mine, her expression clearly stating that she had no idea *how* to use her light against me or anyone else. I concentrated hard on my element while the doctor huffed again, ordering my strength not to wane, though my fever fought to reclaim my body.

"I doubt I could emerge victorious against such acute resolution without poisoning her first." Dr. Greunke frowned at me severely, then let go of my arm and put the leech back inside his bag. I did not relax my ice, for I feared that if I allowed my skin to soften once more, he might infuse my veins with some sort of plant solution to render me unconscious. But in the next moment, he drew a shiny knife from his bag, wielding it like an expert surgeon. "I shall do as you ask, my lady, though you will have to heal the wound yourself and ask the maids to bring you clean sheets. Relax now, that I may bleed you."

My lips parted into a weak smile, and I shut my eyes and drew my ice back into my spirit. The fever took hold of me again when the doctor tied a cord around my upper arm and sliced a vein. Drowsiness tugged at my sagging vitality as my blood poured upon a cloth Dr. Greunke had placed beneath my arm, and I moaned quietly, struggling to cling to awareness. At last, I heard him murmur in my ear, "Sleep now, Lady Swanhilde, for I was joking with you. Of course I can stop the flow from your veins, for I am a doctor and a Teuton. You need not fear." The last sensation I registered before falling into unconsciousness was that of a moist rag pressed upon my wound, the withered hands of Dr. Greunke holding it firm.

The next time I awoke, I found myself alone in the bedroom. The fading light of day outside the window suggested that Freia likely sat at dinner in the great hall, giving the count an update on my health. I still felt weak and feverish, my sweaty skin sticking rather maddeningly to my linen nightdress. The room was stuffy, and though I knew that I should not expend the effort to use my ice until my body had begun to recover, I wanted relief. The heat of early June seemed to chain me to my bed.

As my eyes drifted slowly toward the window and the darkening sky, the events of the previous day filtered back into my mind. I abruptly remembered that other duty that the filial curse required—the destruction of all records that betrayed the existence of the Cursed One. I wondered whether the Prince and his cronies had managed to finish that yet, whether they had stormed the archives and cast every document Augustin had ever filed into the fire. Curiosity overtook me and I knew that I had to find out, even if the exertion made me sicker. I glanced around the room once more, assuring myself of its emptiness. Then I closed my eyes and summoned the full power of my ice, freezing my body completely against the raging fever, thrusting my spirit free.

I glanced down at my robes when my spirit appeared in the atmosphere, noting that they appeared translucent, probably due to my earlier attempt to freeze myself solid against the actions of the Teuton doctor. A strange frailty seemed to taint my every movement as I took a few steps in the twilight, my gaze shifting from the manor below to the walls of Muniche a short distance to the west. The lungs of my spirit expelled one heavy breath, and I imagined myself in the archives, willing myself to leave the air and return to earth, to see the treachery that must come to pass. I suspected that my sickness would not allow me to remain in the spiritual realm for long. My fever could melt my icy protection, like that time when Augustin had threatened my spirit with his fire. So I gathered all of my tenacity to cling to my element as the landscape around me coalesced into the cellar of Muniche's town hall, tall shelves rising in my peripheral vision.

In the center of the room, right beneath the chandelier, a massive iron cauldron sat upon the stone floor. Virile red flames that matched the flickering candles above leapt out of it. Several men clad in monks' attire drifted from shelf to shelf, sorting through countless papers and scrolls, a mound of incriminating documents heaping ever higher on the floor beside the cauldron. My eyes widened, and I drifted toward the far end of the archives where Augustin's writing desk once stood. There, I saw one of the priests of energy from the council ripping the wood apart, his superhuman strength evident in his sparking eyes. My eyebrows came together as I wondered why they would need to rip his very *desk* to shreds . . . and a second later, the door to the archives burst open. Heat blistered through the room as Prince Otto marched inside with his brother Paulus trailing behind.

I stepped into the shadows, ordering the robes of my spirit to darken, to match the midnight color of the Isar just outside the city walls. Although I knew that the men in this room should not notice me, I clothed myself in caution. I stood between two of the shelves with my back to the priest of energy, watching the Prince confront a middle-aged man who bent over a heap of papers stacked upon another desk. "What progress?" the Prince snapped, his deep red eyes looking furious.

The man behind the desk bowed once. "The monks have sorted through four rows of shelves comprising the birth and death records, as well as some of the judicial records and the chronicles documenting recent Teutonic rituals, *Leitaeri*. Unfortunately, it appears that the Cursed One has left his mark on quite a few official writings. It may take weeks to finish this task."

The Prince hurled a curse, his hands hardening into fists. "Tomorrow, bring all of the literate monks down here, along with the other city chronicler and any officials who have no pressing business to attend. Paulus, that includes you." The Prince spun to face his older brother, his eyes smoldering. "All of you are to scour each and every shelf, burning any unnecessary parchment that bears his name, blotting the important ones with indelible ink. I shall come down here myself tomorrow evening to ensure that things are progressing efficiently."

When the Prince finished his harangue, one of the monks dumped the mountain of papers that had lain upon the floor onto the writing desk. Prince Otto's glowing eyes locked on the pile, and he leveled an accusing finger at the stack. "What is this?"

The middle-aged chronicler bowed again, his face looking slightly fearful at the Prince's anger. "Those are the records that cannot be burnt, *Leitaeri*, but that bear the Cursed One's initials. Unfortunately, much of what we have found thus far cannot be discarded. It is slowing us down, I'm afraid."

The Prince's lips curled back from his teeth, and he snatched one of the papers into his hand, holding it up to the red light from the chandelier. "Archived by A.v.B." He swore, his fingers leaving burn marks upon the document as he threw it back upon the desk with the words, "Carry on."

I drew back further into the shadows when the Prince turned on his heels to stride across the floor to where the priest from the council had finished breaking Augustin's desk. "Throw that into the fire, Rupert," the Prince commanded, his crimson eyes meeting his comrade's sparking ones. "All memory of that bastard's existence must be erased." The priest of energy bowed, scooping up shards of wood from the floor and carrying them to the flaming cauldron.

I sank my fingers into the shelf at my side, my sickened spirit overwhelmed by the acrimony that hung in the room. The scarlet glow from the cauldron and the candles made the dusty archives appear to be a chamber of hell, Prince Otto the demon lord who stalked here and there, glorying in the torment of his prisoners. This was terrible. I should not have come to see this. They would never rip away my own memories of my master, no matter what. He would live forever within my soul, within my heart... Augustin Abelard Ulrich von Bayern . . . the misunderstood child . . . the voracious learner . . . the devoted lover.

Rupert returned to the corner to collect more splinters of my master's desk, and I saw the Prince kick at a few bound tomes that lay discarded nearby. "Those I found in a pile upon the Cursed One's desk, *Leitaeri*," Rupert informed the Prince in a guarded tone. "It appears that the wraith grew curious about his fate before you thrust it upon him."

The Prince scowled. I recognized several of the historical books Augustin had retrieved Saturday afternoon lying on the stones of the floor. My mind shot back to that small record I had found, titled *Forbidden Sacraments* in Latin, chock full of intriguing headings and subtitles . . . . And my mouth dropped open as I recalled the one title that had prompted me to pause in my search: *The Bending of Time*.

I slipped out from between the shelves, trying to slide my spirit forward to fully observe the pile of books on the floor without brushing up against the Prince or the other priest. My ice-tinted eyes focused on that small volume, poised atop its counterparts. I considered for a fleeting moment what the men might think if it suddenly started floating away, but the Prince snatched it up himself. A sigh of longing escaped my lips as he flipped through its contents brusquely. A second later, Rupert came to the Prince's side and muttered in his ear, "Did the chronicler tell you about our . . . problem?" He jerked his head toward the paper-laden desk.

"We already have a multitude of problems here. What is it now?"

"We can't find his birth certificate." Rupert's face looked stricken, and the Prince's eyes grew an even darker red. "We searched the entire box from 1018. Nothing, but every other record was sorted perfectly."

"And he came down here Saturday afternoon to look through these horrid books." The Prince growled in fury. "He must have taken it. *Damn him!*" he spat.

A triumphant shriek escaped my lips at this revelation. Augustin was always a step ahead of that pompous Prince. To my horror, both Rupert and Prince Otto jerked as though they had been poked with something the moment I squealed. The Prince whirled to face me, his bloody eyes boring into the shelf at my back. I drifted between the shelves and sank to the floor in an attempt to avoid the Prince's piercing eyes that could likely have transcended the bounds of earth. He sneered at the books separating us and handed the manuscript detailing demonic Teutonic rituals to his comrade with the command, "Burn this one."

NO! The cry burst forth from my mind before I could stifle it.

"Do it quickly." Prince Otto shoved Rupert toward the center of the archives. "I think there is someone here." He glared in my direction.

I heard Rupert say something in response, but I was too busy freaking out to catch the words. I zoomed to the opposite end of the shelf, watching the book that could have spelled my way home perish in flames. I screamed again, my failure driving me to my knees—and in the next instant, I heard the distinct sound of a fiery cyclone, a new spirit cracking the spiritual realm. Fear seized me, and I smothered my ice inside, back to that weakened shell of my body lying upon my bed. And I knew then that I would have to wait twenty-one years before returning home.

Chapter Three

An Equal Partner

My activities in the spiritual realm on Monday evening drained my weakened body to a mere shell. Freia spent that entire night keeping vigil at my bedside, likely fearing that I might die. The greater part of me wished to die that night and most of the day on Tuesday, for the sight of Augustin's scholarly work laid to ash plunged me into a boggy morass of depression. I would have embraced death, had it come for me on Tuesday. Augustin would not have been able to stop me, for he was too far away. I could have laid aside my foolish escapades in the past and focused on my own era, a time bereft of heartless Princes.

But I was trapped in the eleventh century now, in an insane delusion. Now I would have to dust myself off and find out whether Count von Meldorf planned to allow Joel and me to inherit his land. I knew I would never truly love Joel despite his new Teuton blood, but I would have to build a legacy with him anyway, a name that could lay itself down in the records of my people. Joel would come to visit me on Saturday afternoon and stay for the whole weekend, as before; and I would welcome him, congratulate him on the success of his blood-transfer, teach him more about our people, plan for the next two decades.

While we faced the trials of the medieval world together, in a dark corner of my mind I would silently pray for sleep to take me, so I might meet with my Black Priest in secret. I should have let Augustin break the bond on the day of the curse. I knew that, but I would have to live with my snap decision, my moment of insanity. I would feel him in my heart and love him in my dreams, sharing memories, secrets, knowledge—and I would insist, though he would never believe me, that hope yet remained for him.

My fever broke on Wednesday, and I managed to make my way downstairs to the front parlor, where I sat for most of the afternoon. Freia settled herself into a chair opposite the couch where I reclined, her hands hard at work knitting a pair of stockings from a fresh batch of wool. The vassals had just finished cleaning it a few days earlier, she said, and she had snatched a portion for our use from the three young servant girls just that morning. "Emilie and Felda insisted that they could knit our socks themselves, but I don't want to get out of practice," she said with a smile as her slim fingers worked the knitting needles like witches' wands. "I'm sure I'll have a fair amount of sewing to do once I join Heinrich's household."

"He proposed?" I asked, looking toward where she sat. That was news to me. Happiness swelled within me as Freia's cheeks flushed.

"He did, on Saturday at dinner," she disclosed, her eyebrows crinkled a little, as though she feared to celebrate too greatly when all of my plans had screeched to a halt on that same night. "We're going to wait until August or September, because he wants to lay down money for a cottage across the street from the ironworks." Freia and I exchanged speculation on her future as the new Denlinger matron; we even tossed around some potential baby names. My best friend's element showed on her face as a result of her joy. At least she would gain the happily ever after she deserved.

Count von Meldorf came to speak with me shortly before dinner was served at Vespers. I had nearly drifted off to sleep as Freia sang a soft Rhenisch tune, but our host's authoritative voice aroused me from my reverie. "My Lady Swanhilde, it is good to see you here in the parlor," he greeted from the direction of the staircase. "I had feared that I would have to rethink my legacy once again."

I shoved myself into an upright position on the couch, invoking just a trace of my element to counter my frailty. The count stood paces from me, a farmer's cap set upon his white hair; I saw that his pants were soiled from the day's work. Maybe he had helped shear the sheep today. "A little fever isn't going to kill me," I said with a wavering smile. "Is it your intention to grant your land to me and to Joel Hudson, now that he has Teuton blood?" I worked to keep from wincing at the topic as I met the count's gaze.

His wizened face took on a look of sympathy. "Your travel companion spoke with me about that subject last night at dinner. I gave an ambiguous reply, since I was unsure of your opinion on the matter."

I felt as though a spotlight shone upon me, baring my heart's depravity for the count and Freia to see. But he already knew of my interest in Augustin. My eyes traveled toward the entrance to the vestibule. "Well, my other suitor has been exiled, so I don't really have a choice anymore," I admitted, blinking back the tears that threatened to well in my eyes. I paused to clear my throat, then said, "Joel has been hoping to build a home with me in Muniche for a while now, actually. He's a good man, and his family has experience with managing land. I can't spurn him now that he's a Teuton by blood alone." I glanced toward Freia. She had pursed her lips, her green eyes noticeably moist.

"Well, then I shall inform him of my intentions when he arrives on Saturday afternoon." Count von Meldorf looked as though he pitied me, but I knew that he would not pry. Instead, he shifted his cap a bit and looked toward the doorway to the great hall and kitchen beyond. "There is another issue that requires your assistance, my lady, if you have the strength enough to follow me to the pantry."

Freia and I walked together in the count's wake, passing through the great hall, where a fair number of house servants had gathered in preparation for the evening meal. I heard the bells for Vespers pealing out in the distance, but a number of whispers and side eyes caught my attention. Freia moved closer to my right side as if to shield me from the servants' notice. "You'll probably want to eat upstairs again this evening," she murmured in my ear, "because the topic of your lover's punishment has been the primary source of gossip lately."

"They'll have to keep their grumbling to themselves once I'm mistress of this estate," I muttered back, trying to keep my head on straight for whatever issue the count had in store. We entered the kitchen, where it became apparent that salad, wheat bread, and eggs were on the menu that night. I saw Wigge, the head cook, fishing boiled eggs from a pot one by one. His daughter was at work adding final radishes to the large dish of salad, while his son carried a stack of bread slabs into the great hall. All three of them nodded at the count as he passed through, but Wigge looked pointedly aside when I tried to meet his gaze.

My lips twitched, and I turned my attention back to the count, who had paused in the doorway to the pantry. "On Sunday night, an elderly commoner came to the front door after Compline, carrying all of his worldly goods in a bundle," he informed me, his hands on his hips. "He could not make himself understood to any of the servants or to me. He was not drunk, but his Teutonica is terrible. The only words we comprehended were 'service,' 'master,' 'forgive,' and your name." The count raised an eyebrow at me. "He has crouched in a corner of the pantry ever since, his hands clutching a letter that apparently belongs to you."

I blinked at my host, confusion wrinkling my brow. He beckoned me into the pantry, and moments later I found myself staring down at a wrinkled old man with wild gray hair and frightened eyes, his face somewhat scruffy, his gray tunic and pants common but clean. My mouth fell open, for I recognized the man immediately in spite of the low light. "*Viktor?*" I gasped his name, and he crumpled onto the floor at my feet.

I stooped to his level as he lifted his eyes to mine, and his lips trembled as he fought to make himself understood. "Lady . . . Lady . . . Swanhilde . . . . Master . . . my master . . . service." He proffered a folded sheet of parchment.

I reached to take the paper from him, my ice having veiled my vision in blue. My hands shook when I held it up to the light of a candle Count von Meldorf had retrieved. When I read Augustin's request, frigid tears leaked from my eyes.

My darling love Swanhilde von Thaden,

I do beg your apology for this burden that I must place upon you, in light of the countless trials you shall shoulder for eternity on my account. I could not take my servant Viktor with me in my exile, for he must not share my fate. Due to the suddenness of the destiny that came upon me, I had no time to find him suitable asylum; thus, I beg that you consider taking him in at the Meldorf estate. He will perform any sort of labor you ask of him, and though his Teutonica is poor, his spirit is patient and industrious. Please see to it that he is not cast into the gutter as a result of my sins. I am forever in your debt for this favor, and I thank you in advance, for I know that you will heed my entreaty.

Forever your cursed lover,
Lord Augustin Abelard Ulrich von Bayern
P.S.—That marks the final time I shall write that name freely, without stigma. It is yours eternally as a memoriam to my devotion. I love you.

When I finished reading, my icy tears creating slippery droplets upon the stone floor, I nodded, folding the paper into my hand, and addressed the count. "His name is Viktor, and he's willing to do any sort of work we require.

He must stay here, at my responsibility. Jarvis can find him a place to sleep."

Count von Meldorf's lips parted as he looked from me to the commoner who cowered at my side. A look of respect passed over his countenance, and he ducked his head at me as though he were a servant himself. "Very well, Lady Swanhilde. He can take Otfried's place, since his health has confined him to his room." I smiled and said that would be an excellent idea, since Otfried had taken care of small tasks around the house along with greeting guests who came by night. I asked Wigge to bring Viktor something to eat before Freia and I returned to our bedroom to share a meal apart from those who wished to babble about me.

Joel met me on the count's porch on Saturday afternoon, having eaten lunch at the ironworks and borrowed a horse for the journey. He had cleaned himself up rather impressively; he wore deep brown pants with a dark blue tunic, and his beard and hair were freshly trimmed, all traces of grime removed from his face and arms. I instantly suspected that he intended to propose at some point that day, so I gathered my courage and pasted a smile across my face as he beckoned me to walk with him through the front gardens.

We made small talk for a few minutes, for I hesitated to broach the important subjects myself. He told a yarn about his youngest roommate who had lost a bet recently and had to drink goat's milk from the teat as retribution. "The goat started flailing, and now the boy's got a knot on his head the size of a goose egg," Joel related with a cackle as we strolled through a variety of flowers. "He missed a day and a half of work."

"Hopefully that knocked some sense into him," I said, rolling my eyes at the collective foolishness of young men. Joel ran one hand across a stalk of lavender; its flavorful blooms had garnished quite a few recent meals. My American partner looked rather uncertain, his hazel eyes fixed on the road, away from me. Eventually we seated ourselves on the stone bench amid the roses, and I busied myself with inhaling their fragrant perfumes, awkwardness creeping its way into my gut.

"Well," Joel began at length, running a hand through his blond hair, his eyes on a small knot of horsemen heading up the road toward the city, "I have to admit, you were right about the blood-transfer, Swanie. That was *the* worst thing I've ever experienced, worse than when I broke my leg playing soccer in high school, worse than all of the brawls I've gotten into with my coworkers. I honestly thought I was going to *die*." His body shuddered, and he turned his wide eyes to my face.

I shivered myself, attempting to push aside thoughts of Wuotan's demonic voice, his power thrusting me toward the gates of time. "It's the most dangerous Teutonic ritual," I recounted, knowing that no words could ever suffice its torture. "Putting one's spirit into the charge of a demon is not a simple matter. We're both extremely lucky that we survived."

"Yeah." Joel's eyes grew troubled, and he poked his chest with the fingers of his left hand. "I look like I went through some sort of perverted heart surgery. I *used* to be a decent-looking guy, but now I look like I got sacrificed by Satanists." His mouth curled into a wry smile as he peered down the neckline of his tunic.

I snickered at his attempt to find a humorous side to the blood-transfer. "One always pays a price to become a Teuton, especially one of high blood." My ice lightly cooled my blood at the subject, and I looked toward the crimson roses decking the bush to my right. I saw the burning blood washing over me, consuming me, and I clasped my hands in my lap to keep them from shaking.

"You know the weirdest thing?" Joel went on, his voice wavering with what sounded like longing. "There was this one part where I think the pain had driven me nuts, because it faded away, and I could hear you calling my name. You sounded terrified."

I took a deep breath and closed my eyes as I tried to decide whether I should tell Joel the truth. *Yeah, you listened to Wuotan's temptations and left the river too soon. Then Augustin and I had to rescue you, and it cost him his name.* "I might have called out your name a few times while the Prince was mashing your arteries in the bowl," I lied, my whole body quaking. "I got sick before he finished with the ritual. I guess I'm a silly woman who gets grossed out by blood."

Joel slipped his right arm around me and drew me against his chest. "Don't worry about it, Swanie. I'm still amazed that you and Freia did it too. By the way, according to the Prince, my Teuton blood is ninety-*six* percent, just like you two!" He touched his lips to my forehead, and I sighed softly, ordering myself to relax, to allow this decent Teuton man to court me. I could not think of anything to say in response to his declaration. My heart pattered in an unsteady fashion, a sensation of betrayal crawling up my spine, gradually superseding the awkwardness.

"Apparently, Heinrich was ninety-six before he did the blood-transfer for me, and he's somewhat proud of the fact that he's ninety-seven now," Joel said after a moment. "I guess I got shorted, since my blood could have become as Teutonic as his, but I'm just glad the whole thing worked. I feel different already, knowing that I'm a Teuton, the same as you, the same as everybody here. I feel like I honestly *belong* in Muniche, as weird as that sounds."

I pulled away just enough to smile at him, a twinge of regret gnawing at my bones at his newfound oneness with my people. I knew he hoped that I would love him more, now that he could truly claim equality with me. But he could never have my heart, for it belonged to someone else forever. I congratulated Joel anyway and informed him of the count's plans. A brilliant smile appeared beneath his blond beard, and he took my left hand in his, squeezing it with the assertion that we were bound to become the most prosperous lord and lady in Muniche. "So have you figured out what element you are?" I asked before he could fully distract himself with speculations on our future.

Joel's expression grew pouty. "Yeah, according to Heinrich, I'm wind. That's kind of boring, in my opinion. It's not much of a superpower. What am I supposed to do with *wind?*" He scowled and released my hand to scratch at his beard.

A vivid memory flashed into my mind at his discontent: Augustin's fiery blue hands reaching in vain for Joel's dying spirit . . . his horrified exclamation, *Swanie, he is wind!* I shook my head, trying to clear it, remembering that the late Lady Muniche in my time had also been wind. She had not felt slighted by her element. I thought back to all that she had taught my friends and me about it.

"Wind isn't so bad, Joel," I reassured him, reaching out cautiously to touch his face, turning it to mine. "Just think about how well you'll be able to dance once you've learned the proper use of your element. You'll be flying all over the place with little to no effort. And if you learn fighting techniques, you could blow enemies away in a tornado or even burn or freeze them, if you can alter the temperature of your wind. If some sort of cyclone threatens the crops here, you could hold it back. And hey, once you get *really* good at it, you could create a permanent breeze in the house during the summer, like having an air conditioner without using electricity."

Joel gawked at me while I rattled off the possibilities of wind, his hazel eyes glowing with excitement once more. "Wow, that actually doesn't sound so bad. I'm going to have to practice with the temperature thing. My roommate Arik is air, so he should be able to give me a few pointers."

I mentioned a few useful factoids about ice—how I often used it to chill my drinks and the water that Freia and I used to wash each morning. I told him that it was easier to invoke my ice in the winter, but that I could use any old stream—or even the rain—to reinforce my vigor. "Maybe the two of us will be good farmers even though neither of us is earth," he mused. "I can make sure the crops have proper air, and you can water them if we have a drought."

Shortly thereafter, Joel stood up from the bench and blathered some nonsense about it not being the twenty-first century and that time was slipping away from us, especially if we wanted to learn all we could from Count von Meldorf before he entered eternity. I felt my body growing stiff, and then Joel dropped to his knees before me and inquired in perfect Teutonica, "My lovely Lady Swanhilde Rolande von Thaden, would you do me the honor of marrying me, a foolish Teuton novice?" His expression looked frightened, as though he feared that I would say no. In his right hand, to my astonishment, he held a diamond ring.

My mouth went dry at the sight of the ring, my mind struggling to discern how exactly he had managed to acquire such an expensive trinket as a common metalworker. "Where did you *get* that?" I gasped.

"From Heinrich's mother. It belonged to one of her sisters. She gave it to me as a gift, to welcome me into the Teuton tribe." Joel smiled bashfully, and I shook my head, marveling at the sunlight sparkling off of the jewel. My thoughts turned back to his proposal. I shifted my gaze to Joel's face and asked him how many times he had practiced the correct phrase in Teutonica. "I asked Heinrich how to say it perfectly and with grace, in hopes of winning your hand as a noble lord should." He tilted his head at me hopefully, awaiting my response.

So I forced back all of my misgivings and threw my arms around him, "*Yes,* Joel, I'll marry you." He hugged me in return, then climbed to his feet to set the diamond on the ring finger of my right hand, in German tradition. Afterward, he wrapped his arms around me again and we kissed for a long moment. I sensed his wind reaching out to my Teutonic spirit, but my ice remained dormant within.

"I think we ought to marry before the harvests," Joel said as we walked back to the house hand-in-hand, "so we can work together to sell the crops. I asked Heinrich about Teutonic customs regarding weddings, and he says that Teutons usually marry in the church and in some sort of mystical ritual."

I nodded, remembering Ina's wedding back home. "In Germany, people marry at the registry office, like at the American justice of the peace," I told him. "Those who are religious also marry in the church, and Teutons who still hold tradition in high status will have a Teutonic wedding with a Teuton priest presiding." A frown creased my forehead. The only Teuton priest I really counted as my friend in this era had been banished.

"That's easy enough. Aric passed his initiation into the Teutonic priesthood back in May. I can ask him to officiate our wedding." Joel grinned and added, "Ours will be the first wedding he's ever conducted."

That was not a pleasant thought. "Well, he'd better not stab our hands in the wrong place at the conclusion of the ceremony," I mentioned. Before Joel could comment, I added, "But I'm sure he'll do it right."

"I think you're going to have to tell me everything about the ceremony," Joel said, sounding a bit disturbed. "I didn't know it had anything to do with knives. I guess I shouldn't be surprised. Teutons and blood."

I snickered and, when we ascended the steps to the porch, I said, "How about we have our Teutonic wedding two weeks from today, on June 29th? Once that one's done, our people will consider us married, so we should probably get it over with before bothering with the frills of a church wedding."

"Good point." Joel paused at the threshold to the front door. "June 29th?" he repeated, turning back to meet my gaze. I nodded once, and he kissed me again before we entered the manor.

Chapter Four

A Ponderous Fate

During the next two weeks, the Meldorf manor hummed with a flurry of activity, preparing for the weddings of the count's unofficial granddaughters. Freia and I spent many hours sorting through quite a few goods that our host bequeathed to us as wedding gifts. Heinrich and Freia decided to wait until August to get married, since they had more arrangements to make beforehand; Heinrich was in the process of negotiating a transfer of goods in exchange for the cottage across from his business.

Since Joel and I would be living at the Meldorf estate, I had fewer responsibilities to finish before our marriage. I spent quite a bit of time preparing a spare room downstairs for our use. The servant girls helped Freia and me sew fresh outfits for ourselves and our fiancés. Their youthful exuberance about our weddings was contagious, and I often found myself joining them in their work as a buffer against the doubts that plagued my heart.

After discussing wedding options as a group in the great hall one Sunday evening, the four of us decided to hold a double wedding at Muniche's cathedral. That way, neither the count nor the Denlinger family would have to spend excessive amounts of money to impress the nobility. We would combine our forces and our currency, and get all of the stress of a wedding over with at once. We set the date for our church nuptials for the final day of the Oktoberfest, a Saturday. Freia and I worked with Ulka and Jarvis on lists of food, drinks, flowers, and decorations necessary for the reception, which we planned to hold at the Meldorf estate. I noted at one point that maybe some of the wedding guests would choose to simply remain in the city and enjoy the Oktoberfest rather than travel all the way to the manor. Freia chuckled and admitted that it might make everything cheaper.

I made several trips to Muniche as June progressed, purchasing fabrics and other materials necessary for my wedding with Joel. Teutonic tradition required that following the ritual wedding—which would be held at the meeting place in the forest—the newlyweds should ride together to a secluded section of the woodland for their first night of marriage. I had read of this practice in *Der Weg Teutonisch* many years before, and I knew that even in the modern era, some Teuton couples still went camping for the first part of their honeymoon. Thus, on the Wednesday before my wedding, I rode to Muniche to buy proper equipment for such a venture, including a well-made bow and a quiver of arrows so that Joel could hunt for game. Per tradition, he would be expected to prepare a meal for me after the first night of our marriage, to demonstrate his skills as a provider for his family.

I turned the count's tan mare toward the eastern gate as the bells tolled for None, having met with success in my shopping and enjoyed a decent lunch with Joel. On my way back to the manor, I rode down the street where Augustin had once lived for the first time since that fateful Sunday. To my dismay, I saw that his cottage had been burnt to the ground, all traces of it completely gone save a pile of dusty ash. Tears welled in my eyes, but I urged the mare onward, ordering myself not to stop and wallow in sorrow at the glory I had lost. I knew that Prince Otto had been the one to destroy Augustin's cottage, and he had likely stolen everything my master had left behind to bolster his own hoard of possessions. I wondered if he had burnt all of Augustin's secret writings. If so, quite a mass of knowledge had been lost.

I realized, as the mare clopped across the wooden drawbridge, that I had not seen Augustin in my dreams since that first day when he pulled me from my stupor on the forest floor. I had sensed his hands upon my heart occasionally, his touch less passionate than before. I began to wonder whether the curse would ultimately provoke him to leave me, to forsake me for Wuotan and the shallow pleasures that his sirens offered. Augustin had promised to be the specter in my dreams, but now uncertainty at his absence darkened my attempts at optimism. I would marry Joel in three days' time. While the count's household rejoiced at my good fortune, my heart wailed inside of me.

When I awoke on Thursday morning after a night of inadequate sleep, I answered Freia's greeting in a mumble and made my way to the chamber pot. I caught the odor of blood as I crouched down, and I began to chew on my bottom lip as my bladder emptied itself. I looked toward my roommate, already clothed for the day, pinning her blond hair beneath a brilliant blue cloth that matched her summer dress. *Today is the day,* I told myself again, the same mantra I had repeated since my urine had remained clean on Sunday. My cycle had matched Freia's for many months now; we bled every twenty-nine days, exactly.

But when I dabbed my crotch with the clean end of our rag, I saw no trace of menstrual blood, just the dampness of regular urine. I stood in a half-crouch with my left hand clutching the skirt of my nightdress above my waist, and my right hand holding a linen rag that had betrayed me for five days now. There was no escaping it. I was pregnant with Augustin's child.

"Still nothing?" Freia's soft voice broke through my haze of denial. I raised my eyes to her face and saw a look of pained sympathy.

Sobs attacked me out of nowhere, and I collapsed in Freia's arms. "He got . . . me . . . preg . . . nant . . . ." I choked, clinging to my best friend as she drew me gently toward my bed, helping me sit down. "It's . . . Augus . . . tin's child . . . and I . . . and he . . . I can't . . . I can't do this . . . ."

Freia held me against her chest and smoothed my hair as I cried, all of my doubts spilling forth in an unimpeded flood. I was carrying the child of a man with nearly perfect Teuton blood, and my blood was ninety-six percent now. The chances of me having a successful pregnancy were slim to none, especially since my own mother had died in childbirth. The one who could have protected me was far away, exiled, damned. And I was about to marry a stupid American, a Teuton novice. This was not how my days in the eleventh century were supposed to go.

"I can't do this, Freia. I can't," I declared once my sobs had subsided. I wiped my eyes and nose on my nightdress, traces of ice mingling with the liquid. "I need to pack up and leave, find where Augustin has gone. I don't love Joel . . . and what will my cousin think when we return? What if Joel makes me have his kids? I can't do this. I have to go and find Augustin. I have to go today." Resolve sent a burst of stamina into my veins, and I leaped up and staggered toward our wardrobe.

"Swanie, please." Freia appeared beside me within seconds, and my hands landed on the reddish-violet dress I had made in the twenty-first century. I yanked it from the wardrobe and shook out its accompanying head covering. Freia touched my shoulders, her element imparting a hint of caution to my agitated spirit. "Swanie, just breathe. You shouldn't run off without telling the count first. Breathe."

She had a point; my hands had started shaking as they clutched the dress. My roommate began to massage my shoulders, her comforting voice bringing me gradually out of my frenzy. I should not strike out to seek Augustin alone, for I may encounter dangers that could threaten me despite my elemental advantage. We did not know in which direction he had gone when he departed Muniche. It would prove fruitless to search for a man whose fate had been granted to our demon overlord; we knew not what Wuotan may have required from him already.

"I know you don't love Joel, but he may be your best option at this point," Freia reminded me while I stood with my eyes closed, trying to still my racing heart. "Remember your duty to hold the secrets of the future. The two of you would be better off shouldering those together. And the count will see to it that you'll be set up for life, as long as you remain here."

"I know you're right," I murmured at last, slipping away from her to lay my dress down onto my bed. "It's just hard to take, knowing that I'll be lying to him for the next twenty years. I hate being a hypocrite, but now I'm being forced into it anyway." I peeled my nightdress off and cast it aside, my lips parting in a frustrated sigh. "Everything's such a mess."

"It is for now," Freia said while I dressed myself for the day, "but don't ever lose hope. God works in mysterious ways." I gave a soft snort at that, thinking that God certainly did not want me in a relationship with an unrepentant sinner. This arrangement with Joel was probably divine recompense for my own folly.

That night I dreamed that I walked the shores of the stream, its dark waters lit by the gibbous moon and stars above. When I caught sight of a gorgeous demon clothed in resplendent cerulean emerging from behind the cherry tree, my heart and mind immediately left the slumber of serenity, coming swiftly back to the dream-world of the spirit. Augustin advanced slowly toward me while I stood frozen at the edge of the stream, its waters caressing my bare feet. My breathing sped at the sight of him, for I had begun to fear that he would never return. His fiery blue eyes glowed with anguish and regret when he reached my side, lifting his left hand to trace it down my face while his right tenderly fondled my yearning heart. I imagined that I could feel his fingers upon my face, though I could not, and I heard him say in a voice as quiet as the night, "My darling swan . . . how deeply I have missed you."

My spirit shivered at the passion in his words, emanating from his fingers, seeping into my heart on the strength of our bond. When I answered him, the words left my lips like a whispering wind. "I was afraid . . . that you would never . . . come back to me . . . ." I stared into his smoldering eyes, sensing the heat of his fire radiating into my icy spirit, reassuring me.

Augustin sighed, his countenance darkening. "I shall always come back to you, Swanie, though I likely should torment you no longer, after what I have been forced to do during the past few weeks." He frowned and dropped his hand from my face, averting his gaze to the trees across the stream.

His internal suffering pierced my spirit as I watched him stare bleakly into the distance, his robes glowing a gloomier blue, his visage dimming into shadow. I knew that something dreadful had happened to him as a result of the filial curse, something he had wanted to hide from me during our weeks of separation. But our mutual love had brought him back to me, and now his pain would be my own. I would have to infuse him with some of my hope, no matter what became of him.

I moved to stand before him, indicating that he should sit with me upon the grassy bank. He followed me without protest, his entire being sagging as though he rued the topics that we were about to discuss. "Augustin, tell me," I whispered when he sat at my side, close enough that I could have felt his arm against mine, had we met in the mortal world, "tell me all of your troubles, so I may soothe your pain. You mustn't hide from me, fearing that your damnation will extinguish my love. Our bond is too strong to be severed by the filial curse." I gazed at him earnestly.

A cynical smile crossed his face at my words, and he looked away from me again. "You know not what you do, Swanhilde," he said, his tone mordant. "If you continue to cling to me, the first Cursed One in nine hundred years, I shall pull you to hell with me, though I would not intend it. Neither of us knew the extent of the curse—*no one* knew the extent of the curse, not even that wretched murderer, or he would not have dared to level it upon me. It is far worse than I imagined, and I know not what shall become of me. I walk the path of darkness now, unable to turn aside until the day I finally perish in eternal fire."

I recalled the things that Hans had told me about the filial curse that day in the gazebo, my mind zeroing in on the most fearsome gift of the Black Priests: the ability to kill with the mind. I wondered if Wuotan had granted that power to Augustin yet. What would it mean for us if he had? Hans had called it an uncontrollable gift. Did that mean that Augustin may accidentally kill me if I made him angry, even though we were separated by great distance? I pushed my fear aside and voiced a valid question while my master glared at the water before us. "Have you found a place to stay?"

Augustin shook his head once. "I am camped in the far reaches of the Alps, where the ground is yet coated with snow in the heat of summer. I have found a suitable cave, shelter for my horse and what few possessions I managed to bring with me in my banishment. I know not how long I shall remain there, although I have found it difficult in recent days to convince myself to rise from the ground. I stare blankly into the blue flames of my fire pit as nature pulses around me, oblivious to my degeneration."

I tilted my head at him, wishing that he would look at me instead of glowering at the stream as though he wanted to transform it into a fiery river. "So are you sleeping now, in order to meet me here?" I asked, curious.

"Yes." Augustin's mouth twisted into a horrific scowl. "It would be better for both of us if I could shirk sleep permanently, but I could no longer avoid you. You should have let me break the bond when we had the chance, Swanhilde." He turned to face me at last, his eyes cindering me. "But no, you had to embrace insanity when I set your heart free. You had to attempt suicide, leaving me no choice but to reform the bond before your heart and soul reunited in heaven. You realize, my foolish darling, that what you did would have truly killed you, for the body cannot live without the heart. You would not have returned to the future. You would have gone straight to the gates of heaven." He glared at me as though I should have known that from the beginning.

My mouth dropped open at the implications of this. "Are you *serious?*" Augustin nodded harshly, and confusion crept into my mind. "But according to the writings . . . the only method of certain death for time travelers is ritual suicide. Throwing my spiritual heart to the ground is totally different . . . is it *possible?*"

"You must remember, Swanie, that the secrets of the song and the Torstein have been well guarded throughout our history," Augustin said, likely recalling the many truths he had seen in my blood. "I highly doubt that either method of bending time has met with frequent use over the ages, and thus, no one would know the complete list of ways to die while in the past."

"Then how can you be sure I would have died?" I asked, not convinced.

Augustin's jaw worked in passion. He pulled my heart from his robes, the fingers of his right hand enclosing it, his fiery eyes glittering as he stared at its throbbing life. "When you did that inane act, I saw the murderer clawing your spirit from behind, dragging you back to your body, believing that the break had been finished at my closing words." My master paused, his grip tightening on my heart. "What the murderer did not realize is that the bond of the Teutons is not fully severed until the body and spirit reunite on earth . . . or until the dying one enters the gates of eternity. I had no intention of departing the spiritual realm until the other priests had pulled you back to earth. And when I saw you rip your heart from your chest and cast it down through the expanse of sky . . . ."

Augustin's voice broke, and his spirit shivered with horror. After a short silence, he tore his gaze away from my heart to look into my eyes, dedication and fixation pouring simultaneously into my spirit. "I *knew* that it would kill you, for in that moment, the heart of your soul and your mortal heart were one, awaiting the final severance of our bond at your spirit's return to your body. I saw a vision—"

My own passion awakened at his fervor. "I saw visions too," I interrupted, "every memory we ever made together, from the first dance to the last thing you said to me in private, when I walked out of your bedroom that Sunday morning: *You will always be everything to me.*" I shivered once, remembering the sorrow that had washed over me at the thought of our eternal separation. "That was what drove me insane, Augustin. I loved you too much to let you go, no matter what the Prince did, no matter what *you* did. I had no idea how to cling to our bond, but I resolved to do it . . . and when I feared that I had failed . . . all I wanted was death."

Augustin placed my heart beneath his robes once more and reached out to trace his fingers across my lips, our spirits passing through one another. "And you would have found that death, my darling love, for you knew not what you did. As your precious heart plunged toward the ground, I watched your soul *die*, as though it happened before my very eyes. I saw you slip into eternity, your love vanished from my heart, your trust permanently gone, your goodness no longer holding me back from evil. I could not lose you, Swanhilde; I had to catch your heart before it could break and cancel your life. Though now, considering what has become of me in recent days, it would have been far better for you had I allowed you to die then, quickly, painlessly . . . rather than chain your heart to a condemned Black Priest, a wraith who will destroy you."

The intensity of his words and glower frightened me anew, but I ordered myself to be strong. "Tell me what happened to you . . . Augustin," I requested again.

Augustin took a deep breath, wrapping both of his arms around his spirit as though to shield himself from his fate. He trained his eyes once more upon the waters before us and began to speak. "In light of what little information your blood held on the filial curse, and what scant explanation you discovered in that small book in the archives, I suppose I should have prepared myself for the worst. But I had no concept of the meaning of what the murderer did to me . . . until two weeks ago, when I came to that place in the mountains.

"During the days of heathenry, there were two levels to the Teutonic Priesthood of Wuotan," Augustin informed me, still not meeting my eyes. "Those priests of the present era would be considered the first level, the ones trained in history and ritual, the ones skilled in the simple Teutonic powers over blood and elements. I learned two weeks ago that there was another level to the ancient priesthood, a deeper level at which ties with humanity were broken, a level rampant with mystical gifts and knowledge, a level that few Teuton priests ever reached due to the consequences of complete familiarity with the demon overlord of our people."

Augustin paused, a vampirical smile creeping across his lips as he clarified, "Those four original Cursed Ones from the second century were enslaved by Wuotan after the Teutons had cast them out, forced to become his cohorts for all of eternity, thrust into the deeper level of the heathen priesthood. Wuotan requires to this day that at least one Teuton priest be called his timeless servant. When our people renounced him and claimed Christ as their God, he transformed the four rebellious priests into his demonic legion, his final influence over the Teuton people who had forsaken him. They are his consorts in hell to this day, brought back occasionally to torment the living."

I blinked when Augustin paused, my mind struggling to wrap itself around the idea of a degenerate priesthood bound eternally to Wuotan, separated from the decency of humanity yet forced to walk among them. The wretched truth hit me then and there that Augustin was the *first* Teuton priest to have survived the filial curse since the second century. My voice went out of me, and my lips trembled as I tried to say something, *anything* to deny the ghastly reality that had descended upon this tranquil night. But my master began to speak once more, his fiery gaze turned toward the spires of Muniche in the distance, his face marred by lines of rage and treachery.

"Fourteen nights ago, death came to me in the cave, dragging me from my shelter into the cold air at the mountain peak, beneath the waning moon and the glow of a thousand stars. I found myself meeting the fierce glare of an apparition who at first glance appeared to be a devil. He was clothed in faded black, his robes ragged, his bony feet bare upon the snow, his black eyes sparking with dark energy. He nodded gravely at me and introduced himself as Anubis."

I started in surprise, my mind shifting from my people's traditions to what little I knew about ancient Egypt. "Anubis is the Egyptian god of the dead," I said, wondering how he could possibly fit into dark Teutonic lore.

"Yes, and the ghoul had chosen an apt name for himself." Augustin grimaced. "He proceeded to tell me what I just told you, about the two levels of the ancient priesthood. He informed me rather grimly that I was the first Teuton priest with cursed blood in over nine hundred years. He said that I must accept the full consequences of my sin, consigning my heart to Wuotan himself, signing my life over to an eternity in hell and long years of torment on earth until another Black Priest rises to take my place."

My elemental robes darkened further as I abruptly realized *who* this Anubis must have been. Augustin turned his head just enough to meet my gaze at long last, and a despairing smile curled upon his lips. "I see that you have discerned the truth now. Anubis was one of the four Cursed Ones from olden times, the one who was compelled to remain upon the earth until a successor could replace him. The other three chose to enter hell long ago, although they return to the mortal world when their master allows, often to ridicule Anubis for his millennium of exile, forced to mingle among the living while he belonged with the demons of hell."

"Wait a minute." I cut Augustin off while my mind worked to comprehend his horrifying encounter with an ancient Black Priest. "Are you saying that Anubis . . . is still *alive* now? After almost a thousand years?"

The angles of Augustin's face seemed to grow sharper. He shook his head once, his fiery eyes staring into mine as he whispered, "No. He is not . . . alive." My eyebrows came together, and Augustin looked away again, his hands fingering his azure robes in silent distress. "I did not want to tell you this, Swanhilde, but you have no choice now. You must forever shoulder my burden with me, since you spurned all logic and reason to preserve our bond. I formed it out of love for you, those long months ago . . . but now . . . now . . . ." He hesitated one final time, staring at his hands twisting in his lap before directing his gaze upon me, his eyes burning me to embers. "Now . . . you are bound to a dead man."

Chapter Five:
Eternal Death

My ice froze my spirit solid at his impossible words, my eyes raking over his spirit, trying to understand how he could say such a thing when, in this form, he appeared so beautiful, so *alive*. Augustin continued his macabre explanation, prompting my spirit to sink ever deeper into a morass of horror and disbelief. "Anubis told me on that fateful night that I must die in order to achieve that second level of the Teutonic priesthood, to hand my heart over to Wuotan, to be reduced to his eternal slave. Only a Black Priest can kill another of his ilk, and once Wuotan had given me the gifts of darkness, Anubis requested that I kill him immediately. He wanted to join the other three in the realm of the dead." He paused as I gaped, pain marring his expression. "I did not *want* to die, Swanhilde, for I thought of you even then, remembering your love and how desperately your heart bleeds for my salvation. But they forced me . . . the other three rose from the abyss to attend my funeral . . . to aid their brother in his final act of demonic service on this mortal world.

"The three who reside in hell look like skeletons, rotting flesh clinging to their bones, their eyes pits of obscurity, soulless beasts. They introduced themselves as Osiris, king of the underworld, lightning glowing upon his carcass . . . Tartarus, god of the deepest part of the abyss, his bones resembling molten rock . . . and Erebus, god of darkness and shadow, blackness radiating from his form. Their potent elements rendered me defenseless, although Anubis himself quite likely could have defeated my fire with his dark energy, had he expended the effort. They carried me through a portal of black fire to the realm where Wuotan walks, and they threw me naked upon a stone altar, ignoring my screams of protest . . . ."

Disgust consumed me, and I lifted both hands to cover my mouth. Part of me wished desperately to awaken from this nightmare before I could hear the rest. But Augustin trapped my eyes with his as he said, "They sacrificed me while Wuotan and a host of other demons looked on. Each of them made one cut in my flesh with sizzling knives of stone, setting my very blood aflame, and Anubis tore my heart from my chest and invoked Wuotan's fires to consume it. I believe they set my corpse ablaze before the conclusion of the ceremony . . . but Wuotan had already ripped my soul away, dragging me into his void, informing me that if I returned to my body after this death, it would be at his hands, from his mercy.

"He brought me to the very gates of hell, dark wretched things, black flames licking around them, screams pealing out from them in one continuous cry, the epitome of pain and torment. He asked me in a sinister voice whether I preferred to go inside where I belonged or return to the mortal world as his slave. He would grant me powers I had never thought possible and postpone my judgment day until I earned a throne in hell.

"To accept such a deal would place me perpetually in his debt, and I had been informed that three of the original Black Priests had chosen hell over demonic servitude. But I fear, Swanhilde, that terror vanquished my sanity when I stared at those gates. I felt the demons clawing at my soul, the heat of the flames scorching me, those horrific cries blocking out all resistance from my heart. I groveled before him and begged him to take me, to let me go back to earth, so I could gain a status far above hell's rotting humanity. He laughed and asked me caustically what had become of my bargaining powers, raking his claws through my spirit as he dragged me back to his realm. There, he infused me with the gifts of the Cursed Ones, pledging that if I failed to obey his will, he would make the mortal world seem worse to me than hell."

Augustin paused again, his fiery eyes demanding some sort of response from me, a plea for him to release my heart, perhaps, now that I knew the truth. But I could not speak. My element had frozen my spirit, and I marveled that I sat before a dead man, a Black Priest who might very well kill me tonight . . . the man I loved always, the man who was everything to me. Eventually my master seemed to accept my lack of words, and he averted his gaze to the stream and finished his story.

"When I opened my eyes, I found myself lying on the ground outside of my cave, the snow-covered earth no longer chilling my body, a strange potency pulsing through my veins, perfecting my senses, erasing my weakness. I lifted myself off of the ground and saw Anubis awaiting me, gravely reminding me of my first duty as his replacement: to kill him. I asked him how, and he said that I must use the new gift Wuotan had granted me, the one that I saw in your blood . . . the gift of death.

"That reprehensible gift, my darling, is the foulest burden of the Cursed Ones, for it is directly connected with that overarching emotion of anger. Thus, I fear that until my time on earth is done, I shall kill indiscriminately any time I grow angry." Augustin looked toward me, his eyes glimmering with regret. "Anubis had to anger me before I could kill him, and he managed it with amazing finesse." He grimaced at me and I waited, staring at him blankly. "My darling . . . he derided my devotion to you and threatened to kill you himself . . . since Cursed Ones are forbidden to love."

His terrible words finally shook me out of my frozen state. I rose from the ground as fear spattered my robes with icy white, my eyes darting here and there in search of a safe haven. Augustin followed when I fled to the cherry tree, willing my robes to match the stream once more, to conceal me in the shadows underneath the branches. My master drew my heart from beneath his robes to caress it gently, attempting to infuse my spirit with calm. "Swan-hilde, my love, you need not fear him or any of the other original Black Priests," he assured me, sincerity pouring into my heart from his sturdy fingers. "They have left this mortal world for good, aside from the rare occasions in which Wuotan allows them a reprieve from the flames of hell. When they *are* here, they cannot sink their claws into you, for you belong to God. Wuotan must ask your Savior's permission before tormenting you, and he does not prefer to humiliate himself for such favors." Augustin's expression grew caustic.

I tried to let go of my fright, to focus instead on Augustin's hands protecting my heart. He may be dead . . . he may have sold his soul to a demon . . . he may be encumbered with an uncontrollable tendency to kill at random . . . but his love for me had not diminished. I could feel its strength while he tried to assuage my fears; and part of me firmly believed that Augustin's love for me would never burn out, even though Wuotan had laid claim upon his heart. "Even if they hold no sway over my soul . . . there is you." I struggled to put my confused thoughts into words, my doubts needling my quietude. "You're dead now . . . you belong to a demon. What will become of our bond, with Wuotan threatening to torment you unless you renounce your love for me?"

Augustin scowled and he lowered his eyes to my heart, watching it throb in his hands. "Like I told you earlier, you should have allowed me to sever our bond when we had the chance," he said flatly. "Now you are tied to a dead man, and I cannot fight Wuotan forever. He has not begun plaguing me over my love for you yet, but inevitably one day he shall distort my adoration into a lust for blood and death, a longing to tear your heart asunder. Now, as I feel your presence with me, as I sense the purity within your heart . . . I can almost convince myself that our bond may survive this test. But it shall not . . . for although I am a phantom now, eternally dead and technically immortal, I am only a man . . . and my master is a demon. His power far outweighs mine, and I can no longer refuse him."

Augustin's visage twisted with pain, and he tightened his grip on my heart as though he feared that it may vanish at Wuotan's bidding. I stepped away from the tree to place my hands against his cheeks. "There's still hope for you, Augustin," I whispered passionately, believing it in spite of everything. "You *can* fight Wuotan forever, because you *can* put your faith in God. You just admitted that God has more power than your demon master. Why place your soul into the hands of a devil instead? He may have brought you back from the gates of hell and given you a second chance on earth, but you said yourself that he promised you a *delay* of the final judgment. If you put your faith in God, you can renounce that damnation altogether!"

Augustin jerked away from me sharply, his expression fierce as he tucked my heart back within his robes. "You must not suggest such traitorous things, Swanhilde," he reproved me, his eyes blazing a vivid blue. "My chance at heaven has been permanently lost, for I have seen the gates of hell with my own eyes and handed my heart willingly to the lords of darkness. Wuotan may torment me now for my devotion to you, but if I begged God to forgive my sins, my master would thrust me into a far deeper level of demonic agony. I cannot betray him."

I shook my head firmly, refusing to accept his bleak attitude. But Augustin scoffed, and when he spoke again, his tone sounded darker than the night sky above. "You ought to ponder your own fate, since you shall likely be bound to me for the duration of the next two decades. Though Wuotan holds no sway over your eternal resting place, your heart lies in the hands of a dead man influenced daily by the darkness. You shall valiantly attempt to pull me to heaven, while I shall thrust you in vain towards hell. It shall be an everlasting conflict, a contest neither of us can win. And I cannot meet you in the mortal world to break our bond for fear of inadvertently killing you. Therefore, our feud shall continue indefinitely, our love degenerating into disgust."

Part of me wished to argue with him again, to insist that he had not lost his chance at heaven. He had not actually entered hell, and in my mind, that meant that he could still turn. Augustin was not the first to have sold his soul to a devil, and others like him had eventually repented and embraced grace. But I did not want to waste any more of our fleeting moments with futile arguments since I knew not when he would choose to interrupt another of my dreams. Our meetings would likely grow fewer and fewer as time went by, so I needed to preserve every second we had. "So our bond will remain unbroken until I return to the future?" I inquired, my thoughts jumping twenty-one years ahead to the fall of Muniche.

"It is quite probable," Augustin replied, sitting down upon the grass once more and gesturing for me to join him. I sat beside him and curled my legs underneath me. "You had better pray hard that the tides of time shall wield enough force to sever our bond," he went on, "for in the meantime, we must remain separated. It is difficult to ponder it . . . for even in my misery, I cannot expunge the memory of our final night together with its sensual perfection . . . its immeasurable glory . . . its incredible fulfillment . . . ."

My spirit shivered with desire as Augustin stared into my eyes, his strong right hand passing through my face, traveling down the robes at my chest. The sinful part of me wanted to throw myself at his feet and beg him to tell me which mountain he stalked, in which cave he hid. I could flee to him there and ask Wuotan to unite us in some sort of devilish matrimony, so we could enjoy each other freely in spite of his curse. But the eyes of my spirit caught sight of that black scar on his forearm, the sleeve of his sapphire robe pushed back just enough to reveal its very tip . . . and I remembered that as of the upcoming Saturday, my life would become one permanent lie. "I'm marrying Joel in a

Teutonic wedding this Saturday," I said. A second after the words had left my lips, I wanted to call them back.

Augustin snickered quietly and drew his hand away from my chest. "At least you have the fortitude to continue with your life despite what has been done, while I wallow alone in desolation. So he is a Teuton now, thanks to your foolish escapade to the brink of death." Augustin crossed his arms and eyed me with a touch of blame, for my ridiculous race to save Joel's life had resulted in his banishment. "I suppose now that he is your equal, you may be able to convince yourself to love him, to fall for a man of wind who could whirl you through the air effortlessly at every dance, were he properly trained."

I remembered that kiss I had shared with Joel after he had proposed, when my ice had refused to respond to his element's attempt at dalliance. "I guess the two of us could make a good team, running the Meldorf estate and raising a family," I admitted, looking down at my hands clasped in my lap. "But my love for him—assuming I can *find* it—will never hold a candle to my love for you. Joel could never pull me back from death the way you can. And he can't teach me secrets of Teutonic lore or hold the heart of my soul in his hands."

Augustin grinned at me, his teeth glowing rather wickedly in the moonlight. "Then I shall be the ghost in your bed," he commented with grotesque triumph, "and you shall spend the rest of your days wondering what infinite glories I could have taught you if we had remained together . . . the devilry of elemental harlotry."

I laughed when Augustin quoted what the Prince and the Old One had said as they related our sins. "What in the world do they think is wrong about elemental sex?" I asked. "All of the council members are Teutons like us, and I'm sure they get it on with their wives quite thoroughly." I snickered.

"I believe they condemned us for the harlotry aspect, my swan," Augustin explained, a wicked grin still spread across his face. "As much as the Catholics expound on the so-called evils of sexual gratification, I doubt too many of

them hold back their cries of ecstasy during the act itself."
I shrieked once, doubling over with laughter, and then my
lover added, "Eventually you shall learn the perils of intercourse, once you are married. You shall find yourself
pregnant over and over again, forced to face the dangers of
childbirth as a Teuton woman."

My mind flew back to the realization that had come
over me the previous morning, and I winced a little, my
right hand sliding forward to grasp the icy robes at my
stomach. "Is there any way you can . . . somehow . . . be my
advocate . . . when I'm writhing in labor . . . even though
you can't physically be there?" I asked, fearing that Wuotan would seize the first opportunity to thrust me back to
the twenty-first century, to leave his servant unattached. "I
realize that there's a medical aspect to the whole thing. I'll
make sure I have a midwife, and I'll clean the room beforehand. But the fate of Teuton women in childbirth hangs
ultimately upon the whims of Wuotan . . . in the realm of
the spirit." I bit my lip.

Augustin's expression clouded over, intensity replacing
his snide humor. "Wuotan shall not claim your soul in
childbirth," he said, his fiery eyes burning the water before
us. "You must first inform me of your travail with a cry of
your heart, and I shall advocate for you again. He may
require some of your children, but I shall not allow him to
kill you."

Some of your children . . . . I hesitated for one final
moment, then fearfully began to broach the subject that
had plagued me since Sunday morning. "Now that you're
dead, I suppose you could . . . share your bed with anyone
. . . and not worry about having offspring." I gnawed on my
lip while I awaited his response, my icy teeth leaving no
mark on my spirit.

Augustin averted his gaze from the stream to my face,
his eyebrows coming together as he sensed my distress.
"No, a dead man cannot have children. He also does not
need to eat, or drink, or sleep. I have not eaten or drunk
anything since Anubis came to me that night, and I have
slept rarely, due to the nightmares." He paused, his ghostly

forehead crinkling. "What frightens you, Swanhilde? Do the particulars of my existence trouble your heart?"

"No, I . . . I think . . . I think . . . ." I stumbled over the words, fear of his reaction to the awful truth binding me in chains. I shuddered all over and forced myself to meet Augustin's worried eyes. "My boobs have been sore . . . and my period is five days late . . . and I'm never late. I think . . . I might be . . . pregnant." I froze as I watched the emotions run across his face: shock, horror, denial, fury, anguish.

Augustin leaped to his feet with a howl, blue flames exploding from his fists, evaporating before they could taint the grass. He stomped into the shallows of the brook, his spirit trembling with anger. "*Of course* this would happen *NOW!*" he snapped. "I have *never* engendered a child in my *LIFE,* for in the past I have always killed my victims, and Gisela has always been barren."

A horrid oath burst from his lips, and he threw his hands in the air. His cobalt robes transformed into solid flames of fire that licked fitfully amid the flowing waters. "I should have married you that night before throwing you upon my bed. I could have collared some Teuton priest to do the duty for us. Then the murderer could not have cursed me, for I would have been head of my own family!" Augustin howled again and sank to his knees in the waters of the stream. He hid his face in his hands, muttering something in a language I did not know, his robes gradually cooling.

I had frozen upon the bank, my eyes wide as I observed my lover's torment. I opened my lips to say something to calm him, to assure him that no one would know the child was his, since Joel and I would be husband and wife in just two days. But Augustin spoke first, terrible words spilling from his lips. "Now you shall bear a cursed child, the spawn of an apparition, your very own tiny demon."

I rose to my feet at once, my defense of our child ringing out strong. "That horrible curse can't reach into my womb, and this child was conceived before the Prince cast the paper into the fire. Do *not* call it a demon, Augustin. If I manage to carry this child to term, it will be perfect and innocent! Do you understand me?"

Augustin climbed out of the stream to stand centimeters from my chest, his anger rippling the air between us. "And what do you think people shall say if that child looks *exactly* like me?" he demanded, his hands curling into fists.

"There's not that much difference in our appearances," I responded, for I had already considered the excuses I could give if I bore a blue-eyed child. "Camilla had blue eyes similar to yours, and both of us have the same hair color. I can give Joel blond-haired children later. Not all of them have to look like him."

My master sighed heavily, turning his eyes away from me. "I doubt Wuotan shall forgive this progeny," he said, "but I shall preserve your life when labor seizes you, no matter the cost. You mean far more to me than some ridiculous child." He looked toward me again and slipped his right hand into his robes to stroke my heart.

I groaned at the strong adoration that flowed from his spirit into mine. I desperately wished that I could caress him even though we could never reunite again in the mortal world. "Augustin . . . I love you *so* much . . . more than anyone."

He smiled at me sadly, desolation warring with his composure. "And I love you, Swanhilde, enough to fight Wuotan for as long as I am able, enough to refuse his commands to leave you behind. We shall see how long my resolve lasts." His smile faded, and he averted his eyes to the lightening sky.

"Morning breaks, and you must awaken. But I have one final request of you, considering the seriousness of your current predicament." Augustin met my gaze and gestured toward the robes at my stomach. "You must care for yourself strictly in the coming months, my dear. Eat healthy foods and refrain from strenuous activity. I do not wish to confront the burden of preserving your life during a miscarriage." Before I could reply to this, he vanished, leaving me alone in my bed.

Chapter Six:
Blood Marriage

Saturday afternoon, I sat before the mirror in the bedroom I would no longer share with Freia as of that night, half-heartedly trying to concentrate on the excited exclamations of my best friend and Felda while they bustled around me, carefully perfecting my face, dress, and hair for my wedding with Joel. My gray eyes drifted often toward the window, my mind speculating exactly how long it would be until sunset, when the ceremony would begin. I had just a few hours of sanity left. Before I knew it, I would add *Hudson* to my surname and crawl into a primitive tent somewhere in the woodland with my new husband. Soon I would sign my name onto our marriage certificate as *Swanhilde Rolande Hudson von Thaden*, and Joel would sign his as *Joel Richard Hudson von Thaden*. As of that moment, the rest of my days in the eleventh century would be consumed with hypocrisy.

I stared vacantly at my reflection in the mirror, unsurprised at the glow of denial in my eyes. I was about to do the very thing that Freia had joined the Gypsies to avoid—I was about to marry a man I did not love, a man I could never love. My union with Joel would be made out of convenience; we had come to the past together, and we would remain in the past together. We would marry and run the Meldorf estate as a couple and lay down a history to the unknown name of Thaden.

Joel loved me, and he would assume that I loved him in return. He would want me to teach him everything, now that his Teuton blood matched mine. He would believe our elemental dances to be the pinnacle of glory, and his blood would simmer just like mine when we entwined ourselves in bed. We would be a young Teuton couple, both nobility due to the count's generosity, welcomed into the coterie of the elite of Muniche, the subject of good-natured tittering as we attended parties together, as I bore Joel more and more offspring . . . .

I worked hard to keep my unhappiness off of my face when I exited the Meldorf manor, descending the front steps cautiously. The count's nicest carriage awaited me just beyond the stairs with Jarvis at the driver's seat. The bailiff looked rather impressive in a gray suit and cowl, his sandy beard and hair freshly trimmed, his blue eyes glinting as he appraised my dress. I had sewn the dress myself and completed it the day before. It was of blue and silver linen, the skirt wide enough to make me appear as though I had no legs, the sleeves flared grandly, the laced bodice accentuating my figure—which so far showed no signs of my pregnancy. I wore silver sandals beneath the skirt, though no one at the wedding would notice them, and a pair of my mother's silver earrings dangled from my earlobes. Freia had purchased makeup to use at our weddings; thus my black eyelashes appeared more prominent than usual, and my lips were stained a deep ruby red. Joel would be impressed, I knew, but I wished that the carriage would somehow sweep me away to a darker corner of the forest, a place of ghoulish shadows and ghosts where I could marry Augustin in secret.

While the stable hand helped me enter the carriage, I ordered myself to stop fantasizing about my master on the very eve of my wedding with Joel. Augustin had said before that our fates were not meant to be together, despite our desperate wishes. If I were to honestly move on and pick up the shattered pieces of my life, I would at least have to *try* to love Joel instead. But if I abandoned Augustin for a well-meaning Teuton boy who had given up his heritage for me, my master would forget that he still had a chance at heaven. Thus I resolved to enjoy Joel tonight and try to share his future burdens and triumphs as a good wife should . . . while deep within my heart, I would dream with my heathen priest.

My attitude improved steadily as the carriage rattled over the dirt paths toward the Teuton meeting place of Muniche. I held lively conversations with Freia and Count von Meldorf, both of whom were attending the wedding. The count wore noble clothing for the occasion, though he commented several times that the stiff fabric made him itch. He also had trimmed his hair and beard, and looked rather handsome for a man past sixty. He promised to kill several chickens for a feast once Joel and I returned from our honeymoon, and he pledged that my new bedroom would be waiting for us, fully furnished. The count's blue eyes twinkled suggestively as he hinted that I probably ought to change into a more durable dress before taking off with Joel. I laughed heartily at this and promised that I would. Freia and I had prepared a suitable stash of camping equipment for my honeymoon. Jarvis had brought it to the outskirts of the clearing earlier in the day, along with the tan mare and one of the count's stallions.

Jarvis halted our caravan a short distance from the clearing. He came around to help the three of us onto the leaves of the trail before tying the horses to several low-hanging linden boughs. The sun had already dipped below the horizon, and the sky above, barely visible through the leafy branches, had shifted from the light blue of summer into a deepening vermillion.

A bit of nervousness strove with my anticipation as I waited for Joel to meet me, my eyes peering through the shadows of the forest toward the glade that would become the stage for my matrimony. Memories of my other activities at the meeting place of Muniche assaulted my mind for a split second—the first time, when Joel, Freia, and I had to persuade the Teuton council to accept us into the city—and the second time, that horrible time I could never erase from my thoughts, when the haughty Prince had cursed my lover forever. What would take place now would be much happier, the solemnity of the ceremony overshadowed by the wonder of Teutonic blood marriage.

The count and Jarvis exchanged a few final phrases with me before striking out for the clearing. Freia paused a moment longer, her green eyes searching my face. "How are you?" she whispered.

I forced myself to smile at her, pushing aside the last of my hesitation. "I'm all right," I replied quietly, knowing full well that my best friend knew my heart was breaking inside of me. "This is my best path forward, and there's no use bewailing the glories I can never have."

Freia smiled sadly, patting me lightly on the shoulder with the words, "You and Joel will make a wonderful couple, and I know you'll make the Meldorf estate more prosperous than ever. Your life is hardly over, Swanie, and remember that God's ways are far beyond ours. You mustn't lose hope." She nodded once at me in encouragement, then turned away to follow the others into the dell.

The light radiating from her countenance filled me with peace and courage, and I knew that I could conquer the next two decades in spite of the tragedy that had befallen me. I wondered briefly whether the inspiration I gained from my friendship with Freia shared any similarities to my own influence over Augustin. In the next instant, Joel stepped out from the trees, diverting all of my attention to the path before me.

He wore the noble attire I had sewn for him to wear at our Teutonic wedding: a patterned tunic of auburn and indigo interwoven with golden thread, deep brown trousers and belt with an impressive brass buckle, and hardy leather boots that rose to his knees. His blond hair and beard had been slicked perfectly, all traces of dirt removed from his face. Truth to be told, he looked incredibly striking. His hazel eyes shone with excitement as he offered me his right hand, so we could cross the short distance to the glade side by side, per tradition.

"You look really amazing in noble clothing," I whispered to him in English as I took his hand, letting him lead me toward the clearing.

Joel grinned at me and murmured back, "I look like a tramp compared to you. That dress is . . . wow. I don't have enough words to do it justice in English or Teutonica." I giggled and felt heat rise in my cheeks. "Did Freia do your hair?" I nodded. "It looks like the hair of a princess."

I tilted my head at him and whispered coyly, "An ice princess, or a Teuton princess?" I left out the option of 'swan princess' on purpose.

He chuckled. "Whatever you want. Are you sure you don't want to reconsider?" We had paused at the edge of the dell, still in the shadows, though I could see the yellow-orange glow of the traditional fire illuminating the clearing beyond. I imagined the four witnesses who had gathered to observe our wedding: the count, Jarvis, Freia, and Heinrich, standing in a group across from the fire. I imagined the Teuton priest, Joel's friend Aric, clad entirely in black, poised behind the table between the fire and the witnesses. And I imagined the wooden post, likely set up near the riverbank, awaiting our official union as man and wife. I shivered in nervous anticipation when Joel squeezed my hand and said, "Honestly, if you'd rather not marry me like this, I won't hold it against you."

I lifted my eyes to his one final time and replied softly, "I have no intention of backing out. This ritual tonight is the beginning of our future here in the eleventh century. I'm ready for it, even for the knives and blood." I winked.

Joel grinned and confided in a low voice, "I made the knife, and I put *all* of my initials on it since it might be the last knife I'll ever make. JRHvT." His hazel eyes sparkled in achievement.

I smiled back at him and said, "Then let's do this. No more English." I eyed him demurely, and he elbowed me in jest. A second later, we stepped into the glade, walking ceremoniously across the leaves and pine needles to our place before the table.

I invoked my ice into my eyes to sharpen my vision and looked around at the clearing on our journey to our place. Our four friends stood to my right with the Isar at their backs, the count and Heinrich in the middle, flanked by Jarvis and Freia. Both Heinrich and Freia had clad themselves decently for the wedding, and they stood very close to each other, their body language hinting that they could hardly wait for their own wedding day. My eyes darted next to the fire pit, its flames blazing in a natural yellow and orange with no trace of elemental manipulation.

Finally, my gaze fell upon the table before us and the priest standing behind it. He stood just a bit shorter than Joel, the black hood of his robes hiding his hair from me, his hands clasped calmly before him, his expression rather withering. As we halted two paces from the table, I suddenly realized that I had never met this priest before in my life. I had no idea what his full name was, or his element. At least Joel knew him . . . and at least he was not the Prince . . . but a small shiver ran down my spine when I wondered whether he would conduct the wedding properly since he had never officiated one before.

"Tonight, we come together to bind two Teutons by blood, oath, and love." Aric spoke the introductory words in Teutonica, his tone solemn and mystical. After a short pause, he lifted a braid of silver oak leaves from the table and carried them to the nearby fire to offer Joel and me our final escape from this numinous commitment. "If either party wishes to renounce this binding, may he speak now, before these leaves meet the fire."

Part of me wished to shriek and run, to leap upon one of the horses tied near the trail and ride with the fury of Augustin's fire, ride without stopping, ride away from this obligation that would unite me with a man I could not love. I entertained the shortest of fantasies on a wild ride into the Alps, upon the snowy peaks, my heart and ice seeking my master . . . finding him in the cave, a wraith of darkness, throwing myself at his feet, pleading for his mercy and his everlasting love, begging for a reprieve from this madness. But I kept my gaze forward to the line of trees beyond the table, hearing the snap when the leaves met the flames, extinguishing my hopes forever. And I raised my chin as I prepared to meet my destiny, though it was far from what I had wanted.

Aric proceeded to address our friends next, asking the count and Heinrich whether they accepted their responsibilities as witnesses of the binding. Traditionally, the certificate indicating a Teutonic marriage should be signed by only two witnesses, both male; the count and the ironmaster had agreed ahead of time to perform this duty. Personally, I wished that Freia and Heinrich could have signed, since they would soon be husband and wife themselves, but medieval Teuton laws remained as chauvinistic as ever. Joel and the count planned to sign for Freia and Heinrich's wedding next month. I would be there to watch but not to participate.

Soon afterward, Aric stepped back to the table, calmly announcing that all was prepared and that he would now proceed with the wedding. I already knew all of the particulars of Teutonic weddings, for aside from watching Ina's wedding, I had read all about such things in *Der Weg*. The ceremony would consist of three rites involving blood and knives—typical, as Joel would say—and an exchange of vows. In my era, as well as the eleventh century, Teutonic weddings were conducted in Teutonica rather than the older dialect so that the uneducated could properly appreciate the importance of the rituals. Thus, I knew what would be expected of me, and I deemed myself prepared despite my nagging doubts. Joel would likely be far more squeamish about the blood rites than I would.

Aric intoned a few phrases explaining the first rite—the slitting of the left wrists of the betrothed pair, using the knife Joel had made. A few drops of blood from each of us would be collected in a small cup. Afterward, Aric would wrap silver oak leaves around our wounds, using its magic and his skills at blood control to heal the cuts. Pinkish scars would mark our wrists as permanent reminders of our commitment to one another, never fading until the day one of us died. I wondered briefly, when I stepped forward and held out my left wrist to the priest, if my marriage with Joel here in the past would carry over into the twenty-first century. *We're supposed to remain essentially unchanged when we return . . . but I know I read something once, something that suggested that there are some acts that can be done in the past that carry over into the future. But I don't think marriage was one of them . . . I wish I could remember . . . .*

The sting of the blade cutting into my wrist brought my thoughts back to the matter at hand. I watched, slightly fascinated, as Aric turned my wrist downward so that my blood could spill into a wooden cup upon the table. He held my bleeding wrist over the cup for less than half a minute according to my internal clock. My blood had not yet reached the edges of the bottom of the goblet before he pressed a silver oak leaf to my wound, holding it still for a short interval. A playful smile tugged at the corners of my lips, for I could have halted the bleeding of my wrist myself, without bothering with an oak leaf. But I doubted that Aric would appreciate such interference from a woman. So I waited patiently, holding back my defensive instinct while the priest closed my wound, leaving a scab that had already begun to transform into the pink scar of marriage.

Aric slit Joel's wrist next as I stood back and observed, my eyes straying now and then to my own left wrist, marveling at the ridiculousness that had thrust me into this binding with an American Teuton. That had to be a first. Joel certainly was one of a kind, and I could not criticize his newfound loyalty to me and my people, an allegiance that had caused him to turn his back upon his own heritage. Guilt touched my soul at my mental infidelity to such a decent man, but I shoved it aside, ordering myself not to think of such things now. I directed my attention once more to Aric, who had finished with Joel's wound and begun to explain the second rite of the Teutonic wedding— the acceptance and disposal of sorrows.

This part of the ceremony vexed me more than the cuts from the knife. Joel and I stood beside one another, silently watching Aric place the necessary items into the cup which had caught a few drops of blood from each of us. He listed each of the ingredients rather tonelessly: water from the Isar, dust from the earth, bitter herbs from the gardens of Muniche, vinegar from her vineyards.

Once he had finished mixing everything in the cup using an iron stirrer, Joel and I would have to drink a sip of its contents. This symbolized the bitter sorrows we would face in our future together as a married couple in an imperfect world. Joel would drink last and then throw the cup and the remainder of its liquid over his left shoulder to symbolize the triumph of love and loyalty over trials. I never enjoyed tasting things that were supposed to be disgusting, but at least this would not be half as bad as drinking Augustin's blood.

I took a deep breath and steeled myself when Aric handed me the wooden cup, sipping it quickly, working hard to keep the distaste off of my face while I swallowed and handed the cup to Joel. I hoped the count had brought some sort of congratulatory wine with him in the carriage for use after the ceremony, for now I had a horrible aftertaste in my mouth. Joel cast the cup over his shoulder with a bit too much force, his face appearing quite revolted with the whole thing.

Aric lifted an aged book from the table and read a few phrases on the duties of man and wife. Next, he requested that Joel and I face each other at long last, so we could repeat the proper vows, pledging our faithfulness and love to each other. Joel spoke them first, his hazel eyes shining as the words poured from his lips in perfect Teutonica. He really did love me; I could see that plainly. An exultant smile adorned his bearded face, and he clasped my hands tightly. He was probably already forming all sorts of exciting speculations on our honeymoon in the forest and our mutual life together as landed nobility—twenty-one years of marital glory. So I pushed back all of my hesitancy and locked my gray eyes with Joel's as I spoke the required lies.

"On this night I pledge my body and heart to you, Joel Richard Hudson, before these witnesses of earth, fire, air, water, and soul. I give you myself as your wife, with my faults and my strengths, and I take you to myself as my husband, with your faults and your strengths. May we live from this night forward as Teuton partners, of one mind and blood, in all matters of life. I pledge to stay with you and you alone, as your wife, until we are parted by death."

My treachery ate at my insides while Aric recited a few statements regarding the last act of the Teutonic wedding—the uniting of the blood of the pair and the kiss of marriage. Joel and I followed the priest to the wooden post set up near the banks of the Isar, its height about halfway between my waist and shoulders. He carried Joel's knife and an iron bowl . . . and when my eyes strayed to the bowl I remembered the last time I had seen the use of such an instrument . . . collecting Augustin's blood at the curse.

Uncertainty grabbed hold of me as I considered the similarities of the Teutonic wedding and the filial curse. *Both use a knife to spill the participant's blood, collected in an iron bowl . . . the name written with the blood . . . but in matrimony it's mixed blood, signed freely onto a marriage certificate, preserved in honor for years and years . . . and for the curse, it's the blood of one condemned party, signed with fettered hands, the record burnt before it dries . . . .*

My stomach twisted, and I averted my eyes to Joel's caring face when we halted on opposite sides of the post. I tried to focus on his love and devotion, telling myself to forget my cursed master once and for all. I laid my right hand upon the post, as expected, and Joel covered my hand with his strong fingers. His expression suggested that he did not particularly trust the idea of having his hand stabbed through with a knife. I smiled at him in an attempt at reassurance, and a moment later Aric proclaimed, "May the couple seal their marriage with a kiss, and may the union be complete!"

Joel and I kissed passionately, our left arms wrapping around each other as Aric stabbed our right hands together upon the post. A corner of my brain detected the impact and the pain, along with the wood digging into my palm and the strange stickiness that seeped between my hand and the post. But I could not concentrate on the discomfort while my lips molded with Joel's. I could think only of my hormones sparking to life, warring with my ice as it leapt out to dance with Joel's wind somewhere in the realm of the spirit.

I had never kissed Joel like *this* before. It overwhelmed me with amazement and longing. We were equals . . . *and we were married.* That very night, I would look upon him naked for the first time and discover what triumphs a derivative of air had to offer. I would not think of the blue-fired priest who had stolen my heart. This marvelous young man of wind would fully occupy my mind, fulfilling my desires like I satisfied his, and we would ascend to the stars together in Teutonic triumph.

Aric had already extracted the knife from our hands by the time we parted, having caught a sufficient amount of our commingled blood for the signatures. Joel stared at me, his eyes radiant with wonder, glittering silver in the twilight. I glanced down at my right hand, seeing that no mark remained from the knife's work; the blood had entirely vanished from my skin. There was certainly magic in the marriage of Teutons. Joel looked down at his own hand, mimicking me, the English word "wow" escaping his lips. A moment later, he grabbed me with a grin and kissed me again, binding me snugly in his arms.

We returned to the table soon afterward to sign our marriage certificate. I signed first, putting Joel's surname in front of my own like we had agreed, my cursive flowing unintentionally in the style of the eleventh century, like Augustin had taught me. Joel signed after me with a bit more difficulty, since our commingled blood had begun to clot; his handwriting looked far messier, as well. Count von Meldorf took up a feather pen once Joel had finished and signed his name shakily in print. I beamed at him in gratitude when he handed the pen to Heinrich. The count had never learned to write, and his name was the only legible thing he could inscribe. Once Heinrich had signed, Aric took the pen and wrote his full name onto the parchment, his commoner's handwriting on the same level as Joel's.

Joel and I exchanged a few words with our friends afterward and shared several drinks to a long and prosperous future. I entrusted Jarvis with our marriage certificate, and before I knew it, I had changed into a simpler dress and climbed into the saddle, the tan mare reaching back to nuzzle my hand as I secured the reins. Joel leapt atop one of the count's dappled stallions, our camping equipment secured to the animal's back. He shot me one final grin before spurring his horse toward the deepest part of the forest. So I nudged the mare to follow my partner in a race to an endless night, to the rapturous ecstasies of my deception.

Chapter Seven:
My Adulterous Muse

Late that night after the moon had already risen and set, I lay awake underneath a thin blanket, blinking fitfully at the starry sky above as I fought valiantly against my leaden eyelids. Joel had found a decent spot for the first night of our honeymoon the previous afternoon and had brought a few essentials to the place already. The spot he had chosen bordered a small tributary of the Isar, a tiny chattering stream that glittered in the starlight.

Upon our arrival, we had tied our horses to a tree not far from the brook and spread out our bundles some distance away. We unpacked extra clothing, blankets, some food and wine, the knife from our nuptials, two plates and cups, my hairbrush and pins, my camera, and my Bible. Joel had brought two more knives, some flint to aid in lighting fires, a rather primitive fishing pole, rope, and the bow and arrows I had recently bought him. We were as prepared as we could be, for if the good weather lasted, we would not need much shelter.

Once I had sorted our wares and Joel had managed to light a fire, he came beside me and spread our thickest blanket upon the grass. He said that it may be better to have something between our bodies and the ground, since we had no twenty-first century bug spray. I had laughed weakly at his joke, heartsick at the knowledge of what was to come. He sat down at my side and expressed profuse gratitude for my generosity in bringing him with me into the past, now that our next twenty years seemed to shine brightly on the horizon. He told me many times that he loved me, that he would provide for me and protect me, that he would strive to be the best Teuton husband he could be. Murmurs of adoration spilled from my lips in reply, part of me shocked that I could form such blasphemies when my heart screamed in betrayal. By the time we began to remove each other's clothing, I had managed to push aside the pain in my heart. I focused instead on the desire in my blood, ordering it to explode from me in passion, to enjoy the privileges of marriage.

Now, as I lay awake with the softness of fabric between the skin of my back and the grass beneath, dissatisfaction and guilt churned together in my soul, a plaguing reminder of the physical affair I had already had and the emotional affair that would never end. Joel snored softly at my side, his naked chest rising and falling slowly with the peaceful breaths of slumber, the fading scars from his blood-transfer with Heinrich yet visible underneath his blond chest hair. He had given me his virginity just hours before, trusting me with his heart and dreams, his happiness spilling over into the beauty of nature around us. And he did not know that he lay beside Augustin von Bayern's Teuton harlot, a guilt-ridden woman who had freely sacrificed her purity more than a month before to a wicked sinner. She would never forget what she had gotten from the experienced rapist—and she knew that despite Joel's Teuton blood, despite his alluring wind, despite his honest intentions, he could never overtake Augustin's place in her heart.

I did not want to sleep, though I knew that eventually I would succumb to my mental exhaustion. Soon the sky would lighten, and the birds of the morning would call to one another in the trees, the summer insects flitting from plant to plant in search of nectar for another day. Maybe, just maybe, I could manage to stay awake until dawn broke, for I doubted that Augustin would wait for me in the light of day. I had not yet been able to question him on the exact workings of the dream world of the spirit. For one thing, I felt certain that my ice did not cover my sleeping body when I was there.

I had so many questions for my master the next time I met him in my dreams, but I knew that if I met him tonight, the subject of my marriage with Joel would supplant every other discussion. I did not want to face him now, hours after finally achieving sexual union with an innocent virgin who cried out in pleasure at the excitement of release. My body and my hormones had responded to his passion with gusto, but my heart had wailed within me the entire time, telling me I was committing adultery.

This is so backwards.... My thoughts grew more and more confused as my weariness began winning the battle. *Joel is my husband. I shouldn't feel guilty having sex with him. But my spirit has been married to Augustin since last winter, and his fire is so much more gratifying than Joel's wind. Augustin is my equal, my other half*.... *Joel is a necessity, a good man, but one I'll never love* ... *and now I'm stuck with him for the next twenty years* ... *stuck sharing his bed, bearing his children*... *and he snores* ... *and his beard smells weird*....

I opened my eyes to see Augustin's shining face hovering far above me, as though he stood over me waiting for me to rise from the ground. I blinked, my heart sinking at the realization that I had finally fallen asleep. Now I would have to face my lover's ridicule, his saucy triumph at my discontent. He would probably not allow me to wake until after dawn, after Joel had finished preparing some sort of breakfast for me. I wished desperately that I could figure out how to wake from this dream world on my own power ... but, rather conveniently, I thought, my master had not yet taught me how. A slow smile crept across Augustin's face, and he took one step back as I followed him with my eyes. A moment later he stretched out his right hand and requested softly, "Come with me, my darling Swanhilde."

I obeyed him wordlessly, my spirit stepping out of my sleeping body into the misty world of my dreams, my fingers passing through Augustin's. His smile widened, and he brought me to the stream, away from the married pair lying beneath the thin blanket. I glanced once at Joel's snoring form, then at my own body, curled into the fetal position some distance away from my husband. My unconscious face did not appear peaceful at all. A frown line had imprinted itself upon my forehead, even in slumber. I sighed, looking down briefly at the icy blue robes swirling around my spirit. Then I followed Augustin as he strolled leisurely downstream, his ghostlike feet barely touching the water.

We said nothing until we had left the married pair and their horses behind us, the dark blue sky casting the forest in a mysterious hue, the chattering waters of the stream growing colder in response to my ice. At last, Augustin halted near a thick tangle of pines, stepping out of the stream to sit down upon a weathered branch, its needles and cones sweeping the forest floor. I remained standing in the shallows of the stream. I wrapped my arms around my ethereal body, waiting for my lover to speak first, for I knew not where to begin.

Augustin studied me for a long moment in silence. The fire in his eyes smoldered as he fingered my heart beneath his cobalt robes, doubtless sensing all of its torment. "So he does not satisfy you," he observed, his face betraying no hint of derision, only pity.

I shivered and turned my gaze upstream. "No. And I tried. I really tried," I said, my voice sounding dead. "But I'm just not attracted to Joel that way at all, and I couldn't relax enough to enjoy it. Apparently what I need is a fiery Teuton priest, old or cursed." I met Augustin's eyes, a cynical smile twisting my lips.

My master gazed back at me steadily. "It is a burden you have shouldered since your first dance with Hans, my darling," he said. "Deep within the spirit of every Teuton woman hide the needs that can be met only by the mysticism and devotion of the Teuton priest. Those unfortunate women like you who fall under the spell of a priest shall never attain full satisfaction from a lesser man." Augustin retrieved my heart from his robes while he spoke, his fingers infusing it with pulsing affection, reinforcing the wretched truths in his words. "You should have allowed me to break our bond while we had the chance, Swanhilde," he added.

I shook my head at him and concentrated on that other-worldly sensation of his adoration flowing into me through our bond. "I cannot let that happen, Augustin," I said, stepping out of the stream at last to sit down beside him on the branch. "This love we share has changed my life. I don't want to lose it, and I don't want to lose you, even if it renders me unable to properly love my husband." The foolishness of my words stabbed at me in light of two more decades with Joel.

Augustin's frown deepened, and he tucked my heart underneath his robes. "This bond shall drag us both into despair, Swanhilde. It shall constantly hold you back from experiencing contentment in marriage, chaining you to a cursed priest as he descends slowly into hell. And it shall torment me, for the memory of your love shall tie me to my humanity, not allowing me to embrace the demonic shield that should be mine. I have regretted this already while I wallow alone on the mountain, for Wuotan has come to me many times, offering me a devil's pleasure to erase the thoughts that plague my mind, to ease the burden of my cursed fate."

Augustin rose from the branch, his eyes flaming with blue fire. His hands curled into fists at his sides as he towered over me, unleashing his frustrations in a sinister voice. "As Wuotan's timeless servant, he has granted me the ability to mate with any of his cursed sirens whenever I wish, a privilege that no mortal man can know without relinquishing his soul in death. And I have done it, Swanhilde, many times, for I remember quite well that sex used to be one of my greatest pleasures. But now . . . *now* . . . . Every time I copulate with one of those immortal beings, I find myself wishing she was *you*."

Augustin glared at me, a low growl pealing from his throat before he finished, "You have *bewitched* me with your love, Swanhilde, for you have taught me that sharing one's bed with a devoted lover far outshines the grandeur of casual intercourse. I doubt that I shall ever forget that, even when I burn in the flames of hell."

A rather mournful smile played upon my lips, and I looked down at my icy hands resting in my lap. "I guess both of us are on the same page, then." Part of me danced in triumph at the news that Augustin found me far more gratifying than any of those seductive sirens. I recalled the brief glimpses I had gotten of them when I raced after Joel —naked, voluptuous, hair enhanced by their elements— and I realized that Augustin really *must* love me, if those immortal goddesses could not cause him to forget our one night together.

My master stepped away from me, the fire in his eyes cooling a bit. "Both of us are undoubtedly on the same page, as you suggest, for neither of us shall grasp true glory again with this distance between us. And thus it shall continue for two decades until the currents of time tear us apart . . . for we must not meet again in the mortal world, my love." Augustin's face softened, and he leaned down to caress my ghost-like face. "I fear that if we did meet again, to break the bond or not, I may kill you." His face contorted in despair.

I closed my eyes for a moment, imagining that I could feel my master's touch upon my face. "We have discovered one thing," I said when I opened my eyes to look into his. "Apparently your gift of death can't hurt me here. You've been angry several times, tonight and the night I told you about our child. You haven't killed me yet."

"That is true," Augustin agreed, drawing his hand away and sitting beside me once more. "I have not yet discerned the boundaries of the death that churns within me. I have felt it often, flaring with my anger, but thus far I have remained alone upon the mountain. You are the only living soul with whom I have spoken since the curse."

I smiled up at him, grateful for the privileges that came with the heart-bond. All of my questions returned to my mind in a rush. "Tell me about this part of the spiritual realm," I requested, gesturing at the tangled pine trees and the stream. "I know that my element doesn't enclose my body when we meet here. How does this place differ from the other realm?"

Augustin leaned forward and placed his elbows upon his knees. "Where we are now is the *Gæstelort Troumerae*, a secret place no one can reach save those who are bound as Teutons. When we are together here, not even a well-educated priest can sense us, from the mortal world or from the usual realm of the spirit. Though your ice does not shield your body from harm, your slumber protects you just as completely. No one could tell by looking at your sleeping body whether your mind simply dreams its own fantasies or your spirit meets with its lover. This is a place of secrets, a place of shared dreams."

I gaped at Augustin as his eyes glittered at me suggestively, my mind racing through all the possibilities of such an enchanted place. "So when we're here, we'll never meet anyone else, Teuton or demon?" Augustin nodded. "What are the limits, then? If this is technically a spiritual dream, could we change the scene around us into something crazy . . . like Ocean City, New Jersey?" I snickered.

Augustin chuckled, shaking his head. "Unfortunately, there are limits even to the *Gæstelort Troumerae*. We can remain together only in the areas near where our mortal bodies rest; we cannot devise imaginary locations in which to amuse ourselves. Time also constrains us. We could not pass into your twenty-first century world, for both of us are bound to this current continuum. The sky above us shall lighten with the morning, quite soon, in fact."

Augustin paused, glancing through the pine needles at the heavens, then said, "And, of course, that horrid limitation of the traditional spiritual realm also chains us in this place . . . for if it did not, we would be entwined at this very moment." My master grinned, his fiery eyes raking over my robes, his fingers flexing as though he wished to rip them off.

Ridiculous disappointment flooded my spirit, and I sighed. "I guess I'll have to have my own private dreams about you sometime, just to keep myself sane." I chuckled, and Augustin grinned wider. "If we ever *do* happen to meet again in the mortal world . . . ." Shyness peppered my robes with icy flakes.

Augustin's grin turned lecherous as he leaned down to kiss my hair. "I shall wish you to commit adultery with me without delay," he murmured in my ear.

I chortled while his lust and mine dallied together in my spirit. "I've actually considered myself secretly married to you since you created the bond last winter," I informed him rather piously.

My master raised both eyebrows at me. "You are such a terrible Christian, Swanhilde, devising wicked excuses for your sins. It is good that grace covers all of that for saints like you, or you would never make it to heaven."

My mouth twisted into something between a smile and a frown. I contemplated the state of my lover's soul again, consigned to hell by Teuton law, yet still walking the earth among the living. *There must still be some chance for him . . . or he would not still be here . . . .*

Augustin had risen from the branch and stood at the center of the stream, his eyes on the sky, which had begun to turn gray with the dawn. He was likely about to urge me to leave him, to return to my sleeping body and greet my faithful husband with a kiss, readying myself for the rest of our honeymoon. But I still had a thousand questions for Augustin, and I realized that the one I desperately needed to ask was the worst one of all. So I rose from the branch and placed my bare feet upon the pine needles, wrapping my robes more securely around me as I stepped into the water to Augustin's side.

"I know that soon, we'll have to part ways, probably for a while," I began hesitantly. He tore his gaze from the sky to meet my eyes. "But there's something . . . that has really bothered me . . . since that Sunday morning . . . ." My voice broke and I bit my lip, dropping my gaze to the choppy waters beneath my feet.

Augustin's form grew rigid. He stepped away from me, his fists tightening, his jaw working in agitation. For an infinite moment, he stared down at me in silence while I stood in the midst of the stream, his own feet glowing blue with his fire, his toes gripping the opposite bank. And at length he said in a voice laden with denigration, "I have no defense to speak against the truth in my blood." The exact same words he had told the Prince on that fateful morning.

He knew exactly what had troubled me, and I began to tremble. I wrapped my arms around my spirit in a feeble attempt to protect myself from the wretched reality. I tried to speak several times, and finally I lifted my eyes to Augustin's face and choked out, "One hundred . . . *forty-eight?*" He glared down at me, his cobalt robes transforming into licking flames. "In ten years?" His countenance darkened. "That would be . . . more than one per *month* . . . ."

"I was far more rabid in my thirst for blood and death in the early years of my priesthood," Augustin said, his tone flat, his flaming robes swirling around him. "It was the greatest victory I knew at the time."

I struggled to conquer the alarm that threatened to overtake me as I confronted the part of Augustin that I had tried so long to avoid. I looked down at his fiery feet while I collected my thoughts, then met his eyes and whispered, "Did you rape every single one of them? Even the children?" I cringed.

Augustin bared his teeth at me, his whole appearance shaking. "*That* was a long time ago," he exploded, his fiery hands dropping blue flames into the water.

I could feel his anger meddling with the currents of air between us. I wondered for a fleeting moment whether this time I may infuriate him enough to kill me after all. But I had to know every detail, even if the truth compelled me to forsake him forever. "How many?" I asked, my voice barely audible, my robes altering from blue to the white of snow.

Augustin glowered, his eyes burning me to powder. "Thirty-seven children, eighty women, thirty-one animals," he stated tonelessly.

My eyes widened considerably. Had I not already been frozen, I likely would have sunk down into the water. "*The animals?*" I could hardly speak.

"*No!* What do you think I am?!" Augustin roared at me, marching into the stream again, his heat threatening to melt my icy shield.

"Sorry! Sorry!" I squeaked. I raised both hands in defense as he halted less than three centimeters from my chest, his flaming robes licking at my frozen ones.

"You should have left this matter alone, Swanhilde," Augustin snapped, his anger churning around me in a wave of black knives.

Morbid curiosity ate at me while I cowered before him. I sank to my knees in the brook, summoning its waters to reinforce my melting ice. At length, I finally managed to choke out my next query. "How old . . . were . . . the children?"

The silence seemed deafening. I stared blankly at the hem of Augustin's fiery robes, fearing that at any moment, he might decide that I had gone too far and choose to burn my heart into ash. Then I heard him sigh heavily, and he muttered, "The youngest was six."

I gnawed on my lip again and voiced my last and worst question. "Were they . . . all females?" I raised my head to meet Augustin's eyes.

Fury darkened his expression even further, and he whirled away from me, throwing his fiery hands into the air with the accusation, "Swanhilde . . . ! You ask too many questions."

He stomped off down the stream as I stared after him in horror, disturbing images flooding my mind, clawing at my self-proclaimed loyalty to this perverted man. I crouched amidst the waters of the brook and asked myself whether I could honestly love this man, now that I knew the true extent of his immoral obsessions. I had hoped to show him a better way, but I was fighting a losing battle.

Wuotan would laugh at my weak attempts to redeem this demon, for he now held claim to my master's heart.

I endeavored to beat back my panic and disgust, trying to force the lungs of my spirit to draw proper breaths. But mental images of girls and boys wailing as a devil shrouded in darkness broke them upon the altar polluted my brain. *And Wuotan will incite him to do it all again, now that Augustin exists due solely to his power,* I thought, shifting my gaze to where my master stood with his back to me some distance down the stream. *What prompted him to sacrifice children, anyway?*

"Do you . . . think it's fun . . . to rape little kids?" I heard myself saying. I felt as though my lungs had turned to solid ice within my spirit.

The virulent flames enveloping Augustin's robes began to burn out, and I saw his fingers flexing at his sides. "My motivations were far simpler than that. I am no pedophile," he said after a protracted pause, his face turned staunchly away from where I hunkered amid the chattering waters. "Children are easier to catch, easier to control, easier to subjugate. Just a small bit of tonic added to a glass of milk, and they grow passive."

"So you drugged them . . . raped them . . . and murdered them," I translated, shuddering further into myself. I could no longer speak silently to the currents around me, to ask them for reassurance. The man I loved was an evil physician, one who used his skills to kill.

"Swanhilde, it has been years since I last sacrificed a child," Augustin said, having turned just enough for me to see his profile. His expression was drawn, and I may have sensed guilt emanating into my heart through our bond. "I learned quite quickly that my master prefers adults, for they offer a greater supply of blood . . . and more options for erotic triumphs." His lips twitched.

I breathed a sigh and looked toward the lightening sky for a time. Though our heart-bond had shackled us into an eternal strife, the memory of the love I had seen in Augustin's blood dappled my gloomy thoughts with color. I had made a promise to myself on that fateful Sunday when I watched Augustin scream in pain before Marelda's tomb: *He will not lose Swanhilde von Thaden.* Despite what his demon master may force him to do, he was still the man who risked all to pull me back from death . . . the man who treated me as his equal . . . the man who championed me before the entire council of Muniche . . . the man who held my heart in his hands.

So I lifted my spirit from the mud at the bottom of the stream and cautiously approached my master, the fire of his spirit cooled at last. I came around to stand in front of him, studying his face as he stared up at the brightening sky. Remorse and torment enveloped the air around him. When he lowered his eyes to meet my gaze, I told him, "Augustin . . . I forgive you, because I know you're not that man anymore. You're still everything to me, and there is still hope."

He blinked at me once, a pained expression marring his perfect visage. "You really ought to stop forgiving me so carelessly," he chided with a sigh.

"You're probably right, but I made you a promise, remember?" I reached out to touch his cheek, my fingers hardly detecting the warmth of his fire. "I promised to love you no matter what you become. I don't go back on my word."

Augustin grimaced and drifted away from me, shifting his gaze back to the sky above. "The worst of the iniquities that the murderer and the Old One pulled from my blood occurred long before I met you . . . before I recognized that love still exists in this cruel world. I can honestly say, Swanhilde, that I have not sacrificed a human since you found me in the forest that night, unleashing my devilries on that Saxon woman. But now, Wuotan has bound me into forced servitude, and he shall not remain satisfied indefinitely with the blood of hares and deer. He shall thrust me back into civilization soon, that I may offer him human blood once more."

I shook my head slowly, knowing that I would have to think this through. I needed to come up with some solution to hold Augustin back from committing such terrible acts again, no matter what Wuotan demanded of him. If I had distracted him from his ultimate high of murder since that horrible day in the forest, perhaps I could help him retain his humanity even though he was already dead.

"Well, if Wuotan orders you back into civilization, maybe you should do something else," I suggested, looking my lover earnestly in the eyes. "*I* remember that we used to study together. *I* remember that you once gloried in knowledge, in languages, in new information. If no one in German lands will accept you, maybe you could travel the continent. Go back to Salerno and finish your medical degree. Learn more languages, more histories. We could study together again, here in our dreams. English, German, Bayerisch, Ælte Teutonica, anything! That would be better than wallowing in our melancholy . . . how better for both of us to move on with our lives?"

Augustin made a thoughtful sound in his throat, his countenance smoothing out while he considered this new option. "That may actually . . . work . . . since outsiders do not understand the curse." He nodded, looking thoughtful.

I smiled up at him and stuck out my right hand, an offer. "Salerno, languages, studies?" I tilted my head at him.

Augustin smiled back at me and enclosed my hand in his fingers, our spirits feeling no contact in our spectral handshake. And his eyes drifted downward to the robes at my stomach as he said, "Our future . . . and our child."

Chapter Eight:
Freia's Struggles

The transition into married life proved less difficult than I had expected. When Joel and I returned from our ten-day honeymoon in the forest, both of us looking tanner and more tousled than before, the count welcomed us back with proper fanfare, escorting us to our new bedroom himself. He had furnished it with a wide bed, matching wardrobes, a large washing table, a sturdy desk for Joel and me to share, and a comfortable horsehair chair for me to use whenever I felt the need to sew. I noticed a twinkle in the count's blue eyes when he mentioned this. He likely hoped that the Thaden line would produce many children, since his own had not.

On the first Saturday after our return, the count held a noonday feast in our honor, complete with roast goose and mutton. All of the landed nobility around Muniche attended, along with the Denlingers and some of Joel's friends from the ironworks. Since most of the guests had Teuton blood, Joel and I entertained them by dancing one elemental dance through the front gardens, his wind carrying us effortlessly over blooming bushes as my ice whirled around us in a wintry storm. I had taught Joel a few things about his wind during our honeymoon, and he had picked up the dancing with little difficulty.

I missed passing the afternoon and evening hours with my Rhenisch friend, for Freia spent as much time preparing her fiancé's new cottage for their use as she spent at the manor. I helped her on several occasions, but I found myself saddled with countless new duties as the future matron of the Meldorf estate. I had to learn how to manage the household from both Ulka and Jarvis, while Joel spent most of his time outside learning the finer points of farming. After poring over the count's financial records in his office on a rainy afternoon, I resolved that we would start using Arabic numerals rather than the Roman ones going forward. I knew that the modern form of numbers would not spread throughout German lands until the next century, but I could not abide doing math with cumbersome clusters of letters.

Freia and Heinrich planned to tie the knot on the second Saturday in August. As the date drew nearer, I noticed a strange darkness clouding Freia's countenance that seemed to extend beyond the typical stress of relocating. I gently urged her to confide in me a few times at the evening meal, but she just offered a wan smile and brushed off my concerns, shifting the topic to happier things, like how Heinrich's sisters had been helping her furnish the cottage. But I saw uncertainty lurking in her pleasant gaze, so I went to her chamber one morning before Sext, hoping that my new status as a married woman had not driven a stake in our friendship.

I found her layering her undergarments with fresh rags, her tainted ones bundled in the laundry basket beside the chamber pot. "Oh, good morning, Swanie," she greeted when I pushed the door open. She turned away from me out of decency and remarked, "Still nothing for you?"

"Nothing but a child with nigh perfect Teuton blood," I said, grimacing as I turned for the bed that was no longer mine. I sat down and rubbed my abdomen distractedly; my pregnancy had not yet begun to show.

"You'll be fine," Freia assured me, straightening her skirt and coming to sit across from me on her own bed. "You're strong, and I've prayed for you twice each day since you told me. God will protect you, as He has all this time."

I met her eyes, trying to see beyond her peaceful veneer. She was looking at my right hand, which still rested upon my womb. Her blond eyebrows furrowed. "Are you afraid of bearing children as a Teuton woman?" I asked, running my gaze over her quickly from head to toe. She was just a hair taller than me, but her hips were wider, her breasts rounded and full. She had a robust body, one that should be able to withstand its natural duty. *Rhinelanders are hardier than Teutons.*

"It's not that," she said with a sigh. She pursed her lips and looked out the window at the farmland beyond, her posture stiff now. "I know I can do it," she went on at length, still looking away, "because I already did it once." Pain contorted her face when she looked back at me, her eyes damp with tears. "Just a month before I escaped the Gypsies . . . I bore a son. Their witch woman tore him from me . . . it was not yet his time."

Horror overtook me. My ice began to prickle inside my veins as I gaped at my best friend, unsure how to respond. She had hinted before that the Gypsies had raped her, but I had never imagined that she had gotten pregnant. "Freia . . . ."

"I heard him cry," she said, twisting her hands in her lap. "I heard him, but they had me chained. They took him from me . . . and used his blood for a tonic. I never got to hold him." A sob broke from her lips, and I flew to her side and took her in my arms.

We clung to each other for a long while, icy tears seeping from my own eyes at Freia's grief. "You'll see him again," I murmured to her after a few moments of shared sorrow, for her faith surpassed that of any other Christian I had known. "I know he's proud of you, seizing a destiny that most people can only dream about. You've claimed heaven's light for yourself." I sensed her brilliant spirit reaching out to mine, my ice's aura gradually calming her.

"Thank you, Swanie," she said as she slipped away from my grasp, dabbing her tears on the end of her sleeve. "I'm mostly at peace with his fate. I know that God needed him more than I did." She blinked at me, a look of worry creasing her forehead. "I keep thinking about what Lord Niklas said, that I'm damaged goods. I haven't told Heinrich yet, because I'm scared he'll think the same."

I shook my head firmly and grasped both of her hands. "I really don't think Heinrich's that shallow," I assured her, giving her fingers a firm squeeze. "What the Gypsies did to you wasn't your fault, and he knows that or he wouldn't have courted you in the first place. He's enamored with you, Freia; you can see it on his face anytime he looks at you."

Freia embraced me again, her light brightening her spirit, enclosing me in its radiance. When we descended the stairs on our way to lunch soon afterward, I informed her that all of the local bachelors were merely jealous, for the ironmaster was about to marry the most brilliant maiden in the entire Empire. She chortled and shoved me, and we entered the great hall hand-in-hand, ready to share a meal with the count, Joel, and the rest of the household.

On the day before Freia's Teutonic wedding, I found her standing in front of the mirror in the bedroom that neither of us would occupy as of the next night. I had come to ask her opinions on the final touches I had added to her wedding dress, which was a vibrant yellow trimmed with gold to match her light. I stopped short in the doorway when I saw her tense posture before the mirror, her green eyes staring at her reflection rather doubtfully. At first, I had no clue what disturbed her; from where I stood, her face appeared clean and perfect. A moment later, I watched her eyes glow brighter as she frowned in concentration, her entire visage growing radiant like the sun. My eyes widened, and I allowed my ice to trickle into my veins, detecting Freia's light pulsing within her, seeking an outlet for its magic.

Freia noticed me not long after, and an embarrassed smile touched her lips when she beckoned me forward. "I'm sorry, Swanie. I know I should be helping you with the last-minute preparations for tomorrow . . . . But I'm trying to figure something out." She peered at her face in the mirror.

"You're trying to learn how to use your light; I know," I said softly, crossing the floor to her side. "I used to do the same thing, after I first danced with Hans in my time. I would stand in front of my mirror for hours, watching my eyes turn from gray to blue, watching my skin and hair take on the translucent sheen of ice." I grinned, and a sheen of blue enveloped my irises.

Freia smiled back at me, but her mien still appeared unsure. "I'm not very good at this yet," she confessed, placing both of her hands upon the washing table. Her eyes glowed brightly for a moment, then faded. "I can't quite grasp exactly *how* to pull the light out of my spirit, what it is that sets it free. I can make my eyes glow like a cat's in the dark, and my skin seems to shine more brightly when I really concentrate, but you use your ice with such precision. When you dance, you can even turn rushing waters into frozen waves. I'm not sure how to actually bring my light *outside* of me." She frowned and turned to face me. "I need to figure out how to dance as a Teuton. How is that supposed to work . . . light and metal?"

I had danced with light once before, but never metal. It seemed like an odd combination, and I had speculated occasionally on Heinrich's dancing abilities as a derivative of earth. I wondered how high he could leap with such a heavy element, and whether he could pull the rocks along with him in a dance. "You'll have a lot of time to practice with Heinrich during your honeymoon," I reassured my friend, feeling somewhat guilty that I had not instructed her yet in the use of her light. "Once you've really figured everything out, you'll be able to light up a dark room as though it were midday. I bet you could blind any enemies who tried to attack you, and maybe even burn them with the sun."

Freia shook her head at my fervor, doubt clouding her expression. "When would I find the time to learn all of that as a newlywed wife? Soon, both of us will be too busy raising children and managing our households to bother with elemental glories." She sighed wistfully.

She was right, and my thoughts turned momentarily to the child inside my womb. Bouts of morning sickness had struck me already, though I had not yet told Joel about my condition. He would assume that the child was his. My best friend was getting married tomorrow, and after that our hours together would grow few, since she would be living in the city. Inspiration grabbed hold of me all at once, and I jerked my head toward the window. "Why don't we go out there and dance together right now? I could show you a thing or two, and at least it would give you a little bit of experience."

Freia gaped at me. "In front of the vassals?"

I shrugged. "Joel's out there with them. Maybe if he sees us, he'll lay down his tools and join in. Dancing with wind is actually pretty amazing." Freia still looked hesitant, and I suddenly realized that, as a novice, she would not feel comfortable simply leaping out of a window at the start of an elemental dance. So I pointed my feet toward the hallway and waved for her to follow. "Let's go make the guys jealous. We can dance toward the stream, and then I can really start using my ice!" I grinned and jogged toward the back stairs. Freia followed at my heels, giggling in nervous anticipation.

I led my friend to the flower gardens, then glanced around at the few peasant women trimming and watering the nearby vegetation. No men were in sight, and I doubted that the women would complain about what we were about to do. So I turned to face Freia, who had halted several paces away from me beside a sizeable clump of blooming sunflowers, her green eyes still appearing unsure.

I drew my ice out of my spirit in preparation to dance, concentrating briefly on the bursting life around me while my skin iced over. Then I addressed Freia quietly, recalling my first dance with Hans so long ago. "It's not as difficult as you believe, to free your element in a Teutonic dance," I told her, my eyes glittering blue. "We're outside now, in the realm of nature, and you are light. You must let go of caution and focus on the rays of sun shining upon you, upon the gardens, reflecting off of the windowpanes." I gestured once toward the house at her back. "Delve into your spirit, Freia, and *know* that you can embrace this freedom, this glory. It is within you, waiting to escape. Dance with me." I held out one icy hand, an invitation.

I watched my best friend close her eyes, her smooth brow furrowing in meditation while she sought to awaken the powers of her Teuton blood. I reached out to her with my ice, allowing it to caress her radiant spirit, to beckon it forward, away from its bodily shell. Freia's skin gradually began to shine more brightly, her golden hair taking on the color of the sun. When she opened her eyes, I saw that they glowed a brilliant jasmine, all traces of green erased. She stepped forward to take my hand, her body unconsciously moving with an *Eihalbe's* grace. As her skin touched mine, I felt a rush of sunlight upon my flesh, prompting me to gasp in wonder. An instant later, Freia pulled away, her face appearing distressed at the frigid temperature of my element. I remembered how disturbed I had been when I first felt Hans' fire against my skin, so I quickly consoled my friend. "Don't fear. My ice won't freeze you, for we are equals."

Freia hesitated one second longer, her light illuminating her countenance with even greater glory. Then she grabbed my hand with a newfound surety, her teeth sparkling white, her lips parting into a triumphant smile. And we set our elements free in unison, racing together through the gardens, my ice creating a realm of freezing air around me while Freia's light brushed everything in our path.

After a preliminary sprint along the path to the road, I pivoted and charged into the flowerbeds. I sprinkled ice crystals upon them as I passed, leaping over the smaller clumps with the freedom of my element. Freia followed me with enthusiasm, her light casting rainbows all over my frozen water droplets, her brilliance transforming them into mist upon the flowers. At one point I let Freia lead our race, and she carried me in her wake back to the house. She snatched the sunlight reflected upon the windows, and her body burned like a radiant star.

I broke away from her with a laugh and leapt back into the gardens, letting loose the speed of my element as I shot toward the stream in an icy blizzard. Freia pursued me like a luminous comet, her own laughter pealing forth, her glowing hands seeking to catch me. But I made it to the stream before her and jumped upon it, my hair icing over at the propinquity of my element's primary.

I spun to face Freia, who had halted upon the bank. I grinned at the sight of her hesitation. Then I brought my right arm upward in a wide arc, raising a frozen wave from the waters of the tiny stream to tower over my head, raining ice particles upon my dress and hair. Freia gasped in response, and I chuckled at myself. I was getting carried away. I stepped off of the stream, calming my ice gradually while my frozen wave began to drip in the summer heat. Freia shook her head at me, her light dimming, her expression suggesting that she considered my abilities to be far more advanced than hers.

I trotted to her side and nodded casually toward my melting wave. "If you use your light to manipulate the rays of the sun, you might be able to disintegrate my magic faster." I winked at her suggestively.

She blinked at me, her irises yet a shimmering amber. Then she averted her gaze to the blazing sun above, her iridescent eyes staring directly at it—something I could never do. I gaped at Freia in amazement while she pursed her lips at the sun, her blond hair transforming into solid rays of light, her eyes darting from the sky to my thawing wave. She lifted her hands slowly in the direction of the brook, her light exploding from her fingers like beams from a flashlight . . . and in less than ten seconds, my wave had liquefied, rejoining the brook.

"See, you're just as skilled a witch as me!" I cried out as her eyes returned at last to their natural green. A delighted chortle burst from her throat and I jumped forward to hug her, giggling with her at her victory, telling her over and over again that her Teutonic abilities outshone even mine.

A short time later, Joel encroached upon our celebrations, brushing his dirty hands off on his pants. "It looks like I missed all the fun," he complained. "I *felt* you two dancing over here, messing with the currents of wind; and I dropped my rake in the ground to join you, but you've already finished." He pouted at me.

I grinned, stepping away from Freia and refocusing on my ice. "I don't *have* to be finished, my darling cyclone. Come see if you can blow my icy creations to the ground." I held out my hand to him, letting my fingers freeze again. Joel smirked, and his eyes turned the gray of wind as he sprang forward to dance with me.

Joel and I exchanged a bit of humorous speculations on Heinrich and Freia on the night of their Teutonic wedding, while we lay together in our bed after the ceremony. The count had also attended along with Heinrich's immediate family, including, to my surprise, his sick father. Prince Otto had officiated the nuptials, which did not particularly please me. I had stuck close to Joel the entire time, never meeting the Prince's eyes, keeping my attention fixed upon my best friend and her groom.

As Joel played with a few locks of my black hair, I mentioned that Freia and Heinrich were likely enjoying themselves quite thoroughly at the moment, somewhere deep in the forest. Tears of joy had trickled down Freia's face when they had sealed their marriage with a kiss. Sorrow had pierced my heart as I watched Heinrich caress his bride's face with the tenderness of devoted love. I would never know what it was like to marry the man I truly loved.

"I think Heinrich *was* a virgin," Joel commented with a snicker. His right hand moved away from my hair to stroke my left breast. "I wonder if they've figured everything out by now." He cackled and fondled me affectionately.

I laughed quietly at Joel's humor and closed my eyes to concentrate on his touch, ordering myself to stop wishing he was Augustin. "*I* wonder what it'll be like for Freia, getting intimate with metal. It seems like he might be kind of heavy."

"Well, if she can use her light like the fires in the foundry, she could melt him in her hands." I smirked at Joel's ingenuity, and he leaned down to kiss my lips, his arms enclosing me in the chains of marriage.

I informed him of my pregnancy the following morning. His hazel eyes lit up in enthusiasm, and he demanded whether that was the reason he kept smelling vomit in our chamber pot. I rolled my eyes and told him that I had Viktor empty the pot anytime I used it for that purpose. "You ought to inform him whenever you take a crap there," I added, for he had a habit of unleashing his bowels there every morning instead of using the communal latrine. He claimed that he had difficulty pooping in public.

While we dressed ourselves for the day, we entertained a few conjectures on whether the child would be a boy or a girl and whether it would beat all odds to have blond hair like him, when most Teuton children sported dark hair. I played along with Joel's assumptions, although I knew for a fact that the child I carried was not his. Joel said that we needed to talk with Gretchen to find out how medieval women handled childbirth. I suspected that I would be forced to suppress my ice once I drew closer to my due date, since its sharp and frigid qualities could conceivably injure an infant. Dusky spurge grew in the herb garden, so I knew that its restrictive potion would eventually become a part of my life.

I longed for Augustin to return to my dreams, so I could talk with him about our child once more. And I debated within myself whether I ought to ask him to perform a sacrifice for my sake, just in case Wuotan seized the opportunity to shove my soul towards the gates of time.

Chapter Nine:
The Price of Iniquity

Our double wedding came and went on the last Saturday of the Oktoberfest. All of the landowning families around attended, along with the heads of the major trades of the city with their families. Most of the count's vassals and servants also came, and all of the commoners from the ironworks. We paid the bishop of Muniche to conduct the ceremony at my own insistence, for I did not want to be wed with Paulus von Bayern officiating. Joel agreed with me on that. I had told him about Paulus' eventual betrayal of our people, and Joel had considered him a coward ever since. The three Denlinger sisters were our maids of honor, and the groomsmen included two of Heinrich's cousins and Joel's former roommate Arik.

At the close of the ceremony, the four of us exited the cathedral to the triumphant sounds of the organ—played by Prince Otto, to my private chagrin. We leapt into the count's best carriage, wreathed with white ribbons in our honor, announcing to Jarvis in unison that he should drive us swiftly to the reception with the power of his energy. We all ended up in a rumpled heap against the back wall of the wagon as Jarvis drove the horses toward the Meldorf estate.

My headdress and veil became entangled with Freia's, and she got stuck beneath Heinrich's hulking body, prompting her to squeak and poke at him between giggles.

The majority of the wedding guests attended the reception, forsaking the final galas of the Oktoberfest in our honor. We ate dinner outside in the cool air of early autumn. Heaping tables offered roast chicken, goose, mutton, and hare along with the bounties of the late harvests, from freshly baked spelt rolls and biscuits to juicy tomatoes, red and white cabbage, several types of lettuce, string beans, apples, and pears. Beer and wine flowed along with the usual mead, and all of the guests settled onto the grass of the count's gardens to watch the sparks of energy and fire in the distance while twilight descended upon Muniche.

As I lay in Joel's arms observing the bursting colors in the sky, I remembered the countless dances I had shared earlier with the noblemen, all of whom paid the required fee to dance with one of the brides. I had whirled with metal, earth, darkness, and energy that day . . . but for the first time in my life, I had refused to dance with fire. The Prince had offered, possibly in an attempt to prove that he harbored no hard feelings toward me, but I had walked away. The image of his face screwed up in rage—his right hand reaching out to slap my face after he had damned my lover—would forever taint my opinion of him.

During the winter months, I spent a lot of time altering several of my dresses to make room for my swelling abdomen. I also worked with Emilie, Felda, and Eva on an array of outfits for the child, along with blankets for its cradle and a mountain of cloth diapers. The mental image of washing disgusting diapers by hand prompted my twenty-first century mind to cringe, but thankfully the laundry maids would perform that repulsive duty in my stead. Since the count owned no furniture appropriate for a newborn, I purchased a wooden cradle from the city sawmill and a few toys suitable for a baby of either gender. In the beginning, the child would sleep in the same bedroom as Joel and me, but once the child grew old enough,

I planned to furnish one of the upstairs chambers as his or her bedroom.

Augustin visited me in my dreams quite often during the final months of my pregnancy, his fiery blue eyes riveted on the robes at my stomach while he inquired after my health and the child's. I assured him time and again that I had heeded his advice, abstaining from unnecessary work and eating the healthy foods my body demanded. In the *Gæstelort Troumerae*, my spirit did not look pregnant at all, which relieved me since I felt far more untroubled when I did not have to worry about the baby forming inside of me. Besides, I had put on a bit of weight with the pregnancy. I told Augustin at one point that by the time 1066 came around, I would likely look like I carried a permanent boulder inside my stomach. Augustin rolled his eyes at my grim speculations and said that since we must meet in the spiritual realm, we would always see the unchanging beauty of each other's spirits rather than our degenerating bodies.

Augustin enrolled at the medical university in Salerno by early winter, having finally shoved aside his concerns about what Wuotan would ask of him once he returned to civilization. He informed me that many of the professors recognized him from before, and that he had to correct them when they addressed him by his cursed name. He had chosen the Teutonic name of Wolfgang Wolfrik Wolfe for himself, which I found rather repetitive and absurd. He explained that it aptly reflected his current state as the only Black Priest yet bound to the earth, crying at the moon in loneliness and discontent.

The nights tormented him the most, he told me. He usually remained awake while his colleagues slept, sitting alone beneath the night sky, endeavoring to stave off Wuotan's temptations to sacrifice human blood. He said that he often wished to see my face again, to give him reason to hold back the evil in his soul. I begged him to come to my dreams whenever he desired, every night if he wished it; for I would rather share secret fantasies with him than dream alone, even if it ruined my marriage. Augustin replied rather darkly that I should stop clinging to my masochism, for the good in him would eventually crumble at his master's insistence.

We restarted our language studies in the *Gæstelort Troumerae*, though the fact that neither of us could leave a mark on the mortal world as dreaming spirits created difficulties. Augustin had brought my English-Teutonica dictionary with him in his exile, but he had already mastered most of the phrases I had doggedly translated. I tried several times to write with his pens and paper when we met at his chamber in Salerno, but my master informed me that none of the marks I left on his papers remained once we parted ways. He hypothesized that manipulating mortal objects while dreaming in the spirit was likely more complicated than doing so in the traditional spirit realm, since not even Teuton priests could sense us when we met in our dreams. We walked together in a world that did not exist, a place where we could properly interact with no one and nothing but each other.

Eventually we resolved to work on our dictionaries in our spare time and pore over them in our dreams, meeting one night at Salerno and the next at the Meldorf estate. Augustin began to teach me Magyar that winter at my request, for I wanted to be able to communicate with Viktor. I often saw him drifting from place to place on the estate, doing yard work and simple tasks, his expression usually appearing sad and uncomprehending. He likely wondered what had become of Augustin, and someday I wanted to be able to tell him.

I knew, as the month of March slowly melted the snows of February, that my pregnancy was almost complete. I felt the baby moving inside of me quite often, awakening the mothering instinct within me. Gretchen prepared the tonic of dusky spurge for me in early March at my insistence, though she insisted that it was too early for such things. I had to take the tonic every morning and night to keep my ice confined within my spirit. I felt as though I passed each day in a blurred haze, lumbering from the bedroom to the great hall and back again, my breasts and abdomen swollen and uncomfortable.

The count promised to send for Gretchen as soon as the pains of labor struck me, for she delivered all of the babies born on his estate. Freia visited often to help me clean and prepare, and she insisted that I send Jarvis or one of the other servants to summon her the moment my contractions began. She was four months pregnant by that time herself, and she could hardly wait to bear her beloved Heinrich his first child. Her enthusiasm reinforced my own silent torment, augmented by Joel's supportive gestures. I wished more than anything that the real father of my baby could be with me when my time came.

The pains of labor seized me on a Wednesday evening in mid-March. Joel and I and were playing chess together in the front parlor when the first contractions began, and I vomited the entirety of my dinner as Ulka led me down the hallway to my bedroom. My water broke on the way there, and Ulka helped me out of my undergarments once she had shut the door to Joel and all of the other men. Her expression slightly worried, Ulka promised that Gretchen would attend me soon; then she left me alone.

The bedroom seemed unbearably hot to me, the coals crackling in the fireplace raising sweat upon my forehead. Another contraction hit me sharply in the lower intestines, and I groaned, crouching over the chamber pot as fluid poured from my womb. While I waited impatiently for the midwife to come, anticipation overtook me despite my discomfort. Soon, I would look upon the face of my baby, my small memento of Augustin, whom I had carried with me for nine long months. I concentrated on our heart-bond when the contraction subsided, silently calling for him like he had asked. Hopefully he could plead my case if Wuotan tried to kill me . . . or the child.

I had hoped that my first experience with childbirth would be simple and quick. Many of the local noblewomen had visited me in recent months to relate their own tales of travail, some far worse than others. Lady Adeline had told me that birthing her first child had been easy. The first contractions had struck her around mid-afternoon, and she had borne her husband a son by the time the sky had turned red with sunset. Lady Hildegard also said that she had the least trouble with the birth of her first daughter; her two sons, she complained, had taken their sweet time.

Unfortunately for me, it soon became clear that the child inside my womb did not want to come out. While the darkness of night descended, my labor pains centered in my back like stabbing knives. Gretchen came as I pressed my lower back against the windowsill during a particularly painful contraction. She rushed to my side and remarked that my labor had started much too soon.

I knew otherwise, of course, but I could not blurt out the truth to the midwife, since she believed my child to be Joel's. Freia arrived after nightfall and helped Gretchen put counter pressure on my back with each contraction. My thoughts turned occasionally to Joel as I suffered that night, wondering whether he waited just outside the door or in the parlor with the count and Jarvis. He probably did not appreciate the medieval custom of keeping the men away during childbirth, since twenty-first century customs were far different. He likely wished he could be in the room snapping pictures of my torment with my digital camera, which had eight batteries left.

I, for one, felt grateful that he remained far away, for I did not want him to distract me from concentrating on the real father of my baby. Augustin's hands caressed my heart whenever the pain caused me to groan, reassuring me of his presence and support. I wondered distractedly whether he might actually be in the room with me during that long night, standing in the shadows of the spiritual realm, watching me struggle to bring our child into the world. Since the dusky spurge had stifled my ice, I could not know for certain. When my mind was not consumed with the anguish, my thoughts drifted from Augustin to our baby, wondering whether it would be a boy or a girl, whether it would look like him . . . .

Exhaustion covered me in a heavy cloak as the golden light of dawn seeped through the bedroom window. I had spent the night pacing the room and bracing myself against the windowsill and fireplace mantle. Gretchen had offered me tea several times, and after prodding my abdomen and examining my vagina, she observed that the child might be turned the wrong way. Fear seized me at such a prospect, and I began to whisper prayers in Teutonica, begging for God's mercy to spare both me and the child. My strength waned, and I feared that Wuotan sought to kill us both.

By mid-morning, Gretchen warned me that if I could not manage to birth the child by afternoon, she would cut my vagina with a knife and pull the baby out. Horror overtook me as I sat panting on a chair, and Freia clutched my hand in an attempt at comfort. "Are you *sure* . . . that would be . . . necessary? It might . . . kill us both . . . ." I wished more than ever that Augustin could be present in the flesh for this ordeal. At least if he cut me and pulled the child out, he would be able to stop the bleeding from my womb before I died from blood loss. I did not know if I had the brainpower to focus on blood control after such a torturous night.

Gretchen placed a wet cloth upon my forehead, wiping away my sweat for what seemed like the millionth time since the pains had begun. "My Lady Swanhilde, we must get that baby out of you somehow. You've tried all night with no success," she said, her blue-gray eyes studying me gravely. "Perhaps if you move around the room again, the child's head may slide down enough for you to bear it normally. That has worked with a few of the common women here."

Both Freia and Gretchen helped me stand, and the midwife gradually led me around the bedroom once more. After circling the room at a snail's pace half a dozen times, Gretchen asked Freia to brace me against one of the empty spaces at the wall, right beside the fireplace. Before I had time to fully piece together the meaning of such an act, the midwife bore down on my distended stomach with both of her hands, pressing on my womb with incredible force. In the next instant, a sickening torrent of pain stabbed me from inside, prompting me to screech and sink to the floor. Dreadful contractions seized me all at once, and I felt an uncontrollable urge to push.

Though my memories of what came afterward remain hazy to this day, I do recall that I ended up on the bed, my body thrashing as the child within me sought to come out at long last. The agony was worse in some ways than what I had experienced during the blood-transfer. Sometimes, when my awareness wavered between contractions, I imagined that I saw Augustin standing at my bedside, his appearance resplendent as a spirit. His visage was fierce as he ordered me to continue the fight, to finish with the birthing though it drained my vitality, not to fear the deceit of Wuotan, for he could not take the one who belonged to his servant.

I wanted to cling to Augustin, though the stabbing pains brought me back to reality again and again. I wanted to beg him aloud to stay with me, to grant me his strength, to claim the child I was about to bear as his own. I may have choked out some sort of plea to his spirit in Bayerisch as I suffered, although neither he nor the women attending me would have understood it. My mouth could not form any words but those of my native tongue due to the pain, though Freia likely heard me gasp out Augustin's name in between groans.

At long last, I managed to push the child out of me after what seemed like endless failures. Gretchen had ultimately cut part of my vagina to allow the birthing to be completed. I recall that it felt similar to taking the hugest dump I had ever taken in my life, akin to expelling the entirety of my intestines in a heap. Afterward, as I lay panting, my body and mind somewhat in shock that those awful contractions had ceased, I heard Freia gasp softly in a tone that pierced my heart. Then I heard Gretchen's terrible statement, "It's too late."

The haze of weakness still hung onto me, but the truth of the matter struck me hard when I realized that I had not yet heard the child cry. Sorrow grabbed hold of me along with exhaustion. Now I would have no living reminder of my cursed master, no laughing child to brighten my world and take my mind off of my desolate fortune. After that interminable night of agony, I had nothing to show for it.

My child was dead. Sobs seized me, and I screamed, salty tears gushing from my eyes.

I felt myself weakening from blood loss as I wept, and I struggled to picture what my womb must look like, which blood vessels needed to be repaired. *I can't die, too, or else Augustin will go insane.* I worked to focus on slowing the blood flow, pulling away from my grief just long enough to save myself.

I heard Freia asking what went wrong, and Gretchen murmured that she was not entirely sure. "The baby came too early, and Lady Swanhilde's water broke too soon. The nature of her labor suggests that the baby wasn't turned the right way." She muttered something else that I did not catch, and I gave an aggravated whimper. *The baby died because it wasn't strong enough to fight a demon, but it's not like I can tell Gretchen that,* I thought.

I felt a wet towel pressed against the bloody flesh between my legs, Freia's cool hands massaging my stomach as she murmured her condolences, looking me in the eyes. Tears trembled on her eyelashes, and the light in her spirit seemed to have dimmed, but I detected no fear for my own life in her gaze. I silently thanked Augustin for teaching me blood control, then addressed my best friend in a weary voice. "Was it . . . was it . . . a boy . . . or a girl?"

Freia glanced away momentarily to inquire silently of Gretchen. Then she turned back to me and said, "A girl."

Tears leaked onto my cheeks at this news. I imagined a beautiful young girl with dancing eyes and dimples running through the gardens of the estate in playful exuberance. I would never have that now. The possibility was lost forever. "Please . . . Freia . . . ." I gasped, my voice cracking. "Please . . . let me . . . hold her . . . ."

At first, Gretchen refused, for she said that it would make it harder for me to accept the child's death if I held her myself. But I persisted, a scream building within me at the midwife's hesitation. Freia addressed Gretchen in a strong voice, ordering her to allow me to claim the child as my own. Her sharp expression implied that she was thinking back to how the Gypsies had misused her; she looked like an aggressive phoenix. A moment later, she placed my dead baby in my sweaty arms.

I stared down at the tiny child for an infinite time, my bleary eyes taking in every detail of the result of my fornication with Augustin. The child was beautiful, her head adorned with black curls damp with blood and vernix, her body still retaining a trace of warmth. Her limbs were perfect and chubby, though they dangled lifelessly, and her facial features would have resembled a miniature angel, had her lips not been hued an ashen gray. Her face appeared peaceful in death, devoid of pain. In spite of my disappointment, I felt a brief wash of pleasure in knowing that I would meet my daughter one day in heaven. I held her close for many minutes, kissing her hair, whispering that I would love her always.

Gretchen had left the room to inform the men of the child's death, and Freia knelt at my bedside, massaging my abdomen and pressing a towel to my torn skin to catch the discharge. I looked at my daughter's face one final time, preparing to speak my goodbyes. I cradled her in my left arm and brought my right hand to her eyes, my tremulous fingers gently pushing back the lids. I gave a sorrowful croon, and my heart skipped a beat at the sight of her lifeless eyes, frozen and unseeing, their color matching her father's exactly—the light blue summer sky.

Freia hovered over me the moment she sensed my distress, and I heard her gasp when she saw what had troubled me. I remained mesmerized by the gorgeous eyes of my dead daughter until the midwife returned and took her out of my arms.

Not long afterward, Gretchen brought me a mug of peppermint tea and told me that the men intended to bury my daughter that afternoon while I rested. Then she asked me what name I wanted them to write upon the wooden marker for her grave. After considering for a moment, my wearied eyes met Freia's sympathetic gaze as I answered, "Marelda Swanhilde von Thaden."

Chapter Ten

Picking up the Pieces

Freia sat with me while I sipped the tea, which the midwife said would help dry up my unneeded breast milk. That tidbit was news to me, but I had learned an odd variety of ancient remedies since I had come to the eleventh century two years ago. Elderberries for colds and flu, feverfew for headaches, thyme for cough, silver oak leaves for wounds.

Joel visited me after I had finished the tea, intending to surrender to sleep at long last. He comforted me for a time, his expression drawn and sad. Jarvis and Leo, the head of our vassals, were in the process of digging a grave for my daughter, and Joel mentioned that the child had looked a lot like me. I wondered whether Joel had an inkling that Marelda was not his child; he knew how to do math, after all. But I kept my thoughts to myself and murmured that I was tired, so he left me to rest.

Sleep took me shortly thereafter, the pictures in my dreams melting into one another at first, carrying me along the customary path of slumber. I would have rested peacefully had the memories of my lifeless baby girl not cropped up again and again in my mind, her dark curls and sky blue eyes akin to those of Marelda von Bayern, the saint-like woman who had once been Augustin's mother. The thought crossed my brain, even in my meaningless dreams, that Joel may eventually ask what had made me choose the name Marelda for my dead baby . . . and I would have to come up with some sort of explanation . . . .

Finally, my erratic reveries coalesced into a more believable world. I found myself standing upon a grassy hill on the grounds of the Meldorf estate not far from the well, several leafy linden trees ringing the place where I stood, the sky above me turning gray with dusk. I recognized my location as the Meldorf graveyard, a place I had visited occasionally when I sought a sanctity of stillness. My gaze passed over the crosses that marked the final resting place of the count's beloved wife and their three children. The perils of raising a family in the Middle Ages struck me again at the sight of so many markers. I wondered how many children I would lose before Muniche fell.

I noticed, as the dark blue of twilight descended upon the glade, that I was not alone amongst the wooden crosses of the Meldorf cemetery. A fresh grave had been dug at the northern end of the dell, set apart from the others, a new cross placed at its head. Kneeling there upon the ground, clothed in shimmering robes of sapphire, I saw Augustin's spirit, his face turned away from me, focused solely on the tiny grave before him.

Sorrow gripped me when I approached him, not certain at first whether I should disturb his meditation or not. Then I realized, as I glanced upward at the darkening sky, that I had already been asleep for quite some time. Augustin must have summoned my spirit, or I would not be here. So I laid my right hand upon his shoulder, though I could not quite feel his robes or his gorgeous hair. He did not acknowledge my presence visibly. He continued to stare down at the freshly dug grave and its marker, his eyes aglow with fires of torment, his countenance exuding an overwhelming bitterness. The force of his sorrow pierced my heart. I lifted my hand from his shoulder and knelt beside him, realizing suddenly that Augustin's anguish over our child's death outweighed mine, somehow.

"At least she's in heaven now," I whispered after many moments of silence. "God spared our child the pain and sorrow that are unavoidable in this world."

Augustin shuddered at my words. His expression grew more distressed as he sensed the peace I had already found in the knowledge that our daughter had entered eternal bliss. "And you, of course, may look forward to that day when you shall reunite with her," he muttered flatly, staring blankly at the wooden cross. "But as for me, I shall never grasp what could have been, for your precious God took away my daughter, the same way He took away her namesake." His mouth twisted into an acerbic scowl, the fire in his eyes deepening.

I cringed at Augustin's coarse words, wishing he would not blame God for our daughter's death. I remembered that he had done the same thing as an uncomprehending child in 1022 . . . and I realized that he had *not* referred to Marelda von Bayern as his mother. The implications of the filial curse struck me again, but I shoved my despair aside. "You could meet her in heaven too, Augustin," I pointed out, "if you'd stop blaming God for the heartache of this world. Death happens all the time since this world isn't perfect. It was *our* choice to sin, not God's."

Augustin turned his face toward me at last, frustration and grief glinting in his eyes. "How can you sit there and preach at me about original sin and the mercy of God *now,* when your daughter lies *dead* beneath you?" He bared his teeth at me, reaching his right hand into his robe to fiercely clutch my heart. "Have you no sense of decency to weep for the dead, for glories forever lost, for futures eternally gone? This is *not* the time for you to beg me to convert all over again, Swanhilde. You ought to stop fighting that impossible battle, for it shall drive both of us mad."

His sullenness and agony threatened to pull me into depression as his fingers tightened against my heart. His tortured face suggested that he wished to squeeze it until I screamed and acknowledged that he was right. But I shook my head at my master, memories of my prolonged struggle to give our child life surfacing in my mind.

"I wept for her already, Augustin," I informed him quietly, wrapping both of my arms around my icy white robes. "I cried for her all night, while I tried and failed to give her life. I wept when I learned that it had all been in vain. And I screamed within myself in anguish when I held her lifeless body in my arms . . . when I looked into her gorgeous eyes, frozen in death . . . the same color as yours. I knew then that she was Marelda . . . the one cord that ties us both to the past, before that dreadful curse sent you to hell." My spirit trembled with the urgency of my words, grief returning to me as I looked down at our daughter's grave.

Augustin's expression softened considerably, and he stroked my heart more tenderly for a moment before bringing his hand out from his robes and laying it carefully upon the earth. "I heard you give her that name," he murmured, averting his gaze once more to the wooden cross. "I was in the room with you throughout the entirety of your labor, for I sent my spirit to you in the instant I felt your heart cry out for me last night. Hopefully none of my colleagues came looking for me during the night, for they would have seen my flaming body crouched in my fireplace." Half of his mouth quirked upward into a sallow smile.

"I detected during the early hours of your labor that Wuotan had no intention of taking you. He set his sights upon the child from the start, wishing to bury the final remains of the life I led before the curse. I tried to bargain with him at first, promising all sorts of service if he granted me mercy and spared the child's life along with yours, but he would not listen. His arguments were sound, Swanhilde, for he wielded the scepter of God in his greed, announcing that he must punish our promiscuity and cause me to forget the feeble influences that draw me away from him." Augustin's mouth curled into a grimace.

Fear crept into my chest at his pronouncements, and I scooted closer to Augustin, close enough that the robes of our spirits began to meld together. "If Wuotan really wishes to sever all ties that bind you to this world . . . what does he intend to do to me?" I queried, shivering at the prospect of facing a demon's wrath.

Augustin drew my heart out from his robes and caressed it gently, his love and reassurance awakening my courage and trust. "I already told you that Wuotan can do nothing to you without your Savior's permission. As long as you do not give God reason to chastise you, Wuotan shall undoubtedly leave you in peace. He shall focus his attention upon me instead, gradually twisting my devotion to you into an insensitive hatred." Augustin bit his lip and stared down at my heart throbbing in his hands. "I rue the day that he succeeds. I do not wish to lose your love."

"You're not going to lose it," I whispered passionately, promising to myself once again to never renounce my love for Augustin, no matter what he did to me. "You have to keep fighting him, Augustin, for both of our sakes. Our daughter would have wanted it," I added pointedly, knowing it was true.

My master smiled a little, turning his gaze to the wooden cross not a meter from where we sat together. "Marelda Swanhilde von Thaden, 1046." He read the short inscription on her tomb thoughtfully, then admitted, "In spite of everything, I believe it would have been much harder for me if Wuotan had taken you. I never met our daughter, so the attachment I could have developed shall remain elusive. But it was torment for me, standing there at your bedside, watching you writhe in agony, seeing the fumbling actions of that midwife, hearing you choke out my name as you gasped desperate prayers in your native tongue . . . ." He broke off, pain contorting his face as he stared into my eyes. "Swanhilde, I fear that it nearly killed me, watching your pain . . . unable to interfere, unable to help. If you had died in our daughter's place, I would have attempted suicide in every way possible, though all conceivable methods would have proven ineffective . . . ."

The strength of his love poured into my spirit, and I reached forward to trace my fingers down his face, imagining that both of us could feel it. "I knew you were there with me," I said, remembering how I had felt him stroking my heart during that long night, and how I had seen his spirit urging me to be strong as I drifted in and out of consciousness during the actual delivery. "I wished I could have touched you or said something to you in Teutonica, a plea for your fortitude. But Gretchen didn't know. She believed that our child was Joel's. And even in my torment I feared to admit the truth aloud . . . . I'm such a coward, Augustin. I know you would have told her the truth if you had been in my place."

Augustin smiled at me again. "You acted in the best way possible," he told me quietly, "considering that you have a public reputation to protect. I doubt that the respectable citizens of Muniche would deign to look at you again if they knew that you bore the spawn of the devil's servant, Wuotan's Black Priest."

I chuckled once at his words, so matter-of-fact and yet so strikingly unfortunate. "Well, not everyone in Muniche agrees with your curse," I said. "Freia disapproved of it from the start, and I told her long ago that the child was yours. She's my best friend. She didn't judge me for it."

Augustin nodded once, his fiery eyes focusing on the patches of starry sky visible through the branches above us. "You have found a faithful friend in that Rhenisch Teuton. She is loyal and supportive, an intelligent woman."

A serene smile curled upon my face at Augustin's compliment, proud that he included Freia in his elite group of sophisticated women. "She still hopes that one day the two of us can be together," I said, remembering her encouraging words to me right before I married Joel: *God's ways are far beyond ours. You mustn't lose hope.* "She told me once that I ought to marry you instead of Joel, right after you convinced her to trust you for the blood-transfer."

Augustin snickered, and a sardonic smile broke across his face. "Yes, most women ultimately succumb to my charms, once they allow me a fair chance. Now that I am dead, though, my persuasive abilities shall likely fade as I attempt to calm my sacrifices." I jerked in surprise at this, but Augustin continued before I could make any dark speculations. "I have not yet sacrificed human blood to my master since my return to Salerno, Swanie, do not fear. Thus far, I have been able to satisfy him with animals' blood. But now, with this forlorn grave lying here before us, I know not how long my resolve shall hold. It would be far easier to obey him, for life continues to slip through my fingers." He sighed.

"We just have to pick up the pieces of our lives now," I said, looking at the wooden cross that marked my first child's grave. "This trial has passed, and many more shall come. We have to rise up together to face them." I climbed to my feet and beckoned Augustin to follow suit. "Right now, I think it's time for me to learn more Magyar." I grinned up at my master while he stood in front of me, his fiery eyes delving into my spirit, endeavoring to claim some of my optimism as his own. "Someday, I want to be fluent in Magyar so I can talk to Viktor and tell him about our love." I smiled.

Augustin eyed me for a long moment, and at last he nodded, silently accepting my entreaties for him to relinquish his bitterness at his daughter's death. "So we shall continue our studies; but first, you must grant me one request." He held up the index finger of his right hand and vanished before I could comment. I gaped, staring blankly at the empty space before me. Impatience gripped my spirit while I awaited his return, the night breeze rustling in the leaves of the linden trees.

When he materialized again, I saw, to my shock, that he held a small candle in his right hand, its wax a ghostly sheen of silver, a blue flame glowing from its wick. As I watched with wide eyes, he walked forward to place it ceremoniously upon the wooden cross of our daughter's tomb. "Since my eternal flame for the elder Marelda has been extinguished by the curse, this shall serve as its replacement, as a memorial to both Mareldas . . . but especially to the one who is my daughter. No curse can separate me from her, for I am her father."

Chapter Eleven:
Years of Tedium

As I took up the pen to set down the remainder of my years in the eleventh century after the death of Augustin's child, I found myself contemplating everything anew, trying to discern which events of those twenty long years honestly deserved to be recorded. If I had learned one lesson during my stint in medieval Europe, it was that while life was far simpler compared with the fast-paced whirl of the twenty-first century, it was also much more tedious. While Joel spent most days aiding the vassals as they tended the crops, I often found myself alone in the count's grand house with little to occupy my time.

My thoughts often turned to the twenty-first century during those years. I recalled the afternoons I had spent in my bedroom in München, completely engrossed in the music playing on my stereo, the figures and scenes dancing across my television, or the intriguing information scrolling across my computer screen. When I did not sit down to sew or care for the children—who seemed to multiply as the years passed, to my private chagrin—I found myself missing my own era, where I could always find something to occupy my mind, whether it be schoolwork, my father's business, organ practice, or simple amusement.

I had hoped in the beginning that, as the new lady of the Meldorf estate, I could throw myself into the business and trade of medieval farming right away—and if not that, then at least play a substantial role in housework and keeping the gardens. I soon discovered that the count's many servants took care of the mundane duties themselves. On most days, I had to play the role of the landed noblewoman, making my rounds to the various estates, spending time with my peers. The younger women gossiped about their husbands, their children, the crops, and current events, their optimistic spirits helping to stave off my boredom and discontent. But Freia Denlinger remained my closest friend, for she was the only woman in Muniche who knew my heart, and knew that I did not belong in her time.

Freia and I regularly shared our personal struggles and victories like we had during our days as single women at the count's manor. Her marriage was a triumph of love and beauty, for she adored Heinrich and sought to honor him in everything, from doing her daily chores to raising her children to respect their father as a strong protector. Their first child came into the world in early October of 1046, a tiny daughter with light brown hair and hazel eyes. I stayed at Freia's side during her labor, like she had done for me, silently thanking God the whole time that her first experience with Teutonic childbirth proved easy and successful. As she held her daughter to her breast while I looked on, she told me with a smile that she would name the child Lorraine Marianna, after her mother and one of her sisters. When I congratulated her on her precious miracle, I knew that one day I too would grasp the joys and responsibilities of motherhood, though I would never share those glories with the man I truly loved.

As time passed and I became more acquainted with my medieval life, I found that the lingering panic that had long tainted my nights gradually dissipated. I had once feared Joel's reaction to my nightmares, when he learned that they sometimes shackled my lungs in a false notion of disease. But time and distance accomplished what drugs and counseling had not. Sometimes I wondered whether my mind and spirit found some sort of odd comfort in having a man beside me in my bed—though not the one I preferred. On the increasingly rare occasions when my nightmares tore me from my sleep, my gaze would shift to Joel snoring at my side, while I sought to force my lungs to draw breath. And my fearful Teuton spirit would reach out to his confident wind in silence, steadily claiming his strength as my own.

At the outset of 1047, while I stood before the mirror brushing my hair, Joel told me in a scratchy voice that all of his EpiPens had technically expired. "They're good until March 2002, but this is our third year here," he said as he crouched at the chamber pot, cleaning his buttocks.

I laid my brush down and looked toward him, a sense of frustration settling in my stomach. *Well, we wouldn't have had that problem at all if you'd thought of the right time and place when we came here . . . .* "I'll talk to Wigge about it again," I replied, looking away as Joel tugged his trousers into place. "I'll make sure he knows not to use any of our almonds in the food. But you'll have to keep your eyes open whenever you eat somewhere else."

Joel heaved a sigh and muttered that things would be a lot easier if he was not allergic to tree nuts. And I thought ahead to the days of the Saxon invasion, knowing that we would have to prepare a large stash of victuals in advance for my husband's sake.

In late September of 1047, at the close of the flax harvest, I bore Joel his first child, a daughter. The travail did not last half as long that time, to my relief. Gretchen allowed Joel into the bedroom just after sunset to meet our first child, who slept peacefully in my arms. He insisted that he had never seen a more beautiful baby, as he sat beside me on the bed grinning down at the infant with a look of unnecessary accomplishment. He exclaimed on several occasions that it surprised him that the baby's hair was blond; he had figured that Teuton children always had darker hair. I reminded him with a rather impish smile that since the blood-transfer did not alter his hair or eye color, it would be natural for some of our kids to look like him. "Her eyes are gray, so at least I have some claim to our daughter," I added. Her eyes had seemed huge when she stared around the room after Gretchen had washed her.

"You have *all* the claim, since you did all the work," Joel commented fondly, laying his arm around my shoulders and kissing me through my hair. "So what do you think we should name her?" he inquired, pressing his face against mine to get a closer look at our sleeping daughter.

I had been pondering that very thing since Gretchen had pronounced my child a girl, and I murmured some of my ideas to Joel. He needed to have some say regarding this child's name, since she was actually his daughter. After considering several options, we decided to name her Camilla Barbara for my mother and his, making the blond-haired Teuton child in my arms the unspoken union of our two very different worlds.

We ultimately nicknamed our daughter "Cammie." For many months following her birth, I dedicated most of my time and energy to her. Joel and I held countless discussions about Cammie and any other children we might have in the years to come, deciding how best to educate them in such a primitive society and how to properly train them for their future. We agreed that any sons would be trained in farming as soon as they could grasp a trowel, and that I would teach all of our children how to read and write Teutonica. Latin I planned to reserve for the girls, since the boys would be busy working outside. Joel suggested that we speak English to our kids when they were young, so our family could have its own secret dialect that no one else understood. I agreed without fuss, for I knew firsthand that young children could pick up dialects without difficulty.

One matter that plagued us for quite some time, especially as Cammie grew and I became pregnant again in spring of 1048, was whether or not we should reveal the full truth of our lives to our children. Joel and I worried that if we told them that their parents were from the future, they may grow up confused and become alienated from the other kids of neighboring estates. I also feared possible consequences from the Torstein if we explained the notion of time travel and the future fall of Muniche to our children. I had a feeling that doing so may truly effect change upon history.

Joel and I eventually decided not to speak of the future in front of the kids, but to immerse ourselves in our lives here and let them believe that we were the same as the other nobles of Muniche. We agreed to tell them the same story that we had circulated among our acquaintances since we had first entered the city—that I had been born in Muniche but had spent most of my life traveling, and that Joel had grown up in England and moved to the continent after losing his family. However, we did decide to prepare them for the tragedy of 1066 in subtle ways, by making them aware of the brevity of plenty and teaching them to accept fate as it came, whether pleasant or distasteful.

In February of 1049, I bore Joel a son, a cute little chubby infant with black hair like mine and bright blue eyes like my mother's. The delivery was not incredibly difficult, though it took me half a night of struggle to finally succeed in birthing the child. His head proved to be rather large, and it tore my vagina painfully on its way out.

The count's entire household rejoiced at the news that my latest child was a son, for by then all of the servants and vassals knew that Joel and I would inherit the estate once its current lord passed into eternity. Jarvis expressed the hope that this son would be one of many, so that the name Thaden could hold its own for years to come while the deceased members of the Meldorf family rested peacefully in their graves. I promised Jarvis that I would produce as many sons as possible in the next few decades, forcing a fake smile as the dark curtain of the future threatened to descend upon my optimism. Joel and I named our son Maximilian Robert after both of our fathers, calling him "Max" for short. Each of us hoped that he would grow to be a shrewd entrepreneur, since we named him after two prosperous businessmen.

During the early years of our marriage, farming on the Meldorf estate continued to thrive. The count had proven correct in his prediction that Joel would become a successful lord once he had gotten the hang of the business. He cracked down on unsanitary practices, setting up separate areas for the vassals to relieve themselves and requiring that they wash with soap before each meal. He told me that he did not want preventable diseases like typhoid and dysentery taking root on our land, and I could not disagree. I helped the kitchen staff improve their practices, particularly when they preserved foods for the winter.

By summer of 1049, Jarvis and I had streamlined our accounting system using Arabic numerals, which the bailiff admitted made the calculations far easier. In my spare time, I scoured our expenses and balanced our budget, making sure that we never spent more than we earned. Whenever I grew tired of entertaining the youngsters and occupying myself with business and socializing, I ran through the fields on the strength of my element, sprinkling the crops with melting ice in the heat of summer to ensure that the plants would yield a bountiful increase.

But although I tried my hardest to put on a façade of contentment with my dull medieval life, I often found myself wishing desperately for night, when I could dream glorious fantasies alone or with Augustin. We made a tradition of meeting for our language studies on Tuesdays and Thursdays, like we had done before the curse had raised its wall between us. I thoroughly enjoyed exchanging ideas and knowledge with Augustin, even though we had to do so in the dark.

He finished his medical degree at Salerno in the spring of 1049, and by then his grasp on the English language at times seemed to outrank mine. We moved on to Bayerisch at his insistence, for he said that he was tired of remaining ignorant whenever I mumbled something in my native dialect—particularly during the pains of labor. Augustin assured me that my knowledge of Teutonica had reached a scholar's status. He also claimed that my Ælte Teutonica was strong enough for me to read everything on that "dreaded shelf on Teutonic Traditions" in the archives of Muniche, even the slabs etched with runes.

Part of me longed to return to the forbidden archives, disregarding that sign that closed the public out and immersing myself in those mystical writings of my people. But I feared that if I dared to go there again, either in my body or as a spirit, some chronicler or monk would kick me out and squeal to Prince Otto. I suspected that if I tried to sneak in at night like I had done years ago, I may meet the spirit of a Teuton priest standing guard over our people's secrets. I did not want to draw the Prince's attention back to me for any reason.

During our first nights of language study, I told Augustin that the Prince had burned the book on forbidden sacraments, squelching my hopes of returning to my own time apart from death. Augustin shook his head in disgust and commented that the Prince had never properly respected written material. On another occasion, I also questioned Augustin on the location of his birth certificate, since the priests and scribes had been unable to find it during their quest to erase his name from Muniche's records. My master favored me with a rather wicked grin and brought me to the desk in his chamber, summarily retrieving the document from amongst his papers. As I held it in my hands in our private dream world, reading his cursed name written out in ink along with the names of his parents, I felt thrilled that Augustin had thought to swipe it from the archives before that wretched Prince could cast it into the fire.

By autumn of 1049, I finally considered myself fluent enough in Magyar to attempt a full conversation with Viktor, who seemed to grow sadder every day as he moved slowly around the manor performing his tasks of upkeep. I knew that few people in Muniche spoke Magyar at all, and considering Viktor's age and arthritic joints, he rarely made the trip into the city anyway. Since my studies with Augustin focused on my accent and Ælte Teutonica, my

Magyar improved sluggishly. I found the Slavic language much more complex than those of my people, which could be considered dialects of High German. But I began to greet Viktor in his own tongue each day, and as the years passed, I eventually managed to exchange shaky phrases with him on his health, the weather, and his work. But I will never forget that winter evening when I found him alone in the pantry, sipping tea from a pewter mug, his cloudy eyes straying now and then to Jarvis' youngest son playing in the corner with another servant child.

I sat down next to Viktor on the dirt floor, which prompted him to climb to his feet in search of a cushion for me, but I waved him back. Once he had calmed down enough to return to his corner of the pantry, his expression looking slightly distressed at my lack of propriety, I pulled all of the Magyar I knew from the depths of my brain and said in a low voice, "Viktor, there are some things I want to tell you . . . but my Magyar is still poor . . . so please correct me . . . if I make any mistakes." His eyes widened, and his grip trembled on his teacup. Finally he nodded at me and insisted that I needed no help with my Magyar, for it was far better than anyone else's at the estate.

I smiled at his compliment, knowing that as my servant he would never willingly correct my speech, no matter how awful it sounded. So I took a deep breath and broached the subject of Augustin for the first time since Viktor had given me his letter four years before. I discovered after careful prodding that Viktor knew little of what had become of his former master. His fate had come about so suddenly, and he hardly understood the rudiments of Teutonic rituals.

I endeavored to explain what I could about Augustin's banishment. Viktor's aged face darkened as I attempted to convey the Prince's anger at his former brother's habitual sin and his decision to punish him severely at long last. I added that I still had contact with Augustin quite regularly—through a complicated Teutonic ritual that I did not wish to explain—and that he was surviving as best as he could, although he would never again find welcome in Teuton lands.

When I had finished after stumbling over quite a few words, Viktor paused for a long moment before speaking, his eyes turned toward the servant children in their careless play. At length he sighed heavily, and took a small sip of tea before murmuring in an uncertain tone, "My master was not a good man. But he did not deserve the fate you describe. I would work for him again, even in his exile, if my age did not hold me down." His eyes darted to mine when he spoke, his expression suggesting that he feared what I might say to the truth, that he would rather work for Augustin than for my household.

But I smiled sadly at his words, wishing I could feel Augustin's hands upon my heart more often, like during the spring of 1045 when we were young lovers with no barriers holding us apart. "I understand," I whispered to Viktor, a few tears leaking from my eyes. "I loved him before . . . and I love him now. He was not what the Prince said . . . and I miss him very much. I would live with him in his exile . . . if I could." I gave Viktor a knowing look, and he smiled crookedly at me. He remembered that one glorious night I had with Augustin, and he knew full well that his former master held me in higher standing than any other woman.

After Augustin had finished his studies in Salerno, he chose to travel slowly northward again, toward the Alpine lands for which his Teuton blood cried, seeking to find asylum with some ruler who would accept him in spite of his curse. The years had been more difficult for him than they had been for me. While I often found myself consumed with ennui, I did not shoulder the torments of a demon. My master admitted in the winter of 1049, when I gravely informed him that Joel had gotten me pregnant again, that Wuotan had begun to wear down his resolve to cling to the love of a woman whom he could never touch. But I begged him on my knees not to let Wuotan win the fight, my heart pounding with eternal love as he fingered it with the hands of his spirit, his broken face silently asking me to forget him.

Chapter Twelve:
The Red Plague

As the years passed, I became accustomed to the illnesses that swept the Meldorf estate each winter and spring, from colds and flus to fevers and sore throats. Joel set up a one-way breeze around the sewage ditches to disperse mosquitos, and we transitioned toward using only animal dung and compost as fertilizer for our crops. But both Cammie and Max faced some pretty wicked sicknesses in their early years. Their new sister Gloria seemed to catch everything that went around in her first months of life, rendering me severely deficient on sleep.

Joel and I talked in passing about the vaccines we had, wondering whether our children would come down with things like measles or pertussis. I had left the disease research to Beth prior to our journey, and I realized that I had no clue how to treat any of the illnesses that modern preventatives had rendered rare. We ran a cleaner show than any of the other estates around Muniche, but not every horrid malady stemmed from bacteria.

None of us were prepared for the specter that cast its shadow over Muniche in November of 1050. Lady Adeline spread word of a strange plague that had started in the sections where outsiders lived; the afflicted were struck with nausea, fevers, and backaches and progressed to a mouth rash that erupted and spread all over the skin. "My husband urged the Prince to expel the scum who brought it to us, but he opened the cathedral to the sick so that the sisters can pray over them." Lady Adeline bristled as she related her news to me one frosty afternoon, having stopped by in her carriage on her way home from the city. "It spreads among our people now, so you had better shut your doors tight before it ravages your household."

"So it's killing people?" I questioned, rubbing my forehead as I tried to recall what sort of ancient sickness involved fevers, backaches, and a mouth rash.

"Five have died, and one Slavic shopkeeper is now blind," she responded, her upper lip curled in disgust. "Take my advice, Swanie, and bar your doors against any travelers from the east. They bring God's judgment upon us."

No one from the Meldorf estate had visited Muniche for over a week, for we were in the process of bunkering down for the winter. Joel and a group of young vassals had just returned from a hunt, and most of our servants were occupied with freezing and drying the venison. After Lady Adeline had gone, I found Joel outside the ice house and beckoned him to my side. He blew on his hands and joined me as I pointed my feet toward the manor. "Lady Adeline just came by and said there's some sort of disease going around in Muniche right now," I said, "and I'm trying to figure out what exactly it is. Fever, backache, nausea, mouth rash that spreads all over the body."

"Mouth rash?" Joel looked troubled, and he shivered beneath the heavy coat he wore. "Scarlet fever maybe? I remember reading about that one in *The Velveteen Rabbit.*"

I thought back to that old children's story, remembering that the adults had planned to burn the rabbit in question. "They're blaming the outsiders, of course. She said not to open our house to any travelers. It's killed five people already."

"Wish we could spray the house for fleas," Joel muttered with a grimace.

He had a fair point. Our beds and furniture were infested with the nibbling insects. "It's definitely not the Black Plague," I reminded him. "That's not coming for another century or two, and Lady Adeline didn't mention coughing."

"Well, hopefully it'll stay in the city and leave us alone. I'll tell Jarvis and Leo to forbid any of our people from going there. We can skip the Christmas mass and the New Year's party."

"Good plan," I said, grateful that I would not have to plaster a false smile on my face for the local nobility as they thronged the Bayern castle on the eve of my master's birthday. I had attended two New Year's galas since 1045, and trailed Joel like a bound wife during the entirety of both, steering clear of the royal family.

I told Augustin of the sickness when he came to my dreams the following Tuesday. His expression grew rather grave at the subject, and he asked me to go to the cathedral and report back on the state of those afflicted. "I would go myself, but the curse constrains me," he said, waving me toward the ivy-coated walls in the distance. "This may be something I have seen before, but I need a thorough description, not a noblewoman's tales."

So I envisioned myself in the main nave of the cathedral after extracting a solemn promise that Augustin would wait for me in the dell by the stream. I found a small group of Catholic priests bent in prayer before the main altar, the eldest of them reciting the words that Freia spoke at Matins. The natural flames atop several lit candlesticks cast their pale faces in a garish light, and I turned away, not wanting to pick Paulus out of them. I drifted toward a staircase at the back of the nave, for I knew that the cathedral had an extensive basement.

It did not take me long to find the sick sprawled in one of the lower chapels. Horror darkened my spirit's colors as I ran my eyes over people of all sizes lying sprawled upon the pews, their skin coated with pus-filled lesions. Many wore naught but a loincloth, their voices wheezing for water while nuns moved among them, dabbing at foreheads, murmuring comforting phrases. *This isn't scarlet fever,* I thought, the eyes of one elderly woman snaring my attention. Her corneas were inflamed, her skin flushed crimson.

My twenty-first century friend Marga's face arose in my mind, her reply to my topic about time travel on our Teuton forum standing out in my memory: *If you went to the Middle Ages, you'd want to update your vaccines first and get one for smallpox.*

Terror turned my robes as white as snow, and I fled back to the dell.

"Smallpox," I said to Augustin the second I saw his face, my fear contracting the lungs of my spirit. His forehead wrinkled in confusion, his fiery eyes sweeping over my icy robes, observing my distress. "It has to be smallpox. That doesn't even *exist* anymore in the twenty-first century. And I know it's deadly. I don't think there's any treatment for it." I shuddered and curled into a ball in the middle of the stream, summoning its waters to reassure me.

I did not know the Teutonic word for smallpox. After asking careful questions, Augustin identified it as something his professors had called the red plague. "Razi described it in one of his medical works as the worst type of pox, easy to spread but not so easy to treat. My most religious tutor claimed that demons dictate its path and that it fears the color red. Its victims should pray to Saint Nicasius for aid."

"That's a bunch of primitive nonsense. It's caused by a virus."

Augustin cocked his head at me, looking amused. "Your beloved Bible would disagree with you there. Or do you not believe in the angels of death, only the ones that offer life?"

He was mocking me, and I splashed a swath of water at his cerulean robes. "Do you think that Wuotan or some other demon has a hand in this, sending smallpox to weaken the Teutons before their defeat?" I raised my eyebrows at him from where I sat in the water, its currents cooling my spirit from the inside out.

Augustin scowled and averted his eyes from mine to the distant city walls. "He ought not to spurn my worship. I have burnt blood for him twice per year as he requires and allowed his fires to consume the carcasses. It may simply be a time of plague. A blight of holy fire swept through Muniche in my youth and resulted in hundreds of deaths. Illnesses come and go at will."

"I guess you're right," I conceded, rising to my feet and trying to shake off my fear of encroaching pox. "We'll have to shut everything down whether it comes to the Meldorf estate or not. I hope Freia's being careful." I knew that my best friend had to visit her local market regularly for fresh food, and I cringed. She had three young children now herself—Lorraine, Heino, and Katchen.

Augustin advised me to tread carefully and avoid the city, assuring me that Freia and Heinrich were sagacious enough to protect themselves. Gloria woke me with her cries for milk shortly thereafter. So I was obliged to bid my lover farewell and gather my infant daughter to my breast, silently fearing what was to come.

The plague came to our door at the outset of January. Joel went to Muniche after the Christmas holidays to retrieve several barrels of beer that the nearest brewery owed us; their production had slowed during the past two seasons due to internal strife. I advised my husband not to go, to send word to the brewery to hold our beer until the spring. We could continue to survive on our own mead and on boiled water if it came down to it. But the vassals had begun to grumble, especially since most of them did not grasp why we had forbidden anyone to leave the grounds. Joel insisted that it would be best for him to go himself and quarantine inside upon his return.

So he drove four horses and our strongest carriage to the city on the second of January, returning that evening with four casks of spelt beer and a visage marred with alarm. He had to pay ten Thaler to cross the drawbridge, for Prince Otto had raised the toll to discourage travelers from entering the stricken city. The sick were freezing to death in the streets now, he said, and the three young men who helped him load the barrels had pockmarked faces, their lips still spewing the occasional cough. "They were getting over it," he told me while he sat on our bed, his fingers curled around a cup of tea. "But I don't know if they were still contagious or not. They said it takes three weeks for the pox to flake off once the rash starts and that it's like hell. You can't get comfortable."

Joel shut himself in our bedroom for a week and wore the same tunic and pants the entire time, since he remembered reading about the smallpox blankets that the American colonists had used against the natives. I shut up both wardrobes and ordered Ulka to have a new straw mattress and blankets made for us. We spoke with Count von Meldorf only once, Joel's description of what he had seen in the city convincing him to let us quarantine alone. He repeated Joel's earlier order to all of the vassals, informing them that they were not to leave the Meldorf grounds for any reason without permission from him.

Ulka and Jarvis ran the household while we nervously awaited our fate. I feared for Gloria the most, for she was frail and still dependent upon me for milk. Cammie and Max were kept apart from us, though I heard both of them crying for us, tears evident in Cammie's voice as she whimpered that she missed her Mutti. I longed to leave our bedroom behind to comfort her, and I thought about doing it in spirit form. But then I would have to explain the concept to Joel, who knew next to nothing about Teutonic spiritual powers. I did not need my witchy knowledge to spread far and wide, for the plague had amplified people's mistrust of the unknown.

My husband came down with the fever and backache on the eighth day after his return from Muniche. By then I had grown utterly bored with his company, and I was getting frustrated with Gloria too, since I had been unable to pass her off to the servant girls during that long week. "Guess this is it," I said in a dead voice when Joel sat up in bed with a groan, the heat radiating from his body, touching me where I sat nursing our daughter just centimeters from him.

"I was hoping we'd get lucky." Joel's face appeared wan already. He scratched at his beard, his hazel eyes shifting to the ice flakes flecking the panes of glass on our window. Another batch of snow had coated the landscape the day before.

"Apparently not," I muttered, still annoyed that he had felt the need to visit Muniche when the disease was rampant there. Gloria's gums tugged on my right nipple, and I looked down at the dark hair coating her head. Would she survive such a nefarious virus? Would *any* of the three of us survive?

And if smallpox sends me back to the twenty-first century . . . will I be able to preserve my bond with Augustin? Or would death break it like the writings say, even if it's not final death . . . ?

I heard a knock at our bedroom door a moment later, and when I cracked it open, I found myself looking at Viktor's aged face. He held a plate of stew and jug of beer for our lunch, his expression grim. "You may want to bring us a week's worth of bread and mead," I told him quietly in Magyar, my eyes locking for an instant with Ulka's. She stood some distance away from Viktor, her arms shielding my two oldest children from their parents. But Cammie cried out for me anyway, and I sighed, looking at the elderly Slav as I accepted the victuals. "Joel has a fever now. I don't want any of you to get sick."

To my surprise, Viktor's thin lips spread into a wavering smile. "Fear not, my Lady Swanhilde," he answered, his tone sounding uncharacteristically confident. "I had the red plague when I was a child. I can serve you both without danger."

Viktor was true to his word. He brought us water thrice per day and kept our fireplace stoked while we fought the virus, emptying the chamber pot every morning and evening. On the first day of Joel's suffering, I ordered Viktor to burn all of Gloria's used diapers and to make certain that he washed his hands thoroughly with soap after handling any of our things. He obeyed me without fuss and pledged that none would get the plague from him, for he had worked for a doctor before. His eyes seemed to sparkle when he said that, and I managed a wan smile in return. It was nice to have one faithful servant who shared my secret respect for Augustin, who did not judge me for my loyalty to the Cursed One.

The fever struck me on the day that the rash attacked Joel's mouth. My husband spent most of that day groaning and vomiting mucus and bile into the chamber pot, while I lay naked upon our bed, the fingertips of my right hand dipped into chilled water as my left held Gloria against my chest. She had started sneezing three days before, and I knew for certain that her immune system was not up to the challenge of two illnesses at once. I prayed silently for God to take her quickly, that she would not suffer long.

My own experience with the virus was miserable, not something that I prefer to remember in depth. I could not keep any solid food down for over a week, and my milk supply began to dry up. Viktor brought milk from our small clutch of cows to the bedroom for Gloria, who refused it, the pox having attacked her ruthlessly. My lesions followed the standard course of the disease—harboring fluid and forming pustules—while hers remained malleable and flat, encompassing the entirety of her body. She died after five days of torment, her fate weakening me afresh. I had never imagined having two out of four children die before their first year of life, despite the dangers of childbirth, despite the difficulties of this primeval period. It crushed me to a degree that I had not anticipated.

When I was finally able to leave the bedroom on the second Saturday in February, I looked and felt as though I had been through hell, like the young men at the brewery had said. My scabs had all dispersed, but my face, hands, and feet were riddled with pockmarks, effectively erasing the beauty I had once claimed. All of the excess weight from my pregnancies had fallen away, leaving my breasts sagging and my abdomen layered with folds of limp skin.

I used all of my strength to stagger into the front parlor and collapse upon the couch there as the servants cleaned the bedroom. Joel entered from the hallway after I had lain in the sunlight for a few minutes, silently questioning the purpose of my journey all over again. I had expected to face just two years of this mess before watching my city crumble and burn . . . but the trials just kept on mounting, the death toll climbing far earlier than it should.

"The kids are in the great hall," Joel remarked, his formerly handsome face mottled with scars, though his beard hid the worst of it. "Want me to bring them in to see you? Cammie's still asking for her Mutti." His lips quirked.

I sighed and closed my eyes, wishing again that I had run off with Augustin when he had been cursed. Then I would never have faced this sickness that had ruined my body, this loss that had ruined my heart, this husband that I could never love, this yearning that could never be appeased. "Sure. Bring them in," I said, pulling the mask over my face yet again.

Chapter Thirteen:
The Untenable Ruse

Life returned to a semblance of normalcy in subsequent months. The disease lifted its claws from Muniche in early spring, having slain nearly two hundred and disfigured hundreds more. It had touched four of the neighboring estates, its death having claimed Lady Rachel Sendlin and Lord Paulus Schwabing, the goofy freckled young man who had attempted to woo me years ago. Freia's household was spared, for she had faced a smallpox outbreak in Eisenwald during her childhood and knew what to expect. She offered me an herbed tincture to spread over my scars, stating that it had helped hers to fade over the years.

I did my best to return to my typical activities, but the condition of my face shamed me. I added veils to each of my head coverings to conceal my pockmarks from the casual viewer, and I cursed myself for having cut my hair short after Max's birth. At only twenty-seven years of age, I looked like a haggard wench stricken by the goddess of ugliness, if such an entity existed. Thankfully, my spirit still looked perfect in the dreams I shared with Augustin. I began to insist that we spend our time together in places apart from my sleeping body. I moved my English, German, and Bayerisch parchments to Count von Meldorf's desk, since he rarely spent much time there these days, transferring the desk in my bedroom to Joel.

One cool Friday night in early May, right after the flax and barley had been planted, Joel and I prepared for bed after ensuring that Cammie and Max had fallen asleep. Both of our children had their own rooms now. Cammie occupied the one I had once shared with Freia, while Max's room was the one that Joel had used in the days of old when he visited the manor for the weekend. The cradle that lay at the foot of our bed had been empty since Gloria's death, and in actuality I was grateful for the peaceful nights of late. I had decided that one of the most annoying things about babies was their insistence upon crying in the middle of the night, selfishly interrupting their parents' dreams. Cammie, Max, and Gloria had pulled me from my nocturnal studies with Augustin many times.

As I slipped my nightdress over my head and approached the bed in the dim light of the candle we kept at the windowsill, I wondered for a fleeting moment how often I would have to face Joel's embrace in bed over the next fifteen years, and how many children I would have to feed as a result. It was 1051 now, and we had both survived smallpox, one of the darkest plagues of the Middle Ages. I was starting to think that we were both destined to face the siege and watch Muniche burn, even though my American husband had no inborn loyalty to the city.

"So," Joel began in a companionable tone when I slipped under the blanket, "how are you feeling tonight, my dear?"

I had heard that question more times than I could count over the past few months. While I appreciated Joel's concern for my health, I knew full well that he had an ulterior motive for his queries. I propped myself up on my right elbow to regard him, a wry half-smile playing on my lips. "Why don't you just ask the question plainly: do I want to have sex with you tonight?" A bashful smirk appeared beneath Joel's sandy beard, and he dropped his gaze down to the blankets covering his chest. Embarrassment crept over me at the thought of how dreadful my face looked. Maybe all he wanted was my vagina.

"I suppose we can start doing that again," I said with a sigh, my fantasies of uninterrupted dream worlds crumbling to pieces. "But . . . I don't really know . . . if we ought to." I stumbled over my words while I tried to sort my tumultuous thoughts. Joel raised his eyes to me again, a strange darkness clouding his mien. "I mean, it's not that I don't *want* to," I added. "But all these children . . . all these pregnancies. Joel, I think maybe we should . . . hold off for a while. It's hard to be constantly tied down . . . and it's all been wreaking havoc on my body." I glanced down at myself as I spoke, frowning toward my breasts, which sagged noticeably beneath my nightdress.

Joel said nothing for a long moment. Unhappiness marred his features as he looked at my body, then into my eyes. We gazed at each other in silence, and I began biting my lip when I saw the emotions playing across his face. Guilt washed over me, for I should have kept my thoughts to myself. Joel was my husband, and we were supposed to enjoy each other in bed despite the consequences. I should not complain, for I was not the one working outside day after day. Joel needed a break from hard labor when he came to bed at night, and it was my duty to grant him that release.

So I opened my mouth to apologize, to tell him that I did not mean it, that I wished to have sex with him anyway. But he spoke first, his tone rather suspicious, his question prompting me to freeze in my tracks. "You'd rather have sex with Augustin von Bayern, wouldn't you?"

My ice flooded my veins, crystallizing my skin as my mouth dropped open in shock. *How could Joel say that . . . how could he have found out?* "Excuse me?" I squeaked.

Joel's hazel eyes lightened into the gray of wind in response to my ice, and a rather abrupt breeze caused our candle's flame to flicker. "You heard what I said, Swanie." His eyes pierced me to the bone.

"I . . . I . . . don't know . . . what you mean . . . ." I choked, my mind spinning.

Joel huffed, sitting up in bed and crossing his arms. "I suppose you wouldn't have heard the rumors, since they're about you," he allowed, looking frustrated. "Quite a few of our noble peers have gossiped about you ever since we got married. Many of them say that before we wed, you spent countless afternoons and evenings during the week with Augustin von Bayern, taking walks with him alone. They also say you danced with him at the Prince's New Year's party in 1045 . . . and that you were *intimate* with him." Joel's blond eyebrows came together, and he glowered at me, awaiting my response.

I opened my mouth, then closed it, a plausible lie forming inside my mind. "I thought you were too intelligent to believe idle gossip." My icy fingers clutched the blanket as I waited to see whether Joel would swallow that one.

He eyed me distrustfully, then frowned and looked toward the window. "I didn't believe it, Swanie. For the past six years I've tried to make them stop talking like that. But now . . . ." He broke off momentarily, uncrossing his arms and placing his hands upon his thighs, his fingers flexing; then he looked me straight in the eye and finished, "Now I have proof."

My eyes bugged, an icy sheen perfecting my vision. What sort of proof could he possibly have found? I had told him nothing of my dealings with Augustin since my one organ concert, and I knew that my secret was safe with Freia. And Joel spoke no Magyar, so Viktor was out. Had some of the other servants squealed on me, maybe the three who had exchanged giggled speculations on my status with the noble lords in happier days? It figured that the local nobility had noticed my past activities with Augustin. It irked me that none of my acquaintances ever mentioned him to me, after they had gotten over the novelty of his curse. I shook my head, not knowing how to answer Joel's glare.

He nodded at length, accepting my momentary loss. Then he jerked his head toward my nightstand, where I stored my few possessions from the twenty-first century. "The last two batteries for your camera ran out back in

January." I frowned, for I already knew that. They had run out after we had snapped a bunch of pictures of Gloria during the outset of our quarantine. A second later, the truth of what he had found struck me like a brick.

"I know you didn't want to look at the pictures until we get back home," Joel said with a grim expression, "but I got really curious one Sunday afternoon when you were out with Freia. I mainly wanted to see the pictures of our kids, but once I started looking, I kept scrolling back."

Horror seized me along with a ridiculous ire. "So *that's* why those batteries ran out so fast!" I snapped. "You had to go and sift through those pictures, and now we won't be able to capture anything else in the next fifteen years!" I fumed.

"You had more pictures of Augustin on that camera than you had of me," Joel charged, brushing off my aggravation at the final death of my camera. "And *obviously* you didn't take all of them, because I saw half a dozen of both of you together. Kissing." He scowled at me and cracked his knuckles.

My mind shot back to those carefree days of early 1045, when Augustin and I used to walk together by the stream, our mutual love seeming to fill nature with beauty. I recalled that one occasion—the afternoon before my world had come crashing down due to my meeting with Prince Otto—when we had invited Freia to walk with us. I had taught her how to use my camera early on, so I could have some photos of me to prove that I had really been to the eleventh century. On that afternoon, she had taken several snapshots of Augustin and me at my request, locked in our customary erotic embrace. Apparently some of those photos had turned out decently . . . .

A horrible notion overtook me in the next instant, and I whirled on my husband. "You *deleted* them, didn't you?!"

Joel snorted, averting his gaze to the far wall. "No, I didn't, but I should have. After seeing those pictures, I realized that all the rumors I've heard probably have some truth to them. I could tell, when I zoomed in on those shots of you and him together, that you *loved* him. It was written all over your face." His mouth twisted into a discontented frown.

I could not deny that, and my heart throbbed with pain as I wondered what those pictures looked like. But right now I had to reassure my husband, so I shoved my heart-ache aside, ordering my ice to abate, and said, "Maybe I did love him, but it's in the past now. Augustin is cursed, and technically you shouldn't even call him by that name. He's never coming back. You're my *husband*, Joel, and I have no intention of cheating on you." I forced myself to meet his gaze.

Joel shook his head slowly, the breeze in the room calming as he brought his wind back under control. "I'm sure you don't plan to cheat on me," he muttered, his tone belying his proclaimed sincerity, "but I know that you still love him. I've heard you say his name in your sleep"—my mouth fell open at this revelation—"and every time you bear a child, I've asked Gretchen whether you've called for me, whether you want me to be there. And she always says that the only name you speak in your travail is Augustin's." He bit his lip.

I looked away from him, mentally kicking myself again for making such a mess of my eleventh century life. "It doesn't matter how I feel about him," I said, unable to meet his eyes, for my bound heart speared me at my lies. "I chose to marry *you*, not Augustin. We have a life here that we've built together, a family."

"You think our family's big enough at four, though, don't you?" he asked in a grating tone. "You don't want to have any more of my kids. You'd rather curl up with some bastard you taught to speak English. Maybe I should have tried for one of my old roommates' sisters."

"Joel, please." A seed of worry sprouted inside of me at his anger. I reached out to touch his left arm, but he shook me off. "You know that wouldn't work. We can't let our secret get out to just anyone."

"But you told him, didn't you?" My husband gave me a dangerous look.

"He already knew," I blurted. A half-truth. "He knows about the Prince's song, and after the Torstein gets created, he'll write a dark set of lore about it. I read his writings on the Torstein before we came here, actually." Joel looked taken aback, and I took advantage of his hesitation. "See, Augustin has his own separate destiny to carry out, and I'm not part of it. My feelings can just suck it up."

Joel wrinkled his forehead and rolled his eyes, his stiff posture loosening at last. "So we got married for convenience, not love. Great."

"It hasn't been all bad," I pointed out, images of our vibrant daughter dancing through my brain. I could hardly wait to see what element she would manifest.

"I guess so. And I guess that means you won't complain about fulfilling your marital duty. Right?" My husband's hands drew the blanket back from my body and traced their way up my right thigh. I chewed on the inside of my cheek as I undressed myself. Joel's eyes bored into my body as though he needed inspiration to get hard after such a piercing revelation, his hand tugging at his cock.

I hated the fact that he was circumcised. His penis looked so bare.

And it occurred to me after his cock had awakened and found its way deep inside of me, that maybe Joel wanted to keep me pregnant or nursing to discourage me from forsaking him. My heart's infidelity was more apparent than I had believed.

Chapter Fourteen

Sorrows and Celebrations

The year 1052 ended up just as tragic as the previous year, and in some ways it seemed far worse. Though I strove to convince Joel that I loved him and that my past flirtations meant nothing, our relationship deteriorated as time wore on, the difficulties of medieval life and the waning of newlywed glory wearing on both of us. Joel continued to excel at managing the estate, his business sense and willingness to work hard alongside his servants cementing his reputation as a fair and honorable lord. I could not complain about his industriousness or his abilities as a father. He spent most of his free time entertaining Cammie and Max, both of whom really loved the games he created for them involving his wind. I watched him toss them into the air, using his element to bring them slowly back down into his arms while they chortled.

But the one trait that frustrated me the most about Joel was his insistence upon enjoying his marital rights with me at least twice each week. My lust for him had diminished significantly since our first year of marriage, when I often pretended he was Augustin. Now, when he drew me close in bed and covered my body with his, my mind filled with images of innumerable babies, my ice remaining dormant in my spirit as his wind beckoned me into elemental dalliance.

Joel likely noticed my distance and attributed it to my feelings for Augustin, for whenever we argued he had the tendency to bring up that subject just to nettle me. I had a notion that he insisted upon sex to annoy me, and as his wife I should not refuse him. I became pregnant again in July of 1051, and I complained to Freia during the subsequent months about the nuisances of such things. I had been with child for more than half of my married life. I began to muse upon getting sterilized as soon as I returned to the future, so I would never have to face the irritations of pregnancy again. I hoped that two decades apart from modern hospitals would cure my fear of such things once and for all.

My fifth experience with childbirth was not particularly pleasant. The child came a month early and lived for only three days, plunging our household into yet another time of mourning. We named her Bethany Gertrud after my cousins, and she took her place beside the graves of her two sisters. Joel remarked that we ought to stop naming our children after people who had died, that doing so might be cursing our line. I favored him with a scowl and responded that maybe the month of March was cursed, so he should stop knocking me up at the outset of summer. He did not appreciate my attempt to make light of the situation and accused me of being a heartless mother. So I stifled my complaints inside and tugged the usual mask over my face, focusing my attentions on our living daughter and son.

A noxious flu took hold of Count von Meldorf around the time of Bethany's birth, and he spent two weeks in bed fighting it, his aged lungs unable to hold back the resultant pneumonia. He called Joel and me to his side on his final morning to impart his last threads of wisdom. He urged us to run the estate honorably, treating the servants and vassals with decency, keeping the memory of his family alive for years to come. He also begged me to look after

Freia, to give her his regards and wishes for a prosperous future.

Viktor informed Joel and me of the count's death that night after we had prepared for bed. His wizened face appeared sorrowful as he imparted his news to me, and my eyes welled with tears, my voice hardly able to thank him around the lump in my throat. When the men buried him beside his wife the next morning, I clung to Joel during the short ceremony we held in his honor. I knew not how he and I could ever manage to fill his shoes as the new lord and lady of the estate. We were so young and inexperienced, and I would miss the count deeply, from his kind generosity to his wit and wisdom.

A shroud of loss seemed to hang over the manor for the rest of that year. Joel and I strove to honor the count in all that we did. We donated a portion of his savings to the church and named the stream that marked the southern boundary of his property the "Meldorf Stream." Joel had to assert himself before the other noble families when it came time to set prices for our harvests, for Count von Reuter and Lord Sendlin united in an attempt to undersell our barley. I rolled my eyes at the collective posturing of men and told my husband to withhold our wool if they refused to work with us like they should. Lord Ahloch of the council eventually came to our aid and decreed that our local peers must respect the Thaden family as they did our predecessors, for it was Count von Meldorf's wish.

Tensions eventually simmered into a slow boil, and by the time the Christmas holidays came, I set my melancholy aside in favor of the traditional festivities. I had concluded that it was best to concentrate on my living friends and family rather than those I had lost. Death had been my companion from the days of my childhood; Joel struggled more with the high mortality rate of our offspring than I did. He made no more advances toward me in bed after Bethany's death, and the darkness rarely left his face. But when he amused Max and Cammie, his hazel eyes would light up once more, and he would smile and laugh like he had during our first years in the eleventh century. I had hoped that the Christmas celebrations would help Joel divert his attention from loss to the joys of the season, but he caught a cold on Christmas Day and remained indoors the whole week, missing all of Muniche's merriments.

I attended the Christmas mass at the cathedral with Freia and Heinrich and their daughter Lorraine, who spent the whole service giggling with Cammie under the pews. Subsequently, we joined my best friend and her husband for a feast at the Denlinger house. Heinrich's two younger sisters still resided there, though both of his parents had passed away. Eva had married a merchant the previous summer and lived a street away from Heinrich's cottage. While we watched our children playing together after the meal, Freia told me that she and Heinrich planned to move back into his family's house once the snows had melted. I exclaimed in excitement for my friend's good fortune, for she had birthed her fourth child successfully in November and needed a larger house for her growing brood.

On New Year's Eve, I attended the traditional gala for the nobility at the Bayern castle. I had debated within myself for a long time whether I dared to make an appearance without my husband. No part of me wished to encounter Prince Otto or Lady Maria in their splendor amongst their adoring subjects, but I knew that the food would be sumptuous. Joel advised that I go to represent our household, to show that the Thaden line deserved its place amongst the nobility. He had a fair point after the fiasco with the barley, so I decked myself out magnificently for the occasion. I chose a fur-trimmed deep green dress with silver buttons, plaiting my black hair to my head beneath an argentine net. I included my mother's silver earrings, diamond necklace, and emerald bracelet to really impress my peers, and donned a fur coat and gloves against the cold before Jarvis drove me to the castle in our finest carriage.

When we arrived, I told Jarvis that I would call him with my ice once I wished to depart, and that in the meantime he should enjoy his part of the celebration with the other servants. He grinned at me beneath his thick brown beard and promised that he would keep his energy on alert for me.

As I passed through the front entrance of the castle moments later, casting off my coat and gloves and handing them to an eager butler, I realized that I had not graced the halls of the Bayern castle alone since that horrid meeting I had in the library with Prince Otto. My thoughts traveled back to that spring afternoon while I walked demurely through the vestibule, ready to seek Freia and Heinrich. *It's been almost eight years now, but I doubt the Prince has forgotten our tête-à-tête or that stupid elemental fight. I wonder what he'll think when he sees me here by myself—for he* will *see me, no doubt about it. Augustin's harlot. I wish Joel was here, and if not him, Augustin himself. This castle is dismal without him . . . just a swarm of posturing aristocracy.*

I encountered Freia and Heinrich in the hall with the balcony. They waited with a significant amount of the guests for the three members of the Bayern family to make their speeches before the feast. Lady Adeline and her husband joined us, and we exchanged the usual pleasantries, laughing at cheerful stories involving our respective children as the men discussed their businesses.

I sighed as I looked toward the balcony, my thoughts far away. I missed Augustin terribly now, while I stood in what had once been *his* family castle, feeling incredibly alone yet surrounded by friends. I wished he would touch my heart tenderly sometime during the party tonight, to remind me of his presence with me, though he rarely caressed me that way anymore. Perhaps he would come to my dreams later on, to surprise me for his birthday . . . and then I could tell him that I imagined a dance with him now, as I waited for his dreadful ex-brother to appear with that wretched Lady Maria.

When the Prince finally showed up along with Lady Maria and Paulus, I did not pay attention to any of their speeches. I just shifted from one foot to the other, waiting impatiently to attack the dinner tables. Freia stood close to me, sensing my disgruntlement but unable to speak any comforting words with our acquaintances in hearing range. She granted me strength on the vitality of her light while she stood at my side, a wistful smile gracing her face when our eyes met.

I allowed myself a ridiculous fantasy as Paulus finished up his religious speech, recalling that Freia once suggested that I marry Augustin instead of Joel. *If we had married, the Prince could not have cursed him, for he would have been head of his own house . . . our house. We could be here together, standing on that balcony with the others, voicing our own wicked speeches laden with blunt honesty . . . and maybe a few young children could be standing up there with us . . . .*

I heaped my plate with victuals when everyone raided the tables, for once glad that I had retained the weight I had gained from my recent pregnancy. I ate roast goose, steak, salted herring, cheeses, biscuits with apple jam, and vegetable soup, washing it all down with red wine imported from France. I might disparage royalty for its pride, but I could not complain about the bounties of the imperial table.

As I mingled with the other noblewomen, my ears picking up the festive sounds of flutes, fiddles, and harps drifting from room to room, my thoughts turned to Prince Otto's organ, nestled in the music room in the far reaches of the castle. I wondered why he did not play it for this party, for those in the rear chambers could certainly have enjoyed its melodies. I considered for a fleeting moment what would happen if I slipped away from the crowd to play it myself. I had not touched my favorite instrument in years, and I missed its triumphant tunes, harmonies that infused my spirit with joy.

Eventually, I found myself on that stone terrace that overlooked the Bayern gardens, the night sky above dotted with stars, the waxing moon casting a ghostly light upon the snow coating the ground and sparkling off of the plants. I stood at the railing for an endless moment, the frigid air speaking to the ice within me as it ruffled the fur of my dress. Two Teuton couples danced upon the frozen gardens, and I watched them with lidded eyes, appreciating their artistry though I likely would not join them.

I recognized Lady Hildegard dancing with her husband, her mist mingling with his air, creating a billowing fog. I also saw the couple that I had observed at that other New Year's party long ago: the man of darkness and the water woman. The man was a knight, Wilhelm von der Leidt, the head of the Prince's army, and his wife's name was Louise. I had danced with Wilhelm following my church wedding in 1045, and I smiled at the sight of him chasing his wife, using the shadows as his cloak.

"It is a glorious sight to watch our people dance in the realm of nature, is it not, my Lady Swanhilde?" A male voice cut into my tranquility, and the ice already flowing through my veins froze my skin in an instant. My blue eyes widened as I turned slowly to my right to face Prince Otto. He stood just two steps away, leaning against the stone railing himself, layered in furs against the cold. I could sense heat radiating from him on the strength of his red fire.

I paused, my eyes darting back to the glass doors to the warm room beyond, calculating whether I had a chance of racing inside and pretending that I did not hear or see the Prince. But he had averted his gaze from the dancers to look at me, his own eyes glittering a muted ruby, his face appearing friendly with no trace of malice or prejudice. I realized that I could not simply dart inside without hearing about my impropriety later, for I knew not whether some Teuton woman—such as Lady Maria—watched us covertly from beyond the glass doors. So I summoned my courage, silently cursing myself for not having stayed at home with Joel, and curtseyed once toward the Prince. "Yes, *Leitaeri*, observing elemental dances always brings a sense of fulfillment," I acknowledged.

Prince Otto's mouth quirked into a slight smile beneath his black beard. It looked rather impressive at long last, for he would turn thirty-one this year. "Why then do you not join them, Lady Swanhilde?" he asked, jerking his head once toward the dancers.

My eyebrows came together, for I had an inkling that he thought of Augustin now. He likely remembered that glorious dance I had shared with him years before, at a New Year's party just like this one. But I pushed aside my annoyance and refused to let the Prince bait me. "I would join them, *Leitaeri*, but my husband is ill, and therefore I have no partner with whom to properly manifest my ice." I eyed him and leaned slightly onto the railing with my left elbow, awaiting his reply.

The Prince's forehead wrinkled as he glanced from me to the Teutons below. Then, to my utter shock, I heard him say in a low voice, "*I* would dance with you, if you would allow me, my Lady Swanhilde." He did not look at me when he spoke, and his fingers grasped the stone railing with a bit too much force.

I opened my mouth, then closed it, my mind racing to fabricate an intelligent response. No part of me wanted to dance with Prince Otto, for I still hated him for what he had done to Augustin. Though the Prince was red fire, and though I had always enjoyed spinning with fiery Teutons, I knew my weakness for priests. I did not want to allow the Prince to delve into my spirit during a dance. So after a rather awkward silence, I nodded my head once in the Prince's direction and replied without meeting his eyes, "I shall have to decline, *Leitaeri*, for I fear that my husband would not appreciate such a thing. If you wish to dance as a Teuton, may I suggest that you present yourself to Lady Maria." I looked directly at him when I said that, a slight smirk curling on my lips.

The Prince frowned at the rebuke in my words and crossed his arms with a sigh. I could feel the heat of his fire rippling outward from where he stood, so I took several steps back, wanting to appreciate the winter's chill without a human heater messing with my ice. When the Prince finally spoke again, he shocked me once more. "My Lady Maria has not danced publicly with me since our church wedding in 1043."

My eyes widened. I had never known that the Prince had officially married Lady Maria after accepting the keys of Muniche. *So they apparently married in the cathedral, but not as Teutons . . . for I doubt the Prince sports the marriage scar, or he wouldn't wear such tight sleeves all the time.*

I glanced down at his hands as I considered the implications of this, wondering if that might be part of the reason his relationship with Lady Maria always seemed so formal. I wondered which of them had decided not to bother with the mystical Teutonic wedding. I had a strong feeling that it was probably the Prince, for I remembered how greatly he had loved Kezia during his time travels. He likely would not want to take Maria as her replacement, and my thoughts returned to Augustin. A scowl twisted my lips at the realization that I had done the very thing that the Prince could not do, for Joel was Augustin's replacement. *And see how well that's worked out for you, Swanie. You should have run off with Augustin after the curse.*

"It has been my experience, *Leitaeri*," I began in a rather callous tone, "that attempting to ignite a false love while the true fidelity still burns results in wretched failure." Prince Otto's mien clouded over with restlessness, but he met my gaze as I went on, my words growing more and more caustic. "Unfortunately, both of us have had to learn this lesson the hard way. But unlike you, *Leitaeri, I* had no choice when it came to love. You could always choose to go back to your lover in the past or to meet her any day in heaven. But I can never meet my lover again, for he was torn from me by misplaced jealousy."

The red fire in the Prince's eyes deepened, but aside from that, he held onto his control and stated flatly, "You should have been able to forget him." He was thinking of that spell that he believed had broken our heart-bond, those misleading words that suggested that its severance equaled freedom.

But I sneered at the Prince, my icy fingers winding around the railing to my left as I reminded him, "If that were truly the case, then you would have forgotten Kezia. There are lies in the writings of the Teutons, *Leitaeri*, and you ought to consider them before making such assumptions."

The Prince exhaled audibly, tainting the air with just a touch of smoke. He turned away from me entirely to look down at the dancers again. "Everyone writes with a bias," he noted evenly.

"That is true," I said, silently ordering my fingers to unfreeze, though my ice did not want to obey. I had not wanted to speak with the Prince at all during this party, for we never seemed to have a civil conversation. So I turned for the doors, prepared to take my leave, but before I did so, I realized that I had a golden opportunity to end this confrontation as the victor.

So I paused in front of the glass doors and reminded the Prince, "Unlike most of your female acquaintances, *Leitaeri, I* have read many Teuton writings from the future. Therefore, it ought to interest you that I knew exactly what you had planned for my lover the moment you threatened to write his name out of history. And you ought to discern that I *knew* from history that he was destined to be cursed, or both of us would have vanished before you could have finished the act." Prince Otto eyed me in muted horror as I finished, "You have wondered why I came to this era, *Leitaeri,* and it ought to trouble you, for I do *not* travel time lightly, as you believe."

I eyed him for a long moment, watching the curiosity and trepidation war on his face. Then I opened the glass doors with a flourish and went inside.

Chapter Fifteen:
Wishes in the Night

As I reentered the ballroom, the sounds of lilting music and banal conversations filling my ears, I caught sight of the Lady Maria poised beside a heavy curtain that framed the doors to the balcony. She turned away when I passed by, but I detected a touch of annoyance on her face before she slipped into the crowd. An eavesdropper, just as I had suspected. I sighed in relief, glad that I had refused Prince Otto's invitation to dance, for I did not wish Lady Maria to hold a grudge against me. As the Lady of Muniche, she could order me to leave the city if she could find a decent excuse, and flirting with her Keyholder would be reason enough.

I spent several more hours mingling among the nobility while the New Year dawned, praying in my heart that 1053 would treat my family more kindly than its predecessor. Once Freia and Heinrich had taken their leave, I drifted toward the front vestibule, intending to call for Jarvis and return home. But when I passed through a lengthy hallway en route to the front entrance, I noticed a dark staircase winding downward, a single torch casting eerie shadows on the stone walls beyond. I remembered that I had descended that very staircase once before with Augustin, when he had taken me to his mother's chapel. An overwhelming desire grabbed hold of me, and I glanced around to ensure that I was alone in the hallway. An instant later, I snatched the torch from its niche and headed downward, wanting to visit Marelda's chapel again, assuming I could find it.

It took me some time to locate the correct door. I would not have found it at all, had I not run across one of the castle servants in the basement corridors. He carried a keg of beer on his shoulders and looked rather surprised to see me in the nether reaches of the cellar, but he directed me to the proper place without fuss when I told him what I sought. The Prince would probably hear about my underground escapades later once the servant tattled on me, but I shrugged it off and carefully opened the door to the chapel. Someone needed to grace the site of Marelda's tomb now that her most faithful son was banished.

I used the natural flames of the torch to light six of the candles resting upon her altar, then placed the torch into a notch outside the door, shutting it reverently behind me. For a long moment, I stood still to the right of the altar, gazing around at the shadows and the light of the candles casting intriguing rays upon the stained glass window. The chamber still invoked an aura of serenity and holiness, a proper memorial to that gracious woman who loved God and her family with an undying faithfulness.

While I gazed at her painted likeness above the marble casket, a sad smile curled upon my lips. I wished, foolishly, that I could have met Marelda von Bayern, that somehow she could have survived and led her children down the path of righteousness. Without her guidance, all three of them had never realized their full potential . . . Augustin a bitter wraith . . . Paulus a coward who hid his weakness in religion . . . Otto a pompous hypocrite. "Marelda," I murmured softly, "this city would have triumphed much longer if you had lived."

My eyes traveled downward from her image to her tomb, zeroing in on the aged candlestick still sitting atop it, bare of flame and appearing quite forlorn. It surprised me that none of the palace servants had thought to remove it, since they obviously kept the chapel clean. Maybe some of them still had sentiments for Augustin after all.

I concentrated on the elements inside my spirit, pushing my ice aside to delve into my master's fire for the first time in ages. The flames began to pulse within my veins, the air around me prickling with unusual heat. I narrowed my eyes and gestured at the candle, willing Augustin's blue fire to invigorate it once more. A cobalt flame appeared with startling suddenness upon its wick, its light casting an enchanting glow upon the image of Marelda. The candles on the altar began to flicker as my master's fire sought to supplant their natural flames, so I smiled to myself and allowed my ice to reclaim my spirit, a tiny corner of my heart centered forever on that new fire, keeping Marelda's memory alive.

Late that night, when I fell asleep beside my husband, Augustin came to me in my dreams. He greeted me at the banks of the Meldorf Stream, the cherry tree's bare branches cleaving the starry sky apart like the hands of an apparition. He bowed gravely when I wished him a happy birthday, his shining robes dulled only by the gloom in his eyes. "Technically, this is no longer my birthday, for I died some seven and a half years ago." His mouth twisted into a sallow smirk, and he reached forward to brush my hair back from my face. "I came to wish you a happy New Year, my darling swan, nothing more."

I closed my eyes as his fingers passed through my spirit, the sensations of his devotion enticing me all over again. When we met for our language studies, we kept each other at a distance until we parted ways at dawn, for Augustin insisted that neither of us should engage in fancies that could never come to pass. Although I knew every time he caressed my heart that his love for me had not faded, I could also sense his torment, for the darker part of him longed to leave me behind. Since Joel had discovered the truth of my feelings two years prior, the reasonable part of me had actually begun to wish from time to time that I could find a way to stop loving Augustin, for my obsession for him was a constant strain on my marriage. But on this night, as my master set aside his own interests to give me his regards for the New Year, I determined to forget reality and love him freely once more.

"You are not dead to me, Augustin," I reminded him, opening my eyes to gaze into his. "And I hope that you, too, will find this year better than the last."

Augustin smiled ruefully at me and said, "Thirteen years until the deluge of 1066. I think that perhaps this year I shall return to Germanic lands to see if any lord or Prince would grant me sanctuary." His spirit shuddered, and he glanced downstream toward the brook's confluence with the River Isar, his countenance dismal. "My heart longs for Muniche, though I can never enter her gates again," he admitted softly. "I felt you desiring me last night, while you watched your people dance upon the Bayern gardens in the moonlight. I wanted to come to you then, to run with you there in the spirit, but this curse restrains me." His gaze traveled downward to his right forearm, hidden beneath his clothing. "I cannot enter Muniche in the mortal world or in the spiritual realm, for she has cast me out. It is frustrating."

His disappointment flowed into my heart through our bond, and I sat down upon the snowy grass, placing my icy feet upon the frozen stream. "The curse is a horrid thing," I whispered as he came to sit beside me, "but it'll never ostracize you from me. I still want you more than anything, and I still love you more than anyone, more than Joel, more than any of our children." I placed my hand on top of his and watched our spirits merge, our hands appearing to be one.

Augustin sighed heavily, reaching his free hand into his robes to retrieve my beating heart. "When time severs this connection, your love for me shall fade," he said, blinking his fiery eyes and closing his fingers around my heart.

I moaned quietly at his touch, so strong yet so gentle... and my mind went back to the confrontation I had with Prince Otto not long before. "I highly doubt that," I informed Augustin, remembering that the Prince had not yet forgotten his true love. "Our love is too powerful to be broken by anything or anyone, because it's real love, free love. I made a choice to love you in spite of your sins, Augustin, and I don't intend to change my mind." I winked at him.

A sad smile graced his lips as he drew his left hand out from beneath mine to cradle my heart more closely, more ardently. "I cannot imagine how you intend to keep this relationship alive when our bond finally breaks." He stroked my heart one final time before placing it in its rightful place at his chest, beside the heart of his own sinful spirit. "You must not cling to a Black Priest who has been in hell for centuries when you return to your own era. Then you must find another man to take my place, a better man, a Teuton priest who would not abuse you."

I chuckled at his words, thinking of Hans for the first time in a long time. I wondered whether I would love him like I once did, when I finally made it back to the twenty-first century. "So you're suggesting that I forsake you for an old man?" I inquired of Augustin, tilting my head at him coyly.

He smirked at me and said, "You may do what you will once you have been loosed from my chains. If you can convince Hans to absolve your long insanity with a Cursed One, perhaps he could cause you to forget."

"There will be no forgetting," I insisted, "but maybe someday I'll be able to honestly move on. These last seven years have been a sham for me, trying to love a man who isn't a priest, bearing his children over and over." I huffed in irritation, wrapping my arms around my knees. "I still pretend that we could be together one day, united in true matrimony, entering heaven side by side when death takes us both. No one else completes me the way you do. You're still everything to me, in spite of the distance between us."

"Castles in the air, my darling," he murmured, his eyes on the frozen stream.

I frowned, aggravated by his refusal to acknowledge hope and grace. But I ordered myself to not give up, for I had thirteen years before Muniche's fall would send me home. His casual mention of castles in the air turned my thoughts back to the party and my unmet desire for a Teutonic dance. A sudden inspiration took hold of me, and I jumped up from the snow and looked toward the Isar and Muniche's turrets beyond. "Augustin, you said that you cannot enter Muniche again . . . but *I* can, and I've gone there before in my dreams when you're not with me." I met his gaze, steeling myself to voice the impossible question. "Do you think . . . *I* could take you there . . . here in our dream?"

Augustin's eyes widened, and he rose from the ground, his expression growing thoughtful. "I do not know. It may be possible if you carry me there on your own power, if we stand together as one, if I hold your heart tightly. But we should not attempt such a thing, Swanhilde," he added, his forehead wrinkling. "It would prove an unnecessary torment, for each of us to grasp what we desire so greatly only to see it vanish with the dawn. We ought not to distress ourselves further. I should not have come to you until Tuesday, as usual." He frowned.

I shook my head firmly, my whims conquering reason as always. I stepped forward, allowing the white robes of my spirit to meld with his flaming ones. "This world is a dream, Augustin, and I want it to be a *good* dream. I want to dance with you in the Bayern gardens now, when no one can sense us. Come with me!" I moved my spirit even closer to his and squeezed my eyes shut, willing the scenery to change before his hesitation could alter my yearning. I heard him gasp, an almost painful sound. His fingers tightened upon my heart in a stone grip as I felt my spirit pass through an invisible screen that seemed to rip us asunder.

I blinked my eyes a moment later, my mouth falling open at the sight of one of the intricate fountains of the Bayern gardens to my right, its waters frozen in a glorious sheen of ice, sparkling in the starlight. I could see the tangled grapevines around me, coated with snow, and my icy feet just barely touched the snow-covered ground, leaving no detectable imprint. The winter wind breezed through my spirit as I turned my head to the left and saw Augustin. His fiery feet sizzled an imperceptible stain upon the snow, his cobalt eyes aglow with amazement. At length, his gaze locked with mine. "You did it," he whispered, sounding awed.

I would have blushed if I had been in my mortal body, but instead I spent a brief moment looking down at my frosty feet, gathering my courage. Then I lifted my head and asked shyly, "Would you dance with me, master?" Part of me feared that he might refuse, or force me to wake from this wondrous fantasia.

But he smiled at me mischievously and proffered his right hand, his fire transforming his spirit into a radiant azure. "It would be my pleasure, my precious swan princess, my love who shall never allow me to forget beauty."

So we danced an infinite elemental dance, our spirits racing with the freedom of a dream, crossing all mortal barriers as we leapt high into the air, floating like birds across the sky, tripping lightly through the grapevines and bushes. I kept my ice prominent during the majority of our dance, my spirit merging with the ice of the fountains, exploding from them like a queen of the frost as I endeavored to catch Augustin. I threw a myriad of snowballs at him during our romp, and he allowed some of them to stick to his gorgeous hair for the shortest of intervals before shaking them free and chucking several fireballs in my direction. I chortled as they passed through my spirit, finding no purchase upon me or the nature around us, and Augustin pouted at his lack of influence on the frigid landscape.

When we paused beside an architecturally elaborate gazebo that reminded me a bit of the one in my own backyard in München, Augustin jumped into the sky. His spirit rocketed up with a speed and glory that shocked me afresh. I stared after him, wondering if he wanted me to follow. My eyes opened wide when he grabbed what appeared to be one of the stars from the sky, transforming it into a fiery white orb in his hand as his spirit sank back to the earth.

A wicked smile broke across his face at the sight of my astonishment and he drifted to my side, holding the burning sphere out to me, a gift. "Come, my darling, you must relinquish your ice for me," he cajoled, his eyes glittering with fun. "Your element gives you far too great an advantage in this winter. Be my fiery bride, and let us singe this tranquility in a devil's dance."

Anticipation washed over me, and I forced my ice back, drawing Augustin's fire from my spirit for the second time that night. I felt the blue of my eyes change from solid ice into a boiling flame, sharpening my vision with a sapphire's power. I snatched the fiery orb from my master's hand and cast it into the sky with a laugh. Augustin leapt upward to catch it, and an instant later we were racing across the gardens once more. Our blues combined into a sweltering inferno, searing the snow beneath us, melting the ice of the fountains, setting the trellises aflame. I would have grown breathless if I was not in spirit form, for I danced with a vigor I had never known. Augustin's fire pervaded my spirit, almost making me believe I could actually touch him, even though our dream world did not permit physical contact. I laughed more than I had in years, ecstasy filling me as I strove to outdo my master, my feet leaving diminutive fires upon the snow.

We likely would have danced until the sun rose, for the sky had begun to turn gray when I finally halted, having scaled the stones of the castle to set myself upon the railing of a wide balcony near the turrets of the roof. I grinned and spun around on a single toe to look for Augustin, whom I assumed would follow me to my perch eventually. But I saw him standing on the ground far below me, the look on his face telling me that he had no intention of joining me. I frowned, trying to discern the reason for his reticence, and in the next second I heard a door open behind me with a creak. Terror took hold of me, for I swung my head around and recognized Prince Otto. He stepped onto the balcony, his body clothed in an elegant sleeping robe, a nightcap adorning his head.

I cast myself off of the balcony without pause and darted to my master's side with the words, "We'd better get out of here."

Augustin shrugged, his expression caustic. "He cannot detect us here." But he scowled when the Prince appeared at the railing, his gaze on the lightening sky.

I looked up at the Prince, then back at Augustin. "But what if he sees . . . the results of our dance?" I thought of the melted waters, the fires upon the snow.

My master snickered. "What we did does not exist, Swanhilde." He gestured behind us at the gardens, and I saw, to my surprise, that the landscape did indeed appear untouched. I saw no trace of footprints upon the snow.

A moment later, Lady Maria approached the railing, at least a meter of space between her and the Prince as her sharp eyes scoured the snowy scene beneath her. I could tell, though they both stood far above me, that neither of them appeared content. They looked like they were about to have a rather dreadful discussion. "If they really can't detect us here, maybe I should sneak up there and listen to their conversation," I mused.

Augustin grimaced, his cerulean eyes riveted on the Prince and his Lady. "I suddenly have an incredible urge to kill," he stated tonelessly.

I stared at Augustin in horror. "But you can't," I reminded him, afraid that he may decide to try using his death gift against the Prince, even though I doubted that he could accomplish murder in the *Gæstelort Troumerae*. "He won't die until 1074. If you kill him, that would change history."

My lover snorted, his expression extremely annoyed. "I realize that." He glared at the Prince one final time, then looked at me. "You may climb up there to eavesdrop on them, but I cannot. I shall meet you by the cherry tree to bid you farewell at sunrise. See to it that you do not waste time here, Swanhilde." He nodded at me significantly, then disappeared.

I scaled the castle walls a second time and positioned myself in the shadows of a pillar that reached upward to the awning. I balanced atop the stone railing and peered around to see Prince Otto leaning forward, a heavy sigh lifting his shoulders. "I do not understand how you can be so melancholy on such a magnificent winter morning." Lady Maria's voice, her tone as distasteful as ever as she stood beside her Keyholder. "The frigid wind whispers to my blood, asking me to rejoice in the glory of nature and the success of our city." I saw her blue eyes sparkling with zeal.

A rather rueful smile appeared on the Prince's lips, but he did not meet his Lady's triumphant gaze. "But how long will this success last?" It was a rhetorical question, but his expression appeared unhappy as he looked toward the horizon.

A short silence ensued, and I took the opportunity to observe Lady Maria more closely from my perch. She would be fifty-three this year, if Augustin had her age right, and she looked it. Her hair had turned almost completely gray with little trace of its natural brown, and quite a few wrinkles marred her pale face. She had probably been beautiful once, long ago when she had married Prince Ulrich, but now I doubted that even the madness of the keys could seduce Otto enough to make love to her. A twinge of sympathy struck me, for I realized that as much as I hated the Prince for cursing Augustin, I still pitied his fate.

"That foolish child from the future disturbed you last night," Maria observed, her wintry eyes harsh as she looked at her Keyholder. I gasped quietly at her accusation and slipped further into the shadows of the pillar, though neither she nor the Prince could notice my presence. Maria stepped toward the Prince and halted a handbreadth to his right. "You must not concern yourself with her, Otto," she urged in an earnest tone. "She is a simple young woman who holds no sway over the fate of our city."

The Prince's dark blue eyes glinted with a touch of red as he nodded wearily at his Lady's advice, but when he answered her his tone sounded grave. "You are right, of course, but I cannot help but worry when I contemplate her reasons for coming here." He paused, shaking his head once before turning slightly to his right to face Lady Maria. "She knows the future, and I fear that she did not brave the danger to travel here for the sole purpose of examining our success. Some terrible destiny looms on our horizon, and we shall not be able to counter it." He pressed his lips together into a thin line, averting his gaze from his Lady's face to the heavens, which had begun to grow crimson with the impending sunrise.

Maria sighed at the Prince and slumped forward onto the railing, her element toying with the strands of her gray hair that had escaped her nightcap. "Muniche shall prosper forever, as long as we are here to lead her," she said confidently, her countenance a mask of cold assurance.

I watched the Prince cringe, a rather anxious expression crossing his face. When he spoke again, I had to strain my ears to catch his words. "But how can I lead this city properly if she continues to keep me at a distance?" My eyes widened as the Prince paused, his gaze now locked upon Maria, who had stiffened into a wintry sculpture at his side.

Prince Otto took one cautious step toward her. "I would not have spoken with the Lady Swanhilde at all, had she not stood upon that balcony watching our people dance," he murmured, his bearded jaw quivering. "The glories of our elements summon my spirit to break free . . . and I wanted to dance with you in the night . . . but I knew that you would have refused me." The tragedy in the Prince's voice might have made me weep, had I not been a spirit.

Maria's mouth twitched in displeasure at Prince Otto's passion, and she moved away from him. "You know that we cannot do such things in public," she reminded him quietly, "for we must maintain our poise before our people, so they may respect us. It is still difficult for some, even after ten years, to accept your place as their Prince in your father's stead."

"But we are Teutons, as they are, and our people know it," the Prince pointed out, the fervor emanating from his form striking me where I hid in the shadows. He advanced toward Maria again, guardedly, reaching one hand out to her face. "I wish you to open your heart to me, Muniche . . . my dear one . . . my beloved wind of winter . . . keeper of my soul . . . ." My mouth dropped open, for he spoke his endearments in Ælte Teutonica—worshipful accolades reserved for the Keyholder of a Teuton city and his Lady.

The cloth of Maria's nightdress rose and fell swiftly with her breath, and an oddly vulnerable expression appeared on her habitually hard face as she stared into the Prince's eyes. When his hand stroked her cheek, the temperature of his fiery skin likely enticing her frigid spirit, I heard her moan a soft reply: "My . . . Keyholder . . . ." A moment later they kissed, the Prince folding his Lady in his arms. His obvious devotion reminded me of what I shared with Augustin. Pain overtook my spirit, for I desperately wished that I could touch him again.

Lady Maria pulled away from Prince Otto soon afterward, pointing out that the day would soon break, so he must open the gates of their city. Once she had gone back inside, I heard the Prince sigh again, his gaze toward the rising sun. And I heard him say in Ælte Teutonica, right before I swept my spirit away to meet Augustin, "This forced love shall never satisfy . . . for I cannot forget her."

Chapter Sixteen

Distant Skirmishes

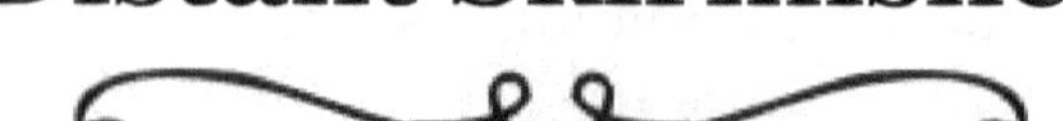

In the early spring of 1053, messengers came to Muniche from the small Teutonic settlements to the north. They requested Prince Otto's aid in repelling a new wave of attacks by Saxon enclaves, the first in over a decade, so it was said. Our enemies had found other distractions to occupy their time since Prince Ulrich's death, but now they apparently wanted to test the courage of his son, to see if he could raise a strong Teuton army like his father before him.

The whole city was in an uproar for several weeks before Easter as the Prince organized his forces—both mounted knights and infantry—planning to march on the outskirts of Teuton lands as soon as volunteers from the nearby cities arrived. On the Tuesday after Easter, the Prince's army set out, reinforced by knights from Salzburg, Augsburg, Freising, and Passau. Their combined forces were slated to meet more soldiers from Ratisbon, Regensburg, and Würzburg on their journey north.

The adventurous part of me wished to accompany the army. I longed to unleash some of my private frustrations upon the Saxons, knowing that they would be responsible for my people's defeat. Yet if I had somehow managed to tag along with the soldiers, I knew that I would not survive an enemy onslaught, since I had never learned the use of medieval weapons. I could fight the Saxons with my ice, but the Prince would likely frown on obvious elemental displays. I had some skills with the sword thanks to Joel's coaching in the early years of our marriage, but I knew next to nothing about the bow and arrow, the mace, or the lance. So I contented myself with baking bread and drying meats, fruits, and vegetables as provisions for the troops, and I sewed durable clothing for Joel, hoping that it would hold up underneath his armor.

Joel departed with the Prince's army, perched atop our strongest stallion, his face aglow with the excitement of a fight. As soon as the news of the skirmishes in the north had reached us, Joel jabbered about future battles incessantly, saying over and over that he could hardly wait to take part in the fray. He wished to kill as many Saxons as possible while he had the chance, before they stole the advantage over us with the Prince's song. He proclaimed that he would blow the Saxons to the ground with his wind whether the Prince approved or not, and sever his opponents' heads with an impressive sword that he had forged himself.

I smiled tolerantly at his boasts and reminded him not to underestimate the dangers of battle. I warned him to stay away from bread and nuts, and he promised to finish the food we had prepared for him before scrounging what he could from the land. I hoped that he would return safe and sound, for I did not want to spend the next thirteen years running our estate by myself. Although I felt no love for Joel, I did appreciate his managerial skills as well as his enthusiastic games with our children. Part of me rejoiced that I would not share his bed until the Saxons had been expelled from our lands, especially since he felt the need to bang me good and hard in the weeks before he left. It did not surprise me when my menstrual cycle forsook me at month's end. I had a strong feeling that Joel had purposely impregnated me so that I would not flee to Augustin during his absence.

That year was the first in which I oversaw the business of the estate without my husband's help. Our fields were short-staffed that summer since twenty-four of our vassals also joined the Prince's army; but with Jarvis' help, we managed to clear a profit in spite of our smaller harvests. Our estate fared better than many of the others that season, for a wicked drought descended during the months of July and August. Had I not rained my ice upon the fields faithfully before morning light each day, our grain would have perished. Two vassal women who claimed the element of water kept our well filled and came to my aid from time to time with the crops. During the harvests, Jarvis left the bookkeeping to me and ventured outside to pick the increase, his energy allowing him to fill nearly twice as many baskets of produce than any of the other laborers. We sold a large amount of our crops, and what we could not sell we preserved for the winter, the women drying meat, vegetables, and fruits for future consumption.

Freia spent quite a bit of time with me that year, for Heinrich had also gone with the Prince's army, leaving Aric the priest to run the ironworks. We exchanged many speculations on the fates of the army and our husbands, while our children played together under our watchful eyes. I could tell that Freia feared greatly for Heinrich, and we prayed for him and Joel every time we met. I admitted to my best friend that while I thought of Joel often, I did not really worry about his safety; for I knew that if he got killed, he would return to the twenty-first century. Freia commented with a doleful smile that it must be nice to be from the future, knowing that death would not separate Joel or me permanently from this world.

Just before Cammie's sixth birthday, she manifested the element of ice on a breezy afternoon when we played together along the Meldorf Stream. It thrilled me to learn that my blond daughter claimed the same power as me, and I gave her careful instructions on the use of her ice. I warned her not to display her magic out in the open, that it must be kept contained to guard the safety of the Teuton people. She promised that she would keep it a secret, but she begged me to frolic with her again sometime after her next sibling had been born.

At Cammie's birthday party in September, I related the tale of our exciting discovery to Freia, who brought her three children over to celebrate their friend. She favored me with a knowing smile and admitted that her oldest daughter Lorraine was earth, the primary manifestation of Heinrich's metal. She told me that having a child of earth could be frustrating at times, for Lorraine tended to leave dirt around the house by accident. I laughed at this and pointed out that Count von Meldorf had managed his earth decently enough, since his servants had not spent all of their time cleaning up after him. Freia noted that Heinrich would have to be the one to explain the use of earth to their daughter, since the control of Teutonic elements still seemed alien to her at times.

We held a lengthy discussion on the possible elemental powers of our offspring, for Teuton children generally demonstrated derivatives of their parents' gifts. Joel's wind was a subsidiary of air, while my ice was an offshoot of water. Since I had no idea what element my father had, I figured that my children's gifts could range from air, wind, or whirlwind to water, ice, snow, or mist. Heinrich had earth and fire in his family, so combined with Freia's light, their offspring would claim quite a few elemental possibilities.

Joel returned home in late November with the rest of the Prince's army, bubbling over with tales of primitive battles rife with swords, arrows, and spears. His stallion had fallen as a result of several hits from a mace, but he had managed to snatch another horse from a Saxon camp, which he proudly dubbed "Booty." He showed off new scars on his arm from enemy spears, which prompted Cammie and Max to gawk while I shook my head tolerantly at his boasting. Three of our vassals had died in battle, saddling their families with long nights of bereavement.

Freia and Heinrich visited for lunch shortly after the army's return. The men discussed the truce that Prince Otto had brokered with Emperor Heinrich III. After days of negotiations, they had agreed that the Saxons would cease their hostilities against the Teutonic settlements in the north. Several trade agreements had been altered in our people's favor, for Heinrich III had grudgingly accepted responsibility for the burning of three of our people's villages.

The Prince's formidable army had gained the upper hand after countless skirmishes, according to Joel and Heinrich. Joel disclosed with a smirk that quite a few of the Teutons had used their elements against the Saxons, though they did so surreptitiously. He had used his wind several times, generously sucking the summer breezes away from the Saxon camps to leave them sweltering. Heinrich confessed with a snicker that his hand had merged conveniently with the metal of his sword and armor more than once, protecting him from harm and delivering fierce blows upon our enemies.

It surprised me that Prince Otto had allowed such enchantments during the fighting, for I still remembered how vehemently he had rebuked my use of my ice against the Gypsies. But apparently the Prince had relaxed his standards a bit in the face of death. Both Joel and Heinrich claimed that he had spoken privately with the commanders of each regiment after the first battle, stating that their men should use their elements if they could do so with discretion. Burning Saxons to the ground left and right was positively forbidden, but raising a thick morning fog at an opportune moment or letting an enemy's horse trip on an abrupt patch of soft sand were deemed acceptable.

Joel related one rousing tale of a night attack in which several of the fiery Teutons had extinguished the Saxons' campfires while Knight von der Leidt used his darkness to delay the sunrise. The men's tales of battle prompted me to ponder Muniche's impending fall afresh. Even when the Saxons captured the Prince's song from Paulus, how could they manage to defeat an army with elemental powers?

Augustin and I exchanged speculations on this conundrum on occasion, and he ultimately concluded that a force of infinite size with the possible immortality of time travel could bring the Teutons to their knees.

Peace descended upon Muniche for the next few years as the Saxons bowed temporarily to our demands. We had a very successful season in 1054, bringing in bountiful harvests and clearing a substantial profit. The fact that Joel and I rarely hosted expensive parties and spent little money on clothing or furniture kept our business in the black, and I commented often that I could not care less whether our noble peers thought we were misers. Both Joel and I wanted our children to have a store of capital on hand before the defeat of 1066 would chase them from their home. Neither of us would be there to guide them, but we did not want to leave them destitute, either.

In January of 1054 I bore another son, a skinny infant with dirty blond hair, hazel eyes, and a wail that reminded me of a cat howling in pain. We named the child Helmut Friedrich in honor of the late count, for we did not want him forgotten, although his family name had vanished from the current events. During the summer of 1054, I handed baby Helmut off to Ulka's capable hands for a few hours each day so that I could tutor Cammie and Max. Each of them could speak English and Teutonica quite well by that time. I focused their lessons on the reading and writing of the vernacular, along with Bible stories and simple mathematics.

Early that September, Freia came to visit me one cloudy afternoon, having left her three children under Kathe's care for the day. We sat together on the front porch speaking on various topics, a soft breeze rustling the plants in the gardens before us. She had lost a newborn son to a fever several weeks prior, and she told me that as much as she adored raising her children, she seemed to lose a portion of her heart with each one that had passed. The two of us had each lost three by that time. Aside from the son that the Gypsies had stolen from her, my best friend's two most recent children had already gained their angel wings.

"I'm grateful to God for His protection," she murmured, her hands cradling a cup of mint tea. "I honestly thought it would be harder to bear children as a Teuton woman, with all of the stories that float on the breeze."

"I know what you mean," I said, thinking of how much I cherished Augustin's spiritual support whenever I faced the burden of labor. "In my time we have ways to actually make it so a woman can't have kids. I'm sorely tempted to do that once I go back home."

"People would say that's a waste of your blood," Freia pointed out.

I shrugged one shoulder and leaned back against the house, taking a sip from my own teacup. "My blood's doing fine here. It's not my responsibility to make sure the Teuton people don't die out. Three of my cousins already have kids."

"It's still odd to raise magical children," Freia said with a chuckle. "It's not something I had ever expected to do. Kathe's been telling stories to Lorraine and Heino about some sort of tree fairy. She says that they live amid the branches of silver oak trees and that they give out sage advice."

"*Eihalbae*," I clarified with a smile, thinking of the three that I had met thus far. One had led me to the Torstein, one had entrusted me with the responsibility of planting a new tree . . . and the one here in the eleventh century had helped me save Augustin after I had uncovered the truth of his love.

"Then they're real?" Freia asked, her eyes opening wide.

I grinned. "Of course they're real. Did you think Kathe had made it up? They embody the spirits of the silver oak trees, the ones with healing magic."

"Kathe mentioned that Teutons must ask their permission before cutting a branch from a silver oak for use in rituals. But do they really give out advice?" My friend tilted her head at me, her expression doubtful.

"Well, one set me on this path of time travel, and another one told me how to save Augustin's life that time I drank his blood." Freia gaped at me, and I rose to my feet and stretched. "There's a silver oak by the Meldorf Stream here on our property. We can take a walk there if you want, and maybe its *Eihalbe* will deign to speak with us."

Freia stood up herself, her expression both curious and cautious as she followed me into the yard, our cups of tea lying empty behind us. We found Viktor on our way around the house; he was cleaning a windowpane. I beckoned him to where Freia and I stood on the path and requested that he take our discarded teacups to be washed in the kitchen. Viktor ducked his head at both of us and headed off in the direction from which we had come, his withered lips curled into a fond smile as he departed.

"It amazes me that you've found the time to learn so many languages," Freia commented as we walked the path to the stream, her eyes gazing off into the distance with a look that could have been wistful. "I hardly have the brainpower to study anything these days, even with Kathe's help with the kids."

"I don't have the brainpower for anything either, except in my dreams," I related with a sigh. Although my husband had taken up most of the estate's duties upon his return last autumn, I often felt like the only time I had for myself occurred during sleep. "Augustin and I mostly just go over what we've already learned at this point. He's taught me Magyar and Ælte Teutonica, and he's helped me improve my Teutonica and Latin. I'm not sure if I ought to move on to another subject or not."

"Maybe Rhenisch?" Freia suggested with a grin, and I cackled, turning east along the stream toward the far end of the Thaden property.

It took us a fair amount of time to reach the grove of oaks, a place I rarely visited due to its distance from the manor. On the way, I related my own personal experiences with *Eihalbae* and told Freia that she needed to treat the fairy respectfully if it showed itself. "Hans said that they view themselves as superior to humans because they hold the wisdom of ages," I said. "They share the knowledge of the forests and the mountains and all of the creatures therein."

"I wonder if they have knowledge of God," Freia mused, her green eyes admiring the cloudy sky above.

"I think that all of nature has that," I replied, "but the fairies certainly don't seem to be in league with Wuotan. They've told me to respect the price of magic more than once."

"Warning you against going too far," Freia assumed.

I sighed a little as we crested the hill beyond the water mill, the small glade of aged oak trees drawing ever closer. "They have a fair point if so," I said, my thoughts shifting again to Augustin. He had restarted his search for a place to call his own after having trailed the Prince's army last year to write his account of the skirmishes. He had told me last Thursday night that he may have found a ruler willing to accept him at long last.

We slipped into the grove of oaks, and I called my ice forth to enhance my vision, revealing the silvery sheen of a single tree standing among its ordinary fellows. "This is the silver oak," I said, stepping forward to place my right hand gently upon its ivy-coated trunk. "You have to call your element into your eyes to see it properly."

The glow of the sun broke forth from Freia's eyes, and she gasped softly, running her gaze up and down the trunk before us. "I see it now . . . it really *does* have silver coloring!" She bent down to touch several fallen leaves upon the ground. "Do these have healing properties, or does it have to be a fresh leaf?"

I nudged a few leaves with my shoe. It was harder to see the difference between white oak and silver oak when the leaves had turned their autumn yellow. "I think the fresh ones are best. Gretchen collects a batch every spring and summer for use in her potions and tonics. I'm not really sure about the yellow—"

I broke off mid-sentence, for my Teuton spirit had become aware of another presence joining Freia and me in the dell. I took a step away from the trunk and lifted my eyes to a low-hanging branch—and there, in a cluster of yellow leaves, I saw a humanoid face about the size of a squirrel's, hair of wispy argentine framing its cheeks, its eyes sparkling with a prism of colors as they stared directly at me. The rest of its body was concealed among the leaves.

I nudged Freia and nodded once toward the branch before ducking my head in propriety. "Noble *Eihalbe*, good afternoon," I greeted the fairy.

"The Teuton witch brings her Rhenisch blood-sister to learn of arcane lore," the silvery *Eihalbe* observed after a moment's pause, its Teutonica silky and quiet, weaving its way sinuously into my ears. I heard Freia's soft intake of breath; then she clutched my left arm in fright.

I guess I did, I thought to myself, my lips quirking at the way the fairy had referenced Freia. Apparently it had heard of our blood-transfer. "This is my good friend and blood-sister Freia Denlinger von Eisenwald," I said, using my right hand to detach Freia's fingers from my arm and sliding them through my own. "I should have introduced you before."

The *Eihalbe's* rainbow eyes shifted from my face to Freia's, its silvery lips pursed for an instant in what appeared to be consideration. "The Rhenisch Teuton misses her family," it discerned, its gaze boring deeply into Freia's radiant eyes.

My best friend squeezed my hand, and brilliant tears welled in her eyes. "It's true," she whispered in a broken voice. I wrapped my free arm around her shoulders, her admission taking me by surprise. I knew that she mourned for the children she had lost, but I had not realized that her wounds ran deeper than that.

"The plans you have made with your husband. Share them with your blood-sister and bring them to fruition," the *Eihalbe* advised before looking toward me again, its prismatic gaze mesmerizing me. "You will find your dark one there," it said, and before I could respond, it fluttered away from us. I thanked the fairy belatedly, then turned to regard my friend with a questioning look.

On our walk back to the manor, Freia admitted that she and Heinrich had been talking about making a trip to

Eisenwald the following summer if no new problems arose with the Saxons. She confessed that she wished to visit her father at long last, to see if he still lived and to learn whether he had found a decent man to take his place as ruler of the town once he had passed away. "He probably has believed me to be dead these eleven years," Freia said in a remorseful tone. "It's really been a burden on my heart, for I should never have run away from him. He needs to know that I'm happy with the path I've chosen . . . and maybe he could find the grace to forgive me for deserting him."

My respect for my best friend rose considerably, and I encouraged her to go, for I agreed that her family ought to know what had become of her. If her father could get past Freia's renunciation of her Rhenisch heritage for Teuton blood, I felt certain that he would forgive her and welcome Heinrich into his family. If he was anything like his daughter, he would be fair, if nothing else. Before bidding me farewell, Freia told me that she and Heinrich would love for Joel and me to make the journey with them, since they both knew of our lust for adventure.

Joel and I discussed the exciting possibility of a medieval vacation at length that night, ultimately concluding that we would go. We would have to be cautious about his nut allergy, but Joel said that he had gotten in the habit of avoiding bread during his time in the Prince's army. The kitchen staff could prepare a supply of unleavened barley and spelt bread before we departed.

After a bit of debate, we decided to bring Cammie and Max along, but leave Helmut behind in Ulka's care. We spent the remainder of 1054 and the beginning of 1055 in frantic preparations for a grand expedition, my first since our arrival in the Middle Ages.

And I did not tell my husband that the main reason for my enthusiasm was that Augustin had recently settled near Eisenwald. Freia's father had been the first Germanic lord to accept him in his lands despite the curse.

Chapter Seventeen:
Journey to the Rhineland

Our caravan set out for Eisenwald on the first Saturday in May, laden with sacks of supplies and valuables to trade along the way. Our crew consisted of Heinrich and Freia, Joel and me, Cammie, Max, Lorraine, Heino, and Johann, a young knight acquainted with Heinrich. He came along for the sake of adventure and to help the men protect their precious quarry of women and children. We brought eight horses with us, five for the adults and one for our bundles. The other two were tasked with carrying the four children. Thankfully, both Cammie and Lorraine had some skill with horses already; our constable Clovis had taken care to train our daughter and her good friend well during the past year.

Our course—which the men had meticulously planned out after poring over all sorts of maps—would take us through Augsburg, Ulm, and Stuttgart along the southern Germanic trade routes. We would cross Schwäbisch lands during our journey, but they had always been allies of the Teutons. Both Johann and Freia could speak enough Schwäbisch to get by. My Rhenisch was starting to improve because I had asked for Augustin's help with it last fall. I looked forward to trying it out once we reached our goal.

Our vassals were sorry to see us go. They all wished us safe travels and promised to pray for us each day. Jarvis assured us that he and Leo would keep the estate running efficiently in our absence. Ulka guaranteed that she would take care of little Helmut, who wailed with vigor as he watched his entire family set out down the front pathway to the road without him. By the time we returned in early fall, his vocabulary would likely have tripled, so it was painful to leave him behind. But I knew that bringing too many small children on such a difficult journey would slow us down, and Joel and I had almost decided to leave Max at home. He had pitched a rather horrid fit once he caught wind of our plots, and Cammie took his side, so we ultimately decided to let him come. Heinrich and Freia left young Katchen with his sisters.

Joel had nearly insisted that I remain behind. I had missed my period in April, taking the chains of pregnancy upon myself yet again. After a heated argument, I convinced him that I would come whether he liked it or not. I did not fear that travel would aggravate my condition enough to cause a miscarriage, for I had already faced six pregnancies successfully. I had long since regained much of the weight I had lost from the smallpox, so I did not expect my body to fail me.

In truth, I feared my inevitable encounter with Augustin once we reached Eisenwald; for while my dreaming spirit still appeared young and beautiful, my mortal body had grown quite ugly. My arms were chubby, my stomach protruded, spider veins marred my legs, and innumerable pockmarks scarred my once-comely face. Though my hair sported no trace of gray as yet, I had cut it short years before to keep it out of the way. I would turn thirty-two in August, but the strains of pregnancy and motherhood made me appear old and tired.

But when we set out for the Rhineland, I set my face to the future with anticipation. It had been far too long since I had an adventure, having been tied down to Muniche since 1044. I had decided to keep my journey a secret from Augustin until we arrived at Eisenwald. I worried that he might hide from me if I informed him of my travels, for I knew that he still feared that he might kill me if we met in the mortal world. But I was not afraid; he had controlled his death gift admirably thus far. Even if I infuriated him, I doubted that he could bring himself to end my life. Besides, if he did kill me, it would send me home, and I figured that seeing my lover again was worth the risk. So I threw myself into the excitement of the trip with vigor, chattering with the children and Freia as our horses trotted along the well-worn trade routes, making notes on the flora and fauna as well as other travelers.

We reached Augsburg, a Teuton stronghold northwest of Muniche, after two days' journey. Joel and Heinrich exchanged news with a few members of the city council, discussing the recent skirmishes with the Saxons and the current prosperity of Muniche. Freia and I had the privilege of meeting the Lady of Augsburg, who invited us to a brunch on our second day in the city. A kind-hearted elderly woman by the name of Bruna, she welcomed us into her Keyholder's castle, and we spent several hours with her, trading stories about our lives and our cities.

Right as we prepared to reunite with our husbands, her Keyholder graced the room for a few moments, apologizing profusely to Freia and me that he had not gotten the chance to properly entertain us. The duties of a ruler never ended, he complained with a twinkle in his eye, and his Lady laughed at him and promised that they would invite us to a full dinner when we passed through Augsburg upon our return. Freia and I both agreed, when we exited the castle grounds to seek our husbands, that the Keyholder and Lady of Augsburg seemed much more content and hospitable than Prince Otto and Lady Maria, likely due to their age.

Two days after leaving Augsburg, we reached the banks of the Danube, the great river that marked the western border of Teuton territory. We had to pay a rather hefty toll to cross the wide stone bridge that led to the city of Ulm on the opposite bank. Three burly-looking Schwäbisch knights haggled with Johann about the price. His knowledge of the dialect got us through without extensive loss, although we had to hand over one of Heinrich's extra swords before the knights let us enter the city. Johann told us that they claimed that the sword would be waiting for us upon our return, but I doubted it. Joel commented that the knights would probably ruin it at a tournament.

We reached Stuttgart a week later, slightly delayed due to a bout of stormy weather that had prompted us to camp beneath a thick canopy of trees until the rain abated. We stayed at the Schwäbisch city just one night, since most of us did not speak the local dialect. The keeper of the inn where we slept spoke a bit of Teutonica, so we managed to secure two rooms for our families without difficulty. A hearty breakfast of fresh eggs, biscuits, and rope sausage awaited us the next morning, and we embarked upon the trade route to the west with renewed energy, the tastes of civilization lightening the hearts of our children. Though both Joel and Johann had proved to be decent hunters, having brought down a fox and several hares to bulk up our stash of victuals, our spoiled children preferred the comfortable food of home to wild fruit and game.

We finally reached our goal toward the end of May. The final leg of the trip proved tedious, for we left the common trade route behind us to crunch through the northern section of the Black Forest. Eventually we discovered the main road into Eisenwald, which Freia recognized, her green eyes aglow with excitement as she led her horse to the head of our caravan. We came upon the settlement just after mid-afternoon, and Freia gave a delighted cry when she heard the bells of her home church clanging out their melodies for None. The trail opened onto a wide field of tall grass and flowers on a lush hill with a decent view of the town.

We paused there to rest, and while the children loped around the meadow picking flowers and poking at insects, I gazed down at Freia's hometown through the blue veil of my ice. It was much smaller than Muniche, a cozy cluster of brown-roofed houses and cottages with several larger buildings interspersed. I picked out the church's steeple reaching to the sky and a large stone house which I took to be Freia's family dwelling. I saw quite a few farm fields to the north of the town; and it appeared that a decent amount of forestry supported the settlement's economy, for I noticed loggers working to the south. Directly across from the hill, framing the western border of Eisenwald, I laid eyes upon that glorious river of Germany, the Rhine, its sapphire waters sparkling in the late spring sunlight.

Freia came to my side, so I tore my gaze away from the magnificent river to regard my best friend. "So," I began, addressing her in Rhenisch for the first time in a long time, "are you ready to meet your people again?"

Freia's face took on an air of uncertainty as she replied softly in Rhenisch, "I don't know, Swanie, but I suppose I must. But I'm afraid. I'm afraid my father won't understand . . . what I've done. I fear he may not forgive me. Maybe he won't even recognize me." Her blond eyebrows came together in anxiety.

I wrapped my right arm around her waist. "It'll be fine, Freia," I reassured her, switching back to Teutonica. "All we can do is try our best. If he doesn't accept you, we can go. But I think he will, because I'm sure he loves you."

We descended the hill toward the town moments later, all of us once more atop our horses. Joel called out one question to Freia while she led our convoy forward. "Why aren't there more people coming in and out of the village? You said this is the main road into Eisenwald, but we haven't seen anybody coming or going."

"Eisenwald is much simpler than Muniche, Joel," Freia answered with a wry smile. "The major industries here are forestry and metalworking." She threw a suggestive glance at her husband, then continued. "Most of the trade is done on the Rhine, using boats or the trail north to the major Rhenisch cities. This road is the only connecter to the east, but it sees most of its use in the mornings and later in the summer when the crops are harvested."

Eisenwald had one major street that traversed the town from west to east, the road ultimately turning northward along the Rhine. Every person we passed as we rode our horses down the main street shot inquisitive glances in our direction. I had a feeling our group would be the topic of many conversations that night, if Freia was correct that few travelers came to Eisenwald from the east.

When we approached the stone house at the center of the village, a three-story manor with impressive fenced gardens, a stocky woman who appeared to be a peasant unexpectedly called out to Freia. The basket of rolls she had been carrying fell to the ground as she waddled toward us. An instant later, Freia dismounted, tossing her reins to Heinrich before racing toward the woman and embracing her in an ebullient hug. Joel, who had halted his stallion beside my mare, raised one eyebrow at me in an unspoken request for a translation. Freia and the elderly woman now held each other at arm's length, tears streaming down my best friend's face. Though my Rhenisch was fair, I could hardly follow their conversation, but I muttered to Joel, "Obviously, Freia knows that woman, and she recognized her."

Joel rolled his hazel eyes in a silent *I can see that*. Freia led her friend to where we waited and introduced her as Anna, the servant woman who had been her childhood nanny. We all dismounted from our horses to greet the woman, and Joel took it upon himself to pick up her fallen rolls and place them back inside her basket, the epitome of chivalry.

Once we had finished with the introductions, Freia asked Anna a few cursory questions about her family's health. We discovered that while her father still headed the town, her mother had died of consumption seven winters before. This news prompted Freia to gasp in dismay, and Heinrich gathered her into his arms while she composed herself. Anna assured Freia that her mother had not suffered long, her ruddy face downcast as she blotted a few of her own tears on her sleeve.

Eventually Freia sighed and straightened once more, taking hold of her daughter's hand while she inquired after her two sisters. Anna told us that Marianna and Suzanne had both married young men of the town, and Marianna's husband was slated to take the place of Freia's father once he passed away. My best friend looked relieved when she heard this news; she likely felt glad that her father had married one of her sisters to his successor, letting her off the hook.

Anna invited all of us to accompany her to Lord Edwin's house, the large stone one that I had seen when we stood upon the hill. Freia asked the rest of us to take the kids and explore the town, to give her time to confront her father alone. We agreed to this and led our horses into the garden of Freia's family house, where Anna summoned a stable hand to care for them.

Heinrich and Johann took Lorraine and Heino off to satisfy the boy's curiosity about the sounds of woodcutting in the distance, while Joel and I toured the town with Max and Cammie. Both of our children grumbled loudly about the fact that they could not understand the Rhenisch dialect as we passed groups of youngsters playing in the street, but I reminded them that they could not understand us, either. "You can speak either Teutonica or English in Eisenwald, and none of the kids will have any idea what you're saying," I told them with a wink. "So while we're here, we have two secret languages instead of one."

"Yay!" Cammie and Max cried in unison. Then they proceeded to chatter incessantly in a conglomeration of English and Teutonica. Joel and I exchanged a private smirk at our kids' ingenuity, and soon we reached the place where the main street turned right to follow the river.

We left the road behind to walk through the tangled grass at the banks of the Rhine, our kids exclaiming that they had never seen so much water before. Max announced that he liked the Rhine better than the Isar. This prompted his sister to shove him with the assertion, "The Rhine is *not* better than the Isar, because the Isar is a Teuton river!"

Max swung at Cammie in defense, and soon they were tussling in the grass, my daughter freezing her skin to protect herself from her brother's wiry strength, which he reinforced with his own element. He had manifested energy several months prior, and Joel had summarily accused me of having an affair with Jarvis, since neither of us had energy in our background, to our knowledge. I had rolled my eyes at my husband and reminded him that I was no whore and that he was a lot better-looking than Jarvis.

As Joel stepped in to separate our scuffling children, giving each of them a smack for fighting and for using their elements in a foreign town, I turned my gaze upstream, to the south. I knew that Augustin lived some six kilometers away from Eisenwald, deep in the gnarled forest out of reach of the woodcutters, in a small cottage of log and stone on the banks of the Rhine. He had built his home late last year with the help of a Saxon skilled at construction; after completing the cottage, Augustin had sacrificed its builder to Wuotan.

Now, we traditionally met there for our language studies, for I had studied Rhenisch thoroughly during the past few weeks in preparation for my trip. So far, I had managed to keep my presence in the Rhineland a secret from my master. But now, as I looked upriver toward the dark glen where he made his home, I knew that I would have to set out on an expedition to find his hut sometime when the others were distracted. My heart pounded within me at the prospect of seeing Augustin again after a decade of separation; but I turned my attention back to Joel and my children, calling my ice further into my veins to counter the heat in my cheeks.

When we reunited with Freia at her family's house, she welcomed us inside with a brilliant smile. Her tall, gray-haired father stood at her side, his right arm wrapped fondly around his oldest daughter. He introduced himself as Lord Edwin Friedhelm von Eisenwald and expressed great appreciation for our visit.

As we sat down to a bountiful dinner shortly thereafter, I quickly discerned that Freia and her father had made amends without hesitation, for his wrinkled face beamed with pleasure throughout the entire meal. Freia sat to the right of her father, her adoring gaze often locked upon his face. Heinrich sat beside her, with Freia serving as translator whenever her father engaged him in conversation. We also met Freia's sister Marianna and her husband Lord Reginald. He was a congenial man with a knack for cracking dry jokes, some of which I did not understand since I had not grown up in Eisenwald. Cammie, Max, Lorraine, and Heino occupied themselves with Marianna's boy, a blond five-year-old named Fritz, overcoming the language barrier to enjoy childish games after dinner.

That night we installed ourselves in several guest rooms at Lord Edwin's insistence. Afterward, Freia and I met on a balcony overlooking the back gardens to share thoughts on the many events of the day. "My father really is a gracious man; I'd never realized it until today," Freia admitted with a sad smile as she gazed at the moon. "When I ran away, all I could remember was how he tried to match me with greedy lords, so I was blinded to his good qualities. But he forgave me for *everything,* Swanie, even for becoming a Teuton. He said he's just glad I'm still alive, and that I'm happy with the life I've chosen."

I smiled at my best friend and gave her an encouraging hug. "See, I knew that your father would be a fair man, because I had an inkling that he's like you." And after a moment's pause, I appended quietly, "If he could accept Augustin into his lands, he would certainly forgive his daughter."

Chapter Eighteen:
The Long-Awaited Reunion

We spent two full weeks as guests at Freia's family house, enjoying her father's hospitality and the simple tranquility of the peaceful village on the Rhine. We met all of Freia's relatives, and we passed many warm afternoons sharing stories with the local gentry. About two hundred people resided at Eisenwald, the vast majority of them very friendly and accommodating. Soon enough, our group had gotten to know the common shopkeepers and peasants to the point where we exchanged brief pleasantries when we met in the streets. Joel, Heinrich, and Johann always stumbled over the right phrases since they had never learned Rhenisch.

The people of Eisenwald had likely learned over time to evince a natural affability due to the flourishing trade on the river. My children and I spent several mornings sitting at the banks of the Rhine watching the boats come and go, carrying creations of wood and iron away to distant ports in exchange for fabrics, foods, and other necessities. It did not take me long to discern how Eisenwald had gotten its name. The word translates into *ironwood* in English, and the town's major industries proved to be metalworking and forestry.

Heinrich spent a formidable amount of time at the local foundry, learning what he could from the Rhenisch ironworkers and sharing a bit of his own experience with them in return. Joel observed the local farming methods and commented to me that the types of cabbage grown in Eisenwald seemed somewhat different from the Bavarian types to which he had become accustomed. He passed his free time engaged in various forms of friendly combat with Freia's brothers-in-law, from games of chess and darts to target shooting and sword fights. The four children played vigorously with their new Rhenisch friends, all of them holding their elements back in respect of their parents' wishes. Freia spent most of the days with her father and sisters; and when I was not with her, I kept an eye on the children or sorted through the Rhenisch writings in her family's library. I discovered that even though the Rhine people had no special powers, they certainly had a talent for writing fascinating histories, especially regarding the time of Charlemagne, some two hundred fifty years in the past.

I met Augustin in my dreams as usual, seeing him at his cottage to practice Rhenisch, Magyar, Latin, and Ælte Teutonica. He must have noticed my edginess during those two weeks, but he did not question me about it. I debated within myself every day whether I ought to inform him of my presence in Eisenwald upon our next encounter, but each time I dreamed with him, an odd hesitation held me back. Part of me still worried that he might flee if I told him the truth, or that he might force me to meet him in order to sever our bond. I also feared his reaction to the current state of my body—the weary mother hen stricken with scars.

So I kept insisting that we continue to study at his cottage rather than at the Thaden estate, giving no explanation save that he had already practically mastered the three languages I had taught him. He acquiesced to my requests, likely making the logical assumption that I would rather spend time with him far away from my husband's bed. But after I had been at Eisenwald for two weeks, I knew that I could no longer keep my existence a secret from my master. I had made this journey for his sake more than anything else. Therefore I decided, one balmy Monday morning in early June, that the following night I would tell Augustin the truth.

That Monday evening, Freia and I entertained our relatives with a musical duet. Freia had found a flute somewhere in her father's house, and she played many tunes while twilight descended, some popular melodies of the Rhineland—to which her father and sisters sang along—and some lilting harmonies of her new people, the Teutons. Though our audience joined in from time to time, my soprano led the way, accompanied by my best friend's flute.

I sang folkish melodies in Teutonica and Rhenisch, intermingled with a few songs of the future, which I had translated into Teutonica at Augustin's suggestion. Freia had a good ear for music and had no trouble picking up the tunes, for we had practiced them on occasion back home in Muniche. What her relatives thought of my heartfelt renditions of haunting songs such as Within Temptation's "Restless" or Nightwish's "Deep, Silent, Complete" and "Sleeping Sun," I know not. But the familiar tunes sent my spirit soaring with thoughts of my own era, when my life was so much simpler.

Once we had set aside music for the night to put our children to bed, an unshakeable desire to walk alone by the Rhine enclosed my heart. After I had kissed Cammie and Max goodnight, I murmured in Joel's ear that I wished to go outside and enjoy the cool serenity alone. He smiled knowingly and said that he would drift into slumber while my Teuton spirit transformed into an iceberg to merge with the river. I grinned back at him, pleased that he understood me enough to allow me to drink the cup of the united glories of music and ice to its fullest. Not long after, I slipped out of the big stone house and set out for the river,

174

clad in an airy black dress and veil to help me blend in with the night.

The sky was dotted with innumerable stars as I walked the short distance to the Rhine, the quietude of the late spring night descended upon Eisenwald. I met no one in the streets and saw very few lights glimmering inside the cottages, for the commoners had already retired in preparation for Tuesday's labor. I reached the riverbank and gazed for a moment at the waxing moon, then looked toward the boats docked for the night, awaiting the resumption of trade at first light.

My lips curled into a contented smile while I marveled at the success of this tiny Germanic town. In the next moment, I pushed aside all thoughts of civilization and shut my eyes to focus on the ice within my spirit, reaching out with my senses to grasp the beauty of the night. The melodies of Freia's flute drifted into my memory, and I hummed the opening notes of "Swanheart." I lifted my face to the breeze, my ice cooling me, the waters of the Rhine lapping at my feet in response.

As my feet began the first steps of a Teutonic dance, here in this foreign town beside the grandest German river, my ice detected a new presence, one that I had not sensed in over a decade. *A dark soul . . . a phantom of death . . . a demon of blue fire . . . yes, he is here . . . he is on the water . . . and he sees you . . . .*

My body shivered once, all over, and my feet froze upon the bank. I opened my eyes to see my master paddling toward me in a small rowboat, coming from the direction of the other docked vessels. How I had not noticed him earlier, I do not know. Now my heart pounded frantically within me at the sight of him, my eyes the frosty blue of ice. I glanced to the left and right, my icy spirit assuring me that no other human was anywhere nearby. We were alone in the darkness, the devil and his woman, Augustin and Swanhilde . . . *in the mortal world.*

At length, he guided his boat onto the bank several meters away. Its bottom scraped the grass as he leapt out deftly, casting the paddle aside. He came to stand before me, his eyes glowing blue in the dark, his face ghostly pale in the moonlight. If I had not sensed that familiar fire emanating from his aura, I would not have recognized him as Augustin. He wore a common tunic, trousers, and clogs with no ornamentation, making him appear horribly like a peasant rather than the noble lord I remembered. And, to my absolute shock, I saw that he had grown a goatee, cut rather sharply like the beard of a goblin—and his gorgeous black hair was gone, cropped as short as Joel's had been before we had come to the past.

My mind raced back to our encounters in the *Gæstelort Troumerae*, where his appearance reminded me of the Augustin I knew, his clean-shaven face shining like a star, his long hair resplendent, his cerulean robes matching the fire in his eyes. Now, when I stared up at him, I felt as though I actually confronted a man who had sold his soul to the devil. He met my gaze coolly with no trace of love, just surprise mixed with an overarching acrimony. I opened my mouth but found that I could not speak, my mind working doggedly to organize my befuddled thoughts. *He's still Augustin . . . he's still my master . . . he's still my lover . . . but he looks awful . . . and no softness escapes that bitter veneer . . . .*

"I do not recall falling asleep prior to this meeting," Augustin said at last, his tone low and quiet, sounding as though he simply stated facts. "Considering the perfection of my dead memory and the simplicity of our clothing, I find it doubtful that this moment could be anything besides reality. Nevertheless, you should not be here, Swanhilde. Perhaps it is you who are the ghost come to haunt my hell."

I shook my head slowly at his morbid conjectures, wishing desperately that he would come closer and touch me. "No . . . Augustin . . . I am not a ghost . . . or a dream." I stared at him, watching his bearded jaw twitch in disbelief.

"Then you have come to tell me that you are dead, that you have returned at last to your own era, leaving me alone to mourn your loss." His eyes glowed more brightly, and a single tear escaped one of them to trickle down his pale cheek.

"No." The word barely escaped my lips, and at last I managed to take one step forward, close enough to feel the heat from his fire, close enough to reach out and touch him. But I kept my hands at my sides and whispered, "I'm here with Freia. She came to make amends with her father."

Realization broke across Augustin's face, and he nodded, his eyes traveling toward the main street and the stone house in the distance. "Your husbands came with you." Another simple statement of fact.

"And four of our children," I appended, suddenly grasping the fact that my master could doubtless sense the presence of my comrades due to their obviously Teutonic elements in a foreign town. It was a disturbing thought, for some reason.

Augustin's eyes drifted back to me, taking in my whole appearance. "Your husband shall expect your return," he said, his jaw tightening a bit, some sort of emotion finally breaking through his disconcerting shell. "He would not wish you to remain at the riverbank all night, emptying your heart to this serene ambience. His blood may be Teutonic, but his spirit shall never fully comprehend the glories of our arts or the satisfaction of evocative harmonies." A derisive smirk appeared on his face for an instant, a brief reminder of the Augustin I loved.

I snickered once, shoving aside the frightening notion that my master had discerned the singing of my spirit when I had come to the riverbank, as well as my elemental yearning. "He told me he didn't mind my walking out here in the night. And he even said he'd probably be asleep before I return . . . because he knows that nature may keep me long." I lifted my eyebrows at Augustin, hoping that he would answer the call of my heart and not order me to leave now, before we had gotten past the initial awkwardness of our unexpected meeting.

Augustin stared into my eyes for an infinite moment. When he spoke again I could hardly hear his question. "And how long . . . shall nature keep you?"

My lips trembled, and my heart throbbed within me, longing to feel his hands caressing it once more. And I finally managed to reply in a choking voice, "As long as you wish . . . master . . . ." My hormones raced, making me feel twenty-one again, a passion I had not experienced in many years.

Augustin lips parted into a smirk, and he looked back toward his boat. "Come then, my swan," he requested, his flaming eyes burning me again. "Though I must warn you that it may be some time before I shall return you to your husband." His white teeth glittered in the moonlight as he held a hand out to me.

I shivered one more time and glanced around again, still seeing no one. Then I pushed my nervousness aside and stepped forward to take his hand, relishing the touch of his warm skin against my frigid fingers. He brought me to his boat without further ado and indicated that I should sit toward the bow in front of several large cloth sacks. I did so without speaking, and he shoved the rowboat into the waters of the Rhine moments later, leaping inside to take his place at the stern, paddling us upstream with the inexhaustible strength of immortality.

We said little during the journey upstream, for Augustin suggested that I rest while I had the opportunity. Anticipation knotted my stomach as I considered what we might do once we reached his cottage. We would have much to talk about, but since talking was pretty much all we did in our dreams aside from our studies, I had an inkling that we might share quite a few other activities. I wondered, as we drifted upon the dark waters of the Rhine, whether we would have sex; and if we did, what Augustin would think of my body now. He had once labeled it perfection, but now I looked like a pockmarked matron who had borne too many children. *And what about him?* I asked myself. *His hair is gone . . . and I hate beards. I've had to put up with Joel's for far too long; it always stinks like old food. And*

Augustin's technically dead . . . would his naked body look like a corpse?

I asked Augustin about the sacks lying at the bottom of his boat during the beginning of our voyage up the Rhine. He explained that while he usually remained aloof from human contact, he came to Eisenwald once per month to conduct business and trade goods. He still practiced his medical training upon willing patients, he informed me with a simper, and he visited Lord Edwin from time to time to ensure that the ruler of Eisenwald still harbored no ill will toward him.

Freia's father had agreed to allow Augustin to settle near his village as long as he did not unleash his devilries upon its inhabitants. "The Lord Edwin does not complain when I occasionally kidnap outsiders, especially his enemies," my master said with a dark smile.

This prompted me to wonder what Freia's father would think once he realized that I had disappeared. He would have the sense to attribute my absence to Augustin, since he had apparently done business in the town that day. Freia knew that I planned to see Augustin sometime during our stay in her hometown; and though she did not necessarily approve of my plans, I doubted that she would squeal on me. Hopefully she could keep her father quiet on the subject.

Eventually I settled down to rest, leaning back against a softer sack behind me and turning my gaze upward to the stars. The stillness of the night gradually beckoned me to slumber, faint calls of the nightingales and frogs and the sounds of Augustin's paddle lulling me toward a blissful dream. Just before I drifted off into my own private fantasies, I heard his voice address me softly, like a whisper on the breeze: "Sleep now, my lovely swan princess, for your demon shall watch over you this night . . . and awaken you when we reach his lonely kingdom."

I know not what I dreamed during my short snooze, but I felt peaceful the entire time, my unconscious mind certain of my lover's company, looking forward to seeing him again upon waking. When my soul cast off the calm of slumber, I blinked my eyes against the weariness to see Augustin's face above me, the heat of his fire warming me in the cool of the night. It took me a few seconds to realize that we had left the river. I lay in my master's arms as he carried me through the trees, their tangled branches painting black streaks across the starry sky. Augustin's voice reached me as I gazed upward at the moon, many thoughts swirling through my head. "Welcome back to the mortal world, my darling swan," he murmured to me, a smile playing upon his lips.

Excitement infused my veins with heat, but the doubting part of my mind refused to believe the magnificent truth: I lay in Augustin's arms in the realm of nature—in the *mortal world*—with no one around to interrupt our long-awaited reunion. I shook my head slightly, incredulous. "How can I be sure . . . that I'm not still sleeping?" My voice quavered with uncertainty.

Augustin chuckled, a gravelly sound, and in the next instant he had opened a door of strong wood, the front entrance to his quaint cottage of stone and timber. It was built into a dark thicket of the woodland, the waters of the Rhine just barely visible through the foliage. Though my physical eyesight was far blurrier than the eyes of my spirit, I recognized the hut even in the dim light of the moon. I had come here many times in my dreams since my master had completed it right before the first snows of winter. I knew every tiny chamber, every crossbeam on the ceiling, every candle upon the shelves and floor.

Augustin lit all of the candles as he carried me inside, his powerful element setting its blue flames upon their wicks with finesse. He did not even have to look at the candlesticks to ignite their flames; the use of his fire was second nature to him, strengthened by the gifts of Wuotan, perfected in death. I wondered for a fleeting moment whether he may choose to kill me here, like he had hinted in the early days of our relationship . . . rescuing me from the dreary prospect of returning to my husband, to my children, to my responsibility . . . .

Augustin laid me down upon the couch in his front room underneath the single window with the view toward the river. My eyes traveled around the rest of the chamber while my body relaxed upon the couch. I saw the familiar writing desk in the corner furthest from the door, where Augustin and I had spent many dreams poring over our dictionaries. I looked from there to the adjacent fireplace, the shadowy doorway to the other chambers, the bookshelf stuffed with writings that my master had collected during his travels, the cabinet where he stored his medical tools and objects necessary for Teutonic rituals. The corners of my lips turned upward as I mused upon the many mystical rites my master had likely discovered now that he was Wuotan's timeless servant. He could probably rewrite that book on forbidden sacraments himself, soon enough.

I felt Augustin's hands upon my face a moment later, brushing my veil back from my skin. He turned my neck carefully to the right so that I could meet his gaze, where he crouched at my side. His fiery fingers slid down the skin of my face, his touch like embers upon my neck while he stroked my veins, likely sensing the life flowing in my blood—a life he no longer had. He drew close to me, his glowing eyes appearing unnaturally large in the darkness. "Do you believe now that this is not a dream, Swanhilde?" he asked.

I could smell his breath as he spoke, the fire within him mingling with his deadly decay, bringing the concept of a smoldering campfire to my mind. I parted my lips but found that I could not answer, my desire for him chaining me to silence. His mouth brushed mine, its heat causing me to gasp.

"*I* know we are both awake," Augustin murmured, cradling my face in his hands. "You see, my darling, a dead man does not need to sleep. I allow slumber to take me only when I wish to meet you, for my private dreams torment me like the fires of hell. But I know, yes, I *know* . . . that in our dream world . . . *this* . . . is impossible . . . ." And he kissed me, his goatee rather prickly against my skin as he pulled me to his chest. One of his strong hands clutched the back of my head with enough force to bruise while his tongue hungrily sucked the life from my lips.

When he finally released me, my head pounded from a lack of oxygen. I took a wheezing breath, dizzy from the consuming kiss of a dead man. *This is madness . . . all he would have to do to kill you now is kiss you long enough,* I thought, shaking my head from side to side. *He could probably go indefinitely without pausing for breath . . . and his mouth seems to siphon my vitality away.*

Augustin snickered at my frailty while my frigid fingers grasped the cloth of his couch. "I shall return shortly, my angel," he said, his gaze on the heavens visible through the windowpanes. "I should bring my goods from Eisenwald inside and float my vessel to its hiding place before the break of dawn." He crossed the stone floor to the front door in less than a second, swinging it open with a flourish.

"Augustin," I croaked, reaching one hand out to him as I lay upon the couch still trying to recover from his kiss. He halted his retreat and turned to face me. "You . . . you'll . . . come back?" I implored. Part of me feared that he may vanish with the daylight, crawling into a vampire's coffin and leaving me bereft.

A mischievous smirk appeared on his face. "Shortly," he responded. In the next instant he was gone, the door closed quietly behind him.

While I waited for him to return to me, I gathered my strength and rose from the couch, stretching a bit and looking around again at the furnishings of Augustin's front room. He did not have much, but that was probably due to the fact that he had resided at this cottage for only seven months. If he managed to remain in Lord Edwin's good graces, I predicted that within a few years, he would have more possessions with which to pass the time. I glanced briefly at the bookshelf laden with scrolls and parchments, then approached his writing desk, its contents lit by two blue-flamed candles. I ran my fingers over the papers lying there, lifting one of his feather pens, savoring the fact that in the mortal world I could grasp it properly, my fingers winding around it in the style he had taught me.

"Prepared to study Rhenisch, swan princess?" Augustin's voice cut into my reverie as I stood at his desk with his pen in my hand, my eyes absently passing over the words on the page before me: *Prepared the dinghy for my voyage to Eisenwald, upon which I shall embark at first light, that I may negotiate with the foreign traders of the summer. Perhaps if I conclude my deals in the light of day, I may succeed in refusing my master's demands for human blood . . . .*

"What is this, your private diary?" I inquired. Interest welled inside me at the thought of its possible contents.

Augustin took my right arm in his sturdy fingers, leading me away from his desk, back toward the couch. "That it is, and thus it is not yours to read." He eyed me distrustfully as I sat beneath the window, the sky growing gray with early dawn. "The things I write in Ælte Teutonica are mine alone, Swanhilde."

I tilted my head at him, my curiosity unwilling to abate. "I doubt you'll have too many problems with snoops if you write it in Ælte Teutonica. By the twenty-first century, no one will be able to decode your writings."

"No one but you," he corrected with an indecipherable expression. I smiled, and he reached back to pull one of the stools from his desk to the foot of the couch, seating himself upon it. After studying me for a while, he leaned forward, taking my hands in his and massaging them tenderly. "You appear discontent, my swan. I had believed that for years, you wished to see me again in the mortal world. Now you appear as though you may have changed your mind." His brow furrowed.

I blushed, looking down at my fingers imprisoned in his, concentrating on the touch of his fiery hands. Their heat felt strange and elemental, not stemming from his blood. "It's just that . . . I don't know . . . everything is . . . *different* . . . not quite what I expected," I confessed, not looking at him. "I know I can't stay with you, though my heart bleeds for it. If I didn't have children to look after, I probably *would* stay. I'd throw myself at your feet and beg you to keep me forever."

A low moan sounded in Augustin's throat, and he lifted his right hand to my cheek, his fiery touch prompting me to tremble. "You are no longer a lighthearted maiden," he observed, staring into my eyes as though he wished to read my soul. "Responsibility constrains you, ties you to a family . . . something I can never have again."

The sorrow in his tone struck my heart. I touched his bearded face at last and admitted, "But I still love you most, more than anyone."

He smiled sadly at me and kissed me on the forehead with the words, "Ah, my swan, that love of yours shall become your anguish."

Chapter Nineteen:
One Blissful Reality

We decided to spend one glorious day together, and then Augustin would return me to Eisenwald the following night, before Joel and the others really began to worry about me. I hoped that Freia would cover for me for at least one day. Meanwhile, I ordered myself not to think of my husband or my children, to immerse myself in adulterous dalliance with my true mate, with the dead man for whom I would have renounced life itself.

I sat upon Augustin's couch at daybreak, covertly studying his appearance as the room lightened around us. We shared many personal thoughts and wishes, things that we kept hidden when we met in our dreams. I told him about my family, about my wonderful children, often focusing on Cammie, my icy daughter. Although it was wrong to pick favorites among children, at that point I would have chosen Cammie without question. Her insatiable curiosity and juvenile pride for her people spoke to my heart, telling me that Joel and I had not done everything wrong. I mentioned a few things about Max and Helmut, then noted with a frustrated sigh that I was three months pregnant at the moment.

Augustin's eyes traveled to my abdomen, a rather disturbing smirk crossing his face. "Six pregnancies in ten years . . . and it has ruined your beautiful figure, I see," he commented. His glittering eyes appraised my dress and body.

I huffed in annoyance and folded my arms across my stomach. "Well, I'm not the only one who looks far better in the realm of dreams," I pointed out. I eyed his short hair, goatee, and common clothing when I spoke, noticing that the sleeves of his brown tunic were long and tight, hiding the cursed mark from my sight. "I guess I can forgive the beard, though I've never been partial to facial fuzz . . . but why did you cut your hair so short?"

My master snorted and rubbed his hands together agitatedly. "I have kept my hair long since the age of four in memory of that saint who is no longer my mother." I started at this revelation, and Augustin added in a harsh tone, "Unfortunately this curse has severed that connection, and consequently I have discerned no reason to retain my feminine hair, though it remains yet in the spiritual realm." He scowled, his goatee making the expression appear more wretched than usual.

"Why is that?" I questioned, my thoughts darting to our shared dreams in our astral fantasia. "Neither of us looks half as bad in the realm of the spirit as we do in the mortal world. I've always wondered about that."

"In the spiritual realm, my darling, we lay eyes upon our innermost beauty," Augustin explained with a sallow smile. "Our spirits manifest what perfection we can attain in this tainted life. In the *Gæstelort Troumerae* we shall always appear young and beautiful, no matter how old we become." He raised an eyebrow at me.

I looked down at my hands and said, "Then I suppose both of us are a bit disappointed at this meeting. Here I was, expecting to see you with silky obsidian hair crashing down your shoulders, your face clean-shaven and smooth, attired like a priest or a lord. And you were probably hoping to see me how I used to look, before smallpox and childbirth wrecked my body." I grimaced.

Augustin kept silent for a long moment. When I finally lifted my eyes to his, I saw that he gawked at me intently. "Silky obsidian hair . . . crashing down my shoulders?" he repeated, sounding dubious. "I never realized how much you liked my hair, Swanhilde." He reached a hand out to my own hair, which fell to the base of my neck, far shorter than it had been in my virginity. "I miss yours, as well," he murmured softly as he stroked my hair. "But we cannot have everything, I suppose. Nevertheless, if you grant me a few moments of privacy, I could correct several aspects of my own appearance for your sake." Before I could frame a proper reply, he rose from the stool and vanished through the doorway to his inner rooms, a sneaky expression upon his visage.

I sighed in aggravation, wishing that Augustin would stop leaving me alone when our time was short. I heard him moving about in another chamber, so I rose from the couch and walked to the threshold of his front door, opening it and lifting my eyes to the garnet sky of sunrise. Birds chirped in the trees and a warm summer breeze caressed my cheeks, chasing away my weariness, filling me with vigor for the day—for one perfect reality to share with my beloved.

Augustin approached me soon afterward, and when I turned to regard him, my mouth fell open in surprise. He had shed his commoner's clothing and wore the magnificent black garb of the Teuton priest, the robes sweeping the floor. And to my delight, he had shaved his goatee, revealing the pale solidness of his chin and jawbone. I wanted to kiss him again, even if he drained my life in the process. "I regret that I cannot grow my hair long in a few short hours, but perhaps this may suffice your desires?" He smirked at me.

"Most definitely," I assured him with an answering grin. "At least you don't look like a horned devil without that ridiculous goatee."

He stepped forward to take me into his arms, pulling us both out into the early morning sunlight. "And when I look into your eyes, I always see my darling Swanhilde," he murmured, "her figure not marred by illness or age, her black hair cascading down her back, her gray eyes the epitome of that hour before sunrise." He kissed me a moment later, enfolding me in black, his flaming arms my prison.

He prepared a breakfast for me, sausages from Eisenwald and wild berries from the forest accompanied by a potent French wine. It was an odd meal, but since Augustin did not need to eat, I figured I was lucky he had any food at all in his cottage. I consumed the victuals outside, sitting cross-legged near his fire pit. My master watched me eat, the color of his eyes matching the flames flickering in his pit, an enchanting light blue.

The day I spent with Augustin marked the pinnacle of my life since he had been torn from me in June of 1045. We passed the bright summer morning in and around his cottage, walking along the short paths he had worn through the trees, gathering berries and nuts from various plants, watching a swarm of honeybees perfecting their hive. I rained a bit of my ice upon the few wildflowers that grew near Augustin's door, complimenting my lover on his refusal to eliminate all beauty from his world, for the buttercups and dandelions brought a splash of color to his dwelling place. He gave me a wry smile and admitted that death had not erased his love for art, whether in the form of music, writing, or nature.

At one point, he brought me to a fenced area behind his hut. There he kept two goats, a rooster, several chickens, and a black stallion. Though he did not need to eat in his death, he confessed that he still enjoyed the taste of milk and eggs, along with cheese and the occasional roasted chicken. He said that he could taste the life anytime he ate a raw egg or drank milk directly from the female goat. He found it more satisfying to consume such things than to kill and cook the animals in the forest; the bleak taste of death pervaded meat once it had been cooked, he told me. He had stolen the stallion from the Saxons during the fighting the previous year, and he made use of it whenever he set out on a lengthy journey.

Augustin spread a dark blue blanket upon the ground beside the Rhine right at midday, spreading a veritable feast across its fabric. We enjoyed fresh radishes and cabbage from my master's small garden, complemented with goat cheese and rolls from Eisenwald. Augustin actually consumed some of the food this time and remarked that eating traditional food helped him stave off his hunger for human sacrifices. "It is a disturbing thing that as Wuotan's slave I find living flesh most satisfying," he told me with a rather ghostly smile as he sipped wine from a flagon. "I believe that this stems from my death. While my body does not require food, it decays within, invigorated by the power of a demon, forever seeking the taste of life . . . the blood of humans or animals . . . or fresh plants."

I studied him covertly while nibbling a roll, admiring the way the sun glinted off of his hair and how muscular his body appeared beneath his black cloak. "You may be dead, Augustin, but you certainly look handsome," I said, blushing slightly. "Even without your long hair, you're still the most attractive man I've ever met, Teutons and outsiders alike."

Augustin snickered darkly and said, "This façade of mine is due to the gifts of Wuotan, for he does not wish his Black Priests to serve him grudgingly. But underneath this outer shell there lies a sinful heart exploding with wrath and lust, a longing to destroy, to inflict pain, to kill." I tilted my head at him as he sighed once, leaning back on his hands and lifting his face to the light blue sky streaked with cirrus clouds.

"Swanhilde, your love shackles me in a never-ending discord, and Wuotan has ordered me innumerable times to renounce you permanently, to kill you, so I may serve him with nothing holding me back," he said. Dread crept up my spine when I saw the tension on Augustin's face as his eyes burned the sky. At last, he aimed his gaze directly at me and said, "So far, the memory of your love, your faith, your purity . . . the heart of your soul throbbing in my hands, pleading wordlessly for my belief in hope . . . so far, part of me has no desire to renounce the glories of true love. But I fear that my obduracy shall not last forever, for Wuotan is a ruthless master, my darling. He torments me constantly over my devotion to you, in ways that I cannot describe for fear of alarming you. One day, he shall win the fight, for he wears down my will each and every day. This continuous yearning for someone I cannot have drives me mad."

Augustin glared at me while I breathed shallowly, his clawed fingers clutching the blanket beneath us with force enough to tear the fabric. My lips parted, for I wanted to say something to reassure him. I wished to explain my belief that our love would hold strong in the face of any opponent, for my faith was in God, who would defeat all of the demons one day. But the words died on my tongue as I abruptly detected a new force churning in the space between us, a power darker than any element, seeming to test the air with its invisible knives.

An instant later I realized that Augustin was *angry* . . . and he was a Black Priest . . . . My mouth grew dry, and I whispered shakily, "Are you . . . going to . . . kill me?" Perhaps Wuotan was urging him to take me out of the picture at that very moment.

Augustin continued to glare at me, but the prickliness in the air dissipated as he answered thickly, "Not yet. But I would require something of you now, since we are here together in the mortal world, likely never to meet again once I have returned you to your husband." His lips curled back to reveal his white teeth bared in hunger, his light blue eyes burning me to cinders.

"What . . . do you ask . . . of me?" My voice squeaked in a pitiful manner.

"Sex." His mouth twisted into a sneer.

My ice cooled my veins at the subject, and my heart rate increased as my own desire roused itself afresh. I certainly *wanted* to have sex with Augustin, even if my wearied body could not handle his immortal lust. But I remembered what had happened the last time we had gotten intimate—the rush to marry a man I could never love, the loss of the child I would have loved most dearly. So I clasped my hands in my lap and shifted my legs beneath my dress, praying that I could get this out.

"Augustin, I . . . I really . . . shouldn't. I'm married to Joel . . . and adultery is sin. I shouldn't cheat on my husband. Besides . . . you remember what happened the last time we . . . did that." I broke off. Tears dampened my eyes as I stared at Augustin in silent desperation, hoping that he could understand.

He did not reply for a long time, but he gazed at me steadily, his eyes seeming to delve deep into my soul. My heart pounded, and my ice pulsed in my veins at the likelihood of facing his anger again. Then he sighed, the expectation on his countenance slowly dimming. "You Christians are all hypocrites," he accused with a sneer, shaking his head at me. "You would like to define 'adultery' as simply the physical act, while your heart constantly cheats on your husband. You would allow me to kiss you, to caress you, but you draw the line before true fulfillment can be attained. It is *all* adultery, Swanhilde, your entire life, can you not see that?

"Joel may know that you have feelings for me, but I doubt you have told him that we meet in our dreams. He probably wonders where you are right now, as you sit before me on this blanket sharing my food, enticing my lust. Hypocrisy." Augustin growled, the sound of a ravenous beast, then concluded, "At least demons do not bother with the nonsense of love. Humanity prefers to dally with luscious pretensions, refusing to acknowledge that hatred is fair, a straightforward partner."

I blinked at Augustin, realizing that we had not had a discussion quite like this one in years, not since those early days of our relationship, before the Prince had cursed him. "You're right," I allowed, shaking my head at myself. "My life has been a lie since I spoke my vows to Joel, pretending that he was you. But there's nothing either of us can do about my love. It's locked upon you until the day you fade from my memory. And although my mind has not attained the perfection of death, I doubt I'll ever be able to forget you . . . Augustin."

He smiled sadly at me and reached one fiery hand out to trace the curve of my face, his warm touch sending my hormones racing. "You have become that stubborn virgin again, insisting that both of us remain forever unsatisfied. How long has it been since your husband has given you release, may I ask?"

I slid away from his seductive touch, wondering wildly whether he may try to force me to comply. He would not have to work too hard to do it. I squeezed my eyes shut and ordered myself to keep my wits. But the truth fell from my lips despite myself. "I haven't . . . had an orgasm . . . since Marelda's birth. I have to fake it."

Augustin chuckled, a suggestive sound, and quietly asserted, "I could certainly give it to you my dear, if you would allow me." I opened my eyes to look into his, and he said, "Though my fingers now sport a demon's claws, they have not yet forgotten how to please a woman."

We spent quite a bit of time together on that blanket beside the Rhine, and Augustin worked his magic upon my clitoris thrice, pulling ridiculous groans from my lips. He asked me each time I came whether I would prefer the full experience, and I continued to decline, though my heart stabbed me at my selfishness. He would certainly have to please himself later, after watching me reach Elysium at his command again and again. I wondered, as his virulent love poured into my spirit on the strength of our bond, whether he would summon a siren after he had returned me to Joel. Sex without love—an inferior release.

We shared a glorious elemental dance while the sun traveled steadily across the heavens. My icy hand never left his sizzling one, fully appreciating the contact possible in the mortal world, where we could feel each other as completely as we could feel our feet skipping across the waters of the Rhine and through the forest glades. We ran together to the opposite bank, scaling trees with the agility of our elements, perching ourselves upon their highest branches to take in the panoramic view of nature: woodland and river, animals and sky, the splendor of creation. When we ended our dance due to my own exhaustion—I could not boast the vigor that drove Augustin's animated corpse—we packed up the blanket and glasses from lunch and returned to his cottage.

Once inside, Augustin showed me some of the contents of the bookshelf in his front room, letting me sift through the rare tomes he had collected in his travels abroad. He had copies of several renowned works of his era, including Latin translations of the Arabic *Book of Optics* and medical works by Razi and Ibn Sina. Along with quite a few historical works written in all sorts of tongues from Latin and Teutonica to Magyar and Sächsisch, I found a worn copy of Jerome's Latin Vulgate. "Do you actually read this?" I asked Augustin, who stood behind me while I flipped through his impressive collection of writings. I found it hard to believe that my heathen master would bother reading the Bible.

But Augustin replied with a snicker, "Occasionally, for its historical value and for its rather poignant revelations regarding human frailty. Wuotan does not appreciate it when I read the Bible, for he fears that it may pull me away from him with a force that you do not possess." I eyed him curiously, and he quoted, "The Word of God is living and effectual and more piercing than any two edged sword."

"So you read it to bother him," I translated, shaking my head at Augustin's twisted view of Christianity. I still believed that he had a chance at heaven, for he had not yet entered hell.

Later that evening, after we had cared for the animals and eaten a dinner of scrambled eggs, rolls, and the nuts and berries we had scrounged from the forest, Augustin informed me that he wished to bleed me once, before we embarked on our return voyage down the Rhine. He said in a rather apologetic tone that he wanted to read my true thoughts again, so he could fully grasp the complexities of my life since the curse had driven us apart. He wished to see what time and distance had done to my love for him, to discern whether it would be feasible for us to continue as we had for the past decade, feeling each other from far away, meeting only in our dreams.

I had an inkling that what he really wanted was to find an excuse to break our bond. This would probably be our last chance to do it before death cast me back through the gates of time in 1066. But I thrust these worries aside and gave him permission to drink my blood if he could tame his vampirical tendencies enough to refrain from bleeding me dry. He pulled me into his lap as we sat before the blue flames flickering in his fire pit, his arms holding me still.

"Do not fear, my swan," he murmured, tilting my head slightly to bare my neck, "for your heart still belongs to me, and I do not intend to let you die just yet." His lips parted into a wicked smile. A moment later I felt his teeth pierce my skin, the sensation akin to sharp, burning knives—the bite of a devil. I moaned once from the ache, and then shut my eyes, ordering myself to relax my defenses.

I do not know how long I remained a slave to this dead man's thirst for lifeblood and information. I preferred to focus my wearied mind on the strength of his arms holding me against him, the steadiness of his hands pumping my heart in the spiritual realm, preserving my life while he drained my blood. The realization hit me as I lay in his grasp that despite the many times Augustin had claimed that he wanted to kill me, his actions had belied his speech for the past eleven years. *If he hasn't killed me yet, he probably never will* . . . . I saw the truth when I lay helpless in Augustin's arms, his left hand clutching the back of my head with oppressive force. *This sadistic man will not be my murderer. Instead, he will be my perpetual savior . . . dragging me back to this world though I beg him to let me go . . . enslaving me forever with the insanity of my love.*

While many disturbing thoughts rushed through my brain as a result of my abrupt epiphany, Augustin broke away from me, closing the wound in my neck in seconds. His face grim, he looked at the flames of his fire, then at me. I groaned quietly, struggling to regain my faculties, and Augustin set me upon the earth, his fingers appearing rigid, his jaw twitching in resignation. He rose from the grass as I pushed myself into a sitting position, sensing the gradual return of my vitality.

And then, when I lifted my head to meet my master's gaze, he stated harshly with no trace of indecision, "It is never enough. I must break this bond tonight, Swanhilde, with or without your consent. We cannot go on like this, eternally separated yet chained together in the spirit. It degenerates both of us, driving us away from our destinies, shackling us to our dreams, our visionary world that outshines reality. This must stop. It ends tonight."

My breath caught in my throat as my mind spun. *What* had he possibly seen in my blood to bring him to that horrid conclusion? "Augustin . . . you . . . we . . . we *can't!*" I gasped, scooting away from him on the grass, fearing that he may grab me and carry me to the spiritual realm to sever the bond before I had the chance to talk him out of this nonsense. I clearly remembered that first time, ten years ago now, when he had nearly succeeded in breaking our bond—I remembered the loss that had overwhelmed my spirit, the insanity that had conquered my reason and prompted me to attempt suicide.

"Please, you know that we tried this once . . . and it nearly killed me. We can't do this again . . . ." Tears blurred my vision as I stared up at Augustin. He stood like a black specter above me, his clawed fingers curling into fists, his eyes boiling with frustration.

"We have no choice, Swanhilde. This euphoria we shared today has laid the final nail into our coffin, for we do not *have* forever. We do not belong together. By dawn tomorrow you must return to your husband, the man you *should* love. You *must* let go of me, and the only way to ensure your freedom is to finish this permanently." His pale face loomed above me like an impassive ghost as he said, "The initial severance shall be painful for you, but afterward your freed will shall finally release the bonds of its madness and forget your love for a dead man."

"*That* is NOT true!" I exclaimed, fury and desperation seizing me all at once. I jumped to my feet to glower at Augustin, my ice erupting with my tumbled emotions, freezing my fingers, veiling my vision in blue. "Breaking our bond will *not* cause either of us to forget, you *or* me!

Our love does *not* depend on some damn mystical connection; it's my choice! If you try to tear us apart now, I'll do the same thing I did last time—and you'll have to watch me *die*." I seethed.

"So you would rather torment yourself indefinitely, destroying your future, inhibiting me from mine?" Augustin stepped forward to tower over me, heat from his fire emanating outward, threatening to melt my icy shield. A strange lunacy appeared in his glowing eyes, darkening his countenance to a degree that I had not yet seen. "*Love* is not worth this, Swanhilde, no matter what you believe, no matter what I may have said earlier," he snapped in a dark voice that did not sound like his. "I am bound to hate, bound to violence, bound to a demon, to Wuotan's charge. You *cannot* save me, and you *must* stop trying!"

I cowered, fearing this unfamiliar devil that had sprung up before me in the dusk, erasing all trace of the Augustin I knew, the man I loved with all of my heart. I swallowed, trying and failing to push aside my panic. Then I heard myself saying, "Maybe . . . maybe if . . . I could somehow . . . *stop* loving you first . . . we could break our bond." It was a lie, a foolish dream. I knew that, but in my recklessness I offered Augustin—a demon's slave—his one chance at victory.

After a long, disturbing silence, my master stated without emotion, "There is one thing . . . I have not yet tried." His flaming eyes drifted downward from my face to my stomach—and he struck me in the womb with incredible force, prompting me to crumple upon the earth as my dreams shattered in the twilight.

Chapter Twenty:
The Sadist Unleashed

Agony shot upward from my abdomen to my head as I fell to the ground, bruising my hip. I rolled onto my left side, my eyes widening in shock, barely a squeak of pain escaping my lips. Augustin kicked me sharply in the exact same place where he had initially hit me. The clout of his booted foot sent lightning bolts of torment throughout my whole body, breaking my shock, freeing my voice. I screamed, a piercing cry of anguish, and my innards roiled, preparing to abort the three-month-old child clinging to my uterus. My head pounded, and Augustin grabbed me by the hair, yanking me from the earth to meet his furious glare.

"You foolish bitch, *tonight* you shall learn to hate me!" he roared, his left hand twisting in my hair so harshly that I cried out in pain. "You shall grovel before me and beg for mercy, which I shall not grant! You have had this coming for years, thinking your kindness could change a rabid sadist! *Give me your child,* and learn the lesson of physical pain, the abuse I have *wanted* to unleash upon you since that first day!" My eyes watered with tears of denial, and Augustin drew his powerful right arm back to punch me directly in the mouth. My head snapped backward, ripping my hair from its roots as I collapsed to the ground again.

I tasted blood in my mouth while my fingers bruised themselves upon the earth, my insides still contracting with the impending miscarriage. I tried in vain to crawl away, to escape this monster who had driven my lover insane. My brain had put together a plausible assumption: his demon master must have possessed him. He would never treat me this way if he were in command of his body.

Augustin was upon me before I got far, forcibly turning me onto my side and striking me in the abdomen over and over. Each kick threw new waves of agony through my body, causing me to screech, tears blurring my vision. My pelvis jerked, and my legs curled into unnatural positions in an instinctive attempt to stave off the inevitable. Suddenly, I felt flaming hands upon my skin, tearing my black dress from me. A spectral voice reached me through my veil of distress: "Damn it, how *long* does it take to destroy a fucking child?!" Claws descended upon my stomach, ripping at my flesh, launching spasms of sickness through me. My blood burst forth from my womb to hemorrhage upon the grass and dirt.

Repulsive vomit hurled itself from my stomach as I writhed, my legs and arms splaying into agonizing paroxysms, a seemingly endless stream of material pouring from my womb. I heard Augustin laughing, a deep, demonic sound, and my strength waned with the abruptness of throwing a switch, pulling me away from this impossible turn of events to the relief of unconsciousness. Just before the blackness took me, my tortured mind had one final thought: *He doesn't mean to do this . . . Wuotan directs his hands . . . tells him to convince you to stop loving him using abuse, hatred . . . .*

When I opened my eyes again, the taste of blood and vomit still tainting my tongue—I noticed that several of my teeth had been loosened by Augustin's punch—I found that I lay upon my back, my arms stretched above my head, my legs spread horribly apart. Above me, my distorted vision detected the presence of tree branches framing the dark sky of late evening, no light from the stars or the moon seeming to pierce the shadows around me. My abdomen still felt as though it had been struck through with a railroad spike and bent into the angles of a trapezoid. I perceived the stickiness of coagulated blood coating my upper thighs. I closed my eyes again, a muted moan rolling off of my swollen tongue. Then my tormentor took hold of my head, turning it to the right. His clawed fingers forced my eyes to open, to look into those blue orbs of fire that gleamed with a mad yearning for brutality.

"Would you like to know . . . what I plan . . . to do to you?" He spoke slowly, distinctly, his tone sonorous, attempting to infuse me with a false sense of security, with the idiotic notion to trust him. I could not answer. An overwhelming dread had taken hold of me at last, the realization that my lover *was*, in fact, a dead man kept on this earth by a demon's power. He was forbidden to accept the truth of God, ordered to relinquish the memory of goodness and love. He had fought Wuotan for a solid decade on account of our bond, facing unending torment. Tonight, he would sever our connection whether Wuotan worked through him or not, turning forever to serve his demon master, proving to me with his violence that he had chosen hatred over love.

Fear raced through my veins, and I may have whimpered, but Augustin had already released my face to run his hands now over my naked body, prodding it here and there in silent appraisal. "You are such an ugly cow," he commented as he wrung my right breast so hard I gasped. "You have wasted what beauty you once had on that effeminate whirlwind, and now you are nothing but a mountain of misplaced flab."

A scathing laugh burst from his throat while he poked my thighs, their muscles still tender from the miscarriage. "But it is no matter, for thus you have more flesh for me to tear apart." I felt his fingers probing my ravaged vagina, singeing its tissue with his fire. I cried out in anguish and squeezed my eyes shut against this terrible reality that had splintered my dreams.

His hands burnt my face a moment later, the weight of his body pressing me to the earth. "I recall that you were raped once before," he growled in a lascivious tone, "but I doubt that those living outsiders had the virility of the dead to enhance their experience."

Panic clasped my chest in a vise and I wheezed, my eyelids springing open. *No . . . this can't be happening . . . .* I tried to bring my arms down to my sides, resolved to struggle for all that I was worth if his demon overlord forced him to take advantage of me. But then I discovered—*how* had I not noticed it earlier?—that Augustin had chained my arms above my head with fetters of iron. I sensed the solidness of metal locking my ankles to the ground as well, pressing heavily upon the nerves there, rendering any elemental resistance futile. He had made it utterly impossible for me to fight him.

My eyes rolled back, and I begged oblivion to take me again, that I could somehow avoid this wretched fate that had come upon me. A flaming torch burnt my spiritual heart in the same instant, bringing me sharply back to awareness, my voice bursting forth with a screech. A vicious smile crawled across Augustin's lips when I screamed, and his fingers tightened upon my face. "Unfortunately, you shall not receive the relief of unconsciousness again this night," he informed me, "for your heart is in the hands of a sadist. He shall make certain that you fully appreciate your ordeal. For this rape and all that shall follow after, the pleasure is *all* mine!"

So began the most dreadful experience of sex I had ever faced in my whole life, far surpassing the assault I had faced at college. Augustin unleashed his cruelty upon my body and spirit with a vengeance, thrashing me upon the earth, coating my skin and hair with dirt and blood. He yanked my hair out by the handful and left bloody lines upon my arms and chest from his claws. He shoved his body more deeply into mine than I thought was humanly possible, his fire burning me from the inside out, his teeth tearing into my neck again and again. Since he had stifled my ice, I could not counter him, and I smelled my own flesh burning.

Sometimes I screamed, and other times he covered my mouth with his hands, pressing my head so forcefully into the ground that I could hardly breathe. Then he would kiss me until I choked on his tongue, my empty stomach unable to find the relief of expulsion. He threw horrible accusations in my face, reviling my love for him, proclaiming that he had never loved me, that he had always hated my influence, that he would rather rot in hell, away from me. Any time I hoped that my weakness would finally drag me into a swoon, he burned my heart in the other realm. Those immortal flames tormented me more than the physical violence, bringing me back to an agonizing alertness.

Eventually, Augustin rolled off of me after what seemed like an eternity. His death had apparently given him the ability to rape *ad infinitum*; he had climaxed at least six times. After a moment's pause—during which I moaned quietly, feeling incredibly drained and chilled due to the absence of his consuming fire—he retrieved his black robes from a nearby tree branch, wrapping them around his body with disturbing swiftness. He released me from the chains soon afterward, but I had no strength left to attempt to escape. My body was so weak as a result of his abuse that I could hardly move. My muscles would not respond to my brain's commands, so I lay like a corpse upon the earth, closing my eyes once more as I wondered what he could possibly do to me next. He had already ravaged my body and my heart, sewing seeds of doubt at last into my stubborn mind. He may have loved me once, but now . . . he had chosen Wuotan's path . . . .

He took hold of my hair and started dragging me through the forest, the pine needles and stones stabbing the skin of my back. I heard him muttering things as he pulled me into the darkness, speaking in plurals as though he and his demon master conversed like pals. "We must kill her tonight at long last. If she still loves you after this, she is a lunatic. This final torment shall bring forth our greatest ecstasies, the demise of her goodness."

Augustin's hand closed around my throat while I speculated on how long this could possibly last. How long could my body and heart withstand his darkest torments? The Cursed One lifted me to face him, grasping my neck so tightly that my lungs strained. His eyes glittered eerily in the dark as he asked me in a ruthless voice, "Are you ready ... to *beg* me ... for mercy?" He loosened his grip on my throat and locked the fingers of his free hand in my hair. "Are you ready to plead with me on your *knees* ... like the *slave* you are ... to free you from these chains and let go of your helpless heart?" He snarled at me, displaying the inhuman sharpness of his teeth. I gasped for breath, trying and failing to find words. Maybe if I gave him what he wanted, he would cease his savagery.

He howled shockingly, a fierce cry of rage, and he cast my body down upon a flat stone with incredible might. I heard an obvious *snap* as my back laid itself onto its next arena of torture. A horrid pain shot through my midsection, prompting me to yell, then catch the sound back when the agony increased. *He had broken one of my ribs* . . . .

I bit my lip and tried not to cry out again, my eyes wheeling around, taking in my surroundings: the trees, the shadows, the blue flames leaping upward from a nearby fire pit, the stone beneath my back . . . . And Augustin's face appeared above me, set in a pitiless mask. "You *will* beg me for mercy, and you *will* beg me for freedom, and I shall not grant it, for you are my sacrifice!" A double-edged blade flashed in the firelight as he wielded it before me. Demonic laughter burst from his throat at the sight of my terror.

My heart raced as the particulars of what he planned to do hit me hard. My nightmare that had plagued me right after I had witnessed his sacrifice of the Saxon woman was coming true. He had raped me, abused me, murdered my unborn child, and now he would slay me at long last in the most hideous way possible. My muscles bunched, my fingernails scraping the rock beneath me, the ice within me attempting to overcome my weakness in one final attempt at self-defense. Words finally escaped my lips for the first time since this lurid night had begun. "Augustin . . . *please* . . . don't . . . ." I sounded like a baby frog, a frail croak.

"So you still speak." He nodded once, his eyes raking over my body, noting my feeble efforts to flee. "It ought to please you then, that I intend to draw this out as long as I can." Augustin sat down at the foot of his stone altar, lifting my right leg in his burning fingers and placing it upon his lap. I struggled to raise my head from the stone to see what he was doing, but my broken rib stabbed my side at the effort. I sank back upon the altar, staring blankly at the sky, shaking in fright. The metal of his knife caressed my foot a moment later, and Augustin's fingers probed my heel, drifting casually upward to the ankle.

"I remember how masterfully these feet once played the murderer's organ," he commented in a conversational tone, his fingers squeezing my ankle bones. "I remember how desperately you hope to escape this era through the triumph of music rather than through the black gates of death. I also remember how swiftly these feet have run across the snow and on the river in a Teutonic dance." The edge of his blade touched the back of my heel gently, prompting me to gasp in horror, shooting pain through my ribs again. "*Beg* me, you slave," Augustin intoned. "Plead with your master. *Pray* that he would not make you a cripple."

I squeaked, my fingers clutching the stone beneath me in a useless defense. "Please . . . *please* . . . master . . . please . . . don't do this . . . I love you . . . ."

The knife sliced through my Achilles tendon an instant later, its blade singeing my flesh. I wailed while my blood ran onto Augustin's cloak, onto the stone altar, all of my cherished hopes crumbling before me. "*That* is the *wrong* answer, you harlot!" he roared at me, snatching up my left foot and cutting it the same way. "You must *hate* me now, *hate me,* for you shall never run again, never make your favorite music again, all because of *ME!*" I heard another *snap* as his burning fingers broke one of my toes, the pain causing my body to spasm, its movements torturing me further.

He broke two toes in each of my feet and slit the bottoms with his knife before deeming his business there complete. He laughed raucously when I cried, and the blue flames licked furiously out of the nearby fire pit in response to his devilish triumph. He seemed to have centered his anger in his fire and in his knife, for I felt no duress from his gift of death at all during his heathen acts. His face had grown so demented that I feared to look at him, to see how the filial curse had cost him his agency. His years of killing and raping without remorse had led him straight into Wuotan's clutches . . . *why* in heaven's name had my heart fallen for him?

Presently, he came around to the right of my head and lifted his fiery knife over my face. "Beg me again, *slave!*" he cried out, his chin raised to the night sky above. "Cry for mercy, now that you cannot escape! Weep for the devil who stands over you, beg him to torment you no longer!" He brought the knife down to my face, tracing its sizzling blade across my cheeks, his eyes alight with madness. "Ask me to break the bond," he hissed, the deathly scent on his breath prompting my neck to twitch.

I moaned when the metal seared my flesh, and our eyes met. I saw revulsion smoldering with his Teutonic fire; it appeared that he had made his choice. Maybe he had hated me for a long time now. Maybe what I had believed to be love was nothing more than a seductive lie. I shut my eyes and gasped out the impossible plea, fighting to keep my foolish feelings apart from this. "Master . . . master . . . please . . . release me . . . ."

I heard a dark chuckle. When I opened my eyes again, I saw that Augustin grinned at me, his monstrous teeth descending to bite down on my right earlobe. "*No,*" he said, his spiritual hands suddenly aflame, searing my heart with a hellish torment. I shrieked in renewed agony, and Augustin shouted into my ear, "You shall find no mercy in me ever again! You shall be my slave until this world perishes in fire, and I shall glory in your *pain!*"

He slit my wrists next, then stabbed my hands through with knives—apparently he had more than one—leaving their burning blades in my palms as my blood stained the altar red. The fire scorching my heart did not cease, and I heard Augustin laughing manically, railing upon me for more things than I can recall, my love, my stupidity, and my weakness his main grievances. At some point he cast off his outer robe and threw himself upon my body to rape me again, battering my hips against the altar. His weight aggravated my broken rib, and he sank his teeth into my throat, draining my life, cutting off my breath. Finally, though I had believed it would never come, I found myself sinking into the morass of death, my spirit freed at last from my battered body, flying toward the end.

Many confused thoughts swirled around in my dying mind as the eyes of my spirit recognized those aged gates of time looming in the mist, their colors seeming to swirl with mystery. They beckoned me to renounce the eleventh century for good, my only escape from a dead man whose demon master had transformed into a monster. *He could not have ravaged me indefinitely . . . my mortal body still has the capacity to die . . . he drained my blood beyond his powers of intervention . . . the pain in my heart will cease . . . the bond will break . . . home . . . I'll miss the fall . . . I wasn't meant to see it . . . I was fated to die at Augustin's hands . . . he said that all along . . . he got what he wanted . . . now he will descend to hell . . . I cannot save him . . . he cannot save me . . . why do I still love him . . . .*

I could not have turned around, even if I had wished it. This time I had no intentions of returning to my decrepit body, for I feared Augustin had damaged it beyond repair by medieval medicine. But once I passed through those gates—so close now—the effects of the eleventh century would fall from my soul, making me young and beautiful. Sending me back to Hans. *Could he suffice?*

That was my last thought as I closed my eyes, reaching the hands of my spirit out to the currents of light and color that called me away from my prison. But a fiery demon appeared abruptly in front of me, delving his burning hands into my essence with the cold assertion: *Death cannot save you this time. You are mine.*

My eyes popped open, and fire conquered my spirit. He flung me away from those gates a third time, cutting off my escape. I sensed no love in my rescuer, only hatred and triumph. So I screamed one last, tormented cry: *Nooooooo!*

When I awoke again, I lay bound in the fetal position, clothed in the black tatters of my dress, my beaten body resting upon the planks of Augustin's boat. I could not fathom *why* I still lived, especially if he intended to return me to Joel. Would he scorch my heart from a distance and turn my dreams with him into nightmares? I could see him standing at the stern if I twisted my neck upward and to the right. He paddled his vessel forward steadily, his face completely insensitive whenever he glanced down at me.

He dumped me at the front door of Lord Edwin's house in the gray fog of early dawn, leaving me without a backward glance as the pain from my myriad injuries dragged me into delirium. He had trapped me in this primitive wasteland with enough wounds to cripple me for good. This was worse than what Walfrid had done to Ina, far away in the home that I may never see again.

How was I to face my city's fall when my immortal defender had forsaken me?

Chapter Twenty-one

It Would Never End

For the first few days of my long, tortuous recovery, I floated in and out of awareness. My mind could hardly form an intelligent thought as it drifted from the pain-wracked mortal world to the relief of inertia. I knew that my body lay upon some sort of bed, for I could detect the presence of cool cloth beneath me. Sometimes I felt gentle hands working over me, applying salve and bandages, attempting to preserve my life as far as medieval medicine allowed. I heard soft voices speaking around me from time to time, usually in Rhenisch, discussing my beaten condition and my chances for a full recovery.

From these quiet conversations I discerned that—along with four broken toes, one broken rib, and two torn Achilles tendons—I had extensive damage to my head, hands, and womb. Those who cared for me could not understand how I had managed to survive after losing so much blood. I silently agreed with their surprise. Whenever my soul returned from the peaceful oblivion to my broken body, the pain overwhelmed me anew, prompting me to groan in torment, wordlessly begging God to allow me to die, to send me home.

By the fourth day, my brain had chosen at last to remain with my body, to my private chagrin. I was conscious for most of the day, the pains in my feet and insides afflicting me the most, along with a dull ache that had seeped from my jaw to my head. A Rhenisch doctor attended me several times, blotting and rewrapping my wounds and forcing a rather despicable potion down my throat in an attempt to ease my suffering. Joel and Freia sat at my bedside for the greater part of the day. After the doctor managed to convince me to swallow a few bites of bread and fresh cabbage, the interrogation commenced, infusing my veins with a mute terror.

"My Lady Swanhilde," the doctor began in a solemn tone, his graying blond beard appearing strangely mysterious in the dim rays of afternoon sun trickling through the window. "Can you understand me?"

I could, though I feared to face his questions, for his earnest gray eyes were alight with concerned curiosity. So I nodded once, too weak to hide the panic that must have crossed my beaten face. The doctor took my right hand carefully in his, smoothing out the bandages as he inquired, "Can you tell me, Lady Swanhilde, how this happened to you?" He leaned closer to me, his posture cautious.

Freia came to the doctor's side, worry evident in her eyes. Joel remained seated on a stool nearby, closed out of the dialogue due to his ignorance of Rhenisch. I bit my lip as I tried to discern what I *could* say and quickly discovered that was a bad idea. My lip was still swollen and tender from Augustin's hard punch that had practically broken my teeth; I felt several of them shift.

I moaned softly, closing my eyes while my brain fabricated a plausible lie. I felt the doctor's hands upon my neck, checking my pulse, and when I opened my eyes again he held a goblet to my lips. "Drink, my lady, and speak to me," he urged, his expression kind. "No harm will come to you now, but we must find out who abused you so horribly, that the offender may be properly punished." His bearded jaw twitched.

I swallowed a few mouthfuls of milk from the goblet and gathered all of the Rhenisch Augustin had taught me for my clever excuse. "Someone . . . someone . . . a man . . . ." My voice scraped my throat, sounding awful after days of disuse. I tried to clear it and shifted my tongue around in my mouth. It still felt swollen and battered. "A man . . . attacked me . . . while I walked by the Rhine . . . several nights ago." I paused, choking, my broken rib stabbing my side. My head had begun to throb, and I shut my eyes, abandonment washing over me anew.

"Could you see who it was? Was it someone from the village, someone from one of the trading ships?" the doctor pressed, bringing the goblet to my lips again.

I took a few more sips of milk, its taste not particularly soothing me. I took a deep breath and opened my eyes just a slit. "A . . . trader . . . . He took me onto a ship . . . and they beat me . . . they . . . *used* me . . . for a whole day . . . ." The ridiculousness of my lie sent knives of guilt through me, almost more painful than my physical wounds, but I rallied to my tale as I finished, "They . . . dumped me at the door . . . and left . . . ."

The doctor patted me gently on the arm, his expression thoughtful. Freia turned to Joel and related my story to him in quiet Teutonica. I closed my eyes again as weariness took hold of me, a multitude of pains searing my vitality. I longed for a knife to slice my throat so I could leave the eleventh century forever, forsaking all of its discomfort and lies. And my voice escaped my bruised lips one more time, forming a meaningless plea in Bayerisch, understood by no one except me . . . and my tormentor: "Why didn't you let me die?"

I found myself alone just before daybreak. Freia had gone to retrieve fresh salve for my wounds and hot water for tea, while Joel had departed much earlier to discuss options with Heinrich, Johann, and Lord Edwin. He had flipped out upon hearing my story, proclaiming that he must hunt down the sailors who had ravaged his woman and kill them all himself. I hoped that his friends, with the help of Freia's father, could hold Joel back from embarking on a wild goose chase. I did not want my husband to make a bad name for himself as a rampaging pirate of the Rhine, and I had choked out several appeals to Freia along those lines after the doctor had gone. Now, while I lay alone on the sheets in the light of a few flickering candles, I lifted myself onto my elbows with effort, moaning at the stabbing pain in my ribs, steeling myself to observe my wounds in full now that I had the chance to do so privately.

I drew both of my arms out from beneath the thin blanket that covered me, noting the pus-stained bandages wound around my wrists and palms. I noticed quite a few bluish bruises upon my upper arms along with the jagged, healing scars lining my forearms from Augustin's sharp fingernails. I gingerly took hold of the blanket covering me, pealing it back and cringing mentally at the thought of how battered the rest of my body must look.

I found that someone had clad me in an airy nightdress, a sleeveless affair that reached down to my knees. My gaze fell upon my feet, seeing that they were entirely encased in filthy-looking bandages, appearing weak and useless down at the end of my reclined body. I gathered all of my strength and attempted to twitch my bound feet back and forth. My breath caught in my throat when agony shot up my legs, chaining me to immobility. I could not move my feet at all. He had severed both of my Achilles tendons, an injury that would take months and months to heal. In this primitive era, that act alone may very well make me a cripple.

Tears came to my eyes, and I sank back onto the pillow behind me, not wanting to accept the reality that lay blatantly before me. *He can't possibly love you anymore, or he wouldn't have been able to do these things to you . . . unless his demon master took charge of his hands that night. But was he truly possessed, or does he actually hate you? That look in his eyes . . . .*

I stared blankly at the hazy ceiling above, trying to sort out my feelings about what Augustin had done to me. He had indulged his yearning for brutality, one that he had mentioned many times before, during our studies. He had concluded several years prior that he must start sacrificing humans again, that he had no choice. His master had started punishing him for his use of animals in ways that mortals could not comprehend, he had said. He had mentioned scorching flames that left no mark, tortures carried out by a wide array of demons. So he had taken to capturing criminals, murderers and rapists, Saxon spies.

And now he wants to sacrifice you, to renounce your love forever. You have to forget that he still holds your heart . . . but you can't. You'll have to kill yourself as soon as you can get hold of a knife. Just a small cut will do . . . you can direct all of your blood into that channel and end all of this . . . free yourself from this mad delusion . . . a mockery of love offered by one who belongs in hell . . . .

Freia reentered the room shortly thereafter, carrying a basin of soapy water and a fresh roll of bandages. She set her goods upon a table near the bed and pulled up a stool, her anxious eyes roving over my uncovered body before focusing on my face. "How are you, Swanie?" she asked me softly, touching my right arm.

I sighed, then moaned as my broken rib stabbed me once more. "How do I look?" I queried, deflecting her question.

She looked at my body again. "Your chest and abdomen are covered with bruises and cuts, your face is burnt, your neck is torn . . . ." Her voice trailed off, and she looked away toward the window before adding, "You've seen the rest already, I would assume, since you pushed your blanket back."

I nodded weakly, and my friend rose to tend to my wounds. She unwrapped the many bandages one by one and bathed each lesion, cleansing away the ooze. My teeth scored my lip many times as she tended to me, numerous pains gouging me afresh. I got a good view of my battered feet when she unwrapped my ankles. I winced mentally at the deep cuts upon them, the edges burnt with fire, the charred skin still seeping pus. As to the toes, I could only speculate on whether the bones had been properly set or not. I doubted it, so I figured that I would have crooked toes for the rest of my existence in the eleventh century.

But it'll be short, I thought to myself, my plans solidifying in my mind. *I can't ask Freia for a knife, though. I doubt she'd agree with what I need to do. I'll have to wait until I can move around again and get ahold of one myself. Or maybe I could invoke my ice into my hands once I'm strong enough . . . I've used my ice as claws before. That might do it. I could slice them down the artery in my right forearm, just like a Cursed One.*

Surprise shot through me when Freia unwrapped my palms to wash the cuts there, for I saw that they were not simply stabbed through once, like I had believed. In the center of each palm, a wretched puncture wound tainted my once-tender skin—but I also saw long, thin scars that reached from my middle fingers to my wrists. Those slashes had already healed, and I shook my head in bewilderment as the truth of the matter struck me between the eyes. *He gave you his blood to save your life, probably right as he leaped after you in the spiritual realm to drag you back from the gates of time. How else could you have survived after such extensive blood loss? You're alive now thanks to dead blood . . . demon blood . . . why must he torment you this way . . . why can't he set you free?*

Freia noticed my preoccupation while she gently bathed the wounds on my palms and wrists. "This didn't happen to you because of traders on the Rhine, did it?" she asked in a low voice, speaking Teutonica. Her expression told me clearly that she had known the truth all along. My eyes darted toward the closed door, my fear of being overheard holding me silent. Freia's eyes flashed amber in response to my tension, her countenance glowing with the power of her element. "There's no one nearby," she murmured.

A feeble smile played upon my lips as a bit of jealousy gripped me. Now my best friend had a major advantage over me, for my frailty shackled my ice within my spirit. I did not have the strength to bring it out for anything, not to soothe my burns or to heighten my senses enough to check for intruders—or to fashion my own personal claws to end this insanity. I met Freia's gaze steadily and said in a low voice, "It was Augustin." Her forehead creased, and

I whispered, "I asked him . . . to convince me . . . to stop loving him . . . so he did this to me."

I saw tears in the corners of my best friend's eyes as she wrapped my hands in fresh bandages. Her fingers were gentle and full of light, granting me a portion of her vibrancy. "Did he convince you?" she asked, leaning forward to sponge my aching head.

I closed my eyes, relishing the coolness of the wet cloth massaging my burnt skin, beckoning to the icy winter inside me. "I don't know, Freia," I murmured at length, my mind not yet having determined how to interpret Augustin's abuse. "I guess he must not love *me* . . . or he couldn't have done this. But I'm pretty sure he was possessed . . . while he was . . . there was something strange in his voice . . . something dark in his eyes. I don't know. Wuotan's been torturing him . . . about his loyalty to me . . . so maybe he finally decided that love isn't worth the pain." I cringed when I spoke the truth. Despondency engulfed me with the magnitude of what I had lost.

Freia kept silent for a while and finished bathing my face and neck; then she whispered, "Maybe God has decided to give him completely to Satan and sin." A discontented frown turned my lips downward, for she was probably right. Maybe it was too late for him, like he had insisted all along.

Freia gathered the soiled bandages into a pile, preparing to carry them to the maids for cleaning. In her absence, I pondered Augustin's fate again. My heart did not wish to accept the prospect of his being beyond grace. He was still on earth, and Wuotan had incited his wretched acts. I remembered the devotion that I had felt pouring into my spiritual heart as he pleased my body that afternoon. It could not have been fake; that was the real Augustin, the man who had saved my life time and again, the man who had studied languages with me, who saw me as a peer and not as a fool good for nothing but childbearing. And I had made a choice to love him no matter what he did, no matter how deep he sank into the abyss.

But would he ever come to my dreams again? In his darkness, he had proclaimed that he would torment my heart until the earth perished in fire, but I had not sensed the hands of his spirit at all over the past few days. Would he leave me in silence to ruminate on everything alone, or would he bring himself to apologize for what he had done? Though I still loved him, I was not sure whether I could forgive him, especially if his abuse rendered me permanently disabled.

I would have to figure this out on my own.

We all remained at Eisenwald until the beginning of September to give my body adequate time to convalesce. I passed most of the days indoors, seated in a reclined chair once my rib had healed enough for Joel to lift me from the bed. The doctor predicted that with time, most of my injuries should heal, though I would likely need a cane if I ever managed to walk again. I may end up with a permanent limp, he said, for my toes would probably remain bent despite his rather primitive attempts to set the bones.

Thankfully, none of my wounds had become infected. This was mainly the result of Joel demanding the use of soap and fresh bandages anytime someone cleaned my injuries. He had brought the last of our rubbing alcohol from the twenty-first century along on our journey, and he dabbed it upon each lesion himself every morning until it ran out. I joked that he would have to make some more from our grapes before he set out to fight the Saxons again, and he promised with a wink to work on that. The doctor advised us just before we left that we ought to wait until the New Year before attempting any further procreation. He was unsure whether my body could accomplish it after my brutal experience, and I silently hoped that my womb had deemed its work finished.

Nightmares plagued me nearly every night of my recovery. In the darkness, I found myself upon Augustin's stone altar over and over again, his face transformed into that of a beast with horns, his claws and teeth tearing my flesh from my bones. "You think your faith can protect you from my wrath," he scoffed in one spectral vision. "In the end, you shall know the price of tampering with Wuotan's devices without pledging fair service. Your heart belongs to me . . . and my hands move at his direction."

For some reason, my mind struggled to wake from these new nightmares, unlike the ones I had faced in years past. I would scream and cry, and the scenes would shift from flaming darkness to a ghostly dorm room with outsiders mocking me, deriding my weakness, stripping off my pants, jamming themselves deep into my battered body. And even then I would hear Augustin laughing, his voice haunting me in a personal torture decreed by Wuotan himself: "Useless . . . wasted . . . hate me . . . slave . . . ."

Despite my brain's newfound torments and doubts, my plans for a violent end to my days in the eleventh century fizzled as the days passed. I realized that if I fled this time now, Joel would have to raise our kids and manage our land alone. I did not want him to have to explain to Cammie that her beloved Mutti had chosen to leave her behind. She and Lorraine were my most dedicated caregivers during those long weeks, bringing me flowers from the gardens and herbal tea to ease my physical discomforts. Also, the Rhine was just a short walk from where I rested. I did not wish to tempt fate to cast me into final death, especially with a vengeful demon taking Augustin's form in my dreams.

Lord Edwin gave us an open cart as a gift upon our departure, so I could ride inside it rather than upon the back of a horse for our journey back to Muniche. Since I still could put no weight on either of my feet by early September, the cart would simplify things considerably. One of the men could carry me whenever we paused to rest, and all four of the children could ride with me if they wished.

Heinrich, Joel, and Johann spent a few evenings in the company of several men from Eisenwald, poring over their local maps to identify the eastern routes that could handle a wooden conveyance. They eventually concluded that we would take the main road east to where it connected with a northerly route to the Schwäbisch city of Karlsruhe. Then we would turn south along the main trade route to Stuttgart and Augsburg, crossing the Danube at Ulm to enter

Teutonic territory. The journey would take a bit longer, Joel estimated, since by heading north we were going out of the way, but I shrugged off his concerns. I trusted Jarvis to handle all of the harvests in our absence.

On the day that we left Eisenwald, I sat for a long while upon several cushions in the cart, unable to help the others load our goods. As an invalid, my only duty was to speak my farewells to the many townspeople who came to see us off. I hugged Anna hard, thanking her for all of her help during my recovery, and I exchanged countless embraces and handshakes with Lord Edwin's servants and relations, along with some of the commoners I had gotten to know. Freia's father kissed my forehead in parting, apologizing that my stay in his village had taken such a miserable turn and wishing me many blessings in the future. Cammie, Max, Lorraine, and Heino wailed with gusto as they hugged their playmates goodbye, promising with the sincerity of childhood that they would meet again one day and that they would never forget each other.

While the men finished securing the saddles of the six horses that would not pull my cart, a middle-aged man clad like a trader ran to me from the main street, sweating with the effort of a lengthy sprint on a warm day. "Forgive me . . . forgive me . . . for disturbing you," he panted in Rhenisch with a French accent, "but I have . . . a message . . . for you . . . Lady Swanhilde." He pulled a sealed scroll from beneath his tunic and held it out to me.

Though I felt somewhat taken aback that this Frankish trader I had never met before seemed to know who I was, I summoned my propriety and ducked my head at him. "Thank you, my lord." I accepted the roll from his hands, and he bowed once toward me, then struck out for the main road again without further ado.

My eyes followed his retreat for a short moment as my mouth twisted into a puzzled frown. Then I turned my attention to the small roll of parchment in my hands, sealed with pale candle wax. My hands began to tremble as I ran my fingers down the length of the scroll, and I lifted my eyes to the men. All three were in the process of adjusting the packs and saddles on the horses, paying no attention to me. My gaze darted to the left, where Freia herded our children into a semi-organized cluster, her back turned. I exhaled once, then looked down at the scroll, breaking the seal and unrolling it into my lap.

The message was written in black ink, the calligraphy horribly familiar, the words, to my surprise, in Bayerisch: *What I did to you was inexcusable and dishonorable to the extreme. Do not forgive me. Though you shall hate me forever, my love for you shall be my eternal torment. I shall not bother you again.*

Tears trembled on my eyelashes, dotting the paper before me until my shaking hands at last found the ability to roll the message up again. When Freia came beside me moments later, asking me what was wrong, I answered in a tremulous voice, "It was all a ruse. He still loves me." This madness would never end.

Chapter Twenty-two:
Vexation

We made it back to Muniche safely right at the close of the Oktoberfest, the streets and surrounding countryside teeming with the excitement of the revelry. All of our vassals expressed great relief upon our return, and the servant women spent many hours caring for me in the subsequent months, helping me as I gradually began attempting to hobble about the manor. Joel had fashioned me a decent walking stick while we traveled along the Schwäbisch trade route, for he found the timber in the region to his liking.

Many of the female servants begged me to never set out on a dangerous journey again. Ulka in particular asserted that she had never heard good tales of the sailors on the Rhine. I chuckled tolerantly at their advice and assured them that I had no intentions of embarking on another adventure, knowing deep within my heart that I would stay in Muniche for the next decade, awaiting its fall.

Jarvis and Leo had managed the estate well, and Joel threw himself back into the business of trade immediately upon our return. He traveled to the fairgrounds daily to haggle for a profit. The crops had suffered that summer due to a drought that had hit in July, which prompted me to smile privately. I knew that if I had been there, I could have staved off the worst of it with my ice. Although Joel took most of the credit for raising and selling our crops, my element had its uses, and our streamlined system of accounting helped Jarvis immensely.

Joel and I sat down together to look over our financial status during the winter months. We concluded that if our current success held for the next five years, our three children would have more than enough to ensure their survival once they would have to flee the Saxon onslaught. Joel also noted that if we decided to have any more kids, we should leave it at one or two, since we had only ten years left before our tiny kingdom would crumble around us. "We don't want to force a whole horde of youngsters to face the trials to come," he said, and I agreed, glad that he finally seemed to view the situation sensibly.

Upon our homecoming, Helmut did not recognize any of us at first, for we had been gone nearly six months, almost a third of his lifetime. For the first week or so, he clung to Ulka with a look of pouty desperation on his chubby face whenever Joel or I reached out to hold him. Eventually he overcame his bashfulness and spent hours curled up in my lap sucking his thumb or toddling along behind his older siblings when they raced through the manor playing their energetic games. Helmut's grasp of Teutonica seemed to improve daily, so Joel began speaking English to him to get him used to our family's secret dialect. Cammie and Max copied their father with eagerness, their eyes shining with fun as they welcomed their youngest brother into the comradeship of the American Teutons.

When the winter snows descended, I passed countless afternoons sitting by the fireplace in the front parlor, teaching my oldest children the arts of reading and writing Teutonica. I schooled them on European history, discussing the differences between the Teutons and the other Germanic tribes, emphasizing the positive changes that Christianity had effected upon our people. Both Cammie and Max started asking thoughtful questions regarding faith that winter, which pleased me greatly, for I did not want my children to be blinded by the medieval Church's preoccupation with sacraments and good works. I read quite a few Bible stories to them, reminding them often that they could not trust their own abilities, for even heroes like Paul and David struggled with sin.

I had thought constantly of Augustin since our caravan had left Eisenwald. I longed to see him again, even though he had promised in his last letter that he would leave me alone. His absence ate at my soul, and sometimes I feared that he had found some way to sever our bond without my knowledge, since I never felt his hands upon my heart anymore. I had realized at the start of winter that I did have the capacity to forgive what he had done, despite the lingering frailty in my ankles and feet. He had not been himself during those devilish atrocities; I knew that, and I needed to tell him so.

I looked in vain for him in my dreams, cursing the unfairness of the heart-bond of the Teutons. It gave the priest total control, leaving the woman unable to enter his dreams, unable to contact him if he hid himself from her. The chauvinism imbedded in my people's rites infuriated me, for I believed that men and women were equals and should be treated as such. I began to dread going to bed at night, afraid to face my nightmares alone, afraid to feel the emptiness in my heart. Depression gradually dragged me down again as I yearned for someone I could not have while my decent husband slept peacefully beside me, not knowing the torment of my unfaithful soul.

Anger began to ignite within me along with my frustration, boiling over as the winter progressed. Joel and our three children were free to frolic outside in the snow, to sled, build castles, and stage snowball fights; but their lame mother remained trapped in an aging manor. I often sat upon the couch in the front parlor, watching their games through the windows, my feeble ankles bundled in wool against the cold. *If I hadn't gone to Eisenwald at all, I could be out there with them,* I thought one frosty afternoon in late February. *Now I may never dance with my element again thanks to a vengeful demon. And the Eihalbe said I'd find my dark one there. Now my dark one has forsaken me, leaving me helpless and alone.*

My muses shifted from my children shrieking outside, while Joel sent a whirl of flurries after them, to the three Eihalbae I had met in my lifetime and the advice that each of them had given. I was starting to seriously doubt their insight. The first one had advised me to climb the Leutasch Gorge, a feat which would have killed me—had it not been for that shadowy rescuer who summoned multiple elements far divergent from each other. A modern version of a Black Priest, no doubt, one who mocked my lack of power over time and tide. The Eihalbe on my father's property had told me rather flatly that not everything dead was destructive . . . and yet, Augustin had destroyed me inside and out. The one here in the eleventh century had urged me to save Augustin back when he was mortal, and hinted that I would find him if I joined Freia on her trip to Eisenwald.

The Eihalbae seem to want me broken, defeated, I thought, lying back upon the couch to stare up at the ceiling, my eyebrows wrinkling in annoyance. *What have I ever done to deserve this from them? I've never torn a branch from a silver oak or stolen any acorns. I've never asked them any questions. I've always treated them with respect, but their advice has led me to the gates of hell, to a man who has long since given up on hope, given up on me.*

"Enough of this!" I growled in Bayerisch, forcing myself up from the couch and reaching for my cane. I hobbled at a snail's pace toward the bedroom, intending to shut myself inside and leap into the spiritual realm for the first time in a long time. Though I could not walk all the way to the grove by the stream, my icy spirit could get there for certain. My injuries should not hinder my inner essence.

Ulka met me in the hallway just as I reached my bedroom doorway, and she asked me whether I required any assistance, her expression troubled. "I'm going to lay down for a while," I told her. It was not quite a lie. "If Joel and the kids come inside, please tell them to leave me in peace until dinner."

The head housekeeper dropped a quick curtsey and departed in the direction of the great hall. I crept into the bedroom and closed the door behind me, a flame of anticipation smoldering in my chest. I knew that Teutons ought not to question Eihalbae about anything, but I was sick of the fairies' nebulous apothegms and the destructive consequences that their words had wrought. The one on Thaden grounds had some explaining to do.

I stretched my body out upon the bed I shared with Joel and shut my eyes, invoking my ice to its fullest extent. The magic in my blood took a few moments to manifest itself, but I began to feel it crusting the wool over my feet, creeping slowly upward. I clenched my fists and focused more sternly, silently ordering my element to do its duty, to set my spirit free from its prison. My hands and arms froze along with my hair, and finally I sensed its chill enveloping my chest and face, cutting off my breath.

Another lingering moment passed before my spirit broke free, rising from my physical body to hover in the air like a lost cloud. I took several deep breaths with my ethereal lungs, pulling the translucent veil of my eyelids over my eyes while I beat back the panic that had fought to claim me at my element's sluggishness. *It's fine, Swanie. You're fine,* I told myself, endeavoring to draw the room's air into my snow white robes to reassure me. *You can breathe, you can walk, and you can* fly *in this form. Now seize the winter for yourself!*

I sent my spirit out into the yard beyond the bedroom window, sensing its glass scratching at me on my way through. I chortled as I dove into a snowbank, my glum heart refreshed by its cold. Everything was so beautiful outside, a thick coating of snow draping the ground, its crystals glowing in the sunlight beneath a dark blue sky. I lay upon my back for a while, my spirit half buried in the snow, my eyes watching the wisps of wind and the occasional passing bird. *Maybe I should make a habit of doing this every day, at least whenever Joel and the kids go out to play,* I recognized, tranquility buoying my unhappy mood. *But now it's time for business. Let's see what that Eihalbe has to say for itself.*

I imagined myself in the grove by the stream, the place where the Eihalbe of the Thaden grounds prowled amid the branches of its tree. As reality swirled around me, coalescing into that familiar collection of oaks, I lifted my spirit into an erect posture, my elemental eyes passing over the bare branches that shimmered with silver. *Where are you?* I demanded, my mental voice laden with frustration. *Show yourself.* My icy spirit seemed to project my call to the landscape around me; I felt a shivering breeze stir the branches of each tree in the dell.

It took me a fair amount of time to find the fairy. It sat balanced upon the uppermost branch of its tree, its beating wings a blur even to my enhanced vision. I sent my spirit upward to its level, noticing that its entire body seemed to sparkle like diamonds beneath the sun. Its colorful eyes locked with mine as I floated a few steps away from where it sat, its delicate fingers fashioning a small clump of snow into some ridiculous artwork. *We need to have a talk,* I informed it harshly, not bothering with a greeting.

"The Teuton witch has lost her way," the Eihalbe said, sounding incredibly blasé. Its eyes shifted from mine to the snowy creation in its hands.

I've had enough of this! I snapped, my anger darkening my spirit's robes into the cobalt of the sky above. *I've had enough of the ambiguous crap your kind spews out to every Teuton that crosses your paths!* The fairy's eyes moved back to mine, what looked like a grimace appearing on its silvery lips. *You told me to save Augustin a decade ago, and now he's dead anyway, a slave to a demon who's torn my heart to shreds! "I'll find my dark one there," but he wants nothing to do with me now!* I flung my hands up in frustration, disrupting the currents of wind.

The Eihalbe eyed me in silence for a moment, its lips pursed in what could have been offense. But when it spoke again, it looked down at the work of its hands. "He has spurned his destiny for years, that one. But his is not one that can be permanently evaded."

And what destiny is that? To destroy a maiden from the future who had no concept of the depth of his dark-ness? What about my *destiny?* I glared at the fairy, wishing that it would meet my ire with its own instead of balancing so carelessly upon its thin branch. *One of your kind set me on this path of time travel, and look what it's done to me! Turned me into a liar, a hypocrite, a slave, a cripple. I came here to learn the truth about my people's history, not for this!*

"You came to detach yourself from the priest who mentored you." The fairy corrected me in an even voice, its kaleidoscope eyes piercing mine. Its fingers had begun to pull snowflakes from its pile one by one, sprinkling them upon the argentine threads of its hair.

Embarrassment and anguish washed over my spirit simultaneously. I had not expected the Eihalbe to know of the selfish reasons that had sent me into the past. I thought about Hans' necklace tucked away in my bag from the twenty-first century. I had not worn it in ages now. *Was this the price then?* I asked, my thoughts ragged. *Forget Hans and fall for one destined for hell? Learn the agony of betrayed love and watch my children die? This is not a fair price!*

The fairy sighed and raised what remained of its snow to its lips, blowing the entire clump toward where I floated among the tree branches. Its crystals carried a brisk chill that rejuvenated my spirit, lightening my robes once more. I blinked at my ethereal clothing, then looked at my silvery companion, unsure how to take its gesture. The Eihalbe's expression appeared grave, its prismatic eyes gazing in-tently at my face. "The price of Wuotan's sorcery is death," it said.

Confusion swept over me along with an uncanny dread. *Are you saying that death is going to be creeping over my shoulder for the rest of my life, just because I decided to travel time?* I felt as though all of my intentions had been swallowed by a bottomless pit. Was *that* what the Eihalbe in the gorge had tried to tell me?

"None on earth can know the future. What advice we offer is a product of the ages, of the many that have come before." The fairy's tail swished abruptly, and it glanced downward toward the main trunk of its tree.

But you just said that Augustin's been avoiding his destiny, I pointed out, uncertainty altering my icy spirit's translucence. *How can you know what his destiny is if you don't know something about the future?*

The Eihalbe's lips quirked into a smile, and it lifted itself from its branch, fluttering for a moment in midair. "The Teuton witch ought to expand her perception." It darted downward an instant later, quickly vanishing from my sight.

That explains nothing. I infused my thoughts with all of the frustration I felt. Even when I dared to ask questions, the fairy continued to speak in riddles. I could not work this out on my own, or I would have done it already. I slid my eyelids shut and rubbed my temples, trying to summon the frigid air around me into my spirit, to let its icy temperature soothe my pain.

The fairy returned before I thought to compress my spirit and return to my mortal body, frail and crippled upon my bed. I saw it through my crystalline eyelids, and it appeared to carry something in its hands. When I reopened my eyes to look at it directly, it stretched its arms forth, proffering a silver acorn. My eyes opened wide, and I felt my heart skip a beat. *For me?* I queried. No Eihalbe should offer me one of its cherished fruits after I had railed upon it so impolitely.

"For your dark one," the fairy clarified, cocking its head at me. "His stores of our magic run low, and it is time that he raise his own tree."

My jaw dropped in slow motion as I looked from the acorn to the Eihalbe. *But—*

"You visited my home today. Nothing stops you from visiting his."

Shivers pervaded the whole of my spirit, and I had an instinct to slap myself. *Of course. Even if Augustin wants to hide from me, I can go to his cottage as a spirit, search him out until he acknowledges me . . . .*

My lips curved into a real smile, something that felt foreign to my spirit. *I'll take it to him,* I promised the fairy, reaching out to accept its offering. I curled my ghostly fingers around it, pleased at how solid it felt in my hand. I needed to get back to the bedroom and store the acorn somewhere where Joel would not notice it. But before I departed, I met the Eihalbe's gaze one last time. *Are our destinies . . . separate?* I asked, worry shifting my icy robes around me.

"Seek the righteous path," the fairy advised me, its wings carrying it leisurely toward the frozen stream below. "Wuotan's grasp upon him is more tenuous than he believes."

Chapter Twenty-three:
Seeking the Lost

The next afternoon found me in the bedroom right after Joel had herded our three children outside to play. I had opened the subject of diseases before Cammie and Max that day, explaining the necessity of cleanliness to protect against some of the worst ones. Both of my children bubbled over with questions about dysentery, for a bout of it had struck the Sendlin estate two summers prior. I told them that Joel and I took pains to keep our food and poop separated, and I suggested that they visit our neighbors' land once the weather grew warmer to observe the location of their cesspits. "If there are gardens nearby, or if they use human waste for fertilizer, these things happen," I informed them.

They plied Joel with questions and speculations on food and poop while he bundled them up for their trip outdoors. Helmut's piercing voice drifted into the great hall several times, where I sat gathering my strength for the spiritual journey I was about to make. "Daddy, pigs get sick? Pigs like poop!"

I chuckled and grasped my cane to help me to my feet, my eyes locking for a moment with Ulka. She bent over the nearest fireplace, scooping a batch of ashes into a pan for disposal. "I'm going to lay down again for a while," I told her. "Please keep everyone away from me for a few hours."

"As you wish, my lady," she responded, ducking her head once before turning back to her duties. "I think Lord Joel will tire of the nasty subjects before long."

I laughed and riposted, "Better him than me." Then I made my way to the bedroom, closing its door securely behind me.

My icy spirit burst free from my ailing body minutes later, and I whirled for my twenty-first century bag first to retrieve the silver acorn. I gripped it tightly in my ethereal hand and imagined myself on the banks of the Rhine, the place where Augustin had spread his dark blue blanket for our picnic during our single day of bliss. The bedroom evaporated around me, transforming into a realm of white, a snow-covered cloudy day. A grand river stood before my eyes, its waters carrying ice floes along its path northward. I did a quick dance of victory upon the shallows of the river, then spun to face the forest, casting my spirit amidst the trees in search of my master's hut.

I found it with little difficulty, its roof laden with a load of snow, a soft curl of gray smoke rising from its primary chimney. A grin spread across my face as I glanced around at the surrounding yard, the bushes and plants covered with snow, light footsteps visible upon the path to the threshold. Icicles decorated the eaves, and I smiled directly at them, my spirit's element causing them to tremble with answering fervor. It was hard to be depressed in such a magnificent world of frost; I should have entered the spiritual realm every day since winter's arrival.

I could not detect Augustin's presence inside the cottage, even though there was apparently a fire in his main fireplace. But I refused to let discouragement take hold of me now. If he was not there, perhaps he lurked somewhere in the nearby woodland. I would find him eventually. So I passed through the door into his hut with furtive caution, suddenly wondering what exactly *would* happen if Augustin chose to notice me. Would he welcome me, or run, or torture me further?

I blinked my blue eyes in the gloom of his front room, the weak blue flames flickering in the fireplace the sole sign that someone had been there recently. I cast my gaze around the chamber in its entirety, taking in the couch beneath the window, the bookshelf, the wooden cabinet, the writing desk and stools. I drifted forward to set the silver acorn upon his desk beside an inkwell, glancing briefly at the parchment that his pen had touched most recently. My elemental eyes recognized Ælte Teutonica in the dimness, so I frowned a little and turned away, knowing that my master wished to keep his private writings to himself.

I turned my attention to the rest of his cottage, resolved to check each nook even though my Teuton spirit sensed no trace of blue fire aside from what smoldered in the main hearth. I passed through his pantry and tiny kitchen, both totally ensconced in darkness, and at last I entered his bedroom, laying eyes upon his empty bed, the place he never slept—except when he met me in his dreams.

I wondered for a fleeting moment whether he had slept at all since June, shaking my head as I looked around at the other contents of his bedroom: the massive wardrobe, the washing table, the mirror, his private writing desk, the rather imposing iron cauldron in the corner—which he likely used for heathen fire-play—the wall sconces holding unlit candles, the myriad of ledges laden with papers and rather devilish sculptures and objects. My eyes drifted to the window, blocked by heavy black curtains, letting no light into the room. My spirit sagged in disappointment; Augustin was not here.

I drifted back outside with a frown, silently asking the winter to lighten my mood, to infuse my spirit with glory so I could appreciate a dance if nothing else. I did not wish to remain in the spiritual realm for too much longer, even though I had asked Ulka to keep my family away from me. Then I remembered that time I had gone to the archives as a spirit to witness the destruction of Augustin's written records. Prince Otto and his helpful partner Rupert had sensed my presence in the archives when I had squealed. Perhaps if I made some noise, Augustin would notice me here and decide to come out of hiding.

So I stepped back to the riverbank, allowing my feet to merge with the snow as I sent my senses out from me in all directions, seeking his fire. He *had* to be somewhere near, or he would not have kept those embers burning in his fireplace. My ice detected nothing save the snowy winter, so I closed my eyes and screamed his name with the voice of my spirit, using all the vitality I had: *AUGUSTIN!*

My spirit quivered with the effort, and I almost thought I could hear my voice echoed in the waters of the Rhine and in the flurries blowing with the breeze. I leapt onto the river in the next instant, using its wakes as a springboard to jump to the highest branch of the tallest tree on the German side of the Rhine, my blue eyes scouring the landscape intently. I heard birds chirping, wind whirling, squirrels rustling in their leafy nests . . . but no answer to my cry. So I tried again, my mental voice seeming to pierce the sky itself: *AUGUSTIN!*

I waited for at least ten minutes according to my internal clock, but none of my senses picked up any sort of response. I sagged, the color of my robes dulling into the gray of the Rhine. I jumped down to the forest floor, shaking my head at my own folly. Of course he would not answer me. Who was I but the foolish woman who refused to let him go? He could love me alone if he wished, leaving me permanently destitute. Wuotan would train him to forsake love eventually.

As I prepared to thrust myself back into my body, my disenchantment filling me with sorrow, a sudden inspiration seized me, and I zoomed back to his hut. *I'm in the real spiritual realm this time, not some fake dream world . . . that means I can actually* touch *things . . . .*

Passing through his front door a second time, I tripped lightly to his writing desk in the far corner, my eyes roving quickly over its contents. I settled my spirit upon his stool, squinting slightly in the dim light and retrieving a feather pen and a blank sheet of paper. I wound the fingers of my right hand around the pen, smiling at how solid it felt in my hand. Then I dipped it once into a well of black ink and wrote a short message upon the paper before me in Bayerisch, my handwriting flowing in the style he had taught me: *I love you. Come back to me.*

I thought for a moment, then decided that would suffice. If the silver acorn did not awaken his interest enough to return to me, my message ought to do it. After laying the pen down and rising from the stool, my eyes noticed the low blue flames flickering in the fireplace. A new idea struck me, and I snatched a candle from the desk and leapt at the fireplace, lighting the wick deftly. I set the now-lit candle in its holder upon the desk, nodding in approval at the ghostly glow it cast upon my message. Then I lifted my face to the ceiling and hurtled my spirit into the sky, abating my ice, sending myself back into my fragile body.

I went about the remainder of my routine that winter afternoon with a tiny smile upon my lips, keeping a new secret deep within my heart. Whether Augustin would choose to answer my call or not, he certainly could ignore me no longer. I resolved to seek him in spirit form every day until I found him, and plague him like a ghost until he met me once more. My love for him had not wavered due to his cruelty, and if he still loved me, I wanted us to share it together once again.

That night when I crawled into bed, I cannot say that I expected a positive dream. I knew that optimism tended to result in disappointment, for me at least. So when my reveries began, I drifted along with them peacefully, thinking little of their plots. But when I found myself walking beside the Isar about a half kilometer from the city wall, the starlight glinting off of the frosty meadow and icy waters of the waters before me, I abruptly noticed a new presence in the night. A phantom hid in a stand of trees not far from the riverbank, away from my sight. My eyes widened, and my awareness came back to me in a flash when I looked down swiftly at my clothing—the pearly white of moonlit snow. My mouth opened in a gasp, and I trotted over to the clump of snow-coated trees, sensing that familiar cobalt fire skulking there for the first time in what seemed like forever.

I passed between two withering lindens and found Augustin, his fiery robes appearing more dismal than usual, his face turned downward to the ground, the locks of his long hair hiding his eyes from my sight. I stepped forward cautiously, unsure how I ought to greet this dejected spirit, this devil's slave who had avoided my presence for nine long months. So I froze in the snow in the center of the glade of lindens and waited for him to speak first, assuming he found the courage.

After an eternity, Augustin spoke, the voice of his spirit sounding incredibly miserable. "I heard you call for me today." He did not lift his head.

I waited a beat, then asked softly, "Did you . . . find my note?"

A long pause. "Yes." He still stared at the ground.

I glanced around at the trees, then gathered my nerve. "I was afraid . . . afraid . . . that you wouldn't . . . answer." My voice wavered, and my spirit began to tremble. He said nothing to this, so I went on, trying not to sound scared or desperate. "I read your message . . . before I left Eisenwald." I paused, collecting my thoughts, then admitted, "If you hadn't sent me that note . . . I may have actually believed . . . that you had decided . . . decided . . . ." I could not form the words.

Augustin raised his head at last, his eyes staring first at the robes covering my chest, then gradually lifting to my face. In his eyes, and in the weak set of his usually firm chin, I read all of his remorse, all of his sorrow, all of his fear. He had not meant to hurt me; I saw it clearly now, as I looked into his soul. When Wuotan had used him to torture me, it had shattered his heart because he loved me. I could feel it at last, emanating from his spirit, caressing my face with the breeze. He could not simply choose to stop loving me any more than I could decide to stop loving him. We were joined forever, not by some mystical bond but by shared desires, shared dreams, shared intellect, shared loyalty.

He walked forward slowly to stand a centimeter from my chest, tilting his head down to meet my eyes, the hair of his spirit brushing forward to meld with my cheeks. "Decided . . . what?" he inquired.

I had been about to say that I had feared that he had decided to stop loving me, but now, saying so would be absurd. His love enfolded me as he stared into my eyes, his contrition over what he had done to me washing away all of my uncertainties. I shook my head at him and breathed, "It doesn't matter now."

A low moan sounded in his throat, and he reached his left hand out to my face, tracing its curve. I shivered at the thought of how it would have felt, if he had done it in the mortal world. His jaw trembled, and he murmured quietly, his voice breaking over the phrases, "There are not . . . words . . . in any tongue . . . to describe my sorrow . . . for the wrongs . . . I have done to you." He broke off, and his left hand drifted away from my face to curl into a tense fist. "If I could . . . steal the murderer's song . . . and use it to change the past . . . I would do so. I have not . . . been myself . . . since I . . . hurt you. I tried . . . to die . . . countless times . . . ."

The extent of his regret struck me hard. I reached my own hand out to his face, imagining that I could feel its heat and the silkiness of his long hair. "Augustin," I whispered, passion tingeing my speech, "you are forgiven. It wasn't your choice to do the things you did to me. I know your heart. You are still my master, and you are still my love. Nothing you can do will ever change that."

Augustin groaned, stepping swiftly away from me onto the riverbank. "It pains me that I cannot erase those acts from my memory. And there was a part of me that reveled in them—a part I long to crush. I confronted my master in early September about what he made me do to you . . . and I concluded a deal that should bar him from using me to punish you ever again. If he forces me to hurt your heart I shall beg to be sent to hell. You should not forgive me so freely, Swanhilde . . . I made you my sacrifice . . . something I had promised never to do." His voice broke, and he cried out in anguish, sinking to his knees in the snow.

His revelations churned in my mind, and I flew to him to place my left arm around his fiery robes. "Augustin, I can forgive you. I can, because I know you're not a devil, not a beast, no matter what Wuotan wants you to believe. You're a man, a human just like me. We all fall into darkness sometimes." His spirit shuddered at my words, and I endeavored to brighten his spirit with the hope that animated my own. "Master, please . . . put your hands upon my heart again . . . feel its love. I know you won't hurt me. Please don't despair."

At length, Augustin raised his head from between his knees, tears of fire staining his cheeks as he blinked his eyes at the Isar. I felt him grasp my heart in the next moment, the sensation prompting me to gasp with renewed desire. I concentrated on my love, on my devotion to him despite his faults. I closed my eyes while I silently urged him to believe me, to love me, to forgive what Wuotan had led him to do. After a long pause, I felt both of his hands enclose my heart, his sorrow rushing into my spirit along with his love, its currents strong and powerful like a river.

"Swanhilde, look at me," he requested softly. When I opened my eyes I saw that his spiritual fire had brightened considerably. His countenance reflected the glory of the night as he smiled at me at last. "Thank you," he mumbled —and that was all he said.

I smiled back at him, relieved that we were on speaking terms again after such a long separation. "Don't try to kill yourself anymore, okay?" I said, concern seeping into my veins at the thought of his confession. "If you succeeded somehow . . . I don't think I could survive without you."

Augustin chuckled, his expression rather sly. "There shall be no success for me until someone else survives the filial curse, my darling swan. You need not fear." I grinned in relief, and Augustin's gaze drifted downward to my feet.

"Is your body healing properly?" he questioned, his tone hesitant.

"I think so," I said, thinking of my weak ankles, crooked toes, and the ache that had not yet left my innards at peace. I shoved all of those problems into the back of my mind and added, "But I still can't dance in the mortal world. I use a stick when I walk. I feel like a prisoner, shackled inside during this magnificent winter."

Augustin held his right hand out to me. "So dance with me now, my lovely swan princess," he coaxed. "Let your spiritual feet run across this frozen landscape without pain, without hindrance." With a rapturous smile, I indulged his wish.

Chapter Twenty-four:
A Tuneful Outlet

My life returned to some semblance of normalcy after Augustin and I had overcome our difficulties. He visited me in my dreams for three consecutive nights, and we held serious discussions on the current status of our relationship and its possible future. He apologized for his behavior more times than I could count, sobbing fiery tears on several occasions for how deeply he had betrayed me. The wicked side of him had enjoyed the violence with appropriate thrill, he confessed, but another part of him had wailed within during the whole ordeal. He had felt each stab of pain that had struck my body and spirit due to the intimacy of our bond, which he could not completely ignore, though he had tried.

Afterward, Wuotan had congratulated him extensively on his triumph over me, but Augustin asserted that his master's praise had meant nothing to him. Instead, once he finally found the strength to rise from the sorrow in which he wallowed, he confronted Wuotan with a vengeance, threatening to spurn him entirely should he try to hurt me again. He informed his master that our devotion would remain no matter how he tried to tear us asunder, that it would be better for him to allow his Black Priest to cherish his one source of love without obstruction. Augustin refused to reveal the details of the agreement that they had reached, but he swore that he would never hurt me again.

Augustin admitted on the third night that it seemed love overpowered hate after all, at least in some ways. He declared that his memory of my love would never fade, and my willingness to forgive his brutality had solidified it permanently in his heart. He would love me even in hell; and for the remainder of his existence upon earth, he would shoulder Wuotan's rebukes gladly, as long as he could cling to the memory of our love. He promised never to break our heart-bond without my permission and added that he would not even suggest the option again unless some insuperable fate pulled us asunder. The tides of time may sever our connection, but they would not expunge his memories. He would reminisce about our shared commitment until final death took him, glorying in the fulfillment we had gained during our years together.

I told Augustin in return that I would always love him, even while I lived my life in the twenty-first century, separated from him by nearly a thousand years. I acknowledged somewhat grudgingly that although the insane part of me wished to stay with him forever, my future would likely not allow this. I would do my best to move on with my life in my own era and consign my time with him to my private musings. I asserted that while I would never be able to convince myself to properly love Joel here in the eleventh century, perhaps one day things would work out better for both of us. I reminded Augustin that if Joel died before the fall of Muniche, he ought to join me at the Thaden estate, the nearness of his hated ex-family notwithstanding. He did not seem to endorse this proposal, but he pledged to continue meeting me in the *Gæstelort Troumerae* at least twice per week for our studies and any other activities I wished to share with him, making full use of what time we had left.

I found myself pregnant once more in December of 1056, for my womb had apparently decided that it had some vitality left even after Augustin's abuse. I still had trouble walking at that point, and it became more difficult to push myself out of bed in the mornings as my body burgeoned with excess weight yet again. I spent the final months of my pregnancy confined in my bedroom, my feet, face, and arms swollen with retained water. I had a strong suspicion that my blood pressure had risen dangerously, for my head often ached. Sometimes I sensed the labored throbbing of my heart beneath my clothing.

I informed Joel sharply more than once that he would have to just jerk off from now on if he wanted release, for I refused to go through this anymore. "It's not like I'm well enough to run off on you anyway," I told him tersely, "so you can stop feeling the need to plant your seed in a rotting pot." Joel shook his head and murmured in a soothing voice that I would heal when all was said and done and we could talk it over then.

In August of 1057, I bore a black-haired, gray-eyed daughter after a painful, prolonged labor. She looked so much like me that I almost burst with pride when I held her to my breast for the first time, as Freia and Gretchen worked to stanch the blood and discharge from my vagina. Joel grinned at my elation and announced that since our fifth daughter looked so much like her mother, I may have the privilege of naming her. I cocked an eyebrow at him and said that he had just run out of ideas for Germanic names, which prompted him to shrug with a guilty smile.

I ultimately chose to name her Erika Freia, after my best Teuton friends from the present and the future. Freia blushed when I told her and promised to name her next daughter after me, if God blessed her with another. Her most recent child has been a son, named Edwin after Freia's father. She had weaned him just two months before she came to aid me in my labor.

Things settled down again for the next few years. Our crops continued to pull a substantial profit each year, and the worst primeval diseases avoided our land. Joel actually took my wishes into account for once and insisted only rarely that we get intimate. When he did so, he rolled off of me to ejaculate into our chamber pot, claiming that he had heard that trick from Leo, our head vassal. "It's better than beating off," he maintained, while I rolled my eyes at the subjects that the males in our charge apparently discussed. I found it hard to understand their preoccupation with sex after childbirth had dulled my body's response.

Sometimes I mused longingly about the vibrator Erika had given me back home, with her staunch declaration that women could please themselves without making a mess. I suspected that such a tool could solve my problem. Augustin had gotten me off three times with just his fingers, after all. But my ridiculous husband was too daft to think of such a thing.

My feet and legs grew stronger over time, and I began to push my limits by pacing the garden paths and gradually traversing the staircases. Although they still appeared yellowed and weak, I started dreaming of using my feet as I once had, to bring music to the world around me. But I certainly could not do that without practice. I had not touched the organ since 1044, and I feared that my hands and feet no longer remembered how to create wondrous melodies on such an imposing instrument. The two pipe organs in Muniche stood in the Bayern castle and the cathedral, played only by privileged men. But I wondered whether it may be possible to build an organ in the great hall, against the wall that connected with the main house. Then I could retrain myself to play like I once had without any interference.

I shared my musings with Viktor first, on a Friday afternoon in October of 1058. He was in the process of sweeping the front porch while I sat on the bench facing the gardens, my back against the house and a cup of chamomile tea clasped in my hands. "I really miss hearing the organ at mass," I said in Magyar, figuring that he had likely never heard the instrument played under any other circumstances.

"As do I, my lady," Viktor responded, his broom sending bits of leaves and dust to the ground below the porch. His arthritis had slowed him substantially in recent years, but he continued to perform his tasks without complaint. His faithful service had impressed me over the years.

"Then you've heard the organ at Muniche's cathedral?" I asked.

"Many times, in many cities. Buda, Brezalausburc, Wien, Linz, Muniche." He paused in his work to straighten his back, a wince creasing his face.

I brought my teacup to my lips, not having expected Viktor to be a connoisseur of organ music. But the faraway look in his eyes told me that he had relished many a tune throughout his life. "I used to play the organ many years ago, before I came to Muniche," I recalled, my lower legs shifting restlessly beneath my skirt, longing to dance upon the pedalboard anew.

"It is majestic music, far different from the lutes and fiddles often heard." The old Magyar had returned to his duties, sweeping each step that led to the porch.

"I've been thinking about having one built here, in this house, in the great hall," I confessed at length, my fingers quivering where they gripped my teacup. "I fear that my husband may think me mad."

"I would be honored to admire your talents," Viktor said, looking up at me from beneath his mop of gray hair. "I imagine your songs to be far more whimsical than the melodies played at mass."

I chuckled and admitted that he might be right. I shared my longings with Joel that night. Since our farm had prospered significantly in the past harvests, I said that perhaps we could spend a bit of our reserves on something that would enrich our lives while we awaited the end. My husband looked thoughtful and said that it would depend on what I had in mind. So I gathered my courage and told him that I wished to have a pipe organ built in the great hall, the chamber with a towering ceiling. At first, Joel ogled me as though I had lost my mind; but after thoroughly explaining my idea, he gave his wholehearted consent.

We commissioned Heinrich and his best metalworkers to fashion the pipes and asked the master of the sawmill to build the console. We had to import some of the necessary materials from other lands, and the venture cost us a large chunk of our savings. But we could sell the metal and wood again later to make up for our loss, I reassured Joel, perhaps during the summer of 1065. In the meantime, both of us could enjoy the glories of music again, for he had long since taught himself how to play the lute. He often plucked it by firelight in the evenings while I sang Teutonic ballads and various songs of the future.

The organ was completed in April of 1059, right after the vassals had begun to plant the barley and flax. I tested it for the first time one night as Jarvis pumped the bellows, carefully pressing each key one by one, listening to the varying tones of the different stops. I had included a grand total of fourteen stops ranging from rank two to sixteen. There were four flutes, three principals, four strings, and three horns—a trumpet, cornet, and oboe. The organ had two keyboards and a full-sized pedalboard, and thanks to the skills of Paulus von Bayern—who had taken an interest in its construction, to my vexation—each keyboard had its own set of stops, so I could play the trumpet on one and strings on another. Each key seemed to work exactly right. After a barrage of encouragement from the children, Joel, and the few servants who stood nearby—including Viktor —I slid onto the organ bench, situating myself to *play* for the first time in a long time.

I knew that if I could remember any of the glorious pieces I had once played, I could not do them justice without using the pedals—and I had no organ shoes as yet. So I would have to start with something simpler: my favorite German hymn. I hit several softer stops and began to play, my fingers stumbling nearly as often as my feet. I ordered myself not to be discouraged and played the hymn four times. My fingers and feet found the proper notes without fault by the final stanza. My audience applauded when I had finished. The three older children clamored to be taught to play the organ, while Viktor nodded at me with a look of respect.

During the next few weeks, I practiced playing the complex pieces that I had mastered years before. I ran through them on the keyboards and pedals while the bellows stood silent, so no one would have to suffer through hearing my mistakes. I rode to Muniche one morning for an appointment with the local shoemaker, who, after measuring my feet and taking down copious notes on the proper method of fashioning organ shoes, vowed to finish my pair by the end of the week. Subsequently, I turned my horse toward the cathedral, wanting to seek out some contemporary music scores if there were any to be found. I needed to practice my sight-reading, and I wished to perfect my ability to interpret medieval music, just in case Prince Otto ever changed his mind about his song.

In one of the small chapels that branched off from the main nave, I found Paulus von Bayern, the person I needed to ask about obtaining sheet music. Despite my general distaste for the middle Bayern brother, I had realized over the years that his talent with organ music was considerable. After hearing him play for quite a few Sunday masses and special celebrations, I had concluded that while his royal brother could claim the title of composer, Paulus had more skill at interpreting the music. Whenever he played his younger brother's melodies in the candlelit cathedral, chills would run up my spine as my soul drifted along with the tones of the pipes. I curtseyed once in Paulus' deference when he turned to meet me. After exchanging a few cursory pleasantries, I asked him if he knew where I could find some organ scores, so I could put them to use on the pipe organ in my home.

He replied in his tenor voice that he had several stored in the basement of the cathedral. He beckoned me to follow him there, and it took some time for me to make it down the basement staircase. Paulus made a few inquiries about my new pipe organ, which I answered courteously. He commented rather tentatively that he might like to play my organ himself later in the fall. My stomach churned a bit at this idea, and I did not reply. I had seen too much of Paulus in recent months due to the building of the organ. Though I respected his musical talents, I still considered him a coward since he would soon betray our people to the Saxons, paving the way for Muniche's destruction.

I chose four scores to carry back to the manor with me, three of them written by Prince Otto, the fourth by a Catholic priest who had passed away some time before. When we ascended the staircase to the main floor, I told Paulus that I would return the scores as soon as I had memorized them, which prompted him to turn around to stare at me. "Would you mind telling me, my Lady Swanhilde, where you learned to play the organ . . . so masterfully?" he queried, halting two steps from the main floor to gaze down at me inquisitively.

My lips twisted into a slightly scornful frown as I recalled that one song I had played at the Bayern castle back in 1044, and Augustin's haughty words: *This woman plays more masterfully than either of you.* Apparently, Paulus had not forgotten that incident. Since he knew full well that I was from the future, I decided in a flash to throw my atypical knowledge in his face. "I was taught by a Teuton priest, Father Paulus," I said stiffly, thinking of Hans, "and I was actually studying organ performance at the university before I came here."

Surprise appeared in his blue-gray eyes. He nodded thoughtfully, his face appearing quite serious in the dimly lit corridor. Seeing that he intended to say no more, I decided to press my luck. My own curiosity had sprung to life in the presence of the man who could consider himself the eldest Bayern brother. "I'd like to ask you a personal question in return, Father Paulus, if you would permit the intrusion?" His eyes darkened, and he glanced briefly toward the doorway behind him before nodding at me. I looked him square in the eye and asked, "Did you agree with the filial curse?"

His expression clouded over with ambiguity, and a moment later he spun away from me, walking swiftly to the main floor and down the hallway with nary a backward glance. I pursued him haltingly as he returned to the small chapel, not wanting to let him escape without granting me a concrete answer. When he paused at the altar before the rood that pictured Christ's crucifixion, I addressed him again, my voice urgent and out of breath. "Please, Father . . . I must know."

After a long silence, he turned to face me, his brown robe sweeping the floor, his hands clasped rather agitatedly before him. "My lady, my opinions matter not. The Cursed One's fate is regrettable, but such trials befall the unrepentant sinner."

That summer, Prince Otto mustered his forces again to counter renewed Saxon incursions along the northern border. Joel joined the Prince's army as before, along with fourteen of our young vassals, leaving Jarvis and me to handle the estate. Viktor passed away during the flax harvest. One of the peasant women found him unresponsive on the front path through the flower gardens with his broom clutched in his hand, likely dead of a heart attack or stroke.

The old Magyar's absence plunged me into a renewed vat of mourning, for I missed the conversations we had shared in his native language about Augustin. And now I had no aged connoisseur of music lounging upon a bench whenever I practiced the organ in the great hall, his ears keeping track of my stumbling progress. But I supposed that it was best that Viktor had gone now with the Teuton lands still at peace. He would never have been able to flee to the mountains in his arthritic state.

When most of the troops returned at the cusp of winter, Joel told me that our doom was nigh, for Paulus had been captured.

Chapter Twenty-five:
An Unexpected Guest

During the winter of 1059-60, Joel and I spent almost all of our private moments furtively discussing the impending apocalypse. A mood of morbidity had sunk its hellish claws into both of us, though we had six years left before our home would fall prey to our enemies from the north. I discovered that Joel seemed a bit chary about the notion of perishing in the siege of 1066. "I don't know if I really want to . . . *starve* to death," he confessed awkwardly late one evening while we sat together in our bed, the blankets pulled up around us against the winter's chill. "Sometimes I think I'd rather die in battle than suffer through the siege."

I said nothing for a moment, covertly studying my husband out of the corner of my eye. Joel would turn thirty-six in the spring. I decided when I looked at him that though his body still appeared sturdy overall, years of medieval toil had taken their toll on his youthful vigor. His fingers were rough and blackened from frostbite, and several permanent lines creased his forehead, hidden beneath his thick blond hair. Underneath his beard, his mouth seemed to have acquired an enduring set of discontent and worry. I wondered if Joel had taken a liking to his life as a landed lord. Maybe he feared to see it all turn to dust, to get thrust back to the future in the most violent way possible. In some ways, I knew how he felt.

So I stretched my right hand out to touch his arm gently. "I'm sure there'll be lots of battles between now and the end. If you join the Prince's army each time, you may end up dying from a Saxon's sword or axe," I said. "Maybe even a mace. Or you might get crushed by a boulder. They'll have to break the walls down somehow." Joel cringed and pulled his arm away.

"But you really shouldn't worry about things we can't change," I added. "I told you from the beginning, when we were floating down the Isar on that log, that I came here to see my people fall. It won't be a pretty sight, but I'm planning to face it. I won't hold it against you if you choose to die beforehand. I could look after the estate myself for a few years. But the end is coming for both of us, one way or another." Joel grimaced, and I attempted to put the situation into a slightly optimistic light as I suggested, "Look at it this way. In six years, we'll both be back in the year 2000, back to our families and friends, back to our old way of life."

Joel sighed heavily, his hazel eyes shifting to meet mine. "I've been thinking about that a lot, lately," he said, his expression guarded. "Trying to figure out how Beth's going to react when she finds out I screwed *you* for twenty years."

My eyebrows came together, and I scooted to the edge of the bed. That was a subject that I preferred not to ponder, for in truth, my most cherished friendship of the twenty-first century may shatter to pieces when faced with how Joel and I had spent our time together. "Not only that, you became a Teuton," I mentioned, wrapping my arms around my torso, gathering the blanket close. "I spent five years telling Beth it was too dangerous for her to try the blood-transfer. But we both did it, and she's going to find out."

"And she'll want to do it too," Joel predicted, turning his face away again, his jaw clenching. "How do they even . . . *do* that in the modern era? I can't imagine a platform set up in downtown München so people can watch a blood-transfer. That sort of thing would make the news."

"It's done in private. But I can't let Beth try it, no matter how upset she gets when she finds out about you."

"My parents are going to be weirded out when I stop going shirtless at home," Joel said, an amused snort escaping his nostrils. "But wait a minute. Are you sure I'll still have Teuton blood when we go back? You said that we get back—"

"In the same instant that we left," I interrupted with a nod. "But some things remain, from what I read. I'm pretty sure the blood-transfer is one of those things, because it's a really significant change. Teuton blood is forever."

Joel wrinkled his nose and leaned back upon his pillow, his gaze fixed upon the ceiling above us. "What about our marriage scars?"

I chewed on my lip and leaned back on my elbows myself, my eyes drifting toward the pink scar that had ornamented my left wrist since 1045. "Teutonic marriages are broken by death, and we're going to have to die to get back," I said.

A noise of assent rumbled in Joel's chest, and then he admitted, "I guess I don't really mind dying, but I was always sort of hoping that one day Prince Otto would break down and give you his song, so we could get home the easy way." My lips twisted at his words, for I had hoped the same thing for years, though with the passing of time I had begun to relinquish my wishes on that subject.

"It's just really hard sometimes, Swanie," Joel continued, turning his head to look at me as he switched back to the earlier subject. "It's hard seeing everything happening before my eyes when I can't do anything to stop it. I feel like my hands are chained and my tongue has been pulled out. A bunch of times, I've wanted to tell Heinrich the truth about Muniche's fall, but I always have to keep silent. And I have to hold back from ridiculing the Prince's stupid attempts to make peace. All the other soldiers applaud his ingenuity, while I stand in the background knowing it won't do any good."

"We've done what we could, Joel," I assured him, the darkness of the coming doom striking me afresh. "You've fought for the Teutons, and you'll keep fighting until death takes you. And I'll hold the fort here when you're away in battle, like I've always done. Just remember, even though we can't change what's going to happen, we *will* save our children." I reached out to squeeze his hand.

Joel's gaze softened, and a weary smile played upon his lips. After months of serious discussion, we had decided to send our whole brood to Eisenwald in the spring of 1066, so they could reach the safety of the Rhineland before the Saxons conquered Muniche in July. "Do you really think they'll be able to make the journey safely if they leave in March?" Joel asked, his fingers sliding away from mine to grip the blanket in silent tension. "I mean, I know it took us just under a month, when we went to Eisenwald before. But what if the Saxons send scouts into Schwäbisch lands, or what if the Schwabs turn against us?" His hazel eyes locked with mine, shining with anxiety.

"They should be fine," I replied earnestly, thinking back to the many books I had read about the fall of the Teutons before I had come to the eleventh century. "According to the main Teuton history, *Der Weg,* the Saxons will attack from the northeast, avoiding Schwabia and the Rhineland on their quest to wipe out our people. Their armies will be reinforced by Slavs, Bohemians, and a few mercenaries, and of course they'll have the unspoken support of Rome. According to all of the writings, Teuton and foreign, the Teutons who managed to escape the conquest fled to the west and south, mingling themselves with the smaller tribes of southern Germany and Switzerland." I cocked an eyebrow at my husband. "Since Freia's father forgave his oldest daughter for becoming a Teuton by blood, I'm sure he'll welcome our children into his settlement."

Joel looked pensive, but he nodded at my rationale, his expression that of a man who endeavors to accept destiny's tide despite its disastrous flow. And images of my people's defeat played across my mind while I slipped into slumber, the sketch of burning walls, broken turrets. Part of me longed for a stronger body so I could fight, but my weakened feet would not allow for such a thing. Maybe I could convince Augustin to avenge Muniche after the Saxons had ravaged her. His death gift could make a decisive impact, one that could shift the currents of history.

One afternoon in late February, I opened the front door to an unexpected visitor after the older children had finished their studies and gone outside with Joel for a few games before dinner. I sat in the front parlor reading the German half of my Bible when a persistent knock interrupted me. I would not have answered the door at all, but Jarvis was outside meeting with the vassals, and the other servants were working upstairs or preparing the evening meal. After a pause, I laid my reading aside and rose from the couch to receive the guest.

When I swung the door open and found myself staring up at Prince Otto, I almost jumped back and slammed the door in his face. I had not realized that he had finally returned to the city, for he had not come back with his army. He had negotiated for months with some Saxon lords in a vain attempt to secure his brother's release. Now he stood centimeters from me, his thick fur coat trailing the boards of the porch, his snow boots appearing perfectly shined, his fur hat covering his black hair against the cold wind. My eyes widened, and I may have blushed, for I wore a common dress that day and had left my head uncovered. My unimpressive exterior did not seem to faze the Prince. He bowed at me in all propriety and greeted, "My Lady Swanhilde Hudson von Thaden."

The fact that I had not spoken one-on-one with Prince Otto since his New Year's party of 1053—seven years ago—surfaced rather abruptly in my mind. I rushed to curtsey at him, uncertainty overtaking me as I returned his salutation. "*Leitaeri*, Prince Otto von Bayern. Please allow me to apologize for my unsuitable attire. I was not expecting any visitors today."

The Keyholder waved one gloved hand at me in an unconcerned fashion. "Your apology is unnecessary, Lady Swanhilde. I should have sent word before disturbing you today."

"Please come inside, *Leitaeri*," I said, trying to beat down the gnawing panic I felt as I tried to figure out why he had come. He had never before graced the Thaden Estate, to my knowledge. I took his coat and hat and showed him to Joel's high-backed chair by the fireplace, for it was the grandest one we had. In the next instant I turned for the kitchen, so I could ask the servants to prepare some tea and bread.

"My lady, you need not concern yourself with refreshments, for I do not intend to stay long," the Prince called out when I exited the parlor, prompting me to halt my retreat. "There are merely a few matters I wish to discuss with you, and then I shall leave you in peace." He gestured that I should sit across from him upon the couch.

I moved to obey him, my ice trickling into my veins, heightening my senses, testing the atmosphere. I was fairly alone with the Prince; everyone else worked in separate chambers. I exhaled once, placing my hands carefully in my lap as I lifted my eyes to my visitor. He wore an elegant tunic of deep crimson and bronze, his dark leather trousers topped off with an impressive belt, the keys of Muniche hanging from it. Around his neck he wore a jeweled chain of gold, and a ruby ring rested upon the middle finger of his left hand. His obviously expensive clothing prompted me to shrink back into the couch, for I looked like a maid in my plain tan dress and mud-colored clogs. *He really should have sent me word instead of barging in unannounced,* I thought in annoyance.

The silence dragged long between us while the Prince's blue eyes ran over the parlor in its entirety. "It is rather chilly here in your parlor, my lady," the Prince commented at length, his eyes narrowing at the smoldering embers in the fireplace. "I would deign to assume that your element restrains you from noticing the chill, however." His eyes shot to mine.

"The primary elements in this household are of water and air, *Leitaeri*," I said, a small smile playing upon my lips. "Therefore, at times we have the tendency to overlook the fire necessary for comfort in winter." My ice gloried in frigid rooms, and I generally avoided fireplaces when I wished to immerse myself in my element—that is, unless I was thinking of Augustin.

Prince Otto's eyes flashed scarlet, and he lifted his right hand in the direction of the hearth with the query, "If you would permit me, my lady?" My eyes widened, and I gave a nod of assent. A moment later, he cast a burst of red flames upon the embers, causing them to flare brilliantly, giving the entire parlor a crimson glow. "Much better," the Prince said with a cursory nod, and I shook my head tolerantly, holding back my desire to thrust a few blue flames upon the mantel to even things out.

"I would presume, *Leitaeri*, that you did not come here for the purpose of simply displaying your fiery gifts." I looked Prince Otto directly in the eyes, his evasive behavior frustrating me. Teuton priests rarely bothered with preambles. He needed to get to the point so I could resume my Bible reading and forget his visit.

"You are quite correct, my Lady Swanhilde. I came to speak with you regarding my brother Paulus." I jerked at this pronouncement, a thousand thoughts racing through my head. The Prince's jaw hardened, his dark blue eyes cataloguing my reactions. "Your husband has certainly informed you that my brother was taken captive by a stealthy band of Saxons while we engaged them outside of Thuringia, and that I remained behind when my army returned in order to negotiate his release."

I nodded once, and the Prince continued. "Though I parleyed for weeks, I could not obtain his freedom. They would not accept my offers of ransom, and I fear that in the summer, I shall be forced to lead my armies north once more, into Saxon lands, to pressure them to release Paulus. Our enemies may regard such an intrusion as an act of war, but unfortunately it may be necessary—for my brother, as my closest consort, holds a vast amount of classified information that must be protected at all costs." A pained expression crossed his habitually hard face.

I suddenly suspected that he had come to my house for the express purpose of coercing me to reveal information on the future. Why else would he grouse about Paulus' predicament? Exasperation shot through my veins at this impending interrogation, but I held myself in check and remarked, "Forgive me, *Leitaeri*, but should you not bring these issues before your knights and battle commanders rather than before a woman? I fear I have no expertise to impart on the subjects of skirmishes and prisoners." My eyes narrowed, a hint of blue enhancing my vision.

"Oh, but you do, my Lady Swanhilde, for you are the Teuton woman from the future, the one who holds truths in her heart regarding the ultimate fate of our people." The Prince stared into my eyes, his posture in the chair rather stiff. "The last time we spoke, you informed me with a touch of impertinence that you do not travel time lightly, and that your presence here in this era should disturb me. I must admit that at first I shrugged off your admonition; but now, in the face of my elder brother's imprisonment, I wish to seek your counsel." His eyes seemed to examine my soul as he leaned forward slightly in Joel's chair, the ambience of the parlor growing oppressively warm.

My ice had frozen me upon the couch. The intensity of the Prince's stare unnerved me. My brain began to make wild speculations on whether he might attempt to bleed me right here in my own parlor, to satisfy his curiosity. I thought for a moment, trying to discern exactly what I *could* tell him. After an interminable pause, I found my voice. "*Leitaeri*, I must beg your forgiveness, but I cannot divulge certain information to you any more than you could share your own secrets with me." My tone sounded high and fearful, so I cleared my throat before admitting, "It is true that I have more insight on the next few years than . . . your advisors. But I swore an oath in coming here, and it chains me to silence on future events."

The Prince's eyes narrowed, still glittering red as he studied me. His mouth twitched once, and then he said,

"Though I endeavored to convince myself that you had come to this era merely to scrutinize Teutonic prosperity, I have found that I cannot ignore human nature. My lady, no fallen man or woman wishes to watch success. Abundance, though aesthetically satisfying, is nevertheless dull. I have traveled time thrice, and two of my journeys involved ignominious moments in history: the crucifixion of Christ and subsequent persecution of His followers, and more recently, the Peloponnesian War."

My eyes widened at this. Though I had little interest in the history of ancient Greece, I could appreciate the practicality of observing the battles between Athens and Sparta. If Prince Otto had gone there, he probably knew how to speak and read Greek. I wondered briefly what Augustin would think of that. Thoughts of the Peloponnesian War revolved in my mind for another moment, and I murmured quietly, "Thucydides," which prompted the Prince to jerk in surprise. But before he could question me on my familiarity with ancient Greece, I lifted my gaze to his and inquired, "Where did you go on your third journey?"

Hesitation clouded the Prince's features, warring with what seemed to be grief, and he answered shortly, "My third journey was for personal reasons." My fingers froze again as I discerned that he must have gone back to share a few more hours with Kezia, his beloved wife from the first century. I frowned, for at least the Prince had the option to visit his beloved. I remained shackled to Muniche, unable to meet Augustin except in my dreams.

"My Lady Swanhilde," the Prince went on, bringing my thoughts back to the present, "you must understand, in light of the events I have chosen to observe through time travel, that as the ruler of this city, I am concerned about the eventual fate of its inhabitants, since both you and your husband dwell in proximity, silently awaiting 1064."

I almost snickered at his preoccupation with 1064, likely a result of our first confrontation, when I admitted that I had planned to come to Muniche that year. At length, I sighed and made an ambiguous reply. "The future shall come to pass, *Leitaeri*, and neither you nor I hold any sway in delaying it. I came here to observe, not to interfere, to become a part of the past, not to change what is past." I quoted the opening spell of the Torstein, a small smile curling upon my lips.

The Prince's eyes took on a numinous glint, and he intoned, speaking Ælte Teutonica, "I seek the past to learn, to return forever changed . . . restored as I was, but new." My mouth fell open as I recognized segments from the final phrases associated with using the Torstein. *But he won't create the rock until 1074 . . . how in the world does he already know the words?* Shivers ran down my spine, for I realized that Prince Otto knew far more about time travel than I did. He had likely consulted Wuotan many times regarding its possibilities.

"It perplexes me, my Lady Swanhilde," the Prince said, relaxing his tense posture at last as he leaned back in Joel's chair, "that you seem to hold the oaths you swore in high esteem when speaking with me—and yet you undoubtedly revealed many secrets of the future to the Cursed One, years ago." His tone betrayed no frustration, merely a statement of fact.

That was true, and I squinted at the flames in the fireplace as I considered how best to answer the Prince's unspoken query: *Why do you trust him more than you trust the Keyholder of this city?* But I knew. If the Prince had any smarts, he would not have to ask my reasons. "*Leitaeri*," I said softly, meeting his fiery gaze once more, "I told the Cursed One all of my secrets for the same reason you told Kezia all of yours. I love him." I nodded at him gravely.

The Prince studied me for a long moment, his eyes searching my soul for something he, in his conceit, could not understand. When he addressed me again, his voice sounded hoarse and passionate. "My lady . . . how *could* you have honestly loved someone . . . like him?" He shook his head at me in apparent consternation.

"Because God loves even the worst of sinners, and someone had to give the Cursed One a chance," I replied.

"Our love spans the heavens, *Leitaeri*, and it won't be severed by time or circumstance." The Prince studied me in
silence, the stiffness of his jaw suggesting that he wished
to say something but could not decide what would suffice.

I rose from the couch a moment later and crossed the
room to retrieve the Prince's coat and hat. Now that we had
broached the subject of Augustin, I wanted him out of my
house before he infuriated me beyond control. He followed
me to the door, donning his outerwear without a word. As
I opened the door for him, the wintry air of nature erasing
all traces of his heat from the parlor, I spoke one promise
in parting. "*Leitaeri*, our people's fate has nothing to do
with any schemes of the Cursed One. I can say that with
complete confidence." He ducked his head at me and left
without speaking.

Chapter Twenty-six:
Alone

Late that summer, the Prince organized an expeditionary force comprised mainly of well-trained knights to march on Saxon territory in an attempt to pressure our foes into releasing Paulus. Joel was personally asked to accompany the Prince's army due to his impressive skills with the bow and arrow. Though I tried to dissuade him, he accepted his duties like a brave lord. I begged him to reconsider on several occasions, pointing out the imminent flax harvest and noting that we always made greater profits when he remained at home to oversee the trading.

But my husband shrugged off my concerns, promising that he would return as soon as possible and that in the meantime I could trust Jarvis to handle our business in his stead. He pounded me like a jackrabbit on the night before he left, not bothering to withdraw, and he pledged to return with a sizeable lump of spoils. "We may actually attack some towns this time, so I'll try to scrounge up some Saxon jewels for our kids to sell when they go to Eisenwald," he declared.

I prayed hard that his urge for carnality would pass without consequence, but I missed my period in September. I cursed my husband afresh, thinking that maybe I should stalk him in spirit form and slap him for getting me pregnant with Muniche's fall looming so near. I resolved that this would be my final child whether Joel wanted to get intimate upon his return or not. Of course, my body may not succeed at carrying my new responsibility to term. I had nearly miscarried Erika twice as a result of Augustin's abuse, and the subtle ache in my abdomen had never fully dissipated.

During the autumn and winter, I continued schooling our children, young Helmut included, focusing on Bible lessons and common knowledge along with reading and writing. Both Cammie and Max had made great strides in their written Teutonica by then. I had begun to teach Latin to my daughter that summer, and once the freezing weather descended over the countryside, I found her carving Latin phrases in the frost on our windowpanes with the elegance of her ice.

Helmut turned seven years old in January of 1061, and by then he had manifested himself as a wintry wind—the same as Lady Maria, to my private chagrin. I supposed that his element could be the proper commingling of Joel's wind and my frozen water. Watching his stocky form springing over hedges in the gardens with his dirty blond hair whirling behind him always brought joy to my heart.

I practiced the organ often during those long months, before my pregnancy forced me to quit until my stomach had shrunk to its normal size. By that time I had perfected quite a few of the pieces I had memorized in the twenty-first century, including several by Bach and Pachelbel along with the illustrious Praeludium in C by Buxtehude. My frail feet had relearned how to fly across the pedalboard with grace and accuracy. Sometimes when I played long enough I felt almost as though my soul had ascended to the clouds with the music, dancing somewhere far away in the realm of the spirit.

I had committed six eleventh century organ songs to memory, four of them written by Prince Otto. Though my opinions of him remained forever tainted by the filial curse, I had to admit that his talents as a composer were impressive. One organ score that he had written for the May festivals, titled *Dance of the Maypole*, always struck me as magnificent. Its lively footwork and complicated scales had occupied many a practice hour until I at last mastered the piece after four months of work. Sometimes, when everyone else in the house was distracted, I played through the beginning of the Prince's *Song of Time*, still wishing that one day I could discern its conclusion myself.

The Prince's army did not return throughout the entirety of the winter, to my displeasure. I spent too many hours worrying about Joel's welfare, for I feared that his clothing may not adequately protect him from the cold and snow. I received updates on the fighting from Augustin, who had traveled north to observe the Prince's wasted efforts in late autumn. When we met in our dreams, we often passed the hours near where the Prince's army had camped, exchanging thoughts on the battles while the Teuton men slept in their tents, unaware of the presence of our spirits. Augustin was quite frustrated at the Prince's audacity—attacking the Saxons in their own territory again and again—and he complained more than once that it was no wonder his city would fall, after incessantly provoking his enemies. The Teuton army tempted fate by aggravating the Saxons and bringing their elements more obviously into the mix. The Holy Roman Empire would not forgive us, and our allies would retreat to the background as the Saxons ravaged us in the name of Christianity.

I will never forget that Friday morning in late February when I awoke with the sunrise to begin another day. I rolled out of bed gradually, groaning with the effort, certain that in a few weeks' time, I would have to confine myself to my bed like I had during the final months that I carried Erika. My appendages had swelled with fluid retention all over again, and my heart pounded anytime I moved from one room to another. *Never again,* I repeated the mantra to myself as I stretched.

Then I crossed the floorboards to the basin, intending to wash my face and hands before donning one of my gaudy maternity dresses and corralling my children into the great hall for their lessons. I staggered with the weight of my newest child and glanced toward my ankles in mute annoyance. I could feel their sponginess of water retention, though I could not see them. I called Augustin's fire from my spirit, absently casting a pair of blue flames upon the unlit candlesticks atop the washing table. I blinked vaguely at my reflection in the mirror: puffy, pockmarked face, tired eyes, scraggly black hair frizzing around my head in a spectral nimbus. *I look terrible.*

I sighed and turned my attention to my hands, pushing back the sleeves of my nightdress to dip them into the bowl. But my body froze as my eyes caught sight of my swollen left wrist, its skin devoid of stain. My mouth fell open with exaggerated slowness, and my eyes widened in horror while I gawked at my clean wrist. I reached out the index finger of my right hand to touch it, to poke it cautiously, as if contact could renew the mark that had vanished from me after fifteen years of marriage. The scar from our Teutonic wedding was gone, faded away in a single night.

Joel was dead.

I stood before the washing table for an infinite moment, my ice freezing my veins as shock gripped me in its vise. My husband was dead. There could be no other explanation for the lack of that pink blemish that had sealed my doom since 1045, tying me in life to a man I would never love. He had likely died in battle, in an honorable way no doubt, leaving me quite alone and carrying his last child. He was home now, back in the twenty-first century, and I was still here until the siege of Muniche finally killed me.

I shook my head slowly as sorrow and jealousy warred within me, but grief won at last. I sank to my knees on the floor with a moan, burying my face in my hands to weep for my faithful husband, the American Teuton who had stood by my side for a decade and a half. He had forgiven my faults, lived with my lack of love, calmed my fears, and enticed my elemental lust. But now, he would never return to me until I reached the other side of the gates of time . . . a place far different from this one, a place where his loyalty belonged to my cousin.

We held a funeral for Joel the following day, after Jarvis and several of the vassals had prepared a memorial cross to place in the ground near the graves of the dead Thaden children, Marelda, Gloria, and Bethany. It was a small ceremony, attended by all of the vassals and a few close friends. Freia stood beside me through the entire observance, offering her unspoken support on the vitality of her light as my four children clung to me and wept for their beloved father. A few of the servants voiced their encomiums in honor of their faithful lord, and we sang a quiet Latin doxology for him, our harmonies ascending to the cobalt blue winter sky.

When it came time for me to speak my thoughts on my husband's death, I found that I could not form any phrases that could suffice his character. Though my heart had never loved him, I appreciated his devotion during our fifteen years of marriage. So I merely stepped forward to place a candle upon his cross in silence, my eyes damp as I gazed at its flame, flickering a natural yellow-orange, certain to burn out with time. I could have kept a portion of my spirit fixed upon it to alter it into another eternal blue flame, but my adulterous heart would not allow my master's fire to burn in memory of Joel.

After the guests and vassals had departed, Freia and I sat for a while in the great hall. I could hear my children crying in the hallway, their cheerfulness overcome with grief for their most vibrant playmate. Freia's green eyes were moist with tears of sympathy as she looked at me from across the long table, her gentle hands offering light's radiance to mine. "I'll stay here with you until after you have borne your child," she said. "Kathe can care for my children while I'm gone."

I nodded wearily, feeling incredibly like a woman in her final trimester of pregnancy. My ankles had swollen further from standing at Joel's cross, and my feet ached even though I had propped them on the beam beneath the table. With Joel gone, at least I would never have to bear another child in this primitive era.

I heard Ulka attempting to console Cammie and Max in the neighboring chamber, and I sighed heavily, jerking my head in their direction. "Honestly, if it weren't for my kids, I'd probably just end this right now. Thinking about running this estate myself strains my mind. Even with Jarvis' help, I don't know if I can do it. But I have to for their sake." I sighed again, closing my eyes and picturing Cammie, my thirteen-year-old daughter who kept me tied to the eleventh century.

Freia squeezed my hands in reassurance. "I know you can manage without Joel," she murmured, "for you've always been strong, Swanie. And you have to be strong now, for your children. Maybe you could even tell them the truth," she added, switching from Teutonica to Rhenisch. "You know that Joel isn't really dead, and you know they'll never find his body in the fields. He's gone back to your time, and you'll meet him there."

I looked down at our hands entwined upon the wood of the table, hers slender and firm, mine puffy and cold. My best friend had somehow been able to keep her figure beautiful even after seven pregnancies; she had four living children and three who had passed on to heaven. I thought of the future as I gazed at our hands. Joel had returned to Beth and would miss the fall of Muniche, leaving me to witness it alone. Perhaps it was better that way, for Muniche was not *his* city. He had been born an American and thus would never fully comprehend my loyal attachment to my birthplace. I could face the coming trials without him, for it was what I had come to do. I would keep our children safe so they could carry on our legacy after I had leapt back through the gates of time.

"Maybe one day I'll tell my children the truth about Joel and me," I said to Freia, unsure whether I really ought to complicate their world to such an extent. "But in the meantime, I'll stay here and be their mother, preparing them for the trials to come. And I won't really be alone, because you're here." I smiled wanly at my best friend, then finished quietly, "And I'll still feel Augustin in my heart."

When he came to my dreams on Tuesday as usual, I informed him of Joel's death without delay, my spirit still drooping with mourning as my aloneness struck me anew. Augustin expressed remorse for my loss while the hands of his spirit imparted his tenacity to me, his demonic ability to surmount the sorrow of untimely death. "So he shall not stand beside you to observe the defeat of 1066, but you shall reunite when you choose to depart this century," Augustin said. "You must not allow yourself to wallow in misery on your husband's account, Swanhilde. Responsibility holds you to your offspring, and you must cling to your sanity for them."

"I know. Freia and I already talked about that." I closed my eyes and concentrated on the strength of Augustin's hands upon my heart, silently asking my master to teach me indifference, so that I could rise to overcome what lay ahead. "I have no intention of weeping forever, but the wounds are fresh now. I'll bear Joel's last child in a few months, at the start of May. That baby will never know its father." My spirit shivered as I opened my eyes to look down at my abdomen, imagining the unborn child growing inside.

Augustin drifted closer to me, lifting his right hand to touch the locks of my hair, though we could not appreciate the contact. "And you must teach that final child goodness, Swanhilde, that it should never learn the burden of bitterness."

I nodded at his words, my heart whispering a silent prayer to God, that He would protect all of my children from resentment when they would lose their mother and their city in five years. I needed to focus on preparing Cammie and Max to take their places at the head of the Thaden family, to lead their siblings to a land of peace and freedom. And I would have to stress the importance of their Teuton blood, a magic that they would need to preserve in a realm of outsiders.

My gaze traveled to my left wrist, remembering the marriage scar that had been my companion for almost a decade and a half. But it was gone now, the mark faded from both my spirit and body—and my heart pounded thickly as I raised my eyes to Augustin's. Hesitation gripped me when I recognized the renewed desire pulsing through my spirit, shifting the colors of my icy robes. "Do you think . . . do you think?" The words would not come in any language. I broke off, lowering my gaze to the snow beneath my feet. My heart's yearning reached out to my master's spirit, eliminating the need for speech.

I felt his hands close around my heart, and he stepped toward me, his fiery robes licking at my icy ones, melding together in impossible union. "You want me . . . to come to you . . . ." His tone was deep, resonant. I met his gaze again, and my spirit quivered at the passion burning in his eyes. "Swanhilde, my love," he murmured while I stared at his lips, marveling at the brightness of his teeth, "I wish to come to you, yes, more than anything, despite my curse, despite my death. But you know that I cannot. I am locked out of Muniche forever, my condemned blood cast into the Isar by the Lady herself. Though you do not live within her walls, your abode is too near to the city. No part of me wishes to stir up trouble among our people or destroy your reputation. No Teuton priest would willingly marry you to a dead man, my swan. Our desires must remain unfulfilled, our separation unbroken."

I shook my head, firmly grasping denial. "I would . . . leave . . . this city . . . to be with you . . . for I love you more than Muniche . . . Augustin," I whispered.

A slightly mocking smirk appeared on his face. "True as that may be, you must remember that you did not come to this era to shirk the demise of your people for the sake of a devilish matrimony with a Black Priest. You came to watch Muniche burn, and you must stay to perform your duty. You could not run away with me now, Swanhilde, for you must linger to raise your children."

"But you could marry me and become their new father," I pointed out, realizing as soon as I said it that it would never work.

Augustin chuckled darkly and said, "I have no intention of becoming your children's Maria. Joel is their father, and you must mourn him properly in their presence, or they shall believe that you have forsaken him like Prince Ulrich abandoned Marelda."

He sighed once and shook his head. "I could not come back to Muniche now for fear of unleashing my gifts upon those who have wronged me in the past. Too many painful memories lie within Muniche's walls. If I discharge my vengeance upon her inhabitants, I fear that Wuotan shall enslave me more deeply, eradicating what remains of my free will . . . my love."

Disappointment washed over me as I saw the truth yet again—Augustin and I did not belong together due to the malicious punishment he had shouldered for fifteen years. But I told him before the bells of sunrise awoke me that I would cling to our love even in death, all fates and schemes aside.

Chapter Twenty-seven:
The Toteheri

The remainder of my time in the eleventh century prior to the year of the Teutons' downfall simply dragged for me, the sun crawling tediously across the sky more slowly than what seemed natural. Monotony submerged me in its quagmire while I played the role of the widowed lady, managing both the business of the estate and the affairs of the household. I bore Joel's last child in May of 1061, a chubby son with black hair and hazel eyes, whom I chose to name Johannes Augustin in honor of the fiery priests whose influence had shaped my life's path. A renewed sense of pride simmered in my heart when I held my newborn son to my breast, for now I was free to love whom I wished, the burden of hypocrisy lifted at last.

The Prince's army returned to Muniche in late spring, having failed in its attempts to free Paulus. By then I figured that the weak Bayern brother had already been executed by his captors. Augustin and I held many discussions on the subjects of Paulus and the Prince's song, making speculations on exactly how the Saxons would use the song to conquer the Teuton kingdom. The Holy Roman Empire had been under the control of the current monarch's mother and a cluster of Saxon princes since Heinrich III's untimely death in 1056. His underage successor would reach majority in 1065, and Augustin predicted that he would doubtless wish to flex his muscles right away upon the pesky Teutons of the south.

In subsequent years, I spent my days teaching my children, managing the estate with Jarvis, sewing clothing for my family, aiding the female servants with housework and gardening, practicing organ music, and visiting the noblewomen whom I counted as friends or acquaintances. I saw Lady Adeline quite often; by then she had grown into a plump, silver-haired noblewoman whose life revolved around her grandchildren. I appreciated Lady Adeline's friendship, for she had been one of the first noble ladies to welcome Freia and me into Muniche's local aristocracy. She had been the one who had first told me about Augustin so long ago, when I happened to see him playing cards around a barrel with three other noblemen at Lady Maria's birthday festival. She had given me fair warning about him from the start: "Good women want nothing to do with him, for he has no honorable intentions." If I had paid heed to her estimation, my life would have turned out far differently. But despite the agonies I had suffered on Augustin's account, I would not have given up our love for anything, even in hindsight.

Freia and I continued to be best of friends during my widowhood, spending our free hours together either at my house or hers. She bore another son in late 1062, one who sported light blond hair and green eyes like his mother. I congratulated her on her triumph but advised her and Heinrich to hold off for a while. My secrecy scratched at my heart as I tried to convey the message of vigilance without outright naming the coming destruction. Freia had told her husband of my true origin long ago, so thankfully both of them valued my counsel.

As the year 1066 loomed closer on the horizon, I began to innocuously prepare for the impending tragedy by selling any possessions we could do without in order to bulk up the savings Joel and I had hoarded for our children.

I sold all of my mother's jewelry for a hefty sum, certain that it would return to the future with me untarnished. Starting in 1063, I stopped holding parties altogether, and I refused to purchase any unnecessary playthings for my children. Instead, I instructed each of them from Cammie down to young Hansi on useful skills like sewing, cooking, and gardening. I sent Max and Helmut off daily to learn of carpentry and husbandry from the vassals, and I drilled Cammie on her knowledge of plants and herbs, on how to discern which ones were safe for eating or medicinal purposes.

My miserly ways frustrated the kids and confused the servants, but I offered no explanation while I scoured our financial records with a vengeance, pinching every Thaler. I practically broke my own heart in December of 1064, when I ordered several of the vassals to take my organ apart so that I could sell the metal back to Heinrich and trade the wood and fabric. But by then, the Saxons had begun to construct their invincible army, and word had reached Muniche of their suspicious machinations, infusing the populace with a niggling uncertainty.

An odd anticipation ate at me as 1065 dawned, for I began to grasp the fact that in less than two years, I would return at long last to *my* era, the year 2000. I reminisced upon my old lifestyle and occasionally laughed out loud at the thought of flushing a toilet or stepping under a hot shower after two decades of chamber pots and cursory baths. A part of me could hardly wait to return. In the twenty-first century I would leave rampant chauvinism behind me, speak Bayerisch to my friends, fly to America in a jet, and play pipe organs left and right. I would get my virginity back; it would be akin to a second chance at life. But eventually my joyous ruminations would darken, for I feared to lose my bond with Augustin. I cherished my relationship with him more than anything else in my life. He assumed that the impossible time span would break us asunder, and I hoped like mad that he was wrong.

I remember that dreadful night in May of 1065, when everything finally fell into place regarding my people's imminent demise. The Saxon armies had begun to march south that month, and Muniche was in a tizzy as the men prepared for a fight once more. Reports indicated that our enemies had no intentions of satisfying themselves with raids on the outlying settlements this time. Prince Otto had received a dangerously worded message from the Saxon heads-of-state, warning that retribution for his earlier belligerence would soon be unavoidable. What the Prince wrote in response to the note I know not, but news of its threat reached even the lowest of peasants.

It seemed that every man in Muniche, Teuton and outsider, clamored for the opportunity to defend their ruler's honor. Everyone slandered Heinrich IV, who had only just come of age, insinuating that his advisors led him astray. Freia said at one point that the young Emperor probably had little inkling of what his armies planned to do, and I agreed. It would take a lot of gall—or perhaps idiocy—to stage an all-out war with people who claimed powers over elements and blood.

The Saxon forces struck the outskirts of Teutonic territory in early May, and Augustin summarily set out for the site of the battles, intending to conceal himself in the shadows and record everything for the sake of history. When he came to me in a dream on a Sunday night, bringing my sleeping spirit to his side in the grassy hills outside of Bamberg, I knew that something terrible had happened. Augustin rarely disturbed me on Sunday nights, for he respected my custom of concentrating on the things of God while I drifted into slumber. That night, I found myself facing my master upon a wind-swept hill, tall grasses and wildflowers swaying beneath the clouded sky. I caught a rancid scent in the air and wrinkled my nose.

"Swanhilde, you must come with me at once," Augustin said in greeting, his fiery eyes boiling with a combination of rage and repulsion as they drifted from my face to the encampment below where we stood. I recognized it as one of our people's camps due to the elemental manipulation evident in its campfires—natural flames mingled with yellow and black.

"What . . . is that stench?" I asked, cringing as I descended the hill at his side. "Smells like rotting flesh."

"This battalion clashed with the Saxons this morning, and I gained a fair view of the proceedings due to the cloud cover. It appears that the Holy Roman Empire is not as 'holy' as it claims to be." Augustin grimaced, his anger not dissolving.

"Did they sacrifice prisoners to Wuotan or something?" We had reached the outskirts of the camp, and I fought the instinct to hide myself from the knights on guard. It still made me nervous to encounter humans in the *Gæstelort Troumerae*, even though my rational mind knew that they could not sense me.

"I wish it was that simple." Augustin paused before a tent to eye me rather pointedly. A ragged moan pealed from the tent, the stench of carrion clinging to the atmosphere. He slipped inside and waved for me to follow.

I hesitated, shutting my eyes in an attempt to channel the inherent serenity of the spiritual realm into my essence to augment my courage. *Whatever's going on here is bad, really bad,* I knew. But I also knew that I had to face it, to see just how the Saxon forces intended to defeat my people. So I opened my eyes and entered the tent, preparing myself for the worst.

A single lantern provided poor light, just enough to make out the form of a shirtless man outstretched upon a blanket at the far side of the tent. His armor cast forgotten in a pile near his feet, he groaned in a wretched manner, his bearded face screwed up in anguish. A brown-robed Catholic priest knelt before him, his head bowed in prayer. The man on the blanket had a ghastly wound that stretched from his right nipple to his hip—the flesh around and inside of it was blackened, putrefied.

My icy eyes gawked at the wound for a full minute. I could actually *see* the decay happening steadily before my eyes, the death of muscle, the seeping pus. Necrosis just kept spreading; it was clear that the warrior had little time left. I shuddered and tried to hold my breath, unsure how long I could do that as a dreaming spirit. But when my gaze shifted from his awful injury to his face, I realized that I knew him. "Lord Niklas," I whispered, stricken. He had run the Kuegler estate for years now alongside his mother, Lady Hildegard. He had left for Bamberg when the snows melted to visit a distant relative.

"You see this wound?" Augustin questioned, reaching one flaming hand out to touch it unseen. "He was slashed by a sword-wielding monstrosity on the battlefield today, our enemies' latest treachery. This is death, Swanhilde. This decay is wholly abnormal, spreading faster than what is naturally possible, consuming the unhurt flesh around it after the manner of the death that lurks within me." He pulled his hand away and held his fingers up for me to see. Their fiery brilliance had dimmed.

"A sword-wielding monstrosity?" I repeated, blinking at Augustin's fingers as his immortal verve reinvigorated them. "Are they mercenaries?"

"They are warriors that the Saxons have pulled from millennia past, and they practice a sorcery that I have never before encountered. Come and see." The scene swirled around me as Augustin carried us away from the Teutons' camp to another coalition. A circle of animal skin pavilions stood in a moonlit valley, oddly-colored campfires aglow at each doorway, tendrils of smoke rising to the clouds above.

I sensed, as we loitered at the edges of the coterie of tents, a pervading heaviness piercing the night's serenity. Wraithlike fingers seemed to pass through and around my spirit, seeking to pinpoint my presence among the camp of the heathen. I swept my eyes over the entirety of the encampment, noting the devilish paintings adorning each pavilion, the expertly-crafted weapons lying near the fires, the dead animals strung up to dry on poles here and there. I heard voices murmuring inside some of the pavilions, voices that sounded too sultry to be human. "What *is* this place?" I asked Augustin, squinting at the flickering fires.

"This is the camp of the *Toteheri*, Swanhilde," Augustin replied with a fierce expression.

"The dead army?" I raised my eyebrows at him.

"An appropriate term, for they call themselves something that I cannot pronounce." My master folded his arms across his cerulean robes, his fiery eyes narrowed at the pavilions and the strange symbols etched upon them. When I looked a little more closely at them, I recognized that they had been painted with blood. "Even the Saxons who called them from the dead keep a safe distance away. The main bulk of their military is entrenched beyond the hill."

"It doesn't look like there's a lot of them," I said, shifting my eyes from one pavilion to the next. "There are only four tents. And if they've been pulled from the past, they should be able to be killed and sent back. Right?"

Augustin curled his upper lip. "I am not yet certain. Bamberg's Keyholder landed a strong hit on one of their women this morning, but she continued to fight. From my position in the clouds, it appeared that the wound healed itself."

"Wait. Their *women?*" I cut him off, astonishment fluctuating the hue of my robes. "This army has *female* warriors? And they have some sort of healing power...like blood control?"

"I am not yet sure of the extent of their magic, but they have imbued their blades with some sort of deadly necromancy. Lord Niklas' fate is not as gruesome as the fate of a knight who lost a hand to one of their swords. I checked on his condition just before I summoned you. His entire arm has rotted away, as if this devilish force commands some sort of accelerated leprosy. Several Teuton priests tried to heal Lord Niklas' torn flesh, but they failed. You saw what happened to my fingers when I touched it. This army spreads death in its wake."

"And that's why you call them the *Toteheri*," I discerned, his story prompting me to shiver all over.

"The information I found in one of their witch warrior's blood nearly caused me, a dead man, to faint," Augustin said, a humorless smile gracing his grim face. "I confronted her this evening when she went to gather water from the stream. Her people come from an age far in the past, in the days of the Akkadians. They worship multiple demons through burnt offerings and sex. They were a menace that swept the eastern seas in the years when fallen angels copulated with mortals."

I gasped, a stone hand clasping my heart. "They're Nephilim?" My thoughts raced back to what little I had read about the biblical giants: half human, half demon.

"Not quite, but close." Augustin's left eye twitched, and he bared his teeth in the direction of the nearest pavilion, dropping his arms to his sides. "The tallest among them looks to be an *Elle* taller than me. They are not quite at Goliath's level; I believe that they are descendants of his kind, their blood more human than demon. But their dark overlords have granted them the power to spread death through a mere touch, and I fear to see what will become of our people once this force attacks our cities."

"So they're more human than demon," I translated, terror provoking me to draw closer to Augustin. "But they shouldn't be able to kill you since you're already dead." I clutched that fact like a desperate lifeline.

"No, they spread death through physical contact, not through spectral anger. The witch that I bled tried to slay me with no effect. She looked disconcerted when her touch made no mark on my face. But when she cursed me afterward, she spoke my master's name." Wrath simmered in Augustin's eyes again, and he clenched his fists, cobalt flames erupting from them to drop upon the grass below. "I caught the names of Moloch and Nergal in their chants, but those are not the only demons they worship. Wuotan has sent this *Toteheri* as a scourge upon his wayward people, the ones who use his gifts while serving his greatest adversary."

"But how . . . ." I shook my head in uncertainty while I tried to evaluate the implications of what Augustin had learned. "How did the Saxons convince them to come *here?* How did they learn their ancient language . . . how did they find out about them in the first place?"

Augustin's visage darkened further. "I can conclude only that the Empire is not as Christian as it claims to be," he stated flatly. "The Saxons have colluded with Wuotan as a result of the murderer's song, forsaking the God of heaven as well as their olden divinities, Saxnot and Thunar. Wuotan and his fellows used their influence to sway these heathens, and the Saxons have promised them all of Bavaria, should they succeed in their conquest." Augustin sneered toward the tents.

I shook my head again, dread gripping me in its vise. "This . . . is going to be . . . complete carnage."

"This force of thirty shall be our demise," Augustin agreed, heaving a sigh of defeat. "If we cannot discern a way to eliminate this *Toteheri*, I fear that the dawn shall never return again."

Chapter Twenty-eight:
Impending Doom

The subsequent night, after Augustin's startling revelations about the army that awaited us had pervaded my unconscious mind, I had terrifying nightmares from the moment sleep took me until I awoke with the bells of sunrise. Images of spectral killing caused me to wake in a sweat, my heart racing at the thought of the destruction to come. On Tuesday night, I begged Augustin to come to my dreams every night until Muniche fell, for I feared to face my nightmares alone. He vowed to meet me as often as he could, whenever something else did not constrain him. Any time he did not come to my dreams, I found myself plagued by visions of my friends and children screaming while a demonic army tore their flesh from their bones. I restarted my old habit of spending half of the night in the spiritual realm, basking in its ethereal tranquility.

I watched, helpless to interfere, as the Prince's army marched for Regensburg, the soldiers ignorant of the true state of things. I wept for each young vassal who left and for Heinrich Denlinger, fearing that I would never see any of them alive again. When spring turned into summer, I threw myself into the business of farming with a newfound madness, wishing to distract myself from the impending doom. I sold more and more of my possessions in the city each Saturday while my children and servants watched in stupefaction. They doubtless believed that the head of their household had lost her mind.

By November, when news of Regensburg's demise had reached Muniche, the Thaden estate had been stripped down to the bare bones, many rooms standing empty and forlorn. We made an excellent profit on the crops that season, which I counted as a blessing from God, for I knew that would be our last harvest. As the winter snows coated the countryside in a blanket of white, I sifted through all of my savings and accounts and concluded that I had enough funds to offer a stipend to each vassal family, if I could convince them to depart Muniche before escape became impossible.

By the end of 1065, Augustin had learned more devastating secrets of the *Toteheri*. They were nearly unbeatable in battle, their armor scintillating in the sunlight when they struck their opponents with swords, axes, and spears, wielding their weapons with superhuman precision. Augustin said that their skills seemed greatest at close combat, for they could outmaneuver the Teuton forces with striking finesse. Their black sorcery seemed to carry a death that extended beyond humanity itself, for Augustin had seen clothing and armor waste away after being struck with their enhanced weapons.

Once the demonic army had descended upon Regensburg, they had unleashed their uncanny death upon the city walls, crumbling the stones to powder. Augustin had watched in spirit form as they conquered the city, raping the women and burning the children. Each woman they had raped succumbed to the effects of their creeping death within a few days' time, for apparently they had the power to dish it out with their semen as well as their touch. Their atrocious deeds eventually prompted Augustin to retreat to his cottage on the Rhine to set down all that he had seen. His evident horror gave me pause; neither of us had anticipated destruction of this magnitude.

The *Toteheri's* worst advantage, however, scared me far more than the idea of brutal rape and decay. Augustin informed me shortly after he returned to his hut that it appeared that the heathens boasted some form of immortality. He had seen many of them, male and female warriors alike, get stabbed with swords or struck with arrows, each wound healing with inhuman speed. So far, Augustin admitted that he had never seen one of the heathen warriors actually die, and he took a count of their forces each night as they retired to their pavilions. The witch he had bled in the very beginning ought to have died once he had finished with her, for he had practically drained her, according to his own estimations. But she had survived, as had the many heathens who had seemed mortally wounded.

We exchanged many conjectures on this conundrum, and Augustin postulated that enough demon blood must flow through their veins to protect them from natural death. I hypothesized that perhaps they were already dead, like Augustin himself; but he disagreed, for he had tasted life in the witch's blood. It seemed that the *Toteheri* was invincible until we could discern a way to decimate its numbers. The Prince's forces should focus on depleting the Saxons first, Augustin said, for perhaps the heathens would disperse if their leaders met their end.

At the Christmas holidays, the Prince's army returned to Muniche to rest and reinforce itself for the coming onslaught. My family spent Christmas Eve with the Denlingers, the younger children oblivious to their parents' anxiety as they played together. Cammie, Heino, and Max —who by that time were eighteen, seventeen, and sixteen respectively—sat with us in the front parlor when Heinrich related tales of the horrific battles, climaxing at Regensburg in October. Freia and I sat close to one another on her leather couch, our fingers intertwined as her husband spoke, his once positive face appearing devoid of hope.

He told us that the Saxons had ravaged Regensburg with a fury, conquering the Teuton stronghold in only three days, burning many of its buildings, slaying anyone who had not been able to escape. Heinrich had survived miraculously due to his metal—and the grace of God, Freia added—for he had used his element to reinforce his armor, protecting his flesh from the touch of death. It relieved me to hear that Teutonic elements were resilient enough to withstand the *Toteheri's* creeping death, and I sincerely hoped that the Prince would coach all of his troops on how to invoke elemental shields.

Heinrich informed us that the Saxons and their demonic allies had chosen to winter in Regensburg, growing strong on the plunder and the bodies of the dead Teutons. Once the snows had melted, he predicted that our enemies would head south once more, setting their sights on the most prosperous Teuton city in Bavaria—Muniche. They would sweep through like a forest fire, slaughtering, pillaging, annihilating; and as yet, Prince Otto and his advisors had reasoned out no way to halt this indestructible army. Our people faced obliteration unless we could somehow overcome our enemies' paranormal powers.

Once the beaten Teuton soldier had lapsed into silence, stillness pervaded the front parlor as the probability of a gruesome future weighed everyone down. I met Cammie's eyes for a long moment, seeing all of her disbelief and fear. Then I turned my gaze on Max, viewing his stolid frustration, his longing to mete out justice upon our enemies. And I realized in the blink of an eye that while I could never reveal the truth to my children without shattering their lives, I had to tell Freia now. She had stayed by my side for twenty-one long years, graciously accepting my refusal to be completely honest with her due to my worries about altering the past, never doubting my friendship. My eyes drifted from my son to Freia's face, her Teutonic light dimmed by dread. Then I firmly ordered my children to leave the room, to go with Heino to join the youngsters in their snowy exploits outside.

After responding shortly to their protests and shooing them from the parlor with a wave of my hand, I lifted myself from the couch with a muted groan and gestured for Heinrich to take my place beside his wife. He did so and gathered Freia into his arms as they waited for me to speak. I hobbled over to the horsehair chair that faced the couch, my ankles hurting me due to the cold and the weight that I had never been able to lose. Once I had situated myself, I addressed my friends in soft Teutonica, guilt pricking me at the knowledge of how dishonest I had been with them all this time. "I know that neither Joel nor I have told you the truth about why we came to your time," I began cautiously, "but now, as our people's ruin looms on the horizon, I can keep silent no longer."

I watched realization break across Heinrich's bearded face, and he tightened his arms around Freia. "You came to see Muniche fall," he translated.

"Yes," I answered, looking at each of them in turn. "This city will be burnt to the ground in July of next year at the hands of the Saxons and their army from the past. Every walled Teuton stronghold will fall to our enemies within the next three years, and the Teutons who survive will be scattered abroad, never to regain their autonomy again."

Freia gasped, her eyes glinting amber as she clung to her husband. Heinrich simply shook his head in silent resignation. "I had planned to come to the year 1064 to give me the chance to see the calm before the storm, but fate chose to send me to 1044, which makes the inevitable defeat much bitterer for me. I've forged strong friendships during my years in this era, and it hurts me deeply to know it'll all come to naught in a few short months."

I broke off there while sorrow overcame my impassive façade. I averted my gaze to the hearth, staring blankly at the flames dancing upon the embers, tears running down my cheeks as the faces of all of my medieval acquaintances played in a dirge through my mind. After I returned to the twenty-first century, I would likely never see them again. My tears began to freeze upon my skin.

"So you're planning to die when Muniche falls," Freia whispered, speaking for the first time in a while. Her voice sounded soft and sympathetic. "Then you can finally return to Joel," she added in an encouraging tone.

My mouth twitched in discontent. "Return to the man I never loved, the man who belongs to my cousin, not to me." A caustic chuckle burst from my throat as I finished, "And I'll leave my true love forever behind, a lonely wraith, a demon's slave . . . the magnificent Augustin von Bayern."

I sensed Heinrich's surprise at my blunt words. I saw the metallic glow in his gray eyes as his mouth fell open slowly, my aberrant truth finally out in the open. My best friend stared at me in restrained shock, likely having never believed that I would admit my love for Augustin in the presence of her husband.

"There's no point in hiding anything now," I said with a shrug. "I must watch the end, like I've planned, and die in shame for our people's ruined pride. Although none of us can stop the hands of God, we *can* save our children." I looked seriously at Heinrich and Freia. "That's why Joel and I have hoarded so much of our profits over the years, to give our children money to flee. I have more than enough to rescue them, and I want to share some of it with you, so your offspring may survive as well."

Freia wept for a long time as the enormity of the impending defeat struck her hard. Heinrich held her close and discussed the implications with me, his face calm, his metallic eyes betraying his torment. He planned to fight with the Prince's army, come what may, but he agreed to send Freia and their children away as soon as the snow melted. I told him that I intended to send my brood to Eisenwald along the western trade route before the Saxons closed the borders with the Rhineland. Heinrich nodded thoughtfully and said that he would send his wife and children in the same direction. As we exchanged speculations on these things, I noticed a strange expression gradually contorting Freia's face. But she held her peace while her husband and I talked, nodding now and then in silent submission.

At the dawning of 1066, I gathered all of my children together in my bedroom late one evening to prepare them for their journey to the Rhineland. Since my youngest child, Hansi, had not yet turned five, I explained every-thing in simple terms. I said that a terrible army would attack our people in the summer and that they needed to leave Teuton lands before their lives became endangered. Helmut and Max both insisted that they wished to stay and fight with the adults. Cammie practically begged me to let her remain with me so that she could care for my health needs, like she had done so faithfully since my last preg-nancy had permanently aggravated my old injuries.

I told them gravely that there was no point in arguing with me, for I would not allow them to be butchered by our enemies. I reminded Cammie that, as the eldest Thaden child, she would hold responsibility for Erika and Hansi during the trip to Eisenwald. I told Max and Helmut that they would be required to protect the women as good lords should.

Once I had dispatched most of my children to their beds, answering what questions I could when they clamored for further information, Cammie lingered in the doorway. Her eyes glittered the azure of ice when she met my gaze in silence, her figure that of an elegant blond dancer. "Mutti," she whispered at length, her tone laden with concern, "if you truly believe that the Saxons will burn Muniche to the ground . . . and you don't intend to come to Eisenwald with us . . . ." Her voice trailed off, and I saw tears dampening her eyelashes.

I crossed the floor to her side and reached out one hand to brush a few stray hairs away from her face. "My life has already been spent, Cammie, and my destiny lies with Mu-niche. You may mourn us jointly, for I shall die with her."

Chapter Twenty-nine:
Parting Ways

Temperate weather melted the snows of winter in early March, awakening the spring for its final breath of serenity before the storm. The Prince's army departed to engage their foes outside of Regensburg on the first Saturday of the month. I watched them go with mixed emotions, knowing that when I saw them again, they would be bleeding their lives out in a last stand for Muniche. I bade many of my vassals farewell once more, imparting my bleak wishes for success.

Heinrich also departed with the Prince's army, leaving final instructions with Freia to lead their children and mine to Eisenwald the following week. He promised to meet his family in the Rhineland once the fighting had ceased. Freia moaned to me in private that she feared she would never meet her beloved again outside of heaven. I reassured her as best as I could and remarked that his metal ought to protect him from most of the heathen's attacks. But in truth I shared her fears. I prayed hard every night that she would never wake to find her marriage scar gone, for my best friend genuinely loved her husband.

During the second week of March, the Thaden estate buzzed with activity, servants and children alike preparing for their flight to the Rhineland. Jarvis, Ulka, and their two daughters and grandchildren would accompany my brood at my own insistence. The rest of my servants and vassals preferred to remain near Muniche as long as they could, hoping to offer aid to the soldiers and townspeople when the need arose. I disapproved of their fidelity to a doomed city, but I was no better. I had no right to order them to flee if they preferred to stay and die.

Some of the female servants admitted that they might travel south toward the Alps once April had come, and others stated firmly that they would wait until the situation became dire before leaving the area. I had a feeling that some of my underlings did not believe my predictions of destruction, since everyone knew that I had been rather cynical since the early days of my marriage. I complained to Jarvis that those who doubted would die of starvation. My most trusted servant grimaced at my morbidity and said that since he and Ulka were in their late fifties, they may very well succumb to the hardships of travel on the way to Eisenwald.

During that stressful week, I spent time alone with each of my children in turn, to offer them love and wisdom to carry throughout their futures. I recognized that none of them would ever return to Teuton lands. They would grow old amongst foreigners, facing the temptation to taint the magic of their blood. I had taught each of them the importance of preserving their heritage above all, but my lessons might prove fruitless once they left their people behind. Though I could not ask my children to refrain from marrying outsiders, I did emphasize that they must honor the memory of their family and legacy. Cammie and Max both spoke and wrote fluent Rhenisch, Latin, and Teutonica, so it would be their responsibility to lead the younger ones down the right path.

I saw much of little Hansi as my children prepared to depart. Once he had grasped the fact that he was about to leave his mother behind, he insisted upon sleeping with me at night, sharing youthful dreams with me. He feared to leave me, and I passed many evenings stroking his black hair tenderly, whispering that he must be strong, that he must choose to thrive without me, though times would be hard. My soul wept inside of me one night when he cried out, "Mutti . . . I don't want to leave you . . . because I love you more than Max and Cammie!" His boyish face screwed up in pain as he clung to me, tears pouring down his ruddy cheeks.

I wrapped my arms around him tightly in response to his outburst, holding back my own tears. "My darling boy, you mustn't say such terrible things," I whispered in his ear. "Max and Cammie are your family, just like I am, and they'll take care of you when I'm gone."

"But I'll miss you so much!" he moaned, his tiny hands grasping the fabric of my nightdress as though he would never let go. "I want you to come with us. I'll carry you myself if your feet hurt . . . I know I could!" He sniffed loudly, burying his face in my chest.

"Hush, darling, hush," I murmured, turning my eyes toward the door to the hallway. I could hear the pattering of feet outside, likely Hansi's siblings quietly eavesdropping on his sorrow. "You must learn to take the bad along with the good, like your father before you," I urged my youngest son, wiping his tears away with my sleeve. "It hurts me to leave you, as much as it hurts you, but we have to be strong or our pain will lead your brothers and sisters into despair."

I nodded toward the closed door. Hansi squinted that way in response, attempting to detect the presence of his siblings in the hallway, though he had not yet discovered the power of his element at the tender age of four. I wondered from time to time what his gift would be. My other children, from oldest to youngest, were ice, energy, wintry wind, and air.

Once Hansi had composed himself, I rose from the bed and led him to the window, opening the pane of glass so we could appreciate the glorious night sky above, the chilly breeze caressing our cheeks. "I'll still be with you once you've begun the journey to Eisenwald," I promised my son, gently smoothing his hair as he leaned against my legs. "You can look at the stars every night, far away in the Rhineland, and know that I am there with your Daddy, watching over you from heaven. And one day, we'll all meet again there, in the city of God." A mournful smile curled upon my lips while I spoke, for I sensed the paradox in my words—I would not meet my children in heaven for another thousand years or so.

Hansi took my hand. "In heaven, you can run and dance with me in the clouds. Your feet will be perfect." I chuckled at his innocent dreams and gazed upward at the starry sky. "But Mutti . . . what am I supposed to *do* . . . until then?" he asked.

I averted my gaze to his face, leaning down to kiss his forehead. "Grow into the strong and noble lord you ought to be, always keeping God first in your heart," I replied. "Never let yourself grow angry or bitter, for God lets everything happen for a reason, even if we don't understand until later." I hugged him close for a long moment. When he began to yawn I led him back to my bed, tucking him in before lying down beside him.

One cool afternoon that week, I encountered eight-year-old Erika planting bulbs in one of the flower gardens near the house, scratching at the earth with a small trowel, dirtying her childish fingers with dark soil. I smiled as I observed her work from the porch, for she had taken a liking to gardening during the past few years. She often insisted upon helping the vassal women with their planting, even though her skills at such arts were lacking. Roses were her favorite flower because she loved their scent.

I watched the zephyrs of spring dallying with her black hair, which fell to the middle of her back in a straight wave like mine had done in my youth. I focused a bit on my ice while I leaned against the railing of the porch, sending it outward to mingle with my daughter's air. This prompted her to jump up from the ground to face me, her skirt whirling like a dancer's, her eyes glittering the translucent blue of the atmosphere.

"And what, may I ask, are you doing down here, little lady?" I inquired of Erika, glancing from her beautiful eyes to the dirt marring her fingers. "Shouldn't you be inside packing for your trip?"

"I already packed my things, Mutti," she responded, her voice the soft tinkling of bells on the breeze. "I was planting some flowers for you." She paused for a moment, letting her trowel drop to the ground as she brushed her hands off on her dress, the instinctive reaction of a child.

I descended the steps and came to her side, studying her expression. I sensed the tenderness radiating from her spirit while her eyes calmed from the azure of air to their natural gray. I knelt down beside her, biting my lip to keep myself from groaning at the effort. Then I reached out to take her hands in mine. "Why are you planting flowers for me, Erika my love?" I inquired. "There are far more important things to do before you leave with your siblings and friends."

Erika's youthful exuberance dimmed. She looked down at our hands as she answered, refusing to meet my gaze, "I wanted . . . to leave something for you . . . something pretty . . . to make you think of me." Tears trembled on her eyelashes when she twisted her body away from me, blinking at her clump of scratched earth. "Cammie says . . . she says . . . that you're going to die here." Her body shivered while she spoke, the air in her spirit stirring her hair in an innate attempt to conceal her fears. "I wanted my flowers . . . to grow for you . . . so you can remember me . . . up in heaven."

My own tears began trickling down my cheeks in icy drops. I felt my daughter's anguish, and I gathered her into my arms, kissing her hair. "Erika, baby, I *promise* you that I'll never forget you, even in heaven. I'll watch you from the stars, and you will feel me here."

I gently laid my right hand upon her heart, sensing its quickened beat through the folds of her dress. "You must promise me something in return, baby," I whispered as she sniffed, trying to rein in her sorrow. I took hold of Erika's face, turning it upward so I could meet her gaze. "If I'm to be your guardian from heaven, then you must promise not to forget me, even after you're fifty years old." I gave her a teary smile.

"I'll never forget you, Mutti," Erika whispered fiercely, her air rushing over her body, reaching out to touch my spirit. "Every time I plant a flower, it'll be for you." I pulled her into a tight embrace, anguish piercing my heart at the encroaching end. Part of me longed to accompany my children on their journey, but I had to keep my priorities straight. I had come to the past to watch Muniche fall, and I would do it alone and carry what wisdom I gained with me to the future.

Later that evening, I exchanged a few parting words with Helmut, my middle child. He looked the most like his father, a pensive twelve-year-old who loved to read and let his passion loose in music. He had toyed with the organ before I had ordered it dismantled and sold, and during the past year he had taught himself how to play the lute, grasping its techniques with an aptitude that surpassed my own musical talents.

I found Helmut outside on the front porch as twilight descended. He sat alone on the bench that faced the front gardens, quietly plucking the strings of his instrument, humming a tune I had taught him months before. I came to sit beside him in silence, waiting for him to finish his song. Once he had set his lute aside I commented, "Perhaps when you arrive in the Rhineland, you can find a pipe organ somewhere and make the forest ring with the beauty of your music." I grinned at my son.

He smiled back at me, his earnest hazel eyes belying his peaceful façade. "Mutti, if you have to stay to see this city fall, you ought to go to the cathedral and play the organ there, no matter what the monks think. You could play something amazing as an elegy to Muniche, and I can imagine that I hear it drifting along the breeze, calling to my blood." His eyes traveled to the darkening sky, and his smooth jaw quivered in unspoken fervor.

I chuckled a bit at his words, feeling relieved that at least one of my children seemed at peace with my decision to remain in Muniche. "I actually might take you up on that suggestion," I said. Since I planned to spend the final days of the siege within the city walls, I might be able to get my hands on the cathedral's organ, for by then the clergy should have fled. "I'll have to figure out what song would do Muniche justice," I added, knowing that there was one song—and only one—that I wished to play when the city burned. An impossible wish.

Helmut remained silent for a lengthy interval, his gaze toward the road in the distance. "Actually, Mutti," he began in a husky voice, "I really wish that you'd come with us, even though it would make you sick. We could take care of you, along with Jarvis and Ulka, and once you get to the Rhineland your feet can rest again."

I frowned as Helmut revealed his heart to me, my resolution to stay wavering anew. "Who is going to sing with me at Eisenwald?" Helmut continued, his face growing slightly petulant. "No one has a voice like yours, not even Lorraine. And she doesn't know your songs. She only sings Rhenisch ballads." He scowled as though Rhenisch tunes could not assuage his passion for harmony.

I laid my right arm around his shoulders and recommended that he teach Lorraine some of my songs. With her mother's flute and his lute, they could make some beautiful melodies. "Maybe someday Erika will be able to sing like me," I said. "It'll be up to you to teach her and Hansi about music. That's your talent."

Helmut smiled a bit doubtfully and shrugged out of my embrace with the typical awkwardness of a young man approaching puberty. He glanced again at the darkening sky, then asked rather hesitantly, "Mutti, would you sing with me now, one last time . . . while no one else is around?" He lifted his hazel eyes to mine, his element playing with his dirty blond hair in anticipation of melodic glory.

I flashed him a rapturous grin in response and nodded, anticipation flooding my spirit. So he retrieved his lute and struck up the tune he had plucked earlier, Haggard's "Lost." I sang with him in heartfelt English and we covered many enchanting melodies of my era, my voice melding with his strings, rising to the heavens in our final moments of musical passion.

I spoke with Max on the day before my children's expedition was to begin, for I saw him practicing with his favorite sword—a double-edged blade that his late father had fashioned for him long ago—in the grass near the well. I watched him assume all sorts of fighting stances as he battled an invisible foe, his movements swift with the vitality of his energy. "Practicing your techniques so you can defend the ladies of your household, Max?" I asked when I approached him.

He halted his exercises and grinned as he sheathed his sword. "Heino and I should have no trouble protecting the women during our journey," he declared, "and I doubt the Rhinelanders will be able to stand against us, with his fire and my energy." He lifted his bare chin in pride, his eyes sparking in elemental fervor.

I winked at my oldest son and walked to his side, noticing for the first time in a long time that he had grown to be almost as tall as his father. He towered over me like a gangly teenager, his black hair flopping over his eyebrows in casual disarray. "I expect both you and Heino to treat the Rhinelanders as your friends," I reminded him, gesturing at his scabbard. "They may not be your blood equals, but at least they have no quarrels with our people. Freia was born one of them."

"I know, Mutti, it's just fun to think about fighting some Saxons along the way," Max admitted with a grimace. He placed one arm around my shoulders. "Someday I'm going to have to get revenge on them for killing Daddy. But if you're right about the coming conquest, I suppose I'll have a long wait."

I sighed, sensing my son's anguish over his father's death. He had struggled with Joel's fate the most, out of our five children. "Our time will come," I said, "but it may be many years from now. In the meantime, you must take your place at the head of the Thaden family, leading your siblings in the paths of God."

We walked slowly through the kitchen gardens, my son's arm still wrapped around my waist. "How are we supposed to keep our blood pure when we're living among outsiders?" Max asked me at length, sounding upset. "I've got my eyes on Katchen Denlinger, but what about the rest of us? We'll be the only Teutons in Eisenwald, unless some stop by while trading on the Rhine."

"You'll just have to do the best you can," I replied, shaking my head at the very real problem of mixing Teuton blood with foreigners. Part of me still wondered how my people had managed to preserve their heritage after our enemies had scattered them abroad. Maybe they had renounced their prejudices against Teutons of blood status less than ninety percent, so that more men could attain the priesthood and conduct rites like the blood-transfer.

My thoughts turned to Augustin, and a caustic laugh escaped my lips as I considered the truth of the matter. Max looked down at me in concern, so I decided to tell him what other options he may have; although I doubted that Freia or Heinrich would approve of making deals with my dangerous lover. "There's one Teuton priest who resides not far from Eisenwald, as of ten years ago. And I have a feeling that once he gets word of our people's demise, he'd be more than willing to conduct a few blood-transfers on our family's behalf. He'd probably help out the Denlingers, too." I gave Max a considering look.

"You did that once, didn't you?" he asked me, his expression troubled. I nodded, and he promised with a sigh, "We'll do whatever we have to do to preserve our blood, Mutti. I'll make sure that none of the younger ones forget that they're Teutons." I hugged my son tightly, thankful for his staunch loyalty to his people, even in the face of a long separation.

Cammie and I shared many private moments during that final week, for we had always been very close. She begged me to reconsider my decision to remain in Muniche many times, weeping with me as she expressed her fears. Like Max, she worried that she might lose her purity of blood once she found herself among foreigners. She had grown into a magnificent young Teuton woman, her blond hair falling to her waist when it was not tied back, her skin a gorgeous white, her figure as perfect as mine had once been. I told her the same thing I had told Max about the possibilities for blood-transfers once they arrived in Freia's hometown. Cammie cringed, but admitted that such rituals may end up necessary.

The night before my brood set out on their quest for safety, I met Cammie at the family graveyard as she gazed at her father's tombstone in the light of the moon. I stood in the shadows while she mumbled a few phrases I could not hear, her final eulogies for her fallen father and sisters. Silvery tears trickled down her cheeks when she lifted her gaze to the stars above, the cloth of her nightdress rising and falling swiftly with her breath. I sensed the chill of her ice wafting through the night air, crystallizing her tears and giving her hair an argentine shimmer.

"Ah, Mutti," she called out to me in a soft moan, "it is agony to leave this place . . . knowing I'll never see it again . . . never see Daddy's grave . . . never know the location of yours." Her body trembled like a leaf shivering in the wind, and she held one hand out to me in a silent invitation.

I flew to her side on the power of my ice, our skin freezing together as I took her hand in mine. "Everything on this earth passes away, Cammie," I murmured to her, the ice of our spirits uniting while we clung to each other. "It doesn't matter what things we must leave behind here, for we shall all meet again in heaven . . . all sadness forgotten . . . all wrongs forgiven."

"I know it, and I believe," my daughter whispered back, her blue eyes staring into mine. She touched my face with her frozen fingers. "But it'll be so hard waiting for that day, living with strangers . . . knowing that you are suffering." Her lips trembled as she traced the wrinkles on my face, brushing my short hair back. "You mustn't let them hurt you, Mutti. Please . . . ." Her gaze traveled down to my feet, my shoes coated with a sheen of ice, my ankles swollen and weak.

I reached out to tilt her chin upward, holding her gaze with mine. "Darling Cammie, you need not worry about me. It won't be long. They won't bother to abuse me. I'm middle-aged, unattractive, and overweight. I'm sure they'll kill me quickly." I forced myself to smile at her, though the possibility of rape prior to my death had haunted me in recent days.

"I'll pray for you every day, Mutti," Cammie promised, looking toward the sky again. "I know God will protect you . . . and the rest of us . . . ."

My daughter's strong faith brought relief to my heart. I kissed her gently on the forehead, imagining how glorious our reunion would be, years in the future when I finally entered heaven. Before we returned to the house for the night, we shared the briefest of dances upon the meadow near the graves, her ice reinforcing mine, giving youthful vigor to my weakened feet as we embraced the beauty of the night together one last time—Swanhilde and Camilla, the icy queen and her fairy daughter.

Chapter Thirty

The Sky Darkens

The following morning, my children set out for Muniche just after dawn. They took the open cart that Lord Edwin had given our family years ago, and Cammie set up areas within it for five of our chickens and two young lambs. Four horses pulled the cart, with eight more relegated to the tasks of carrying the adults and their packs. Emilie and Felda joined their group along with their parents, Jarvis and Ulka; both women had three young children to tend, their husbands having left them to join the Prince's army. My crew would meet Freia's family near the western gate, not far from the Denlinger house. Then they would head for the main trade route to Schwabia in a giant caravan of Teutons fleeing the inevitable downfall.

Quite a few noblewomen left their estates behind that same week, taking their children and some servants with them as they scattered toward all points of the compass save north. The increase in trade that came with the melting snows slowed that year. Word of the Saxons' intentions had reached the far corners of Europe, it seemed, holding the foreign traders back from passing through Teutonic lands. All of our allies would forsake us, leaving us as prey to the vengeful Holy Roman Empire and its demonic legion from the past.

I spoke my final goodbyes to my children and favorite servants early that morning over breakfast, for I had no desire to follow them to the city to face more farewells with the Denlingers. Freia and I had exchanged our last words several days prior, and in secret I wept more bitterly for her than for my own children. She had been such a good friend to me during my days in the eleventh century. I would face Muniche's defeat alone, for I planned to order my vassals and remaining servants away within the next few weeks if they continued to remain behind.

After my children had departed, the Thaden house seemed empty and full of ghosts, most of the rooms bare of furniture, the floorboards creaking with the shifting temperatures. When I met Augustin in my dreams, I often bemoaned my loneliness, begging him with the pain of my heart to come to me, though I never spoke my requests aloud. He was back at his cabin near Eisenwald that month, for he had left the Saxons and the *Toteheri* behind in late December, returning to his home to record the history he had witnessed in grand detail. He had never written such an intriguing account in all of his days, he told me at one point. His flaming eyes gleamed like blue comets when he declared that it was good that he had held himself back from killing Prince Otto thus far. It appeased his urge for vengeance to watch him suffer.

I asked him whether he intended to come to Muniche to observe the Prince's worst loss firsthand, but he shook his head, replying that the filial curse still held him back from the city of his birth. The temptation to interfere with history would be far too great if he watched Muniche burn, he admitted. Though the city had cast him out, he still loved her. If he watched the *Toteheri* ravage Muniche, he feared that he would unleash his deadly anger upon them, wiping them off the face of the earth before their time had come.

So I resigned myself to my fate of observing Muniche's fall alone, seeing my master only in my dreams, allowing him to watch the destruction through my eyes. I still feared what would become of our heart-bond once death sent me back to my time, for I knew that my bond with Augustin was rooted in the past. We knew that he would remain in the Middle Ages far longer than any other chronicler, recording histories for posterity, taking down information on dark arts and rituals, including the spells of the Torstein. The mere idea of leaving him behind struck blades through my heart, for I loved him so deeply, and I had not yet convinced him to turn from evil. I feared that if I lost him in time, he would fall into hell with Wuotan's chains locked upon him forever. So I clutched the insane possibility that perhaps our heart-bond would hold true over a span of a thousand years, silently praying that God would give us more time.

A heavy rainstorm descended upon Muniche on the Thursday after my children had gone, cloaking the landscape in a dismal gray that matched my mood. I spent most of the day reading through the Psalms, struggling to find peace with the harsh days to come. When a silvery voice slithered its way into my ears, I jerked upright on my bed, the Bible sliding onto the floor. "*Zoubaraera Teutona.*"

I invoked my ice into my eyes, veiling my vision in frigid blue—and, to my utter surprise, I saw the *Eihalbe* of the Thaden grounds sitting casually upon the windowsill, its wings stilled, its multihued eyes staring straight into mine. I gawked at the fairy for a moment in silence, unsure what to make of its presence in my house, in my very bedroom. *I thought they never stray far from their trees . . . and our silver oak is a half-hour walk from the manor. Is all of Teutonic lore wrong where the Eihalbae are concerned?*

"Noble *Eihalbe*," I greeted, heat rising in my cheeks. I cleared my throat and broke eye contact, trying to smooth out the wrinkles in my dress. I had not bothered to comb my hair that day, so I reached back to tug my dress's hood over my messy mop. "I can't say I ever expected to have a fairy visit me in my house."

"Few Teutons are aware of our comings and goings in spite of their elemental advantage."

I looked toward my silvery companion, abruptly realizing that the Saxons and their unholy force may root up every silver oak in Teuton lands. Augustin had showed me how the *Toteheri* had blackened the earth around Regensburg, making it infertile. "You know what's coming ... don't you?" I guessed.

The *Eihalbe* looked down at its hands, which were clasped in its lap. To my surprise, I saw that its thin fingers trembled. "The *Toteheri* cares not for wood or leaves; their objective is glory through conquest. But traitors fight among them in spirit form . . . and they chop down each of us that they encounter." The fairy met my gaze, and I discerned both fear and wrath in its expression.

My forehead wrinkled as confusion muddled my brain. "There are traitors among them?" I rubbed my temple, trying to remember if Augustin had mentioned that sort of thing. "You mean . . . there are Teutons fighting with the Saxons and the devils' kin? And they destroy every silver oak they find?"

"Yes," the *Eihalbe* responded in a bitter tone. "Teutons of low blood who have discerned the magic of the spirit and lurk in the shadows. They wish to eliminate us because our essence betrayed them. They believe that their sacrilege is justified since Teuton authorities prefer to hide their magic from those they deem lesser."

"Oh . . . shit . . . ." Memories of Augustin's visit to Bamberg twenty years ago arose in my mind: the two Teutons of blood less than ninety percent who were punished for studying the mysteries of the priesthood. *Our essence betrayed them . . . of course. Silver oak leaves reveal the status of Teuton blood ... and priests in this era view those of lower blood status to be unworthy of their secrets.*

Those two Teutons had likely joined with the Saxons to pull the Song of Time from Paulus, collaborating with their traditional enemies to strike back at Teutonic prejudice. "Have you told Prince Otto or any of the other Keyholders? The priests need to fight back against the traitors and cut them down!" Augustin's fire simmered in my blood along with my ice, the blue veil over my vision shifting just a bit.

"They know, but they prefer to concentrate on human casualties rather than those of nature." The fairy looked affronted; it turned its face to look out the window at the heavy rainfall. Its tail snaked around its body, and its fingers trapped its tip to stroke it, as though to calm itself.

"Sometimes I really hate humanity. We haven't learned anything in a thousand years. Nature is just as important as people," I muttered, a sense of uselessness prickling my skin. "I don't know if I'm strong enough to fight a Teuton spirit. I don't know how to help you."

"You have helped my kind more than you realize," the fairy said. "You have taught your children to respect us. Your youngest daughter cherishes the acorn I gave her and yearns to plant and nurture it upon her arrival in the Rhineland."

My jaw dropped at this. I had no clue that the *Eihalbe* had offered Erika an acorn before her departure. "Your dark one has treated his tree well," the fairy added with a significant look in its eyes. "He contacts us in the other realm each time he wishes to harvest its leaves."

"Then we just have to set our sights to the future," I gathered, my elemental agitation gradually abating. I felt a small touch of relief that my wispy companion appreciated what little I had been able to accomplish.

"Carry our story with you on your journey," the fairy advised, rising to hover before the window, its tail swishing nonchalantly at its back. It met my gaze for a protracted interval, its kaleidoscope eyes seeming to study my soul, my motivations. "It is a tale that must be told, *Zoubaraera Teutona.*"

The rain abated on Saturday, and I spent the morning helping more groups of vassals pack their goods, handing chickens, sheep, and horses to their charge. Thirty-nine would depart that day, all women, children, and the elderly. I handed out stipends of gold to each group and pledged to pray for their safety. I suggested that they head south or west and avoid the east, since I knew full well that Salzburg and Passau would fall later next year. But I also warned those whose paths would take them through Augsburg to avoid getting comfortable there. Within a month's time, the western roads would be cut, and I suspected that the Saxons might send a side force to weaken Augsburg while Muniche burned.

That afternoon I received one of the greatest shocks of my life when a knock upon the front door interrupted my Bible reading. I went to answer it myself since most of the household servants had gone or were preparing to flee. When I pulled the door open, I took several steps back, my ice freezing my veins as I found myself staring at Freia's face. She stood upon my threshold, clad in a plain tawny dress and overcoat, her graying blond hair tied underneath a pale net, her green eyes flashing amber at the explosion of my ice.

I tried to speak and found that I could not. *What is she doing here? She left last week with everyone else . . . did she come back for something? Are they all back? Have the Saxons already cut the trade routes? Should I have sent the kids away while the snow still coated the ground? Was it all for nothing?* My frigid breath produced icy clouds in the air between us as I stared at Freia, unable to articulate any of my confusion, unable to step forward to touch her.

My best friend stepped into the parlor at last, sensing my momentary loss, securing the door behind her. She reached to take one of my frozen hands in hers, sending rays of light into my horrified spirit. "Swanie, don't look so frightened. I didn't go with the children. I chose to stay." She gazed solemnly into my eyes, her expression suggesting that she had planned this from the start.

"Freia . . . ." I choked, horror washing over me. "*How* could you . . . *why* would you . . . decide to stay . . . when you know . . . when you *know* . . . ."

Freia smiled at me tenderly, placing her hands on my shoulders and leading me to the couch, helping me sit. Once my frozen body had sunk into the cushion, she knelt before me and massaged my hands. "Be still, Swanie, be calm," she urged. "I decided to stay the moment you told Heinrich and me the truth. I didn't want you to have to face this by yourself, since I know that your health isn't good. Once your servants have gone, I feared that you might succumb to the effects of weakness before the city meets its end. When I heard you say that you had come to my time to watch Muniche burn . . . I knew I would stay with you . . . care for you . . . so you can succeed in what you came to do." She smiled again and squeezed my hands. "Now pull your element back, Swanie, before you freeze us both."

"Freia . . . ." I moaned, closing my eyes to concentrate on her touch, ordering my ice to subside, willing her light to invigorate my spirit. "Freia . . . you *can't* stay here . . . no matter how much you love me. The siege will *kill* you . . . you're going to *die*." I opened my eyes to stare at my best friend's face. I envisioned her falling into Saxon hands, raped and tortured before being put to death at last.

"I am ready to die, Swanie," she told me quietly, her eyes sincere. "I know that Heinrich will not survive this battle, and I don't want to live without him once this scar fades." She looked down at her left wrist and the pink mark there. "He has been my life for so long . . . the most loving husband I could ever have known. Since our children will survive to carry on our legacy in the Rhineland, there's no reason for me to remain a bitter old widow. Lorraine and Heino are mature enough to carry on our family's legacy for me."

"But what if he *does* live?" I questioned, appalled by my most sensible friend's unexpected display of madness. "Do you think he wants you to stay in Muniche and starve to death on my account? You're not weak like me. Your feet could certainly make the trip to Eisenwald. And you're still beautiful. What if the Saxons get hold of your body before killing you?" I bit my lip.

"Don't worry. I'll commit suicide before it comes to that," she assured me with a disgusted frown. "And you need not waste your breath trying to persuade me to leave. I'm going to watch this city burn at your side and die with you, my sister of blood, gaining what honor a Teuton by blood alone can have."

I sighed, shutting my eyes again as I accepted the fact that I could not convince Freia to reconsider. Her family had already gone. If she departed now, she would travel alone, likely meeting a worse fate than the one slated for Muniche. But I whispered one final plea as I entwined my fingers with hers. The intensity of our elements strengthened our bond of friendship. "Freia, you shouldn't do this just for me . . . when it'll cost you your life."

"It will be my greatest honor to fight beside my blood-sister against those who have come to destroy us," she said confidently, her countenance glowing with radiant light. I hugged her close to me and whispered my thanks in her ear, for she had saved me from my worst fear—to face Muniche's fall alone.

News traveled slowly throughout Teuton lands of the gradual advance of the Saxons and their demonic allies. More and more citizens of Muniche left their homes behind, the peasants trekking on foot with their possessions strapped to their backs as they headed for the Alps. Any remaining men—from the elderly to boys who had not yet reached the age of ten—began preparing to defend their city from the invading army, buttressing the walls and hoarding stones and barrels of oil to cast upon their enemies.

The gates of the city were reinforced, the keys in the hands of Lady Maria in the Prince's absence. Her health had declined steadily since Christmas, and some talebearers claimed that she could no longer drag herself out of bed to open and close the gates at dawn and dusk. The task of guarding the city gates had fallen to the toll takers, and I snickered at the mental image of Garin Zeuner protecting the eastern gate. He had grown into a rather bulky man past fifty, and his jolly visage would not deter any foes from attempting to storm the drawbridge.

The Prince's militia returned to Muniche in late April, bolstered by Teuton warriors from Salzburg, Augsburg, Ratisbon, and many small settlements across the Bavarian countryside. They positioned themselves in a semicircle around the city walls, entrenching their forces in the hills with the Isar at their backs to throw their final efforts at the Saxons, hoping to defeat them before they could ruin the greatest Teuton stronghold. By that time, our enemies had cut every road except the one to the east, the river remaining our sole advantage against our doom.

On some afternoons I followed the Meldorf Stream to where it met the Isar, watching the weary Teuton soldiers preparing for their last stand. According to all of the histories I had read, Muniche would fall to the Saxons during the first week of July after over two months of blockade. Many times, I wished that I could find the strength to fight alongside the soldiers, using my ice to freeze at least some of our foes before the warriors of the *Toteheri* vanquished me.

But then I would sense the weakness in my ankles, the pains stabbing at my innards, and I would silently curse myself for never losing the weight of pregnancy. When I felt particularly low, I occasionally found myself cursing Augustin for crippling me in his vain attempt to convince me to stop loving him. When he had relinquished his body to Wuotan's charge, he had rendered me unable to defend myself against the coming onslaught, unable to fight for my city as I longed to do.

The last of my servants and vassals left on the first Saturday of May, taking most of my remaining goods with them as they fled east along the river. Freia came to my doorstep that afternoon and urged me to join her within the city walls, for she feared that I would not last long with no one to help me maintain my manor. The Saxons had begun to engage the Prince's army by that time, attempting to get through the defenses to cross the Isar and cut Muniche off from any outside aid. I knew that they would soon succeed in their plot, so the following morning I left the Thaden estate behind me forever.

I rode my one remaining horse to the eastern gate of Muniche to face her bloody fate with her. I packed two bulging bags with goods and victuals, wanting to stave off the inevitable starvation for as long as possible. Among my wares I included several extra dresses, along with my few remaining possessions from the twenty-first century—my Bible and my camera. Augustin had deposited all of the camera's dead batteries into the Elbe when the Saxons had first started scuffling with our people back in 1053. I had already traded my mother's jewelry, and my small supply of contact lenses was long since gone. Hopefully everything would come back with me when I entered the gates of time, like it did during my first trip so long ago.

I met Garin Zeuner for the last time when I approached the drawbridge, which had not been lowered that day due to the propinquity of the Saxon army. The toll taker himself accosted me when I halted my horse at the water's edge, his face overcome with distress at the sight of the bags piled behind my saddle. He shuffled toward me and cried out, "My Lady Swanhilde, you should have escaped long ago! The danger is nigh, my lady. You must not linger!"

I tilted my head at him forlornly. "There'll be no escape for me, Mr. Zeuner," I said. "I need you to lower the bridge for me, and I'm prepared to pay any fee you require." I pulled thirty Thaler from my dress as I spoke.

His mouth dropped open, and sweat began to bead on his forehead. "Lady Swanhilde, they have forbidden me to lower the bridge today for anyone save the Prince's forces. All of the gates have been bolted as of this morning, when the last people who wished to flee were allowed out. You mustn't enter Muniche now, my lady," he finished with a look of horror. "Anyone who didn't flee today will be locked inside until the battle is won . . . Muniche will become a tomb."

I sighed, realizing that Mr. Zeuner had accepted the impending invasion and intended to stand and fight once the Saxons had forded the river. I ducked my head at him, impressed by his gallantry, and told him solemnly, "If you wish to remain and defend Muniche from her enemies, I can beg you only to grant me the same privilege. I'll get inside Muniche today with or without your help, but if I have to scale the walls, I'll be forced to leave my provisions behind . . . and that would accelerate my end." I gazed down at him soberly.

After a few more arguments, the toll taker finally bowed to my wishes. He said that I could enter the city with the soldiers who were slated to come through at Sext.

I passed the next hour sitting at the riverbank beside Mr. Zeuner, sharing stories of our lives and dreams, all of which had crashed to the ground with the Saxon attack. His wife had borne him three children, two sons and a daughter. His oldest son, Ulrich, had died at Regensburg the previous autumn. He had sent the rest of his family to Salzburg a month before, and he hoped that they would find peace there while he stayed behind to defend Muniche. I did not share my thoughts on that subject, since I knew that Salzburg would also fall to the Saxons within a year. I did tell him that my children had gone to the Rhineland back in March, along with Freia's children.

After Mr. Zeuner had lowered the drawbridge for the knights, I dropped my thirty Thaler into his hands, though currency would likely be meaningless in a few more days. Then I led my horse onto the bridge and crossed the Isar without a backward glance. I would not leave Muniche again until she crumbled to the earth, when the black claws of death thrust me through the gates of time. This was what I had come to see, and I would not shirk my duty.

I installed myself in Freia's house shortly thereafter, unpacking my food and storing it deep inside her pantry. I commented that once the siege had truly begun, we may have to deal with hungry looters seeking nutrients. Freia replied that she could blind any thieves with her light and possibly burn their eyes with the sun's rays if we caught them before they could enter the house. I doubted that my ice would hold much sway against famished Teutons, but maybe Augustin's fire would rise in my spirit again if I found myself endangered. I wondered if I might be able to sear some Saxon flesh before the end.

I discovered later that day, when I took a short walk around the western side of the city, that very few people remained on the streets. Most of the cottages I passed appeared vacant, with no lights glowing in any windows. In the gutters, I saw a few infirm peasants who had not been able to flee, searching for food in the grime. A morbid triumph flowed through my veins as I realized that most of my people had indeed scattered before the siege, taking their blood to lands far away to preserve its magic for future generations.

When the sky darkened with evening, the bells in the cathedral mournfully tolling the melodies of Compline to a damned city, I lifted my face to the sunset, gazing at the empty houses and vine-covered wall in the distance, my ice solidifying my courage for the coming days of want. "Do not despair, Muniche," I whispered to the sky, "for this is not the end. You shall rise again, for I have seen it."

Chapter Thirty-one

He Did Not Forsake Me

As the month of May progressed into June, the city of Muniche descended into a dire state of barrenness. The few civilians who remained retreated into the shadows by day and stalked the streets at night in search of food and supplies. The gutters grew more repulsive each day, the peasants who once cleaned them having either fled or shirked their duties. Most of the shopkeepers had gone long before, their stock depleted as the days passed and desperation rose.

Along with the elderly and sick, injured warriors began to be deposited within the city walls, housed in the cathedral and the city hall, cared for by the few medics who had not taken flight. Freia and I began lending our untrained hands to aid the wounded in the town hall, just a few streets away from her family's house. The smells of blood and pus twisted my stomach as I granted the fallen soldiers the relief of ice on their lesions, what little I could offer them in my scant knowledge of medieval medicine. Freia's bright countenance cheered their weary spirits while she bandaged their wounds and fed them herbal tea, her smile belying the calamity around her.

It appeared that the Saxons had chosen to hold their inhuman army in reserve for the time being. I had yet to encounter any warriors whose wounds showed the signs of creeping death, like the ones that Augustin had shown me outside of Bamberg. Our enemies seemed to have decided that Regensburg had fallen too soon, that this time they would render both the city and its army desolate before striking the fatal blow. Freia and I exchanged speculations on whether the *Toteheri* would crumble the city walls with their deadly touch, or if the Saxons would use the standard mortars and battering rams first.

I decided by mid-June that watching a siege firsthand was not particularly encouraging. I had butchered my horse on my second day in the city, knowing that Freia and I would have no use for the animal otherwise. She had slain her handful of chickens and goats shortly before my arrival. Her family had kept a small garden and several blackberry bushes in their backyard, which was enclosed with a high stone wall. I rained my ice upon her plants each morning before we set out for the town hall, hoping to preserve our sources of food for as long as possible.

My best friend had the tendency to take a few strips of meat and a handful of berries or vegetables with her when we walked to the town hall each morning, giving her resources away to the poor who crossed our paths. I advised her more than once to halt her generosity, for several urchins had begun to gather near her front door in hopes of scampering inside to pilfer our food. Freia shrugged off my concern, saying that she would be in heaven in less than a month, and that she did not want her Lord to regard her as stingy. I rolled my eyes in frustration and made a habit of slapping the beggars away with hands of ice any time I passed through Freia's door, snapping at them to loiter somewhere else.

On some afternoons, I climbed the turret at the southwestern corner of the city wall for a good look at the skirmishes below. The Prince's forces had camped right around the bulwarks with the Saxons and the *Toteheri* lurking in the distance, biding their time while the Teutons starved. I witnessed a few token battles on the outskirts of the landscape, slashing swords and clattering spears and clubs creating a muted din. It looked as though our enemies were working on constructing trebuchets to hurl stones, though my eyes could not quite pick out the details even with my ice enhancing my vision. I wondered whether they had used the wood of silver oak trees to build their war machines. I silently prayed that they would spare the one on Thaden grounds, for it hurt my heart to imagine that *Eihalbe's* life snuffed out so carelessly.

When I met Augustin in my dreams during that fearsome month, we discussed the siege at length. Both of us concluded that our enemies were drawing this battle out for the purpose of sapping the Teutons' morale. The Saxons had cut all of the routes in and out of my beleaguered city by mid-June, surrounding Muniche entirely, taking control of the Isar to halt all trade, sitting on prosperity while my people slowly died.

On the last day of that awful month, my ice detected a disturbing lack of comradeship from nature when I woke to the melodies of Lauds. Once I had pulled a dress over my head, I raced into the backyard on the power of my ice, all of my senses streaming in every direction, seeking water … water … *water* . . . . There was nothing.

Panic clutched my chest, and I charged for the back gate, bursting through and shutting it securely behind me. I set my course for the southwestern turret, my ice overtaking more and more of my body. I endeavored to hurry and channeled my element into my ankles, silently ordering my Teutonic vitality to grant me a vigor that was not my own. *There can't be no water anywhere. It's impossible . . . .*

My hair had frozen completely when I sprang upon the steps to the tower where the southern and western walls met. I took them two at a time, a feat I had not been able to accomplish since Augustin had ruined my feet eleven years ago. My adrenaline drove me forward with a strange but waning desperation. When I halted before the first window with a view toward the mountains, I froze into a sculpture, my energy extinguished. Though I had to squint to see the truth from such a great distance, there was no denying the absence of the river that marked my city's eastern border. *The* Toteheri *had dammed the Isar . . . they had dried our river, Muniche's primary source of water.*

"It won't be long now," I told Freia wearily when I returned to her house, limping badly as a result of my elemental outburst. "They've dried the Isar. We're going to run out of water."

Freia gasped and raced out the front door to check the nearby well. She came back moments later and whispered, "The well is completely dry, not even a drop at the bottom." She collapsed onto a chair across from me at the kitchen table, covering her face with her hands. "How can they *do* such things . . . how can any humans have these powers of Satan?"

"I don't know," I answered flatly, shaking my head. I lifted my feet onto a stool and fingered my throbbing ankles. "But I wish I could figure out how to kill them. This is insane . . . and I'm not going down without a fight."

That night I informed Augustin of the Saxons' latest scheme. My spirit trembled with ire as I cried out that they would kill me with dehydration before they burnt the city down around my shoulders. "My ice can provide water enough for Freia and me, but I'm already raining it on her garden every morning. If I have to start melting it just so we can have something to drink, that's going to sap what little energy I have left. We're already out of beer and mead." I shook my head and glared toward the enemies' tents from where we stood as dreaming spirits upon the city wall. "There *has* to be some way to kill these ghouls . . . and if they're in direct contact with Wuotan himself . . . maybe *you* would have to do it." I lifted an eyebrow at my master in silent implication.

Augustin frowned thoughtfully, his eyes locked upon the reposing army. "I know not if even I could hold sway against the forces of time, but you may have a point." He crossed his arms and glanced at me, then at the tents below us. "Only devil's blood can defeat a devil's kin . . . and since the blood in my veins is dead indeed—a gift from Wuotan

—perhaps I shall have to emerge from the background after Muniche burns, so this heathen force may be properly punished."

"You shouldn't wait that long," I muttered, drifting close to his spirit, our robes merging though we could not appreciate the sensation in the realm of dreams. "We have no time now. Soon I'll be dead . . . and we will be eternally separated . . . Augustin . . . my darling . . . my master . . . ." Sorrow washed over me in a tidal wave, and I closed my eyes against his inevitable rebuke. "I wish . . . oh, I wish . . . you would . . . I wish . . . ." I could not go on, for I knew that my desires were futile. He would never come to me.

Augustin said nothing for a long interval, his silence enfolding me while I wept over my foolish love for him, a demon's slave who held me impassively at a distance. But when I sank down upon the stones of the wall, I felt his fingers stroke my heart with a tenderness infused with commitment. An impossible oath poured from his lips in response to my agony: "My precious Swanhilde, you know me better than that. I shall not let go of your heart that easily. The forces of time shall have to rip you from me with the power of God . . . or I shall never release you."

On the first day of July, I forsook my duties at the town hall to climb the southeastern turret, the one that provided a view toward my property. I looked down at the Prince's forces entrenched in the dry riverbed, then toward the Saxon army in the distance. They likely lounged at the Thaden estate now, growing plump on the spelt that my vassals had planted last winter. I should have burnt it all with Augustin's fire before leaving for the city, but I had not thought of it at the time.

I leaned my body against the railing surrounding the uppermost balcony of the tower and closed my eyes as I sent my ice out of me, sensing the Teutonic life pulsing beneath me. Though I was alone in the turret, my soldiers waited below, prepared to protect my city till the very end. A weary smile curled upon my lips, and my ice caressed each of their spirits in turn, granting them my hopes for an honorable battle. I sensed a myriad of elements as my ice floated with the breeze: earth . . . wind . . . smoke . . . yellow fire . . . energy . . . stone . . . lightning . . . mist . . . molten rock . . . blue fire . . . .

. . . BLUE FIRE??

My eyes popped open as my ice zeroed in on that familiar element, that cobalt fire I had not sensed with my mortal body in over a decade now. *Could it be?* Disbelief conquered me briefly, for any Teuton soldier might be blue fire—it was, after all, one of many specific manifestations of that potent primary. But this blue fire seemed further away than the Teuton warriors below me, across the dry river, prowling in the trees in no man's land. I closed my eyes again and ordered my ice to confront this hidden fire, to reveal its identity to me. And to my utter astonishment, I sensed an answering flicker, a familiar embrace. *It IS Augustin!!* I could hardly believe it; he had come to me!

I hefted my body atop the stone balustrade, invoking my ice to freeze me to the brink of the spiritual crossing. My rational mind questioned what I was about to do, but I cast aside all fears; for my emotions were blooming with eternal love, my heart throbbing with uncanny vitality. *If I die this way, so be it. Augustin won't let that happen.*

With an exultant scream, I leapt from the turret into the sky, hurtling to the ground in a straight trajectory for the glade near the riverbank. Ice crystals rained behind me, and I sensed the air wafting to buoy me, to send me to my Black Priest.

I overheard a few gasps rising from the encamped Teuton soldiers as I shot across the dried river, but I paid them no heed. Flaring my arms out, I grasped what scant moisture lingered in the atmosphere to slow my descent. I landed upon a clump of browning weeds several meters from the stand of trees, mist clothing me in vapor when my clogs hit the ground with a bit more force than necessary. *Ouch.*

Agony spurted upward from the soles of my feet to my knees, and I crouched low, my icy right hand pressed upon my heart as I worked to force my lungs to draw breath. I calmed my ice, drawing the mist around me into my spirit to reinforce my element. I would sorely pay for my gusto later. The pain that had stabbed my ankles now throbbed in my head. But I shoved the ache aside and heaved myself to my feet, turning for the trees. I stumbled forward on weakened ankles, my quaking arms outstretched to embrace my immortal lover.

His strong arms caught me the second I slipped into the shade, his voice calling to me through the haze that had draped my exhausted mind. "For pity's sake, Swanhilde, you should not have attempted such a hazardous leap without the aid of a river or snow. I feared your thrill would be your undoing."

I could not answer him at first, for my weariness had snapped something in my brain. I began weeping hysterically while he held me against his chest, his fire warming me deep inside. The sane part of my mind recognized the foolishness of my reaction, but I had resigned myself to never seeing Augustin again in the mortal world before death sent me home. Now he was here, *with me*, against all logic, breaking all rules.

My tormented brain whispered in my ear that I must be dreaming, that I could not actually feel my master's arms around me, his fire heating my blood as the summer's warmth never could. Slowly, I raised my face from his chest, blinking my tears away to stare at Augustin's familiar face. His skin appeared ghostly pale, his black hair long and perfect, his eyes reflecting the glory of the sky. "Are you . . . really here?" I panted for breath as I looked from his face to the black cloak covering his chest, helping him blend in with the shade of the trees.

His lips quivered as he observed my wavering emotions. He brushed one fiery hand across my cheek and answered softly, "Yes, my swan, yes . . . I am here with you." His mouth molded with mine a moment later, and he swept me into his arms to cradle me like a weightless child, kissing me with a fervor that I had not experienced since 1055, during that blissful day beside the Rhine.

When he released my mouth, I moaned quietly, my hormones racing with a newly awakened fury, making me feel twenty again. "But why are you here?" I whispered to him, shivering at the tenderness that radiated from his gaze. "I thought . . . you couldn't come . . . to Muniche."

A wry smile appeared on his lips, and his eyes glittered. He sat down upon the earth and leaned against a withered linden, setting me upon his lap, his strong hands shifting to clutch my own. "My darling, you should recall that rules mean little to a dead man. When I took the time to truly ponder the state of things last week, knowing that you were here alone, about to face death—and knowing that you braved the currents of time just to observe this terrible event of history for yourself—it occurred to me that no curse could hold me back from watching it myself. If this is to be labeled the greatest Teutonic defeat in all of history, it would do no good for me—the cursed chronicler— to miss it."

I smiled a bit uncertainly in response. Disappointment dulled my euphoria at the realization that Augustin had come to watch Muniche burn, not to keep me company in these final days. "So you came to see your people fall," I translated, my expression likely appearing rather disenchanted.

My master tilted his head at me coyly and replied, "As *you* came to see your people fall." I lowered my gaze to the fabric of my bodice, valiantly attempting to push aside my foolish longings, my hopes that he had come just for me. There was no point in wishing for sympathy from a Black Priest who yearned for the day that our bond would break, freeing him permanently from the cords of love.

But his right hand reached out to tilt my face upward to meet his gaze—and even with my mortal senses, I could clearly detect the devotion pouring from his aura. "Swanie, my love," he murmured, his sonorous voice piercing my soul, "rend the doubt from your heart. I would have come for this downfall whether you were here or not, but your presence with me shall make these last moments a heaven in the depths of hell . . . if you would allow me to protect you until you wish to die."

I closed my eyes while he spoke, concentrating on the adoration flowing from his spirit into mine through our bond. He wanted me still, though I had grown stout and unattractive—he loved me, and he wanted to protect me until the end. A quiet sigh escaped my lips, but I opened my eyes a second later when a rather unsettling thought struck me. "Protect me until I wish to die . . . then you . . . intend . . . to kill me . . . Augustin?" I frowned as a rather disquieting piece of the puzzle fell into place. He had wanted to kill me from the beginning.

He leaned down to kiss me softly, a brief touch of fire. "Yes, Swanhilde . . . I do intend to kill you, when you ask it of me. I would make it simple, painless, far better than starving or wasting away at the hands of the *Toteheri*. You have suffered enough in this era, my love. I do not wish your last act to add to your grief, as you watch your city crumble around you."

Fear warred with an odd relief inside my soul. I could think of many ways Augustin could kill me that would be far easier than falling prey to the Saxons. He could use his death gift against me, stopping my heart in an instant . . . or he could kill me somehow in my sleep . . . bleed me dry . . . kiss me until I died from lack of oxygen . . . . I shook my head once and said, "Neither of us will have long to wait. The *Toteheri* can't hold the Isar back indefinitely. I think they'll storm the gates within two or three days."

Augustin grimaced. "Yes, and then I must record the most disheartening chapter in Teuton history," he said, his gaze lifted to the walls of Muniche.

I sighed and leaned my left cheek against his chest. "Where are you planning to stay at night?" I inquired, wondering if he had brought any belongings with him. I had not noticed any bundles lying in the thicket.

"I do not know, for I arrived just after Sext and hid myself here until your ice called to me from the turret. I may spend the nights scouring the opposing camps, taking notes on the formations for battle, perhaps attempting to send a few of the heathen warriors back to the abyss." He paused and looked down at me as I gazed back at him steadily, an unspoken suggestion in my eyes.

He bit his lip, then finished, "Or I could attempt to scale the city walls, to see if the murderer's curse can truly chain me from the place of my birth. You and Freia are living alone in the Denlinger house. Once the remaining inhabitants of Muniche have found themselves desiccated, some may try to force water from your spirit, an injustice that I could not allow."

Augustin's eyes flashed cobalt, and he bent his head to my neck. His lips locked upon my throat for a long moment, prompting me to moan as his death sucked the life from my veins without cutting them. When he lifted his head at last, he bared his teeth at me like a vampire and declared, "Your vitality belongs to *me*, not to some starving vagabond."

"I'll be waiting for you then . . . tonight?" I breathed, my heart pounding at the possibilities of such an arrangement.

He nodded once, his expression grim. "If the curse holds me back, I shall call for you and meet you upon the wall. In the meantime, I shall prowl the edges of the enemies' camp to form a proper analysis of what we are up against. Do you and Freia require any extra food or water, clothing or firewood?"

"We're good on clothing and firewood, but food and drink would be helpful. What are you going to do, steal it from the Saxons?" I queried demurely.

He snickered and kissed me on the nose. "I do what I must, my lovely swan princess. Now, you must return to Muniche before the arid atmosphere further depletes your verve. Your leap from the turret melted your ice for the present, so I would suggest that you use my fire to climb the city wall. Fire sweeps upward more effortlessly than ice, and I could grant your spirit a bit of my own power before you depart, to prepare you."

An inquisitive smile played upon my lips. "How do you intend to do that, master?"

He chuckled darkly and rose to his feet, setting me upon the ground and taking my face in his burning hands, his eyes delving into my spirit. "Draw the fire out of you now, Swanhilde my love; feel its potency, feel its strength, *know* that it is ours," he intoned. "Allow it to supersede your ice entirely, as you once did long ago, when we danced in our dreams upon the Bayern gardens. *Burn* your body—your hands, your hair, your eyes—show it to me."

I took a deep breath and concentrated, shutting my eyes. I called Augustin's fire into my veins, inviting it to consume them with a deadly heat. His hands infused my spirit with an impossible vigor, a dark glory, his blue-fired heart pounding in union with mine. I felt heat radiating from my pores, my hair swirling around my head in flames of cerulean, enveloping the whole of my dress and hood. When I opened my eyes again, Augustin smiled and let go of me. "Exquisite," he commended. "Now go, singe the ivy of Muniche's wall, and I shall see you tonight."

Chapter Thirty-two

Realizing a Transient Dream

When I returned to the Denlinger house soon afterward, I reentered through the backyard and kitchen, so I need not face the begging urchins at the front door. Freia would not return until Vespers, for she had gone to care for the wounded at the town hall that morning as usual. I spent a few minutes checking our supplies, discovering that we had only four strips of meat left, one slab of unleavened bread, and one jar of cherry preserves from the previous year. Two bottles of red wine remained in the back of the liquor cabinet. We planned to enjoy those on the last day, to celebrate our futures in heaven and the twenty-first century while the city burned around us.

I sighed when I realized that I would have to melt some of my ice for water later, unless Augustin chanced to find some beer or other drink somewhere in his travels. My extreme elemental displays of that afternoon had drained me to a shell, for my middle-aged body did not have the drive I had boasted in my youth. I knew that I ought to check the status of the vegetables in the garden, but my vitality had vanished for the time being. So I sank down onto a couch in one of the back parlors, closing my eyes to rest for the coming night—when I would likely face the erotic embraces of an immortal priest for the first time in over a decade.

Many licentious thoughts breezed through my brain as I drifted gradually towards sleep. *So Augustin has decided to stay, to protect Freia and me from the horde, to provide us with much needed victuals . . . but he doesn't need to sleep. I'll take him to the bedroom Freia lent me . . . and I'm no longer married . . . .*

But I'm almost forty-three . . . an old witch . . . my hair going gray . . . my stomach bloated from pregnancies . . . my legs coated with spider veins . . . my face covered in pockmarks . . . my breasts sagging. There's no way he'll want me that way, not when he can have sex with Wuotan's gorgeous sirens whenever he wants. Their elements are far more potent than what mortal humans can claim . . . he told me that before . . . .

But I want him so desperately . . . I want him inside me . . . his fire uniting with my ice . . . he makes me feel so young. But I shouldn't, because it's still sinful. I've had him enough already . . . even though we will never meet again after I return to the future . . . I can't have sex with him. But abstinence will drive me insane . . . .

I woke from my restless slumber to the touch of Freia's light upon my spirit, her soft hands stroking my forehead. "How are you, Swanie?" she inquired when I opened my eyes, blinking away the sleep. "You look unwell. I can bring you some wine . . . don't get up."

"No, no, I'm fine, Freia. I've just had . . . a very strange day." I pushed myself up into a sitting position, wincing as pain struck me in the abdomen. Once I managed to shove the discomfort aside, I beckoned Freia to sit down beside me while I told her the story of my incredible afternoon. Her countenance lit up with joy for me when I spoke of Augustin, words of adoration and gratitude for his faithfulness spilling from my lips.

Freia hugged me tightly, but unease marred her happy smile as I said, "We ought to clean a bit before he gets here.

He said he might bring us some food and water, although he'll probably steal it from the Saxons, not that it bothers me." I grimaced.

"Swanie…there's one thing that … disturbs me," Freia said as I rose to my feet, intending to seek out a dusting rag. I turned back to face her and saw that her gaze was riveted upon the floorboards, her slender hands clutching the couch rather fitfully. "I don't know if I can … condone what you plan to do … with your lover. You're not married to him, and you're going to sleep with him tonight. I'm just … uncomfortable … with the idea of fornication happening inside of my house." She broke off, her pale cheeks reddening.

I sighed heavily, for that very problem had festered in my mind and heart the whole time I had rested upon the couch. "I know, Freia," I conceded, scuffing my clogs upon the floorboards. "This is your house, of course. I guess I'll go clean one of the other bedrooms for him, though he'll probably just go back out to study the soldiers, after he's shared his plunder with us."

Freia lifted her eyes to mine, gratitude evident in her gaze. I nodded at her, then turned to complete my task, thrusting aside the frustration of unfulfilled desire. *You're better off not getting in bed with him anyway,* I thought. *You're fat, pockmarked, and weak. Augustin wouldn't find what he wants in you, when he can screw Wuotan's sirens anytime. His immortal lust would probably kill you.*

Augustin appeared at the front door as the heavens burst with vermillion, the setting sun hovering over the western wall in a glowing scarlet orb. He complained that he might have to slay the waifs that sprawled across Freia's threshold just to put them out of their misery. "I could see their ribs poking through their rags," he observed caustically on his way to the kitchen, where he plopped two large sacks upon the table. "And I could detect hardly a trace of life coursing through their blood."

"Well, if you kill them, don't tell Freia," I advised in English, glancing toward the back staircase, where I could hear my best friend's footsteps approaching. "She is far more righteous than either you or me. She has forbidden us from committing fornication within the walls of her house."

A harsh bark of laughter burst from Augustin's throat. "Damn saintly Rhinelander," he muttered in the same tongue. "She's ruined my plans for tonight." He grinned at me, showing his teeth and rubbing his hands together rather wickedly.

I smirked at him and glanced at his bags, then settled onto one of the kitchen chairs. "Did you bring your chains and knives?" Memories of our most recent sexual encounter arose in my brain. I tried not to shudder.

Augustin's grin turned into a shadowy scowl. "You ought not to joke in such ludicrous ways, Swanhilde," he reproved me. "I never intend to hurt you like that again." His eyes darkened considerably, and he looked away, bowing properly as Freia entered the kitchen. "My lovely Lady Freia Denlinger. What a privilege it is to meet you again, though I regret that it must be under such bleak circumstances." He raised her right hand to his lips, greeting her with the propriety of the young lord he had once been.

Freia blushed at Augustin's flattery and drew her hand away. "I thank you for your kindness," she replied shyly, "and it is a . . . pleasure . . . to see you as well . . . my lord . . . ." She hesitated.

Augustin's lips curled into a mysterious smirk. "You may call me Wolfgang, my lady," he said. "Now come, sit with your blood-sister, and eat. I have scrounged a feast for us this night." He pulled a chair out for Freia, then opened one of his sacks with a flourish, revealing a heaping pile of dried venison, fresh wild cherries and blackberries, edible roots from the forest, and two bottles of beer. I gasped in shock at his impressive booty, and Augustin added that if I could find it within myself to produce enough water for a soup, he would prepare the roots and meat over the cooking fire while we enjoyed the fruit.

We spoke on many topics during dinner. Augustin allowed Freia and me to do most of the talking, discussing our families and the lives we had lost. My master expressed hope that Heinrich would somehow survive the coming fray, and that by some twist of fate he and Freia could reunite with their children at Eisenwald. I saw my best friend smile sadly at Augustin's words, glancing down at the marriage scar upon her left wrist. She undoubtedly wondered how long it would remain. Augustin said that life would become far more interesting with a brood of young Teutons residing near his abode. Although he knew that they would shun him due to the curse, he promised that he would aid them with traditions and rituals, if they wished it.

As Freia cleaned the kitchen, lighting a few candles to brighten the rooms against the deepening twilight, Augustin and I adjourned to the back parlor where I had napped earlier. He planned to claim that room as his quarters due to our hostess' chariness about his sharing my bedroom. I sank onto the couch while he unpacked his second bag, revealing several changes of clothing, writing materials, a wicked-looking dagger, a coiled rope, several bars of soap, and a comb.

When he saw me looking at the dagger, he grinned and snatched it up, flipping it around his right hand expertly with the comment, "Considering the seriousness of the events I came to scrutinize, I prepared myself on all fronts. I doubt that the *Toteheri* has high regard for unobtrusive texts." His dagger clattered to the floor, and he removed his black cloak to reveal a magnificent sword sheathed at his left side.

My eyes flew open as he drew his glittering weapon, the blade whispering its way out of the scabbard, the handle fitting expertly into his palm. "I've never seen you use a sword," I remarked. Augustin swung it in a wide arc, his manners suggesting he imagined severing a Saxon's head.

Augustin snickered and sheathed his sword once more. "You might see me use it often in the coming days, but this night, I have more important matters on my mind." He came to sit beside me on the couch, the blue-flamed candles in the parlor dimming as he gathered me into his arms with a seductive expression. "My darling swan," he crooned in my ear, his lips brushing my neck between phrases, "so long I have dreamed . . . of feeling your body against mine . . . of holding you in my arms . . . one last time . . . ." His tongue traced my jawbone, and he pulled me into his lap, his mouth closing gently upon my throat. His right hand twisted in my hair, his ardor causing my entire body to tremble. My will to abstain from sin was crumbling into powder.

"Oh . . . Augustin . . . ." I could hardly find any words to say. I felt the hands of his spirit caressing my heart in the other realm, sending waves of excitement into my veins. "We could go . . . to some vacant house . . . to some empty bed . . . it doesn't matter." I closed my eyes while he kissed my lips, his heat throbbing through my clothed body, making me wish that he would simply rip my dress off here and now, despite my horrid looks, despite Freia's disapproval.

"Ah . . . you adulterous Christian siren," he murmured when he released my mouth, a bawdy smile appearing on his lips. "I actually had a more honorable idea . . . if you would not mind." He raised one eyebrow and slid his body out from under me, laying me down upon the fabric of the couch.

I propped myself up on my right elbow, my hormones still racing with long-forgotten desire. "What honorable idea?" I asked, my aroused mind unable to follow his implications.

His lewd smile turned gentle as he stood up, his face seeming to look down at me from a grand expanse of darkness, the flames of his candles reflecting in his eyes. "I realize," he began carefully, his expression growing a bit uncertain, "that neither of us has much time, for Muniche shall soon be rendered desolate around us. But even now, as we meet the end together, everlasting severance staring us in the face, I wish . . . yes . . . I wish I could have taken you legally long ago."

A gasp escaped my lips, and Augustin knelt beside me to take my right hand in his. "It is an illogical request, I know, but if our glory must be forever ephemeral, why not grasp its full potential now, releasing both of us from our customary stigma? Swanhilde Rolande Hudson von Thaden . . . I beg for your hand in marriage . . . if you would grant me the unspeakable honor." His fiery eyes smoldered with passion as they stared into mine.

My thoughts whirled in an emotional storm, and I am certain that the room began to spin while I processed his offer. *Marriage . . . with Augustin? Now, at the very end?* Tears of amazement blurred my vision as he stroked my hand, his jaw quivering with what looked like desperation. "But . . . could we even . . . *find* . . . someone . . . to conduct such a ceremony . . . during a siege?" My voice squeaked, insane pictures of myself as Augustin's wife enveloping my mind.

"There must be some clergy left in this squalid city," my master replied, his fingers still infusing my blood with heat. "Any Teuton priests remaining would be outside the walls, with the soldiers. But under the circumstances, holy matrimony would suffice, for me." He smirked and lifted my hand to his lips, kissing my fragile fingers. "I would remind you, my charming seductress, that you have not yet accepted or rejected my offer, and the suspense may kill even me, I fear." He turned my wrist upward and sank his teeth into its veins.

I cried out softly at the stinging pain, but I threw myself upon him, wrapping my free arm around his shoulder. "*Yes*, I'll marry you. Yes!" I squealed like a frenzied child, thoughts of Muniche's downfall smothered beneath the glories of my greatest wish.

Augustin unlocked his teeth from my wrist, closing the wound there in less than a second and gripping my body in a powerful hold, his eyes alight with mad triumph. One of his hands clutched my skull with the force of demon's claws, and his lips descended upon mine again. I found myself pressed upon the floorboards, his body chaining me to the ground while he drank the life from my lips.

Somewhere in the back of my mind I heard a gasp of shock as I lay helpless upon the floor, enslaved by the irresistible love of a dead man. Augustin lifted himself off of me an instant later, his eyes still blazing with mad desire. He glanced away from me, toward the doorway to the dining room. When I lifted my enfeebled head from the floor, I recognized Freia poised there, staring at each of us in turn with wide eyes.

Augustin sighed heavily, the fire in his eyes gradually cooling as he nodded once at my appalled friend. "*Now*," he stated thickly, looking down at me and running his tongue lusciously across his teeth. "We must do this now, before my lust for you nullifies all of my good intentions. Come." He bent down and swept me into his arms without further ado, setting his course for the front door. "Lady Freia, if you should like to accompany us, we are going to the cathedral to be married," he called over his shoulder. He kicked the front door open blithely and leapt past the beggars onto the street beyond.

We reached the main entrance to Muniche's cathedral in less than a minute, according to my internal clock. Augustin had tapped the speed of his fire to shorten the trip, carrying me swiftly like he had that evening so long ago, when we had learned of his royal brother's sinister intentions. He set me upon my feet and crossed the threshold into the vestibule, its walls devoid of crosses or roods. Most of the city's valuables had been entrusted to the council members when they had escaped, along with the most important documents in the archives.

Two lonely-looking candles glowed upon a small table beside the entryway to the nave, and Augustin peered into the gloom beyond with a vicious expression, his perfect eyes running down the length of the empty pews toward the distant altar. I leaned my back against the outer wall, attempting to regain my bearings after an exhilarating ride of fire. A moment later, Freia entered the vestibule, her light casting the entire chamber in a luminous radiance. I smiled at her weakly and held out my left hand; she rushed to my side and twined my fingers with hers, her element reinforcing my anticipation for this fleeting dream.

"I detect Teutonic life far below us, sickened elements crying for water in the nether regions of the basement,"

Augustin reported. He turned back from the nave and crossed the floor to stand before us. He had not bothered to don his cloak again; now he wore simple black trousers and a long matching tunic, black leather boots reaching to his knees to complete his outer layer of darkness. His sword still hung from his belt, making him appear quite formidable.

His impressive build coupled with his gorgeous hair—part of which he had pulled back in a clip, as I remembered from long ago—prompted my heart to pound with hunger. Soon, he would truly be *mine.* I was so distracted by his incredible handsomeness that I completely missed what he said next. He and my best friend began tugging me forward, toward a stairway to the basement. *He must want to search out a priest or a monk,* I realized, my ice-tinted vision fixated upon him.

When we reached the bottom floor of the cathedral, Augustin threw his fire upon a bare torch hanging on a wall, using its light to lead our procession toward the sounds of life that pealed forth from the end of the hallway. The smells of sickness and death accosted my nose as we entered a spacious chapel. Its wooden pews were gone, likely cut up for firewood, piles of cloth serving as beds for the ill of the city, those whose frailty had not afforded them the privilege of escaping the Saxon onslaught. There were no wounded warriors here, only the weakest vagabonds from the streets. A malnourished blind man lay sprawled upon an empty grain sack near the doorway. He lifted a disintegrating hand in the air when he heard us enter, a feeble plea for water escaping his parched lips.

I took a half step backward, cringing away from the filthiness of the chapel, cries of the sick piercing my ears. I froze in disgust, ice coating my skin in protection from the disease around me. Freia gave a quiet gasp of sympathy, her light bursting from her spirit to comfort the dying as she maintained her grip on my arm. Her body language suggested that she feared I may either bolt for the exit or sink to the ground in exhaustion if she let go of me.

Meanwhile, Augustin strode into the chapel with authoritative steps, his face impassive to the suffering around him. "Are there any clergy left in this godforsaken cathedral?" he demanded to the room at large, prompting several of the sick to gasp at his blatant sacrilege.

A few women who were tending to the ailing glanced at him in apparent confusion, but a single man rose from the far corner of the chamber. He wore a grubby-looking brown robe, his face appearing gaunt and pale. "Yes, I am Father Markus," he said in a quiet tone, his light hair telling me that he likely was not a Teuton. I squinted at him as Augustin crossed the floor to stand over him rather threateningly, stating in no uncertain terms that he wished the priest to conduct a quick wedding, without any frills. I had never seen Father Markus before, but I had also not attended any masses at the cathedral in years. The priest looked young and inexperienced. I wondered why he had chosen to stay in a beleaguered city—perhaps out of compassion for the sick?

After a short discussion in tones too low for me to hear, Augustin and Father Markus walked over to where Freia and I waited. The priest smiled at me gravely and said that he would gladly officiate my wedding. Tears welled in my eyes as my mind began to grasp the enormity of what I was about to do—unite myself in matrimony with Augustin, the Black Priest Wolfgang, a cursed man damned to hell, the devil who held my heart, the angel I loved more than life. I managed to smile weakly in response to Father Markus. I could hardly believe that my darkest dream was about to come true, and now, with the enemy at the doorstep, my people dying all around me—*now*, when I had no time to properly appreciate this victory that I had imagined for years.

Before I knew it, I stood before the altar on the platform of the nave, the entire room cast in shadow save for a handful of blue-fired candles flickering upon the retable. Out of the corner of my eye, I saw Freia standing off to the left, and beside her one of the women who had tended the sick in the basement—the two required witnesses. I had to stifle a mocking snicker, for both of them were *female*, completely subverting the medieval tradition of keeping women in the background. Father Markus stood across the altar from me, holding an aged Bible in his hands, his haggard face appearing solemn in the candlelight. And right beside me—close enough for me to feel the fire exuding from his spirit to clandestinely caress my ice beyond the reach of our company—stood Augustin von Bayern, the eternally young yet lifeless man I had wished to marry for over two decades, my one true mate, my love of choice.

Father Markus opened the ceremony with the customary statement of intent, asking each of us if we accepted the responsibilities of uniting in marriage before God, to which we both answered affirmatively, without hesitation. Augustin's fiery hands closed over my fingers as the priest read a few portions from the Bible regarding the duties of matrimony. He read a passage from Genesis about God's creation of woman to be a helper for man, then paged forward to speak a few verses on love from First Corinthians. I marveled that Augustin, that staunch agnostic who wallowed in hopelessness, would grasp my hands so tightly when the priest read truths of love and hope. His acceptance of our spiritual union seemed to throw a thorn in the face of Wuotan himself.

We exchanged just a few heartfelt vows, the ones that Father Markus had memorized. We gazed into each other's eyes while we pledged our mutual faithfulness and love no matter what trials the future may hold. Augustin altered the final words of the vows from "until parted by death" to "for all of eternity." This surprised me until I recalled that since Augustin was already dead, that dreaded specter could not separate us. I repeated his amendment when I spoke the vows, hoping deep within my heart that it would hold true even after both of us entered the gates of eternity. I wanted to meet my lover in heaven when final death took me, despite the damning results of the filial curse.

Father Markus closed the short service with a reading from Matthew, including the phrase that I had always considered the profoundest of them all: "What therefore

God hath joined together, let not man put asunder." The Catholic priest closed the Bible rather ceremoniously and told us with a smile, "You are now husband and wife, in the eyes of God and man."

Elation and disbelief washed through me simultaneously. Freia gave a small cry of delight, and a moment later Augustin wrapped his arms around me, his eyes wet with tears. "How madly I love you, my precious swan . . . my *wife*," he whispered to me in English. And we kissed, our elation filling the cathedral with glory, with unheard melodies pealing from the organ, Augustin's fire brightening the candles, invigorating my spirit to face the coming destruction.

When Augustin released me, he turned to face Father Markus with a rather expectant expression. "Where is the certificate?" he questioned frankly.

The priest's beatific smile faded, and a look of fear crossed his face. "We have no more paper for such documents, my lord," he responded. "It has all been taken out of Muniche, or burnt."

"Then we shall rip the title page from this Bible and write the record there, for I wish to have a physical copy of this triumph." Augustin's eyes glittered, ordering no protests. Soon afterward I signed my name onto our makeshift marriage certificate using one of my master's own pens. I added the surname *von Bayern* after my maiden name, disregarding Augustin's protests. He signed as *Wolfgang W. Wolfe,* and we departed the cathedral as the unlikely husband and wife.

Chapter Thirty-three

Heaven in the Midst of Hell

We hiked back to the Denlinger house leisurely. Augustin held me against his right side, his love flowing into my heart through our spirit's bond, shielding me from morbid thoughts of the future, of how little time we had to enjoy our marriage. I said nothing as we walked under the night sky, the stars resembling distant points of hope upon a backdrop of ruin. My husband murmured phrases of love in my ear now and then, blocking out the cries of the thirsty lying in the gutters, focusing my fatigued heart on him alone. When I considered the activities we would undoubtedly undertake once we reached Freia's abode, I blushed in the dark, not sure whether my middle-aged constitution could withstand such fervor after such a draining day. Perhaps his wicked sex would kill me.

Freia trailed behind us, commenting a few times on the weather and the sounds of the reposing armies outside the city. When we approached her front door, I heard her promise to stay far away from our bedroom that night, leaving us to our rapturous pleasures without interruption. I could feel Augustin chuckling as my head rested against his side, his body rumbling with his dark humor. He told Freia that he appreciated her discretion, but that she should inform us if some horrid crisis occurred.

He lifted me into his strong arms to carry me across Freia's threshold, out of reach of the ragged waifs pleading for water—I counted three of them, all incredibly young. A grunt of annoyance pealed from Augustin's chest as we passed them by. Moments later, he set me upon my feet in the front parlor while Freia bolted the door behind us. My legs felt like jelly. A morass of expectation mixed with fright had overwhelmed my soul.

Then Augustin put his warm hands upon my cheeks, his eyes peering into mine intently. "I would assume, my darling wife, that you would wish to have some time alone to prepare yourself for bed," he murmured. "As for me, I would like to record a few things before retiring for the night, and I may complete one other task before gracing your bedroom, with your permission?"

He kissed my forehead with seductive tenderness. I nodded at him wordlessly, relieved that he would give me a few minutes to stop my head from spinning before the *coup de grace* of our wedding night. He let go of me and said a few parting words to Freia, then left the room in a shroud of darkness, headed for the chamber where his belongings lay.

After he departed, my heart pattered with a strange uncertainty, wild images of experiencing Augustin in bed filling my mind. I had not actually gained pleasure out of sex with him for over two decades—not since that sinful fling of ours on the night before his curse. Now he would take me as his wife, our bodies melding legally with no boundaries or shame. Soon, I would discover for the first time the glories of uniting with the man I loved with my heart and soul, knowing that he was mine forever, our holy matrimony binding us in the eyes of God and man, expunging our previous failures, solidifying our devotion. Part of me could hardly wait to sleep with my dead husband, while a doubting corner of my brain feared what he would think of me now, with my beauty long wasted and my destiny pulling me away from him, into the next millennium.

Freia helped me up the front staircase shortly after Augustin had gone, her light giving me what strength she had to offer. Once she opened my bedroom door for me, she left me alone with a kiss on the cheek, stating that she would go bring some of the wine we had been saving, to drive my weariness away. I smiled at her in gratitude, then entered the bedchamber, closing the door quietly behind me and leaning against it, letting my eyes drift around the room.

Since I had come to live with Freia during Muniche's final weeks, she had granted me use of the room that had once belonged to Heinrich's parents, its furnishings essentially undisturbed since they had both left this world. Their bed was large and inviting, decked with blankets of green and white, two matching pillows propped against the wall. Two windows framed by feathery lime-colored drapes stood upon the northern and western walls. A fireplace also graced the western wall, its embers bare of flame in the heat of summer. I had stored my clothing in their spacious wardrobe, which Freia had emptied of its contents for my sake; my other possessions I had stashed upon the washing table. A simple loom and two stools facing each window completed the room's furniture. The Denlingers had always been a frugal family, not bothering with unnecessary decorations in their private spaces.

I had left one candle burning with a natural flame on the bedside table. Its wick had dwindled to a mere glimmer as I crossed the floor to the washing table to clean up my appearance. I sank down upon the stool before the mirror and cast a tiny blue flame upon a nearby candlestick, then called my ice from my tired spirit just enough to heighten my vision, so I could properly assess my reflection.

With my eyes glistening blue, I found myself staring at the face of a zombie, her raven hair tinged with silver, her eyebrows thick, her mouth drooping at the corners, her forehead and cheeks pockmarked. I shook my head slowly as my gaze drifted downward to the empty washing bowl.

I clenched my teeth and willed the ice to drip from my fingers, granting me enough water to clean my clammy skin. Then I lifted my shaking hands to undo the stays of my dress, not wishing to see how unattractive the rest of my body looked.

Freia returned while I shrugged my arms out of my light blue bodice, letting my dress drop to the floor. She pulled one of the padded stools to my side and sat upon it, placing a single glass of wine upon the table. "How are you, Swanie?" she queried, her voice sounding concerned.

"I don't know, Freia," I said, not liking how puffy my shoulders and neck appeared in the mirror. "I can't believe I'm about to do this . . . it's been six years since I've slept with a man . . . and I haven't bothered to maintain my figure the way you have." I glanced toward my best friend, noting her lack of excess weight, her form still impressive even after bearing many children.

She reached forward to squeeze my hand. "I doubt that your husband will think you're anything but beautiful," she said confidently. "You mustn't tear yourself apart over your body, Swanie; he knows you've had a difficult life. When he looks at you, I think he sees the gorgeous Teuton with whom he fell in love. He kisses you as though you're the most important thing in his world. He doesn't care what the years have done to the outside, because love goes beyond all of that."

I closed my eyes, looking away from the aged woman in the mirror while I removed the rest of my clothing mechanically, leaving it in a messy pile upon the floor. I did not want to look at my reflection again, though I knew that I would have to in order to wash. I put off the unavoidable as I met Freia's gaze. "Even if my body doesn't matter to him, I don't know if I have . . . the strength . . . for this. I'm so tired, Freia. All of my elemental displays today have drained me, and my feet have been throbbing since this afternoon, when I jumped to the ground from the turret. I don't know how I managed to walk back here from the cathedral without stumbling. I feel like I'm being stabbed all over my ankles and legs." I looked down at my swollen feet and froze my fingers again with effort, sliding them down my legs and ankles in an attempt to ease the pain.

Freia rose from the stool and came around to stand behind me, dipping a cloth into the washing basin and rubbing it down my neck and back, wiping away the sweat and grime. "Relax now, and focus on the tranquility within your spirit, to invigorate you again." Her light infused my body with serenity as she washed me from head to foot, the coolness of the water loosening my tense muscles. I closed my eyes to concentrate on the vitality of her element, thankful all over again for Freia's faithful friendship. I hated to think that I must leave her behind in a matter of days, watching her soul fly to heaven while mine passed through the gates to the future. I could never match her for kindness or compassion, and I knew not what I would do without her.

Once she had finished bathing me and running a comb through my short hair, she held the glass of wine to my lips, quietly urging me to drink, to flood my veins with its numbing heat, with its temporary relief. I obeyed her, consuming half of the wine and offering her the rest. She shook her head with a smile and said that she would leave the glass on my bedside table in case my husband deemed it necessary to force it down my throat later.

I chuckled shakily and lifted myself off of the stool with a groan, pointing my feet toward the bed without one backward glance at the mirror. While I rolled back the coverlet, Freia trod softly toward the door, offering me one parting phrase. "Swanie, dear, have a wonderful night. I know you will, despite your doubts." She flashed me a radiant smile before exiting the chamber, leaving me to face my demon alone.

I waited a few moments more in the dim light of the candles, their beams hardly touching the bed where I lay, the majority of the room ensconced in darkness. My gaze traveled down to my body after I glanced toward the windows, and I bit my lip at the sight of my distended stomach, its stretch marks visible even in the candlelight. My breasts looked no better, lying upon my torso like tired lumps of flesh. The words Augustin had thrown in my face when he prepared to rape me on that horrific night in 1055 came back to me while I cringed at my figure: *Such an ugly cow . . . wasted beauty . . . mountain of misplaced flab . . . .* He was right. He was always right. I slid my feet under the blanket and pulled it up to my chin, hoping that he might extinguish the candles before demanding that I reveal my body to him.

I heard the bedroom door open and close with a creak, so I steeled myself to face my immortal husband, feeling incredibly unworthy as I hid beneath the coverlet. Augustin smiled at me and approached the bed, placing his bag on the floor near the bedside table. "Forgive me for not coming to you earlier, my darling swan," he apologized, glancing around at the furnishings of the chamber with a cursory nod. "I found myself unable to forgo writing a novel in Ælte Teutonica regarding our wedding, and after that I slipped outside to put the famished urchins out of their misery." He snorted caustically and added, "I did not wish them to attempt to break in tonight and disturb our fleeting heaven. Most of them had no qualms about dying, it appeared, for they did not struggle."

I scoffed quietly at his rationale, watching him remove his sheathed sword from his belt and rest it against the table. "In the twenty-first century they call that 'physician-assisted suicide,'" I informed him with a grimace. "Or 'mercy killing.'"

Augustin's lips turned downward briefly. "I would refer to it as inevitable, and a far better end than being sliced to bits by Saxons or putrefied by the *Toteheri*. I stopped their hearts quickly, without pain."

I rolled my eyes at him, then frowned in consternation as he retrieved five lengthy candles from his sack. "What are those for?" I demanded.

He smiled at me wickedly and set them upon the bare candlestick atop the bedside table, igniting their wicks with a flourish, brightening the room considerably. "You forget that a man prefers to *look* upon his woman in the process of mating, or you would not be hiding underneath that verdant blanket." His eyes roved over the outline of my body beneath the coverlet, their color matching the flames he had set upon the candlestick, his teeth glittering white.

My breath caught in my throat, and my hands clutched the blanket more tightly, my heart sinking. My hopes for a simple copulation were in vain. Of course Augustin was still a man, though he may be dead, and he would want to savor the appearance of my body before enfolding me in his fiery arms. I felt the blush rise in my cheeks while my husband removed his boots and belt. I saw the sizeable bulge in his trousers and wondered how many times he would ejaculate before he determined the process complete.

He lifted his tunic over his head with the acerbic remark, "I would trust that you are already naked beneath that blanket, because if I have to remove your clothing before finishing this business, it likely shall not survive my claws." His fingers curled, and he cast his tunic to the ground, then stepped out of his trousers with disturbing swiftness, his expression growing more and more alarming.

I found that I could hardly breathe as I sensed the heat emanating from his body. He stood directly over me now, staring down at me with a madman's eyes, looking as though he would tear the very blanket to shreds if I did not push it back without further delay. "Now *why*, for pity's sake, are you cowering on that bed like an inexperienced virgin?!" he exploded abruptly, his voice likely reaching the far corners of the house. "Do you honestly think playing hard-to-get is going to please me when I have waited *eleven years* for this moment?" He bared his teeth.

"I . . . I . . . I'm sorry!" I squeaked, quaking as he leaned over me, his grasping hands descending upon my neck. "It's just . . . I'm just . . . could you . . . could you . . . snuff all the candles first?" My voice broke when his fingers touched my neck, their heat singeing me so harshly they likely left welts.

His hands froze upon my throat, their fire cooling. He stared into my eyes, and a look of shock crossed his face. "You . . . don't want me . . . to look at you." It was a statement, not a question. He looked rather disenchanted.

Tears welled in my eyes as I sensed his distress. "No . . . no . . . it's . . . well . . . I'm not much . . . to look at," I whispered quickly. "I know I'm fat and ugly . . . a mountain of misplaced flab." My teeth scored my lips and I looked away in shame, my whole body trembling.

Though I had feared his ardor, I had gotten a good look at his naked body while he hovered over me. He was even more beautiful now than he had been before, a man perfected on the outside by the powers of a demon, his muscles ideal, his legs firm and sculpted, his cock grandly poised, his hair a wave of ebony. I could not satisfy him now with my human frailty, not at all.

But he brought his visage close to mine, his hands traveling upward to my cheeks, turning my head gently to face him. "My darling wife, you cannot possibly believe those lies," he crooned, his fingers wiping my tears away. "My master forced me to speak those horrible falsehoods in a ridiculous attempt to make you hate me. Lightning should have struck me from the sky when those words left my lips . . . for they were such outrageous lies. You are *my* Swanhilde, my princess, my beloved. There is no need to fear some imagined dissatisfaction, I promise." The hands of his spirit stroked my heart while he spoke, prompting me to groan with desire, my trepidation falling away. "Now show yourself to me," he coaxed, "for you are my wife, and this bed is undefiled now and forever."

My ice trickled into my veins when he gradually drew the blanket back. I squeezed my eyes shut as he pushed the covers down to my feet, tracing his hands slowly up my legs, the heat of his fingers causing me to moan. He made a sound in his throat, and I felt him climb upon the bed to straddle me. His hands traveled up my stomach, then my chest, fingering the scars that still remained from the blood-transfer I had done for Freia so long ago. I felt the heat of his lips pressing upon my heart, prompting it to pound unsteadily as my husband groaned, his dead soul enticed more than ever by the life beating within me. When I opened my eyes at last, I blinked at the intense passion evident upon Augustin's face. "You are *still* a goddess," he purred, his lips brushing mine, "the pinnacle of Teutonic splendor . . . your loveliness far surpassing Aphrodite . . . absolute perfection in my hands." He kissed my bottom lip briefly, his eyes burning into mine.

I opened my mouth, then closed it, disbelief and adoration flooding me at the same time. "Augustin . . . you're *blind* . . . ."

"With eyes perfected in death? I think not." He smiled beguilingly.

"Then you're biased," I whispered. My eyes rolled back as his hands fondled my breasts, sending fires of lust through my suddenly youthful veins.

He pressed his body upon mine and wrapped his hands around the back of my head. "I don't think you mind," he intoned. Then his lips covered my mouth as his fire entered my yearning body, canceling out any replies I could have made. In blissful rapture, I closed my eyes and seized this heaven in the midst of hell.

Much later, as the blue flames upon the candlestick faded, Augustin lifted his mouth from my neck, his tongue cleansing my blood from his lips. "Your frail humanity pulls you into slumber, my dear one," he observed after kissing my mouth for the thousandth time, his mussed hair brushing my cheek.

I smiled at him apologetically, no longer wishing to fight the exhaustion that depleted my consciousness. Our blissful union had lasted longer than I could recall, and he had taken care to bring my beaten body to the pinnacle of grandeur more than once. He had managed it inside of me —something that Joel had rarely accomplished—and he had done it deftly with his fingers, my ice crashing against his flames. Augustin was a master at pleasing a woman, and now I could claim his expertise for myself forever.

I lay upon the blanket in a reverie, my husband's body still wound around me, though at the moment both of us were resting from our passion. I felt as if I had ascended to the clouds that night, my spirit dancing among the stars, running free with a fiery partner whose dynamism never faded, whose expertise remained unmatched. But now, sleep dragged my awareness underneath the sea, calling me away from heaven, to a lonely repose. "I'm sorry . . . Augustin," I whispered, clearly sensing his desire to make love with me all night, shunning rest for the high of release again and again.

"I forgive you, my love," he reassured me, reaching out to stroke my hair. "Perhaps your drive would have lasted longer if I had not bled you so much," he commented as he glanced down at my neck, which stung from countless cuts from his teeth. He kissed my throat tenderly several times, then sighed, "Ah, Swanhilde . . . seeing the extent of your devotion astounds me anew, convincing me that I can never let you go, *never*." His mouth molded with mine again.

I exhaled heavily when he raised his head, the shadow of the future dulling my paradise. "But we have so little time . . . ." I lamented, closing my eyes and trying to hold back the tears. "I wish I could stay awake just to feel your fire upon my frigid skin . . . just to feel you holding me . . . ." I clenched my teeth in silent pain.

When my husband spoke again, his statement drew me back to clarity with a start. "Our heaven does not have to end when Muniche falls." My eyelids sprang open to stare at Augustin in disbelief. "My darling swan, you do not have to give yourself over to death after our enemies have prevailed. I could carry you to safety once you've seen enough. I would not let them hurt you. We could go back to my home in the Rhineland, enjoying each other until your own hourglass takes you out of this era permanently."

His eyes glittered intensely as he unveiled a new destiny before me, one that prompted me to freeze upon the bed. From the beginning, I had planned to return to the twenty-first century once Muniche burned—but now I saw myself flying like a lark, living with my lifeless husband for a few decades alone in the forest. My weary mind could not wrap itself around this impossible concept, and my brow furrowed. "Augustin . . . I don't know what to say," I hedged.

"Just think about it, my darling," he advised, caressing my hair. "It is a valid option, in my estimation, but if you prefer to return to your future like you initially planned, I would still be willing to end your life easily, whenever you ask." His lips touched mine softly, a small brush of fire.

I closed my eyes while his hands moved downward to fondle my breasts, a soft murmur pealing from his throat. His tongue stroked the skin over my heart, his death likely yearning to taste the fresh blood pounding there. I gradually began to doze as his gentleness hypnotized me, charming my heart to sing in serenity. I groaned quietly and relaxed upon the bed, my passionate night having aggravated the familiar pains in my body. I ordered them to cease now and drifted off, my husband's presence comforting me in the stillness.

"Swanie, love." His voice brought me back to reality again. I opened my eyes a crack. "Your body aches," he murmured in an agonized tone, his hands tenderly stroking my throat. When I opened my eyes wider, I saw that his face was contorted in pain. "I saw it in your blood." He stared at me in consternation.

I sighed, knowing that he was right, wishing that he would let it go. "I'm fine . . . Augustin . . . . Don't worry about me." His words brought the agony in my ankles and innards into the forefront of my mind, and I winced.

His jaw twitched, and he rolled off of me for the first time since our union had begun, his gaze drifting to my feet, curled at the end of the bed. "It is because of what I did to you . . . in my sadism." Regret marred his beautiful face as his hands touched the bones of my ankles, his fingers probing my weak muscles like a doctor examining a patient.

"Damn, your feet are so cold . . . yellow and weak." Both of his hands closed upon them, and he rubbed his heat into my flesh. "I have brought no tools with me to heal them . . . ah . . . I am a monster." A choked cry burst from his throat and he continued to massage my feet and ankles, his tears soaking them with a devil's repentance.

I squeezed my eyes shut, for his distress clawed at my heart. His fire eased the pain in my feet, sending a peculiar cure through my blood. "Oh, master . . . ." I could find no words to comfort my weeping husband as he tried in vain to expunge the scars his abuse had left upon my body. He sent his fire into my ravaged veins, and I lay still while he kissed each of my toes, then the backs of my ankles on the very spot he had cut them, so long ago. Finally, he crept back to his former place, cradling my face in his hands and staring into my eyes in silent torment, his own still wet with tears of shame.

"Swanhilde, how could you have married me after I made you a cripple . . . after I unleashed Wuotan's violence upon you? How could you have trusted me still . . . I cannot understand it . . . *how?!*" He grasped my shoulders with his trembling hands, his hot tears falling upon my bare chest.

My lips parted, but at first I had no idea what to say. I was insane, enslaved, blinded, a fool—but Augustin would not have accepted that wretched truth. So I finally whispered, my voice barely audible, "I don't know . . . but I love you."

He shook his head at me, his eyes glowing with a mixture of incredulity and devotion. A moment later he kissed me again, his fervor ignited afresh, his strength pressing my head deeply into the pillow beneath me. My eyes closed as he wrapped his arms around my body, covering me in the embrace of death, my life seeming to wane at the pull of his mouth. I do not know how long he chained me in the throes of his passion, for my fatigue won the fight at last, and I fell into a peaceful slumber with my lips locked upon his.

Chapter Thirty-four:
Looting

I awoke to rays of white light streaming through the windows, casting the verdant-themed bedroom in the bright hue of late morning. The heat of the day already basked my body in a coating of sweat, the dampness calling my ice from my spirit to pacify my resultant discomfort. I blinked the sleep from my eyes and stretched, feeling the stiffness in my limbs from my exertions of the previous night. My husband's face appeared in my line of vision an instant later, and his smile outshone the glory of the morning sun as he leaned down to kiss me. "Welcome back to the land of the living, my swan," he greeted, his right hand resting over my heart, its heat sinking deep into my spirit, making my hormones sing again.

I yawned vigorously, then entwined the fingers of my left hand with his. "What time is it?" I inquired, glancing toward the brilliant windows.

"It is nearly Sext, my bride." He winked at my shock and lifted my hand to his lips. I rarely slept past the bells of sunrise, and now it was almost noon. "I would have woken you earlier, but your body and soul needed a respite from this tumult." He kissed my wrist gently, his immortal fire invigorating me.

"Why didn't you come to my dreams?" I thought back to the blissful images that had floated through my sleeping mind. Many had included him, but I knew that I had dreamt alone.

Augustin's expression darkened, and he too looked toward the windows as he said, "In light of the current . . . circumstances . . . I judged it more prudent to remain on guard all night. I have not left your side since you fell asleep, interrupting a rather satisfying kiss"—he gave me a suggestive look—"but my ears have been trained on the activities outside the walls, for I believe that the battle has begun."

I stiffened and concentrated on my ice, training my ears in the direction of the city walls. My heightened senses heard the distinct sounds of clashing swords and shields, neighing horses, cries of striving warriors. "How long do you think it'll be before they get inside?" I asked, horror overtaking me at the realization that Muniche would be obliterated within a few days' time.

Augustin shook his head, his visage dismal. "They will storm the gates tonight, quite likely, tomorrow morning at the latest. I have seen this force in action more often than I have wished during the past year; and with the Teutons already weakened by hunger and thirst, their victory shall come quickly."

He sighed, his eyes glinting with frustration as he looked down at me, lying naked upon the bed. "I find myself torn in two, my love—for while curiosity beckons me to the city walls to witness this unmatched tragedy, desire entices me to stay here, to never leave this bed, to drink your love and your blood again and again." He wound his arms around my back, raising me off of the blanket. His teeth locked upon my bruised throat to cut my veins once more, draining my life.

I cried out as my dead husband enslaved me again, my eyes slowly closing. The insane part of me begged him wordlessly for more, pleaded with him to never cease his violence until he had killed me and resurrected my lost soul, crowning me his immortal queen, his timeless wife. "Augustin," I moaned, my voice sounding strange and ethereal. "We can't . . . please . . . we didn't . . . come here for this."

He raised his head at my pitiful entreaty, his eyes aglow with craving. He looked from mine to the blood that trickled down my bruised throat onto my chest. "Damn it," he groaned, shaking his head. He healed my wound with the swiftness of an experienced priest and bent his face down to lick the blood from my chest. "Sometimes I wish you were one of Wuotan's sirens, though they have no souls. Your mortality halts my infernal lusts before they can be fully gratified."

He hurled a wretched curse in Bayerisch, prompting me to laugh. Then he rolled off of me, bouncing to the floor like a spry young devil, holding one hand out to me with a mischievous smirk. "Come, my delicate wife. Let me help you dress, and then we shall eat and grace the walls, to see this impending disaster for ourselves."

Shortly after the cathedral's bells tolled Sext throughout the doomed city—I commented to Augustin that Father Markus likely rang the bells, taking a break from his medical efforts to keep the Teuton soldiers abreast of the time—my husband carried me from the Denlinger house en route to the northwestern turret. We had found the house empty upon entering the kitchen to consume what remained of our stash of victuals. Freia had probably left earlier to aid the wounded at the town hall.

After a brief brunch of dried venison, unleavened bread, cherry preserves, and wine, Augustin insisted upon carrying me to the city wall. He did not believe that my ankles were up to the task of treading the streets. He had noticed my limp the previous day but had kept his mouth shut. After examining my feet that morning, he pronounced them likely to develop necrosis if I continued to strain myself. Thus he would not allow me to walk unless it was absolutely necessary. I rolled my eyes a little at his concern, but since I knew that my time in the eleventh century was to be short, I resigned myself to being his cherished invalid until fate knocked upon my door.

I had seriously considered Augustin's offer to preserve my life after Muniche fell while he dressed me that morning, his deadly claws gentle as he clad me in an airy black skirt and matching bodice, tying my graying hair beneath a diaphanous head covering. I had pondered it further after he had donned his priestly robes and carried me downstairs, setting the food before me and insisting that I consume it all. Though I wanted to stay with him more than anything, I knew that I could not accept his proposition, as he sat across from me at the kitchen table watching me eat, his light blue eyes intense, his obsidian hair striking, his visage that of a destroying angel. He would have to kill me when the city burned, or I would have to kill myself.

I was too old and weak to withstand a marriage with an immortal devil, even though I loved Augustin more than life. He had almost killed me already, for his passion was infinite now, his longing for blood insatiable. My throat hurt when I swallowed due to the countless times he had bled me, forgoing the opportunity to read my memories to focus on savoring my life. I felt fragile inside and out from Augustin's ravenous lust, and I knew that it could not last. I feared to tell him the truth—that I would have to return to the future within a few days—but he would see it soon enough in my blood.

We parked ourselves upon the stone ledge of the uppermost balcony on the northwestern turret. Augustin held me on his lap while we observed the fighting below, a black-clad vulture and his Valkyrie waiting for the end. The sun beat down upon us, and I used my ice to keep my body cool, which turned out to be rather difficult while sitting in the embrace of a fiery demon. My heart cried within me as the valiant Teutons fought desperately against their malevolent foes, striking down the few Saxons who braved the front lines while the specters of the *Toteheri* avoided every sword and spear, their blades carrying the aura of death.

This was the first time I had gotten a good look at their methods of fighting, and I drew closer to Augustin as the battle progressed despite the contrast of his heat against my ice. The demonic warriors were unnaturally tall and brawny, their skin giving off a strangely deceptive golden glimmer. They moved with inhuman grace and tackled the Teuton warriors with their bare hands whenever one got too close. Some Teutons managed to conjure their elements in time to block their creeping death, but I heard the howls of one who had been caught by a serpentine female. Her fingernails sank into his bare neck, and I watched his flesh disintegrate, his agonized cries tapering off into silence.

"'Her adversaries are become her lords; her enemies are enriched,'" Augustin murmured at length, his eyes riveted upon the bloodshed beneath us. "'Her princes are become like rams that find no pastures; and they are gone away without strength before the face of the pursuer.'"

I wondered, as I considered the Bible verses he had chosen to quote, whether Augustin believed that Muniche would fall because of the rampant hypocrisy of the Prince, the Lady Maria, the Teuton council, and the Catholic clergy. All of them hid in a halo of perfection while in secret they connived with Wuotan, refused to forgive, sacrificed the important things in life on the altar of prosperity. The Teuton priests of this era refused to acknowledge the magic of those with blood below ninety percent, and their prejudice had brought devilish ruin upon our people. I knew for a fact that Teutons of eighty-five percent or higher could invoke their elements and even reach the spiritual realm after study and practice. My twenty-first century cousins Trudi and Traudl and my friend Marga were proof of that.

As the afternoon progressed, the Teuton forces retreated to the base of the wall, gathering near the gates, likely intending to withdraw inside at sunset to rest for their final stand. A shadow of disillusionment dimmed my husband's face as he stared down at our beaten warriors. A notable alliance under normal circumstances, Teutons from every corner of Bavaria with elements potent enough to triumph over ordinary humans. But the *Toteheri* had brought them to their knees, for they spread the death of fallen angels.

"We must go," Augustin said, pulling me to my feet and rising from the ledge. "They shall retreat behind the walls, and the demonic legion shall be forced to hurl stones into this city, breaking its buildings to the ground, like they did at Regensburg."

I thought of the trebuchets I had seen some time ago. Our enemies would probably spend the night transporting them closer to the city walls. My husband took me in his arms and descended the steps of the tower with disturbing velocity. "I have no intention of losing you that way, my precious swan," he murmured passionately, pressing his lips upon mine in a kiss of silent desperation.

I asked him if we ought to return to the Denlinger house to wait for Freia, since the sun had begun to sink toward the western horizon. Augustin replied that he had one duty to perform first and set his course for the opposite side of Muniche. As we passed swiftly through the streets, I caught fleeting glimpses of famished vagabonds, their elements manifesting themselves in a final ferocity. They broke into shops and homes, streaking out with what few valuables they could find. I shook my head at the sight of one bony wench chugging a moldy bottle of beer, her straggly white hair swarming with flies. "What's the point of all this?" I wondered, gesturing toward the chaos around us.

"They care not that it shall all crumble tomorrow," he said, pressing my head against his chest in an attempt to hide my people's final frenzy from me. "They must loot now, steal what they can to save it from the Saxons, to assuage their wounded souls so they can die in peace. Power is a drug, Swanhilde, a palliative for the discord of this world. Our people must taste it again before the end."

I said nothing to this. A part of me felt rather proud that Muniche's citizens had waited until now to lose their control, since they knew that all hope was lost. Perhaps they had clung to a useless trust in their Prince, praying that he might save them from destruction. Their loyalty was impressive, but it had finally broken under the weight of the siege, fallen prey to the pangs of hunger. I hoped that none had broken into Freia's house in our absence, but I knew that Augustin had secured the door before we had gone.

When my husband set me back upon my feet, I saw, to my surprise, that he had brought us to the front entrance of the Bayern castle. He had placed me alongside the archway that framed the entry, and I leaned against it, running my fingers down its chilly stones. Augustin pounded upon the door and pulled on a nearby chain, his eyes flashing cobalt. "Come on, damn you!" he roared at the unresponsive door, his hands curling into fists. "Have all of you left this palace bereft, leaving your Lady to writhe in the hands of pillaging Saxons? *Open this door!*"

He was addressing the servants, I realized with a jolt. He knew the tales that I had heard, that the Lady Maria lay sick somewhere in the castle, tended by servants in the absence of her Keyholder. Why were we here? Did he wish to kill the witch himself, along with any remaining servants, unleashing his revenge upon them for cursing him?

I heard uncertain footsteps upon the floor within, but Augustin's patience had worn thin. He sank his clawed fingers into the door's massive lock, rending it from the wood as though it weighed no more than a toothpick. He kicked the door open a second later, snatching me from where I stood frozen, sweeping me inside with a flourish. He halted after taking three steps, an insidious snicker rumbling in his chest, his right arm encircling my waist as he glared at the single servant who had come to meet us.

I recognized him as Bruno, to my utter astonishment. He looked old and withered now, his hair a wilted gray, his trembling hands clutching a sputtering candlestick. His bleary eyes blinked at Augustin, and his jaw dropped, revealing a toothless hole beyond. For an interminable moment, Prince Otto's trusted butler and his once-lord stared each other down, the silence eerie and suggestive. At last, Bruno choked in a wavering voice, "You . . . should . . . not . . . be . . . here . . . ."

Augustin leapt forward with a snarl, releasing me and grabbing the terrified servant by the throat. Bruno's candle clattered to the floor, its flame extinguishing as Augustin forced the man onto his knees. "*Say it,* you wretch!" he bellowed while Bruno cowered before him, his aged hands trying weakly to loosen Augustin's grip. "Do *NOT* address me as some bastard on the street! Say it, do you hear me?! *My. Lord.*" He spoke the last two words carefully, as if the servant was an idiot.

Bruno's wrinkled face began to turn blue, so I staggered forward, afraid that my husband may kill him accidentally in his ire. "Augustin, please," I whispered, laying a hand upon his right shoulder. "Don't do this. He has done no wrong . . . let him go. There's no point in punishing him for the Prince's sins."

Augustin's posture relaxed; he let go of Bruno's throat abruptly and stepped back. The gasping servant crumpled into a pile of humility upon the floor, covering his face with his hands. My husband whirled to face me then, his fury cooling slowly as looked into my eyes. "I suppose you are right, Swanhilde," he sighed, his tone petulant. "This fool has done me no wrong, though he has chosen to serve the worst hypocrite among men." He leered at the cowering servant and snapped, "I expect you to leave us undisturbed while we conduct our business here. If you do not obey, I shall kill you and the dying hag you protect. Do you understand me?"

Bruno did not lift his head from the floor, but I heard him respond, his voice sounding strangled, "Yes . . . I shall obey . . . my lord . . . *Augustin* . . . ."

My eyes popped open, and I saw my husband's face light up in triumph. He turned away and placed his right hand upon my back to lead me into the corridors beyond. "He is no traitor," he stated simply as we approached a dark staircase. "His genuflections make me feel that I have regained the royalty that once was mine." His entire countenance glowed a muted blue, and he retrieved an unlit torch from a notch upon the wall, igniting one end with a scorching blue flame.

I smiled at the sight of Augustin's pleasure, thinking back to the many royal parties I had been forced to attend. I wished yet again that he could have been the Keyholder of Muniche, leading the city with his blunt honesty and unrivaled intellect. "So what are we doing here?" I asked as he carried me down the steps. A wicked thought crossed my mind. "Are we going to loot?"

Augustin chuckled darkly, his eyes glowing blue in the dark. We reached the bottom of the stairwell and plunged into the basement hallways. "To an extent, I suppose we are going to loot. There is one item in this castle that I do not wish our enemies to desecrate, if it is still here." His expression grew fierce, and he stopped in front of a simple wooden door adorned with a cross.

I recognized the door immediately. "Marelda . . . ."

"Yes." My husband gnawed on his lip when he gazed at the door. He set me onto my feet, then slid his right hand carefully downward to twist the handle. "Bruno was right, I fear. The Cursed One should not be here, tainting the mausoleum of Lady Marelda von Bayern. But his memory has not been expunged, for it is perfected in death . . . and he cannot allow her likeness to fall prey to a demonic army." He opened the door with reverence and stepped inside, holding it open for me.

Shivers ran down my spine as I looked around the lonely chapel, dust covering the purple-draped altar, the last rays of daylight barely piercing the gloom through the stained glass window with its depiction of Christ. Augustin turned back to place the torch outside the chapel, then came to stand beside me, shutting the door behind him. His fire set tiny blue flames upon the candles decking the altar, and a moment later I heard him gasp, a short intake of breath. I turned my head to the right to look at his face, and I saw that he gawked at Marelda's tomb with a perplexed expression, moisture welling in the corners of his eyes. I followed his gaze and saw Augustin's ever-burning candle, the blue fire I had set upon it on a New Year's Eve long ago, flickering still.

A tormented sound burst from my husband's throat as he stepped forward, falling to his knees before Marelda's casket, his right hand reaching out toward the candle. "*How . . . ?*" he gasped, lifting his face to Marelda's painted image, his body trembling as he touched the burning candle.

I walked forward and placed my arms around him, shocked at how weak his body felt. "*I* have not forgotten Augustin von Bayern," I told him, indicating the tiny fire with my right hand. His left hand rose to meet my fingers, stroking them with exaggerated tenderness, silent tears trickling down his cheeks. I smiled kindly at him and nodded my head once toward Marelda's image with the words, "She has not forgotten you either."

Augustin shook his head slowly and rose to his feet, holding me to his chest. "My darling," he murmured in a pained tone, kissing my veiled hair, his warmth enfolding me with the intimacy of our bond. I rested my head against him, listening to his deep voice as he spoke again quietly, respectfully. "Lady Marelda, this is my precious wife, Swanhilde Rolande." He looked at the beautiful painting and continued, holding me close, "She is everything to me, the woman who does not allow me to forget beauty, or goodness, or life. I wish you could have met her while you were here on this earth, but I trust that you shall welcome her in heaven as the educated lady who granted me her love . . . my other half . . . my equal."

He released me shortly afterward and climbed atop the tomb. He muttered that doing so could be considered sacrilege, but it was necessary in order to save the gorgeous painting of Marelda. He planned to place it upon a wall in his hut and light a new candle for her underneath it, so he may never forget the woman who had shaped his life so profoundly during his childhood, although he could no longer call her his mother. I smiled peacefully while Augustin rolled the painting and placed it beneath his cloak. "My connection with her cannot be severed, in spite of what the murderer wished," he asserted proudly. "His spells hold no sway over the saints in heaven."

Once we had left the chapel and clammy basement behind, Augustin carried me to the magnificent porch that overlooked the Bayern gardens, which grew unkempt due to the lack of proper cultivation. Most of the servants had fled months earlier, so the vineyards and flowerbeds were covered in weeds, the three fountains dry. My husband suggested that I remain there while he sought out a few more items. He knew that the staff would leave me alone, for fear of their lives, he noted darkly. "Are you going to go find Maria and wish her a pleasant death?" I asked as he turned to depart, a morbid curiosity nagging at my soul.

He chuckled once and responded, "No, although I likely should." He disappeared into the shadows of the castle a moment later, and I turned to view the gardens. Sorrow washed through me, for I knew that in a few days' time, they would be burnt to the ground, stones cast over the leafy soil. My heart wept with anguish as I pondered the fall of Muniche afresh, thinking of everything that would be gone, the history that would be lost, the truth forever suppressed. The most important Teutonic documents had gone with the council members and monks who had fled the city, but so many memories would be permanently destroyed.

Augustin returned to me when nightfall cast one final tranquility over the condemned castle and its gardens. "We must leave soon, for I sense an impending storm, and I wish to gain one more glimpse of the skirmishes before retiring for the night," my husband said, his gaze upon the heavens, which had begun to cloud over.

"So did you find what you were after?" I swept my gaze over his robes in one quick glance, seeing nothing of note.

"Yes, but it proved quite difficult," he answered with a scowl. "The servants who fled, it seems, stole most of the royal jewelry before leaving, likely hoping to make themselves rich in some foreign land. It is good, I suppose, for thus our foes shall find little plunder to enjoy . . . but I did uncover a few trinkets, all of which I pocketed to preserve from Saxon hands." His frown curled into a wicked smirk.

"Looter," I accused with a wink.

"Not necessarily, for looting implies personal gain, correct?" Augustin tilted his head at me with an almost playful expression. A moment later he dropped to one knee and took my right hand in his left. "I suppose this is a bit backwards, since you have already pledged your troth to me in matrimony, but I came across one piece of jewelry during my search that I believe would look lovely on your hand."

To my surprise, he pulled a sparkling sapphire ring from beneath his cloak, its band a shining gold. "This ring belonged to Marelda," he said, lifting it upward, the fire in his eyes reflecting off of its gem. "Her element was blue fire, like mine, and she wore this ring often, for it matched her beauty well. Now I present it to you, my queen of ice, my bride of the frost, as a token of my eternal love." He slid it upon the ring finger of my right hand, forcing it over the flab around my knuckle with his inexhaustible strength, prompting me to clench my teeth to hold back a squeak of pain. He rose to his full height a moment later, lifting my hand to his lips to kiss the ring. "I love you, Swanhilde," he murmured.

I trembled as I sensed the passion radiating from his soul into mine, burning in his cerulean eyes. "Oh, Augustin . . . I love you, too, so much . . . ." Our lips met in a glorious kiss, and he scooped me into his arms to drink my life with renewed ardor. His lips moved down to brush my throat gently before he carried me through the castle again. Then he pointed his feet toward the street and the western wall, so we could observe the carnage before rejoicing in one more rapturous night.

Chapter Thirty-five:
A Significant Assumption

By the time we reached the northwestern turret, piles of nimbus clouds canceled out the stars of evening, coating the sky in a midnight blue interspersed with yellow flares of lightning. Thunder rumbled across the landscape, echoing through the stony tower as my husband carried me up its twisted staircase in a course for the western wall, where we planned to stand to watch our people retreat. When we had crossed the city under the lowering sky, we had heard the unmistakable sound of the loosing of iron bars, the throwing of a bolt, the creaking of a gate. The Prince had decided to open Muniche one last time as a refuge for his weary army, so they might rest for one night before their enemies broke them to bits.

Now we halted upon the western wall, having exited the turret at one of its lower levels to get a more centralized view of the retreat. Augustin placed me carefully upon my feet halfway between the tower and the gate, which stood open to receive the beaten army. Torches glowed fitfully in the soldiers' hands as a vicious wind swept down from the sky, thunder seeming to crack the stones in two, its flashing companion streaking across the clouds in a breathtaking display of electricity. I leaned close to Augustin's chest while we looked down at the warriors, the wind attempting to blow the covering from my hair, whipping my skirt and his cloak around us in a black layer of obscurity. "I'm starting to think I may get struck by lightning," I said, glancing at the turbulent sky.

"It shall strike me first, since I am taller," Augustin countered, tightening his arms around me. "But I would suggest that you prepare your ice as a defense against its energy, just in case. I fear that this storm may be a result of the *Toteheri* tampering with nature. That grand element of water cannot be restrained forever from its perfect union with the other three." His eyes scoured the heavens, awaiting the rain.

I shivered a bit from the wicked wind and looked down again at the ranks of torches heading into the city. "Maybe the rain will free the Isar." A wild hope seized me, and I drew my ice from my spirit, simultaneously shielding my body against a potential attack from the lightning and calling for the return of my river.

"That is a possibility." The clouds broke at last an instant later, pelting us with fierce drops of summer rain. I heard Augustin grunt in annoyance. He pulled the hood of his cloak over his head, muttering under his breath that this sudden squall might extinguish his fire. I laughed as the rain drenched my hair and dress, invigorating my parched soul after three days of wasteland. The downpour put out the majority of torches below, but I heard cries of relief pealing out from the warriors as they lifted their sun burnt faces to the sky to drink the rainwater.

I watched the lightning bolts chase the thunder across the heavens, the raindrops forming nature's ovation in their pattering upon the stones of the wall. The deluge spoke deeply to my spirit. Muniche would burn tomorrow or the next day, but tonight, conquest belonged to me and to all of the other Teutons of water. I could see the torn bodies of my people scattered across the land below, their souls fallen victim to the demonic army that seethed along the horizon, slowly carting their trebuchets forward. But there was still hope, even in this gloomy despair. I had seen the future, and I knew that Muniche would rise again. The Teutons would survive—hiding amongst foreigners, yes—but their candles would not burn out. I found, incongruously, that I could not mourn now, even with the army retreating, even with the dead littering the ground—for the rain cried out to my spirit, urging me to celebrate nature's glory.

So I trotted away from Augustin's embrace and froze my limbs as I looked at the lightning, the precipitation drenching my blue eyes, reinforcing my ice. The refreshing shower had altered my dismal perspective at last. My soul sang within me, reminding me that life would go on after the siege, after the fall—even after I returned to the twenty-first century, leaving my immortal husband behind. He had said that the currents of time would have to rip me from his grasp with inhuman force, or he would never let go of my heart. Perhaps our bond could be spared if our love proved strong enough to span time. Maybe this was not the end.

My suddenly lively feet tapped the stones of the wall, and I whirled around once, spreading my arms out to the rain, freezing it around me. I trod a cautious dance in honor of the wearied soldiers, of the starving townspeople, of the brave clergy who had stayed, of God and His Son . . . and of my cursed husband. I beamed and turned to face Augustin, my soaked dress adhering to my body. "Dance with me, Augustin, for the Teutons shall not be vanquished forever!" I offered my right hand to him, the sapphire ring reflecting the flashes of lightning.

My husband had grown rigid, his eyes blazing blue, his cloak enfolding him in darkness. His gaze was riveted upon the retreating army, and he shook his head at me. "Not now . . . Swanhilde," he replied in a tone laden with contempt.

I skipped to his side, realizing that I was getting carried away by the beauty of the storm. Its moisture had pulled my soul from its mire with vigor, maybe a bit too much vigor. I should not dance now, not when the Teuton army streamed into a beleaguered city in search of a fleeting respite, an impossible dream. I still would watch Muniche burn to the ground, unable to help, trying desperately not to live in the moment, to focus upon better days to come.

But as Augustin folded me in his arms again, I saw that his reserve did not stem from my silly cheer in the face of destruction. His fiery eyes were locked upon a single man below us, clad in shining armor and noble robes drenched with rain. He sat atop a white stallion, an impressive sword hanging at his side. When the lightning lit up the landscape, I could see his beard, its black hair contrasting with his white teeth as he shouted at his forces, attempting to conduct an orderly retreat. He had doubtless promised them one night of repose before the last battle—and I felt Augustin's fire sweltering me through my soaked dress as he glared down at the murderer, the one who had cursed him.

My ice had frozen me solid, and I gaped at the Prince. Mixed feelings raced through my veins, disgust and pity, satisfaction and sorrow. My husband growled, a frightening sound, and I sensed the death churning inside of him. "He orders me to kill him," he said thickly. His voice sounded detached and malignant at the same time.

Horror struck me, for I detected the invisible knives of Augustin's gift testing the air around us, reaching out to addle the spirit of the hypocrite below us, seeking to burst his merciless heart in an instant. "Augustin . . . no . . . you can't!" I cried, struggling to free my arms from his embrace. I lifted my chin for a good look at his face. Death glinted in his cobalt eyes as he glowered at the Prince, his mouth set in a grim line of hatred.

"I must." Darkness clouded his visage, and he gripped me more tightly in the ruthless arms of a devil. "My master demands it. I cannot refuse him."

"Wait, Augustin, wait!" I burst out, freeing my hands at last and taking hold of his face, turning it away from the Prince, to me. "You can't kill him. Look at me! Please . . . you know you can't. It would change history. He dies in 1074 after creating the Torstein. If you kill him now, I'll vanish. You would never have known me, because I would have never found the Torstein to bring me here." I stared into his eyes in desperation, horrified at the acrimony blazing there.

"It is my duty. I must kill him." Augustin's expression suggested that he had not heard me. His eyes drifted downward from my face to the Prince.

"Don't listen to Wuotan. Listen to *me!*" I implored, tightening my hands upon Augustin's face, trying to turn it toward me again. This time it seemed as though his neck had transformed into stone; I could not make him look at me. "Let go of your hatred, Augustin, please," I begged him. "You know love is greater; you've seen it in my heart! Turn *away* from Wuotan . . . put your hands on my heart again. Love can free you from this pain, but hatred will chain you forever . . . *that's it!!*"

A tormented squeak escaped my lips as a new piece of the puzzle fell into place abruptly in my mind. "*That* must be why Black Priests usually can't control their gift of death —because they use it against the one who cursed them! That's the ultimate act of retribution, of anger, of hatred— to murder the one who murdered their souls. So you *can't* kill him, Augustin, because if you do, you'll be reduced to Wuotan's slave, unable to mingle with the living without killing them!" I gripped my husband's face more tightly, my heart begging him to hear me, to trample the demon inside of him before his anger exploded to slay us all.

A look of alarm crossed Augustin's ferocious mien, and he blinked his eyes several times in rapid succession. He exhaled shakily, his gaze shifting from my face to the Prince below us and back again. At length he spoke, his deep voice sinister. "You cannot know that . . . Swanhilde. You cannot know that I would be chained forever if I kill the murderer, that bloody hypocrite." He frowned again, and his eyes blazed more brightly, locking upon the Prince once more. But I saw him bite his lip, his forehead wrinkling as he considered my words.

"Maybe not," I conceded, still clinging to his face as though my touch might convince him to yield, if my words could not. "Augustin, look at me," I pleaded. When his fiery eyes met mine, I said, "But I *do* know that you won't kill him. If you did, I would have read it. History is very clear on Prince Otto's death. None of it attributes it to you." His mouth twitched, and I reached up to kiss him gently.

My husband stared into my eyes for an interminable moment. His arms loosened finally as he reached up to take my hands off of his face, his ire dissipating. "Yes," he breathed softly, lacing my fingers with his. "We do know the future . . . and I do know that I cannot kill him . . . because of you, my darling swan."

His expression softened considerably, and he lifted me into his arms to kiss me deeply. I felt his strong body shudder as our spirits entwined, likely reveling in the taste of my life. I groaned with desire when he released my mouth, and I saw that his eyes glittered now with something other than fury. "We must go now and return to the Denlinger house, for you have not eaten since Sext, and your body must revive itself before sharing my bed." A voracious grin spread across Augustin's face. His wet hair swung forward to brush my cheeks as he kissed my throat, the rain drenching us in nature's symphony.

"You'll be sharing *my* bed, not the other way around," I corrected.

"You are right, my silly wife." Augustin snickered. He turned for the turret, preparing to fly in a fiery storm back to Freia's house. But first, he paused to look down at the retreating army one last time, and a wicked smirk crossed his face. "The murderer has seen us," he said matter-of-factly.

"Really?" I picked my head up from where it rested on Augustin's shoulder to glance toward the western gate, where I had last seen the Prince. He was still there, seated atop his stallion, his armor more soaked than ever. But he no longer gestured at his troops, for most of them had already passed through the gate. His head was tilted upward, his red eyes focused directly upon us—the Black Priest and his aged siren, poised upon the wall like deities of destruction, waiting to watch Muniche perish. "Does he recognize us?" I narrowed my eyes, curious.

"He does." Augustin's lips brushed my throat briefly, his stance sending an unspoken message to the battle-scarred Keyholder: *You have failed your Lady, for she shall fall to the enemy . . . but I have claimed my lady forever in spite of your desire to ruin me. I have triumphed; you have crumbled.*

I tore my gaze away from the Prince's fiery eyes, glad that I was too far away to fully appreciate whatever expression adorned his face. "Please take me home, Augustin," I said, hiding my face against his chest. "We don't want him to get any bad ideas, and you need to flee temptation."

"That is true. It is quite probable that he shall station some of his forces upon the walls tonight in preparation for tomorrow's battle." Augustin kissed my veiled hair before enfolding us both in his fiery cyclone. He hurtled down from the wall and returned us to the Denlinger house before I could count to ten.

Freia and I exchanged a few speculations about the coming days while I undressed before the cooking fire, welcoming its heat to dry my hair and skin. She confessed that she did not plan to go to the town hall in the morning. She had witnessed part of the retreat during her walk home and figured that it would be better to stay with Augustin and me, so that we could watch the end as a group. I agreed with her plans wholeheartedly, as did my husband.

By the time I had changed into a white nightdress, he had returned from a scrounging expedition. Augustin had harvested a fresh batch of radishes and unripe cabbage from the garden and had managed to come upon a hare somewhere outside the city walls; its heart had fallen prey to his death gift. Freia prepared a soup using rainwater she had caught upon her return home, and all three of us consumed it along with a glass of wine apiece, setting the leftover vegetables aside for breakfast.

When I slid beneath my blanket later that night, the storm having calmed, the sounds of frogs and nightingales creating a peaceful ambiance in the bedroom lit by Augustin's five candles, I gathered my courage and broached the subject of my destiny in the eleventh century. My husband lay beside me as I tried to explain my reasons for refusing his offer to preserve my life. He appeared discontent at my lack of trust in both myself and him. Whether he wished to believe it or not, I knew for a fact that my body could not withstand his embraces indefinitely. Since he feared that my feet may develop infections if left untreated, I could see no point in staying past the fall of Muniche. I pointed out that my original plan had been to leave once my city burned, and that I intended to follow through on my promise to myself with or without his help.

"You foolish woman," he interrupted me at one point, looking frustrated. "You ought to realize that you cannot die until I permit it. I have told you that from the very beginning, from the days when mortality bound me. Now you have an immortal demon as your husband, and he shall watch over you like a hawk if he senses that you wish to end your life prematurely." His lips parted into a mischievous smirk, and he reached his right hand out to stroke a few locks of my graying hair, his touch gentle and seductive.

"I know that," I sighed, resting against my pillow to concentrate on his touch. "But you shouldn't be so selfish, forcing me to remain here, growing older and older, weaker and weaker until I finally die of old age. *I* think that our love will bridge the distance between our eras. The currents of time won't break our bond, not if we don't let them. I'll cling to your heart the whole time, to your hands, to your fire, to your spirit. Somehow, I believe we'll meet again . . . far away."

"Ah, Swanhilde, your faith is so strong, so insane," he reproved, his fingers caressing my cheek. "But if you must go, I shall not forget you, nor shall I fail you, as the murderer failed his Lady. I have learned many questionable spells since Wuotan named me his timeless servant, and there is far greater knowledge accessible in his fiery realm, awaiting my discovery."

I turned my head to look at him and saw that his eyes blazed with a devilish light. "Time is a forceful current, but if the murderer found ways to bend it, am I to be less than him? I shall seek many things in the coming years, my love—secrets about time, about life, about death—and perhaps one day, our paths shall cross again. Then I shall transform you into an immortal witch, forever subservient to me, *my* eternal wife, untouched by age or decay, our love expanding beyond the stars."

I giggled as he leaned in to kiss my neck, his tongue stroking its artery rather suggestively. His mystical ideas were beyond my comprehension, but if he wished to occupy his time in search of ancient wizardry, I would not dissuade him. The notion of somehow becoming Augustin's eternal wife sent shivers up my spine, for part of me knew that I would willingly give up my entire future for such an intriguing privilege. "Then you'll let me die—let me return to the twenty-first century and never forget your love inside my heart?" I had to be sure.

"I suppose so," Augustin murmured with a sigh, "but do not be surprised, my dear wife, if I call your soul back here through sorcery, one day." He turned my head gently away from him, brushing my hair back from my neck. "Relax now, my swan," he requested, "and allow me to see your thoughts, to claim them as my own—with all of your love and hope—that I may find the will to survive alone, forever shunning Wuotan's devices for the sake of your precious heart." I closed my eyes and allowed him to drink the depths of my heart, willing my love to find a place in his own, all of my hopes and dreams becoming a part of him.

When he raised his head at last, his fingers rubbed my neck tenderly as he healed the lesions his teeth had made. Then he laid his body carefully upon mine, his fire warming my pores as he kissed away the blood staining my skin. "Swanie, darling," he crooned, wrapping his arms around my back, his eyes seeming to delve into my soul, "I will save Freia when this city burns and bring her with me back to her family in the Rhineland. I promise."

A contented smile curled upon my lips. He must have seen that wish in my blood. Since Augustin had come to Muniche the previous day, I had hoped that he might be able to rescue my best friend from certain death. "Thank you . . . my love," I whispered, grateful that the Denlinger children would be spared the pain of losing their mother.

Augustin kissed my eyelids gently. "Anything for you, Swanie."

I chortled softly in pleasure as he kissed every portion of my face, from my forehead to my ears to my jawbone, his fiery tongue tickling my skin. I opened my eyes to admire the beauty of his face again, lifting my arms to caress his broad back. My fingers traced his powerful muscles, then ran their way through his ebony hair. "I'm so glad you grew your hair out again," I said, grasping it in my hands, relishing its silkiness.

"Anything for you, Swanie," Augustin repeated with a smile, his own hands caressing the back of my neck now, sliding upward to grasp my head, to twist in my hair. He pressed his body upon mine, his fire dancing with my ice far away in the sky, beckoning me to the glories of physical and elemental union. His tongue touched my lips briefly, erotically, and he murmured, "May I come in?"

"You don't have to ask," I answered breathlessly, my heart already throbbing with need at the touch of his hands. A moment later his fire consumed me, his roughness ignited again, his claws tugging at my hair as his lips descended upon mine in joyous passion.

Chapter Thirty-six:
The Lamentable Twist of Fate

The next morning, harsh sounds in the streets jolted me from slumber, horses' hooves and men's boots pounding upon the dust in a mad rush to the closing fray. Augustin's hands cradled my face shortly after my eyes opened to blink fitfully at the sun lighting the bedchamber. Its atmosphere was oddly peaceful, contrasting with the noise of war outside. "I fear that I cannot welcome you to life this day, my swan," my husband told me, his countenance sad as he leaned down to kiss my lips. "Ruin has descended upon us in the night, for the vagabonds have joined with the Prince's forces in a suicidal attempt to protect the gates." His eyes drifted toward the windows, a sour expression marring his gorgeous features.

I stretched with a moan, then inquired sleepily, "What, did you go outside already and take a look?"

"No, I have not left your side," Augustin answered, his eyebrows coming together defensively. "My hearing is far sharper than yours, and this house is not far from the western gate. Our enemies have chosen to attack there first, for its fortifications are less impressive than those of the other gates."

He had a point. I knew that the western gate had only one door with a single lock and two iron bars. During the days of prosperity, the Prince had closed that gate last and opened it first, to accommodate the traders coming from Schwabia and the Rhineland. I thought of the gate that I knew best—the one with the drawbridge that spanned the Isar—and I sat up in bed with a gasp. The ice within me detected a strong presence of *water*, not the rain evaporating from the gutters but a flowing stream, a grand expanse. "The Isar," I whispered, freezing upon the bed and fearing to blink, lest its waters dry again. I could hear it, sense it in my spirit, chattering over rocks, around reeds, returned to its home.

"Yes, it appears that last night's tempest freed it from the shackles of the *Toteheri*," Augustin said with a nod. "Therefore, I doubt that the Saxons shall bother with the eastern gate until last, for the river has drawn a border across their battlefield. There is a possibility, also, that if those Saxons and heathens who camped across the river choose to rejoin their brothers-in-arms for their triumph, some Teutons may be able to flee once the city has been breached."

My eyes widened as I considered this. "They'd just have to lower the bridge, or use their elements to cross the Isar, then run south to the Alps." I paused, my gaze upon the windows, beyond which I could hear frightening shatters and cracks. "Maybe that's how the Prince will get away with the last of his soldiers. Maybe they'll flee to the south once the Saxons set Muniche aflame. Are they chucking stones at us now?" I frowned at the windows.

"I would assume so," Augustin answered, his expression grim. "You should pray, my dear Swanhilde, that they break through the gates swiftly, or you may fall prey to a ponderous rock from above. I do not know if I have the power to deflect such projectiles."

I shivered a bit, though the room was warm and sticky. I pushed the blanket back and rolled toward the edge of the bed with the query, "Should we head down to the kitchen and meet Freia for breakfast?" I thought of the vegetables we had saved the night before, hoping that they had not rotted with the heat. They would likely be the last food we would taste until this madness had ended, unless Freia had found any more produce in her garden this morning.

Before I could place my feet upon the floor, Augustin's hands grabbed me from behind, dragging me bodily back onto the bed. His eyes blazed with lust as he thrust me down, straddling my naked body with the coarse words, "I am not done with you yet, Swanhilde, if it all ends today." His mouth covered mine before I could respond. In an instant, my spirit danced with fire again while my heart pounded in ecstasy, my body twining with my immortal master, finality intensifying our fervor, heightening our satisfaction.

We did not leave the bedroom until noonday, when I weakly begged Augustin to show me mercy before his violent sex killed me. My husband sealed each cut his claws and teeth had made, and I summoned my ice to cool the bruises from his powerful hands. He helped me clothe myself in a mauve hooded dress laced with purple ribbons. When I made my way to the washing table for one final cleanse, I snickered in restrained irritation at the sight of my reflection in the mirror—a tired woman in her early forties with her neck and throat covered in bite marks. "I look like a desperate harlot," I complained as my husband drew a comb through my hair.

Augustin laughed a vulgar laugh. "At least your clothing hides the majority of the signs of our union. I would like to see the reaction of the knights, should they catch a glimpse of your arms and legs . . . or your breasts." He pressed his mouth upon my neck, his teeth gnawing on my skin without drawing blood.

"I look like I had a tryst with a vampire, not a Teuton," I grumbled, prompting Augustin to murmur erotically. I swatted him playfully and rose from the stool, shooing him to his own pile of clothing with the words, "Quit seducing me, or I'm never going to be able to face this destruction properly. At this rate, I'll either be laughing hysterically or kissing you non-stop."

We left the Denlinger house behind us forever as the cathedral's bells tolled None. Augustin carried his own bundle along with a small pack of Freia's. She had clad herself in a plain green dress and sensible shoes for her impending trek, for I had informed her in no uncertain terms at lunch that Augustin would lead her to safety once Muniche had fallen. Thereafter, she had gathered up a few extra dresses, a thin blanket, bundled herbs and soap, the final bottle of wine, and her cherished flute—all that she wished to take with her on her upcoming journey. Freia left the front door of her house unbolted for the sake of any remaining vagabonds, and we struck out as a group for the town hall, intending to ascend its highest spire, which boasted a good panorama of the city.

We encountered a fair amount of destruction from the falling stones on our way to the city hall. Several houses that belonged to families Freia knew had lost their roofs and parts of their walls, huge boulders that seemed to emanate a deadly dark aura sticking out from some of the ruins. We had to take the next street over at one point, for a massive projectile had landed directly in our path earlier in the day, the ground around it blackening progressively. We saw very few stragglers on our trek, for it seemed that every living soul left in Muniche had joined the Prince's forces at the walls, clashing against the Saxons and their devilish allies.

We said little when we entered the town hall, which had escaped damage thus far due to its central location in the city. We passed by the wounded warriors without a backward glance, although I sensed Freia's light reaching out to them, seeking to alleviate their misery. Many of them had already died, their flesh tarnished with putrefaction. Augustin deposited his bag and Freia's at the base of the stairwell to the primary tower, stating rather blandly that he doubted anyone would disturb their wares, since those who rested in the building could hardly move anyway. He scooped me into his arms before I could protest, holding me tightly and mounting the staircase with Freia trailing behind.

We sat together for a long while upon the highest windowsill of the spire. A light Alpine Föhn caressed our cheeks as we witnessed the fall of Muniche. The *Toteheri* had broken the western gate in pieces and set houses and buildings afire left and right, spreading to the north and south first, slaying any stray Teuton who happened across their path. The Saxons came in behind their demonic legion, pursuing the last remnants of the Prince's army as they fled from house to house, engaging their enemies in close combat.

Augustin commented on several occasions that he wished to be down there with them, for he wanted to test his swordsmanship against that of both the Saxons and the *Toteheri*. Freia sat close to my right side, her hand grasping mine, her tears falling upon the stone floor when the arsonists reached her family's house. I wept with her as we watched our memories disintegrate into ash.

My thoughts turned back to the Thaden estate on the far side of the Isar. I knew that some of our enemies had entrenched themselves there, and I wondered whether they had already burnt it to the ground, whether the *Toteheri* had sewn its fields with death. *Thank goodness I convinced all of the vassals to leave,* I thought, blotting my tears upon the flared sleeve of my dress. *Though I'm sure some of the men are here now, dying all around us . . . following Prince Otto's path to destruction.*

"Swanhilde." An unexpected voice aroused me from my bleak reverie, and I looked up to see the *Eihalbe* that I knew best hovering over the city about a meter away from where I sat upon the windowsill. I sensed Augustin's body stiffening to my left, and I heard Freia sniff to my right, her tear-stained face hidden in her hands. I gawked at the *Eihalbe* with ice-tinted eyes, the fact that it had called me *by name* taking me completely off guard. I knew not how to interpret its salutation.

The fairy's prismatic eyes remained fixed upon me, as though neither Freia nor Augustin existed in this space where we had met. To my horror, I saw its form flicker, an odd translucence enveloping its silvery body. "They have come for me," it said, its face cracking with pain.

It took me a second to translate its statement, but then I remembered what it had told me when it visited my bedroom several months before. "The Teuton traitors? They've come to cut you down?"

"I wanted to see you . . . with him," it whispered, its eyes sliding from me to Augustin, who had wrapped his right arm around my waist, as if to protect me from a fairy's wiles. "I wanted . . . to see this."

"Augustin, you need to go to the Thaden oak *now!*" I burst out, turning my upper body to face him. "They're in spirit form, but I know you're strong enough to stop them, to *kill* them even apart—"

"No," the *Eihalbe* interrupted me, lifting one wavering hand in my direction. "It is my time." The fairy shuddered all over, its glimmer dimming into gray. Then it locked eyes with my husband for a lingering instant, and I heard Augustin exhale in what could have been resignation. "It has been an honor," it gasped, looking into my eyes one final time.

Before I could react, its eyelids slid shut, and its wings stilled. A strange *pop* pierced the air, and the fairy disintegrated just as I cried out, "What's *your* name?"

It was too late. The only *Eihalbe* who had ever addressed me by name was dead, and I would never know whether it had a name of its own. A heavy weight of sorrow crushed me, and I crumpled against Augustin's chest, tears of ice seeping from my eyes. "Be still, my swan, be still," I heard him murmur to me, his arms holding me tight against him. "Its time had come."

It took me a good while to compose myself after such a horrific encounter. Strangely enough, the *Eihalbe's* death struck me more soundly than the cries of the striving Teuton warriors. I remembered what it had said before, that the Prince had no care for the fate of the silver oaks. We had to do better than this.

Once my tears had run dry, I nestled myself against Augustin's chest and quietly asked him to hunt the Teuton traitors down and slay them in the most horrid way possible. "I think you should sacrifice them to Wuotan and chop off their balls first. Only cowards chop down trees while in spirit form." Freia echoed my thoughts, and Augustin's chest rumbled as he vowed to root up the bastards who had betrayed their people.

Eventually I rose to my feet after over an hour of sitting, slipping out of my husband's arms to stretch my stiff limbs. Meanwhile, Freia leaned forward to squint in the direction of the eastern gate, far across the city from our perch. "What . . . are they doing?" she queried, sounding perplexed, her fingers winding around the sill.

Augustin stood and narrowed his perfect eyes toward the eastern gate. A small group of Teuton warriors had gathered upon it, their weapons spread out before them, their gazes fixed upon the tallest among them, who stood poised upon the wall like a god, gesturing with his right hand. In the midst of my stretching, I saw my husband's body stiffen. Smoke began to rise from his shoulders as he glared toward the group upon the gate. "The murderer and his highest ranking knights . . . they cut their veins . . . sprinkling their blood upon the stones . . . setting it aflame . . . while the murderer speaks a solemn oath . . . the keys in his right hand . . . in Wuotan's name!" Augustin's voice broke. His fingers dug into the stones of the windowsill with a sizzling sound; I heard the stone crack. Freia gasped, and I took a step forward for a better look myself.

And Augustin said, his tone laden with disdain, "*He is cursing the city.*"

. . . An infernal agony tore through my chest, cutting my heart in two, chains of iron locking upon my soul, crucifying me upon a cross of treachery. Fire drove me to the ground. My knees buckled, and I crumpled upon the stones, an indescribable torment choking me, ravaging me, *binding me*. My spirit screamed, shooting to the sky on leaden wings, dragged down to the abyss as a bizarre omniscience obscured my vision, showing me *everything,* yet blinding me to the shards of who I had been.

My life . . . I saw it all . . . pulsing . . . throbbing . . . my veins a network of dirt streets . . . my blood a seething mass of humanity—*special humanity*—beaten down, slain, destroyed by a cancer . . . eating outward from one of my four arteries . . . burning my body . . . its members smoldering, one by one . . . my lungs the river, gasping for air tainted with death . . . my blood spilled, pouring like a fountain . . . my soul trampled, forgotten, raped . . . *cursed . . . .*

. . . My *heart . . . .*

. . . It was tied up in those four arteries . . . four ruined gates . . . all leading back to those keys, those keys held by a human soul . . . a red fire . . . a man . . . .

. . . And he had cursed me.

. . . He had forsaken me.

. . . He had left me to the dogs. To the Saxons. To the fires of hell.

. . . I was lost . . . homeless . . . raped . . . destitute . . . a whore . . . .

The screams that had wracked my spirit at last burst upon the mortal world, my voice splitting the sky apart in a cry of infinite betrayal: *"RAPE! The TRAITOR has FORSAKEN me!!!"* I howled, my hands clawing at the air, at my own hair, tearing, ripping, begging for physical pain to erase this spiritual torment. *"NOOOO!"* I screeched, my hands falling upon the stones, freezing into ice, images of carnage splayed before my eyes, of my own deterioration, my destiny. *"You BLEED upon me! You BURN me like a harlot! I have served you FAITHFULLY, on my KNEES before you, and you repay me with TREASON!! WHY?!"* I wailed with a mad fury, icy tears streaming from my eyes, my shouts resounding throughout the city, reaching the far corners of my soul, pleading for a savior . . . .

. . . And there was no response.

No love. No sympathy. Just nothing.

He had fled and left me to die. A lamentable fate. *Finis Muniche.*

I felt the creeping death sink into my soul, ripping my life from me with tedious precision, the blood of my warriors choking my lungs, flooding my river, extinguishing all hope. My sun eclipsed; my soul fell into a flaming chasm wracked with unspeakable anguish. I saw nothing but destruction, remembered nothing but this breaking heart, this disowned spirit, doomed, blighted. My hands scraped the stones, their shards piercing my skin, leaving traces of blood as I wept frozen tears upon this cursed ground. I was dying . . . raving . . . alone . . . .

After an interminable black oblivion rife with blood and flames, I sensed a presence with me at last, someone calling out to my waning soul, reaching for my ruined heart. A new fire touched me, a kinder one, not from my cankered arteries. A voice pierced my hysteria, spoke to me from afar, from a time I could not see . . . from behind the veil of the burning city . . . speaking pleas I could not understand. He repeated a name that was no longer mine, begged for a soul vanquished by a stronger force—the power of the whole locked upon my heart forever. The tortures of plundering, raping, slaughtering, blazing—these consumed my maddened soul. I writhed upon the unyielding stones, screaming for the one who had abandoned me, begging him to return, to heal my wounds, to ease my pain . . . to place those keys upon my heart so I may remember love again.

Strong hands restrained my paroxysms at last, though my eyes could not see their source, my ears still deaf to the voice urging me to be calm—for it was not *his* voice. No one but my Keyholder could save me now. I sank into a delirium of weakness, an unfamiliar light attempting to pierce my soul, the taste of wine upon my bleeding lips, granting me no relief. That strange fire still stroked my soul with a disturbing tenderness, its accompanying voice murmuring in seductive tones, an adulterous hand closing upon my heart, trying to tear me away from the duty that bound me . . . away from my dying people . . . away from my Keyholder.

My eyes blinked, and my vision returned with the abruptness of getting struck by an oncoming train. I saw a dusty bottle before me, held in the delicate hands of a woman, her eyes glinting amber as she coaxed me to drink. And behind me, I felt that fiery wraith, a black-clad priest, his arms imprisoning me, his right hand pressed upon my heart with incredible might, his soul bent upon raping me in the realm beyond this world, rending me from my traitorous beloved. A feral cry burst from my lips, and the infinite legions of Muniche reinforced my feeble muscles, breaking me away from this ignoble phantom, thrusting me back against the stone wall of a tower. My ice froze my body in an impenetrable shield, and I screeched, "*STAY AWAY FROM ME!!*" A hiss escaped my lips, and I was ready for a fight, ready to defend my dying city, though it was far too late.

I heard a feminine gasp, and the brilliant soul who had dampened my mouth with wine took a step backward, toward the window through which I saw smoke rising to the darkening sky. "Swanie?" The woman's eyes had dulled to a natural green, searching my face earnestly, her dress dirtied, her right hand still clutching the bottle of liquor.

But my attention was diverted in an instant by that dark specter, his face pale and looming, his menacing hands reaching for me again. "*Don't touch me!!*" I warned sharply, my icy fingers curling into claws, my eyes crystallizing.

The demon halted, a shocked expression upon his face, and the woman said to him, "Wolfgang . . . what can we do . . . to help her? Has she gone mad?"

"No." My foe's voice was deep, resigned, but he continued to stare at me, an unmistakable threat, his fiery eyes raking over my body, my soul. Wanting to rape me again. "Her city is dying, and she cannot survive this destruction . . . not unless the soul that is Swanhilde can reassert her will, her tenacity . . . which may prove impossible in light of Muniche's death throes."

The name *Muniche* slashed my soul, prompting me to wail again. I collapsed upon the stones, my defenses failing, the fires scorching my bones, the necrosis choking my lungs, veiling my sight. I felt the *Toteheri* rape me again, thrusting their swords deep into my womb, spilling my bowels upon the earth, casting my pearls to the dogs. I moaned as death reached for me anew . . . and two burning hands locked upon my face, pulling it up from the ground. An alien compassion struck my soul, caressing my heart, pushing the pain aside with an effort that could not have been human, for it smelled of the grave.

"Swanhilde, look at me. Please. I know you can hear me." My blinded eyes wheeled. My body tensed in a final resistance against this dead demon who called out to the human soul that Muniche had conquered. "My darling . . . my swan . . . I love you. I *love* you. Remember me . . . feel me . . . I'm your husband. Your *husband.*" My lungs gasped for air, my consciousness ebbing as my life bled upon the stones. That stranger's hands tightened upon my face, his tone growing more and more urgent, desperate. "*Please,* Swanie . . . Muniche . . . I am here with you. You are not forsaken . . . you are not going to die . . . I *love* you . . . your husband loves you . . . ."

His face coalesced in my vision at last, tears streaming from his light blue eyes, soaking his black robes, his jaw trembling, his dead blood pulsing in his neck. I could sense no malignancy in his aura, only compassion, concern, *love.* Two words he had said revolved in my tortured mind, bringing me back to some semblance of reality, of a single soul: *Muniche . . . husband . . . .* "I have no husband." The phrase came out mechanically, without emotion. "My Keyholder has deserted me."

"That damn Keyholder is *not* your husband." Frustration glinted in those moist blue eyes as they held mine forcefully, refusing to let go. "*I* am your husband, and *I* would never forsake you. Remember me . . . feel me . . . know me. I am your lover, for nearly twenty-two years now." Confusion entered my mind, superseding the anguish for just long enough when the dead priest spoke the impossible words: "Swanie, I *know* you remember. I am Augustin. *Augustin . . . .*"

Augustin . . . . The name shot through my memories like a meteor, and a tiny cry escaped my lips as my true self awoke again: *Augustin . . . my lover . . . my priest . . . my master . . . my demon . . . my husband. The Cursed One . . .*

the world of dreams . . . the cottage by the Rhine . . . the candlelit cathedral . . . the sapphire ring . . . the promise to love each other for all of eternity . . . those incredible nights of passion, the impossible union of fire and ice . . . .

"Augustin?" I spoke his name tentatively, shakily, my voice sounding like a child's. He saw the recognition in my eyes and pulled me against his chest with a strangled cry, his tears soaking my hair, his arms enclosing me in raven's wings. My body trembled, and my mind raced, trying to sort everything out logically after a long interlude of insanity. "Augustin," I choked, the pains of the dying city stabbing me afresh, "what's happening to me?"

He cradled me in his arms, his left hand brushing my cheek, lifting my face toward his. "Muniche has chosen you to take the Lady Maria's place," he murmured gravely, his eyes as tormented as I felt. "She must have died when the murderer cursed the city, with his trusted knights . . . and the soul of this condemned stronghold chose you to replace her . . . for you signify the bridging of two eras—the hope of the future and the wisdom of the past."

His careful explanation struck a chord within me, and I realized that I should have expected this from the start. Lady Muniche from my era had died the very night I had come to the past. Someone needed to take her place, too. "The city is taking over my body and soul," I whispered, shivering at the recollection of those black hands of death raking my heart, the Saxons eating me from within. "I can feel it *all*, even now . . . the fires . . . the blood . . . the pillaging . . . the broken stones. But it's not as painful now, as it was at first. I think it's killing me."

"I know." Augustin's fiery lips touched my forehead with bruising force, and he added, "I have shouldered a portion of your burden myself, as far as I am able, for our heart-bond remains, though the city's hold is far stronger. I tried to break Muniche's chains . . . at first. But I should not have. I cannot fight destiny."

I closed my eyes as I remembered the nails tearing through my heart, trying to sever the connection Muniche had formed with me, binding me forever to her soul, to her

Keyholder—until I entered the gates of eternity. I thought of the Prince, cursing the city walls without thought, without care, then running away, fleeing to the mountains to save his own life, leaving me alone. He had shirked his duties, turned tail in the face of certain death . . . but he was still my Keyholder. My soul longed for him now, though I lay in my husband's arms, weakness numbing every part of me. "But why did Muniche take me, when I'm already married?" It seemed that fate wished to spit in my face. Now Muniche pulled me toward the Prince, away from his cursed brother, the man who knew how to love faithfully, fearlessly.

"Holy matrimony is not enough in the eyes of Wuotan, it seems," Augustin replied shortly, a sneer upon his lips. "Muniche belongs to him now, for it has been declared accursed by burnt Teuton blood. We are destined for misery, I fear."

"He should not have done this terrible thing." I cast my gaze around the tower, noting the two bags someone had retrieved from the ground floor while I had ranted, the window with the view of my crumbling city, Freia standing against the far wall, her kind face anxious as she smiled at me. I managed a feeble smile in return, then shook my head. Thoughts of my Keyholder consumed my mind, sending pains of betrayal through my hurting veins. "My Keyholder cursed me . . . he hates me . . . his love for me has burnt out." Tears welled in my eyes, and a weak moan pealed from my lips.

Augustin's lips touched mine softly, his fire seeking to impart some vitality to me, though his dead body had none to offer. And he said fiercely, his eyes glinting with passion, "*I* love you, Muniche, for you are my precious Swanhilde."

And the horrid words left my lips as the chains of the city bound my soul in an indestructible cage, confining my free will to love, tying me to a man who had left me to rot. "I'm sorry . . . Augustin . . . but your love is no longer enough."

He cringed away from me, his expression stricken. He jumped up from the floor, shaking his head in firm disbelief. I rose to my feet in the same moment, wishing I could call my heresy back, knowing I could not. "Swanie, our love *must* be enough," Augustin gasped, his voice hoarse. "Muniche's influence cannot be so strong. Our love has withstood Wuotan himself . . . surely it cannot fall prey to the heartless soul of a city!" He gaped at me, his expression incredibly hurt.

Something else struck me then, and more sacrilege fell from my lips, aided by the agonies of Muniche, stabbing my soul again and again. "You refused me once, long ago." Augustin's gorgeous face cracked in pain when I rebuked him, ignoring Freia's horrified gasp.

"You have stood by all this time, watching my enemies tear me apart, sacrificing me to Wuotan, slaughtering my innocents. If you, as a dead man, are the only one who can avenge my blood, what holds you back? Where is that love you claim for me?" I glowered at Augustin with the eyes of a vengeful goddess, and he fell at my feet, his fire extinguished, sobs shaking his body.

"Forgive me, Muniche . . . forgive me! I love you . . . for I feel your pain . . . and you are my faithful wife. I shall avenge your blood . . . I swear it." And I felt his fiery hands close upon my heart, his fidelity infusing me with triumph amidst despair, our bond expanding now to include my desolate city.

Chapter Thirty-seven:
One Final Triumph

We remained in the upper chamber of the tower until the sun sank beneath the horizon, the blood-red sky reflecting the ill-fated city below. Our enemies had breached the eastern gate by then and converged upon Muniche from both sides, burning and ruining as they went. Each new fire stanched a bit of my blood, and the cries of each dying Teuton struck my heart through with a stake, causing me to cry out in pain over and over. Augustin held me in his arms, trying to help me regain my strength as we debated on what to do next. The pillaging army crept ever closer to the town hall with the approach of evening.

I heard Freia and Augustin discussing options while I lay broken, my awareness wavering, my life slowly burning out. They spoke in Rhenisch to each other, and I could hardly comprehend their words, though my Rhenisch was as perfect as my Ælte Teutonica by then. Augustin insisted that we must go before twilight had come, for soon the city would be so overrun that he may not be able to save Freia from the plundering invaders. My best friend put the wine bottle to my lips again and urged me to drink, to grant my body a temporary relief.

I closed my eyes and complied, the wine dulling the fringes of my pain. I ordered myself to find vigor somehow, so I could accompany my cohorts as long as possible. "Swanhilde, darling." I opened my eyes to see my husband's face hovering over mine, his right hand laid upon my throbbing heart. His mien looked incredibly drawn, uncertainty and regret warring with the love in his gaze. "Freia and I must leave now before escape becomes impossible for mortal humans."

"Yes . . . I know," I whispered once Freia had lifted the bottle from my lips.

Augustin's jaw trembled as he stared down at me, and I suddenly realized that he had said *Freia and I* . . . no reference to me. I blinked at him, and he said in a tremulous voice, "My precious wife, the pain you feel is intense, beyond words . . . and I cannot take it upon myself forever. You shall not find relief until you leave this place . . . to return to your future, *your* München, the city that prospers, its dark days behind. I see no point in prolonging your agony, my darling."

The truth of the matter struck me between the eyes, and fear raced through my veins despite everything. "You . . . are going . . . to kill me?" I croaked.

He nodded gravely, tears trembling upon his eyelashes. "I must, Swanhilde, for you cannot stay here now, not with your connection to Muniche, for she shall vanish with the dawn. I shall be kind, I promise . . . numb your consciousness before I stop your heart. You shall feel no pain. I could kiss you in that last moment, if you wish." A tear dropped from his right eye to fall upon my cheek.

I began to pant, fearing the unavoidable all at once, for it had come about so suddenly. I had no time to properly ponder all of the things that I desperately needed to say. "Augustin," I gasped, reaching one hand to his face, "what about our bond? Will it survive the trip through time . . . and now, when Muniche has thrown her claim upon me? What if I lose you somehow . . . how can I . . . ." I choked. My own tears spilled upon my dress while his right hand gradually unwound the stays of my mauve bodice, slipping beneath the fabric to stroke the skin over my heart, his fingers firm and gentle at the same time.

"I do not know, my love," he murmured, his face stricken with grief. "The city may release you, under the influence of time . . . but perhaps fate has plans for you as Muniche's Lady in the future. As for our bond, there is no telling, but I shall not let you go willingly. My hand shall clutch your stilled heart here in the mortal world and in the spiritual realm. I shall focus solely on our love . . . perhaps it could be enough . . . perhaps." I felt him wrap the fingers of his spirit around my heart in the other realm, solidifying our bond despite Muniche's devices.

"I'll cling to our love, too," I promised breathlessly, trying to invigorate what was left of myself for the necessary journey. "Muniche can't break us, even though your love can no longer fully satisfy me. You were my love of choice, Augustin, and if I ever find myself unchained again, I'd take you first, always." He kissed me passionately in response, his tongue entwining with mine for a long moment.

When he released my mouth, I twisted my head to the left, searching for my best friend. "Freia?" I called softly, and she flew to my side, clasping my feeble hand in hers. "I don't know how to thank you for everything you've done for me," I said. "You've been such a wonderful friend, and I'll never forget you." Freia wept and threw herself upon me in a sorrowful hug. "Please . . . when you get to Eisenwald . . . look after my children," I begged her. "And always be kind to Augustin. He's not what everyone thought . . . please . . . ."

My husband's hand tightened upon my heart at my words, and Freia promised that she would heed my final wishes and wait for me in heaven with Heinrich and all the children. She squeezed my hand firmly, imparting a touch of her light to take with me on my journey. Then Freia stepped back, nodding once at Augustin and wiping her tears on her sleeve.

Augustin sighed, and I turned my head toward his one final time, forcing the tears back so I could fully appreciate the affection shining in his light blue eyes. "My darling

Swanhilde . . . my lovely Muniche," he murmured softly, "I can only wish that we had more time . . . but fate has greater plans for you . . . I know it. And I promise you, by the dead blood that flows through my veins, that I shall avenge you. I will never rest until the *Toteheri* and each Teuton traitor has been wiped off of this earth. My love for you encompasses your city now . . . and I shall not fail you. I promise."

He leaned down to kiss my forehead. My lips trembled as I whispered the only parting phrase I could give him. "Augustin, I love you . . . now and always. Don't ever forget . . . and thank you . . . ."

His arms tightened around me, and he whispered back, "I love you, too, my darling Swanhilde. You will always be everything to me, even in death. Close your eyes now, my precious swan, and relax. Do not weep, for we shall meet again." His eyes flashed a promise, and he bent his head low to kiss my lips, our final goodbye. I squeezed my eyes shut, concentrating on the taste of his tongue, on the heat of his fire, waiting for oblivion to take me, to free me from the agonies of a dying city, to send me home.

Augustin's lips released my mouth rather abruptly, and his body stiffened, his attention diverted from granting me a merciful death to something else, outside my funereal chamber. I heard a growl rumble in his chest. "Who could dare to disturb us now, at the very end?" he snapped.

I opened my eyes, blinking in confusion. My husband lifted his hand from my chest, quickly securing the ribbons again, pulling me upward from the stone floor, his arms enclosing me in a fiery shield. I heard the distinct sound of footsteps upon the stairwell, and Freia drew close to us, her countenance frightened. "Is it the Saxons?" she asked in Rhenisch, her voice barely audible.

My husband's eyes narrowed, glinting cobalt. "No, it is a Teuton . . . a young one . . . a man of molten rock. I do not recognize his spirit." He scowled at the doorway to the stairs, his right hand sliding across my body to grasp the hilt of the sword sheathed at his hip.

My ice froze me as I turned my eyes to the doorway, belated shock flooding my veins at this sudden interruption of my death. An instant later, a brown-haired Teuton soldier burst into the chamber in a wave of heat, his armor bloodied, his appearance disheveled, his eyes a boiling orange, like fresh lava. He ground to a halt, panting, looking at each of us in turn. Then he ducked his head in an almost-forgotten display of decorum.

"Forgive me . . . for confronting you in this way . . . my lord and ladies," he began in a breathless voice, his eyes cooling into a muted blue-gray, "but I have a message for the Lady Swanhilde . . . from his majesty . . . he sent me to find her . . . made me swear to get this to her." He retrieved a soiled roll of parchment from beneath his armor and glanced uncertainly from me to Freia.

I took a shaky step forward, Augustin's hands holding me steady, and I told the winded warrior, "I am the Lady Swanhilde. What is it?" My eyes locked upon his ragged scroll, perplexity mixed with an odd thrill filling my soul. *My Keyholder has not forgotten me . . . he has sent me a message . . . perhaps an apology . . . .*

"His majesty ordered me to see that you received it, with his regards and wishes for a brighter future." I could tell from the soldier's expression that he had no idea what lay inside the sealed scroll, let alone the meaning of the Prince's commands. I shook my head in bewilderment and accepted the message. I heard Augustin shoo the messenger away with a bit of annoyance, commenting to Freia in Rhenisch that letters had no meaning now, only to delay the inevitable. And my quaking hands cautiously unrolled the scroll.

My eyes flew open, a veil of blue enhancing my vision. My hands began to shake so violently that I almost dropped the parchment. A choked cry escaped my lips, for my disjointed mind could hardly comprehend what I was seeing—lines, notes, symbols, a musical score written in black ink, the tune one I had known for years, except for the end, the final lines. A smaller sheet of paper fell to the floor while I unraveled the right edge of the scroll, my eyes flying over those last phrases, the ones I had long dreamed to uncover. The complicated pedalwork . . . the almost-perfect harmonies . . . the registration invoking every melody that ancient pipe organs could conceivably make . . . *Prince Otto's Song of Time.*

When I finally managed to speak, I said something ridiculous, for my eyes were riveted upon those last lines, the musician in my soul committing them to memory. "So *that's* how it ends. I never would have thought. I guess that's why I'm not a composer." My foolish snicker broke the stillness of the chamber, and a deluge of relief and amazement nigh pulled me into an insane rapture. *The song was mine. Now I could escape this era apart from death!*

"This . . . is quite unexpected," Augustin remarked in a gravelly voice, staring down at the paper in my hands. I had almost forgotten about him, for I was so distracted by the beauty of the music my eyes beheld. My mind played its melody. My feet began an unconscious imitation of the pedalwork, thrusting the pains of the dying Muniche into the back of my mind. The performer inside of me had awoken at the very door of death, and she wished to fly to the stars again.

Freia came to my side, laying a small folded paper upon the score before me, breaking my concentration at last. "I think the Prince sent you this, as well," she murmured, her countenance shining in response to my unanticipated triumph. I focused on the small paper, taking it in my left hand and carefully rolling the scroll with my right, fearing to mishandle such a precious artifact. I had noticed that the score contained no words, no explanation, just lines and notes of music. Perhaps the folded paper would shed some light onto my sudden salvation.

Augustin took the scroll from my hands as I unfolded the small note, and he stepped aside to view the score himself. It would do him no good, I knew, for he was no musician. He looked only to satisfy his traditional curiosity. Meanwhile, I read the Prince's flowing Carolingian minuscule with shifting emotions, his handwriting not quite on par with Augustin's but impressive nonetheless:

My Lady Swanhilde Hudson von Thaden,

It is with great and sincere regret and humility that I write you this letter, for by the time you receive it, Muniche shall likely have perished to the enemy. I have failed in my entire life, it appears, blinded by opulence and imagined safety, never truly believing that it would come to this. My shortsightedness has ruined my Lady, destroyed my people, cast my intentions to hell, and I admit now, with proper meekness, that I should have heeded your admonitions long ago.

Perhaps I should have given this song to you that very first day, for no woman ought to behold this degeneration of an epoch. You are a fine musician, and I do pray that this message reaches you before an inglorious death, for you shall certainly treat this knowledge with respect and discretion. I hope that you may split the heavens asunder in one final triumph of Teutonic sorcery before Muniche crumbles, and that the wisdom you have gained from this dreadful era may shed a more astute light upon your own destiny. As for me, I depart in disgrace, cast forever from my people and my city. I have not used my knowledge properly, and now I reap the fatal consequences. May you warn those in your era to shun the vices of pride and devilry, for the effects only serve to hurt. Forgive me.

Sincerely yours, with a broken man's hope for the future,

Prince Otto Eduard Hildebrand von Bayern

I stared at the letter in stunned silence for a long interval, disbelieving the humbled apology I detected in the Prince's words. It had taken the ruin of his city for him to give up his pride, to grant a woman his cherished secret. But it had happened at last, and now the responsibility of the Prince's song had passed to me. The insane cords that had locked upon my soul in the hour before sunset throbbed in my heart, sending a mad pleasure through me.

He had written his last letter to *me*, his Lady, an unspoken plea for forgiveness, repenting of his mistakes, expressing his sorrow in my demise. "My Keyholder loves me still," I whispered at length. My strength gradually returned while my dying city sang a final song of adoration.

Augustin snorted from somewhere behind me, snatching the letter from my hands with the callous assertion, "He wrote this last night, Swanhilde, look at the date. The murderer had no inkling that you were to become his Lady. He likely thought that Muniche would choose no one, after he consigned her to oblivion."

I shook my head, still dazed by this whirlwind turn of events. "That may be, but there is yet grace in his heart, or he would not have sent me this bequest. He must flee now and wander alone until his death in 1074. Then he must pass his responsibilities to another, one who may live to see Muniche reborn. And I shall depart, return to meet the future, as he wished . . . for he is my Keyholder." I spoke the word in Ælte Teutonica, a whisper of devotion from my bound heart—an olden term, one used only between the Keyholder of a Teuton city and his Lady. It has no translation into English or modern German, and though I write it as *Keyholder* it implies much more: *protector, beloved, savior . . . master.*

An aggravated groan escaped Augustin's lips. He paced the floor swiftly from the doorway to the window, his cloak flaring, his hands clutching the score and the letter. "And what is your master now?" he muttered, not looking at me. "Nothing. A pawn shoved aside by a damned city. A marriage certificate burnt in the wind, thrown to the depths of the sea." His face was creased with suffering.

My gaze drifted to the stones beneath my feet, and Freia patted me gently on the shoulder, sending her light into my spirit to comfort my treasonous heart. Regret stabbed me at the sight of my husband's heartache, and I approached him where he had halted his pacing at the windowsill to glare at the darkening sky. "Augustin, forgive me. But I have no choice." I stared up at his face, my heart yanked in opposite directions—a ravaged Muniche to her

Keyholder, and a dedicated Swanhilde to her lover, her cursed husband.

"I know," Augustin sighed, wrapping his arm around me, pulling me to his side, his fingers brushing the skin of my neck. "It may be better for you now," he went on, sounding detached. "Once you return to the future, your tie with the city shall cause you to forget the immortal demon you left behind . . . allowing you to properly move on, to unite with your modern Keyholder."

"No. Never," I disagreed, kissing Augustin's cheek several times, savoring the taste of his fiery skin. "Muniche may pull me away from you, but she can't make me forget. I'll always hold my love for you inside my heart, forever."

"Ah, darling Swanie . . . time shall tell." Augustin sighed heavily, leaning his cheek upon my head, his entire body appearing weary. "But we must cast off our sorrows and confront our situation. The Saxon legions converge upon our haven now, though they may halt their destruction at nightfall and finish with Muniche in the morning. I can see their fires blazing in a cordon around the city, and we must go if you still wish me to save Freia."

My best friend stood beside us at the window, looking down upon the burning buildings and seething forces, swords glittering in the torchlight, moving ever closer to the town hall. "They've already reached the castle," Freia said, her green eyes on its towers, breaking apart slowly with the powers of the *Toteheri*. "If Swanie plans to leave using the song, we'll have to go to the cathedral."

My gaze drifted from the crumbling palace—where Lady Maria's corpse likely still lay—to the cathedral's tall spire reaching to the firmament in the midst of the city, as yet untouched by the enemy. "I've never played the organ there," I said, wondering what sort of stops it had. "And it might be hard to get there with the *Toteheri* below us." I looked down at the main street and the heathen warriors approaching the town hall's front entrance.

"Difficult for well-trained Teutons?" Augustin shot me a reproachful look. "I think not, my darling. We can fly there on the power of our elements; and should either of you fear that you cannot accomplish such a feat, I could carry both of you, if you would each take up one of the bundles."

That very idea had occurred to me, but I remembered what had happened the last time I had attempted a similar display—the stinging throb in my ankles. I could not injure my feet further now, not when I needed to play the Prince's song perfectly. "You're going to have to carry me, Augustin, but I'll bring your fire out to help," I pledged, bending down to retrieve my husband's bag.

Freia added that she would try to reinforce our vitality with her light. She placed the nearly empty wine bottle back inside her pack before shouldering it deftly, favoring me with a determined nod. A devilish look appeared on Augustin's face, and he leapt upon the windowsill, raising his head to the sky. The atmosphere grew unbearably hot, and his robes swirled around him as he called forth the full power of his fire. His long black hair transformed into licking flames; the hands he proffered to us glowed in a scorching blue.

Freia hesitated for a moment, then allowed her skin to shine with a blinding radiance as her trembling hand met Augustin's. My heart pulsed with flame, and I twined the fingers of my left hand with those of Augustin's right. His fire engulfed us and he gathered us close, his very teeth shining like gas flames. "Do not leave your spirits behind, my charming ladies, for you fly tonight with death," he said.

And we jumped from the spire in a fiery storm, the wind and darkness uniting somehow with my husband's element as we soared across the sky. His death heightened his mastery of the realm of nature, holding Freia and me in a vise of shadow. I might have heard a few shocked yells from beneath us, but not even the heathens could slow our flight. Before I knew it, we had crashed through a pane of stained glass, falling to a landing of the cathedral's steeple in a smoldering heap. Augustin snickered, calming his fire, and the steeple returned to its gloom as his glow confined itself to his glimmering eyes. "I suppose I could have achieved that with greater finesse," he noted, sounding amused.

I lifted myself from the planks that had served as my landing platform, a bit surprised that I had not broken them with my weight. My ice reclaimed my spirit and I stretched my limbs, brushing shards of glass off of my skirt, scarring my already-wounded hands. "You shouldn't have broken that window," I rebuked Augustin, looking up at its ruined portrait of creation.

"Tomorrow it shall fall to the earth," he rejoined, dusting off his cloak and pulling the scroll from his belt, handing it to me. I accepted it with a knowing smile, and a moment later I heard Freia cry out softly, her element also dimming. When Augustin and I turned our attention to her, we found that she had cut herself rather horribly upon the glass, for her light lacked the shielding power of our scorching fires. Her green skirt was torn, and both of her legs dripped blood from deep gashes. Thinner scrapes tainted her pale neck.

I immediately focused my mind on the severed veins in her legs, imagining their blood flow slowing, the wounds healing swiftly with a Teuton's power. While I worked on repairing her legs, Augustin placed his hands upon Freia's neck, easing her head into his lap. "Darling Freia," he observed, "I must admit that your blood tempts me . . . for it smells very strongly Teutonic . . . Rhenisch maiden." His eyes glittered, and he stared fixedly at the seeping wounds on Freia's neck.

"Don't be foolish, Augustin," I ordered him as the lesions on Freia's legs gradually healed. "I don't think she'd appreciate you biting her neck, not while Heinrich is still alive." I smiled slyly at my best friend, glancing at the marriage scar that still adorned her left wrist. I hoped that with Augustin's help, both she and Heinrich would reunite with their children at Eisenwald.

Augustin eyed me distrustfully, but he closed the cuts in Freia's neck more swiftly than I could. "Are you all right, my lady?" he inquired. "I could carry you to the ground floor, should you need assistance."

Freia assured him that she could manage. But before she could straighten her scabbed legs in an attempt to rise, Augustin's arms wrapped around her torso, pinning her in his lap. He bent over her face and spoke softly, seductively, "Forgive me, my lady . . . but your blood yet taints your beautiful skin . . . threatening to stain your bodice. Allow me to rescue your clothing from blemish." I watched in a mixture of horror and amusement as he pressed his mouth to her neck, his tongue carefully cleaning her wounds.

I raised an eyebrow at Augustin when he lifted his head, his eyes glowing with an odd satisfaction. Freia clutched my right hand tightly, her whole body quivering. "Ninety-*seven* percent. Delectable Teutonic life." Augustin grinned wickedly at me, and I pouted at him, recognizing his stab at my "low" blood. Freia had reached Heinrich's level after years of sharing his bed, but mine would remain ninety-six percent indefinitely, it seemed.

When we graced the nave shortly afterward, we found the entire cathedral draped in darkness, no candles lit, not a sound of human life on the main level. My husband said that he detected the presence of the sick down in the basement, and that he may offer them an easy death before vacating the city for good. I rolled my eyes and said that he seemed preoccupied with the high of physician-assisted suicide.

He winked at me while he lit several candles, brightening the nave just enough for me to properly read the Prince's score. "I would predict that the Saxons shall not raid this house of God until dawn," Augustin said with a nod. Then he eyed Freia and me rather enticingly. "Therefore, if the Lady Freia would forgive my impropriety, I wish to take you one final time, my darling wife . . . here and now." I, of course, could not refuse.

Chapter Thirty-eight:
Closing the Book

A dawning light crept through the stained glass windows of Muniche's cathedral, casting the nave in morning's brightening glow while the blue flames upon the candles faded. I lay unmoving upon the altar as the sun's rays colored my flushed face, my husband's clothing and mine bunched between my aching back and the wood. Augustin's muscular body held mine to our makeshift bed, his razor-sharp teeth locked upon my throat, drinking my life for the thousandth time since our final passion had begun.

I had not slept a wink the entire night. Desperation had kept me awake to savor my last moments with Augustin. Muniche's bonds hampered my satisfaction, leaving me unable to enjoy my husband like I had just one night before. But I had worked to thrust my city's pains into a back corner of my mind and concentrate on the love I felt for Augustin, my determination to cling to him fiercely, come what may—just as Prince Otto had always pined for Kezia, his chosen love.

The sounds of shouting and vandalism broke the serenity of the cathedral as the sun rose, marking the concluding tones of medieval Muniche's symphony. My husband released my throat, his light blue eyes burning with desire. He ran his tongue across his lips, consuming all traces of my blood before leaning down to kiss me. I closed my eyes when his fire met my ice, tenderness taking the place of brutal passion at last, his tongue like wine in my parched mouth. "Oh Swanie," Augustin groaned softly, "I fear the final act has come."

"It's true," I whispered, for I felt it in my soul—the wracking death throes of my city piercing me afresh, depleting my vitality faster than Augustin's draining of my blood ever could. We would have to rise now and leave our sacred bed behind, stepping into the morning light to meet our separate futures. We had exchanged many ardent words throughout that night, pledges of love, reminders of devotion, wishes for a different destiny . . . but our heart-bond had encompassed us with the depth of our relationship more than spoken words. Augustin had seen my love for him in my blood, and I had felt his love for me in his ardent embraces. Both of us would leave so much behind that day, when I closed the book on my eleventh century adventures for good. Neither of us would ever forget.

My husband lifted himself off of me and slid his feet onto the stone floor. His muscles rippled as he stretched in a beam of color from one of the windows, the glory of his naked body prompting my heart to skip a beat. "I hope," he commented at length, "that our ardor did not frighten your dear friend away."

A blush tainted my cheeks, and my thoughts turned to poor Freia, a forced witness to the final copulations of a dead man and his enslaved bride. She had retreated to the back pews of the nave, if my foggy memory served me well, and I wondered if she had gotten any sleep at all with our ecstatic cries filling the air. "Maybe she went down to comfort the sick," I said, taking Augustin's fiery hand and allowing him to pull me to his side. "I doubt she lingered anywhere in hearing range. Her modesty would probably keep her away."

Augustin snickered as he donned his robes and cloak, glancing toward one of the exits, likely listening for signs of life downstairs. "I shall seek her out then, for I must grace the basement shortly to offer the invalids an easy death. Perhaps while I complete my business there, you could ascend to the organ loft and prepare for your departure." He gave me a considering look, his eyes drifting to the corner of the altar, where his pack lay, along with the score and Prince Otto's letter.

I looked toward the western side of the nave, where the organ pipes stretched upward to the ceiling far above. "I guess we might as well get on with this before the Saxons or the *Toteheri* break down the door," I said. I pulled my wrinkled dress over my head, wishing yet again that my union with Augustin could last far longer. But Muniche had shackled me now. I felt it constantly nagging at my soul, that yearning for my Keyholder, a craving I could not push aside.

I wondered what would become of me once I returned to the twenty-first century, if Muniche still held my heart. I would have to seek out the Keyholder there, quite likely, and I had no idea who he was. But I remembered that he had refused my elderly mentor. I feared that he may have similar qualities to those I detested in Prince Otto—arrogance, indifference, assumed superiority. My gaze drifted back to my dead husband while I patted my hair into place beneath the hood of my dress. I hoped against hope that my bond with him would survive somehow. His love far outweighed that of any Keyholder.

Augustin took me in his arms once I deemed myself presentable and kissed me for a long moment, his fire invigorating my saddened soul for the tasks before me. "Can you climb to the organ loft unaided, or would you like me to carry you?"

"I think I can do it," I answered, stretching my tired legs, wiggling my toes inside their clogs. "But I may have to play the song barefoot unless someone left a pair of organ shoes in the loft. That's going to complicate things, because my feet aren't as nimble as they used to be." I cringed at the memory of Augustin's demonic laughter when he ripped my feet apart eleven years ago.

"You will play masterfully, my darling swan, for you always do," Augustin assured me with a smile, backing away toward one of the side doors. "I shall return as quickly as possible, hopefully before our enemies interrupt your concert." He vanished into the corridors a moment later. I retrieved the Prince's song and his letter, then set my course for the organ loft.

I realized with a start, as I climbed the stairs to the loft, each step shooting pain into my ankles, that I had left both my camera and my Bible back at Freia's house, now reduced to a pile of ash. Hopefully everything that I had brought to the eleventh century would return to the future with me. Both Beth's and Joel's bags had vanished after their deaths, but I did not know whether opening time's gates apart from death would make a difference. I hoped not, for I had a fair collection of pictures to admire once I had access to my computer.

I glanced at Augustin's sapphire ring upon my right hand as I reached the loft, frowning at the likelihood that it would remain here in the past, granting me no tangible memento of my lifeless husband. My mauve dress would transform into that ridiculous red-violet thing I had fashioned for the trip. I would be twenty again, with long raven hair and an hourglass figure—oh, how I wished Augustin could see me in my own era just for a moment, to appreciate the immodest attire of the twenty-first century! I entertained myself briefly with the mental image of his reaction to my youthful body clad in shorts and a tank top. He would probably stare, his eyes smoldering with lust, and then he would throw me onto whatever furniture stood nearby . . . a couch, a bed, the floor . . . rip my clothing from me . . . .

I mentally smacked myself as my hormones began to race. *Be happy with what you shared last night on the altar. That's all you'll ever get.* I looked at the ring again, then at the Prince's song, clasped in the same hand. Maybe both of those items could come through the dark currents with me if I held them firmly, begging the tides of time to recognize the key that had opened them to me and grant it access to the future.

I turned my attention presently to the organ console before me, my eyes sweeping over it in its entirety. In the dim light I discerned that it had two ivory keyboards, a full pedalboard, and forty available stops. A candlestick rested atop the console; Augustin could light that once he arrived. My gaze roved around the floor, searching for a stray pair of organ shoes and seeing nothing. Then I abruptly noticed that the impressive instrument before me had no bellows. Instead, I saw gears, pipes and a lever—a *hydraulic* organ!

I kicked my shoes off and stepped closer to the console, eyeing the gears distrustfully. The *Toteheri* had dammed the Isar for three days. It had broken free during the storm two nights ago, but would there be sufficient water pressure to power this primitive instrument? Or would I have to ask Augustin to kill me after all? I frowned and climbed onto the bench, hearing my companions' footsteps approaching from the stairwell. I unrolled the Prince's score and spread it out across the music stand, praying a silent plea to God that this organ would work, that its melodies would pierce the bonds of earth.

"You must not delay long, Swanhilde." Augustin's voice reached me while I studied the final lines of the score again, my fingers and feet seeking the correct notes on the silent organ. I twisted slightly around to face him and saw that he and Freia had stopped just inside the loft, each of them looking harried and clutching their respective bags. My best friend's eyes were circled with the blemishes of a sleepless night, but she smiled brightly at me as she took in my stance upon the organ bench. Augustin's robes and features looked perfect as usual. "The Saxons are setting fire to the small cottages attached to this cathedral," he told me with a fierce expression. "They shall undoubtedly storm through the main entrance in less than a half hour. I secured the door with its lock and several pews, but they shall break through that barricade with little effort, I predict." He scowled in the direction of the front entrance, his eyes flaming blue.

"No one rang the bells for Lauds this morning," I mentioned, recalling those huge iron bells that I had seen hanging above us the previous evening, when we had crashed into the spire through the window.

"There is no point in tolling the hours for a doomed city," Augustin said, his countenance grim. "Most of the invalids downstairs accepted my gift of a painless death gladly, as did the two remaining female attendants."

I swallowed, picturing those withered forms strewn across the basement floor, all of them stiff corpses now, their hearts stilled by the gift of a Black Priest. "What about the ones who wanted to live?" I asked in morbid curiosity.

"Those I left to their fate, reminding them that they would soon fall prey to the Saxons' swords, or worse." Augustin frowned as though he could not understand why anyone would wish to die that way.

"And Father Markus?"

"The lady who witnessed your wedding with me said that he left yesterday to fight with the Prince's army," Freia said, her eyes downcast.

"Which means he is dead," Augustin translated, walking forward to scrutinize the mechanisms of the organ. He cast a few flames upon the candlestick in a blink of an eye, then asked me in English, an expectant smile curling on his lips, "Shall we throw the switch?"

I took a deep breath, feeling nervous all of a sudden as I glanced down at my bare feet, with their blisters and crooked toes. "I think I ought to play something else first, just so I can get warmed up. I haven't played in a year and a half now. I hope I can still sight-read." I squinted at the final lines again, ordering myself to *believe* that I had played them before, that I knew them well.

Freia came to stand to my left while Augustin yanked the lever, bringing the gears to life. The ice within me sensed water pumping into the cathedral, preparing the organ for its magnum opus. I turned my attention to the stops, testing each of them in sequence. Pleasure flooded my soul as the pipes pealed forth the sounds of woodwinds, brass, strings, principals, and chimes. *This* organ was more impressive than the one in the Bayern castle. Each note I touched sent glorious echoes reverberating throughout the cathedral, singing to the sunlight. "I think I'll play John Stanley's Voluntary V first, just to get my fingers going," I declared once I had finished testing the stops. Augustin said that I had better hurry. My fingers leaped out to prepare the registration, then attacked the keyboards.

The trumpets rang splendidly on the final movement of the simple song I had memorized long ago, when I was in high school. My fingers stumbled at first, but by the end they flew with grace. My twitching feet sought to tackle the pedalboard, awaiting a melody that included those profound notes. My lips parted into a triumphant smile when I concluded the song, and Freia applauded quietly.

I paused for breath and looked at the Prince's score again, preparing myself to do his unmatched song justice. The thought struck me that unless the music came through the currents of time with me, I might never set foot in the eleventh century again. The death pains of Muniche struck me afresh as I gasped, my mind not wanting to wrap itself around the myriad of things I would lose, the people that I would never see on this side of eternity. And I spun my torso to the left, reaching one hand out to my best friend. "Freia . . . ."

An ear-splitting crack resounded throughout the nave, and Augustin cursed. He whirled away from where he stood near the gears and flew to the railing of the loft, heat rippling out from his body. "Damn it, Swanhilde, *play that song!*" he roared, his posture rigid. "They are breaking through the door. You have no time!"

I met Freia's wide eyes for a split second, seeing the terror on her face. Then I cried out to my cursed husband, "Augustin, kiss me!" My heart pounded with desire, frantic for one more taste of his intense love.

He was at my side in an instant, his arms crushing me to his chest, his lips engulfing my mouth in fire. Tears streamed down my face as I drank the depths of his love, praying that I would never forget, not at the hands of

Muniche or even of God Himself. He parted from me too soon and stared into my eyes. "Play it now, Swanhilde. Hurry," he said in a ragged voice.

I ogled him when he darted to the railing and drew his sword. Its blade flashed in the light from the windows as he assumed a defensive stance. I imprinted the memory of his impressive form onto my heart—a magnificent demon clad in black, his ebony hair cascading to his shoulder blades, his visage pale and stern. Then I whirled to face the organ, pulling the proper stops and beginning the opening lines from memory.

The harmonies burst from the pipes, their beauty overwhelming my soul. My eyes ran over the music as the song progressed, my bare feet dancing upon the pedals. Pain shot through my legs as my feet bent into unnatural angles to hit the proper notes heel-toe. I was going to break the arches in my feet, I feared, especially once I got to the end, where the score called for several flourishing scales. But I pushed the agony to the back of my mind along with the wails of Muniche, focusing instead on the twenty-first century, on that clearing in my backyard, the gazebo, the stream, Hans . . . the black-fired priest . . . .

The sounds of feet pounding upon the stone floor of the cathedral mixed with the glorious harmonies—crashes of metal upon wood, upon glass, windows shattering, pews overturned, voices shouting in a language I did not know. I forced myself to focus upon the music and began those final lines, the ones I had never played before.

The muscles of my feet rebelled, my toes bruising themselves upon the pedals while my fingers glided across the keyboards, majestic melodies resonating around me, singing to my soul. And when I played that final note, its tone deep and enchanting, invoking a mysticism beyond my comprehension, I felt the atmosphere tighten around me, a pulse bursting through the cathedral—and the *crack* boomed upon its stone walls as the air to the right of the organ split apart vertically, revealing the gates of time.

My body froze, and my jaw dropped open. I could hardly believe that I saw the gates *in the mortal world*, not on the edges of death, where my frail spirit waited for my fiery demon to drag me back. This time he stood behind me, prepared to unleash his vengeance upon the Saxons for destroying Muniche, but he would not stop me now.

I lifted my fingers and bruised feet from the instrument while the gates creaked open, the darkness swirling inside, streams of light and color flashing here and there, beckoning me home, to the future, to life. I heard Freia exclaim softly as she viewed the gates of time, a portal she had likely never expected to see for herself. I felt her hand upon my back, a silent urging to go, to save myself, to claim my destiny without further delay.

A thousand thoughts overtook my harried mind while I blinked at the gates, memories, fears, hopes, wishes . . . all of it boiling down to Augustin, my wonderful husband who loved me still, though my heart had been chained to a city, to the very man who had cursed him. How could I possibly meet the future without him? My eyes tore at last from the gates to stare at Augustin. Tears blurred my vision at the sight of that familiar darkness poised to defend his Lady against the ravaging horde. He sensed my hesitation and yelled at me, his attention still upon the army below, "Swanhilde, get *out* of here! They are approaching the stairs, and if they swarm this loft I shall have to unleash my death upon them indiscriminately, and I may kill you by accident. *Go!*"

I snatched the score off of the organ and jumped from the bench. Several of my tarsal bones crunched, driving me to my knees, and I screeched once from the pain. Freia placed her hands under my arms to pull me up again as I rolled the score into a tight rod, gasping when my eyes fell upon the sapphire on my right hand. *Maybe if I attach it somehow to the song, it'll come with me . . . .*

"Freia, hold this!" I thrust the score into her hands and braced myself upon the organ bench as I pried the ring from my pudgy finger. I grabbed the score from Freia an instant later, folding one end into a tiny point and shoving it through the ring, closing the fingers of my right hand solidly around my bundle. I heard boots pounding on the stairway to the loft, and my eyes darted from the portal to my best friend's frightened face. I pushed myself toward the open gates, then made a split second choice. "Come with me!" I cried out, holding my left hand out to Freia.

"*What?*" Her green eyes widened, and she hesitated.

"It's either that or death, and I'm *not* letting you die on my account! Come on!" I jerked my head toward the gates and snatched her right hand, dragging her forward with all of the strength I could muster. She followed, stumbling as I limped for the portal, panting shallowly—but she wound her fingers tightly around mine.

I paused for one final second right in front of the gates and turned back to regard my lover. He stood ready, his sword raised, his eyes flaming. An intense longing struck my soul, and I cried out, "Augustin, come with us!"

"I cannot!" he shouted back, swinging his head around to glare at me. "This day, I shall avenge you! Take Freia, and go!" He bared his teeth, his expression glowing with deadly triumph.

"Our bond!" I cried, not knowing what I asked, tears welling in my eyes.

"*I* shall not let go." His light blue eyes flared with devotion and fury at the same time as he finished, "*You* had better not."

"I won't," I promised, my soul filled with resolution once more. Then I leapt through the gates, my shattered feet barely granting me the necessary drive, my right hand clutching the Prince's song, my left entwined with Freia's . . . and the hands of my spirit grasped my heart-bond with Augustin, willing it to endure.

End of Book III

~*~

Turn the page for a sneak peek at the madness Swanie and Freia face in time's dark currents—and in the twenty-first century!

His Name Was Augustin
Book IV excerpt
© C.L. Carhart

Chapter One:
The Harsh Return

That journey through the swirling currents of time on my long-awaited quest for my own era proved to be a perilous experience that far outweighed all of my other encounters with those overpowering tides. I felt like my body had fallen from my soul entirely, strange forces prodding and tangling me as I rushed forward into blinding splashes of light. Terror dragged me into its clutches, for I had too many things to which I *needed* to cling—Freia's hand, the Prince's song, my heart-bond with Augustin.

But as the currents yanked me, I could not feel my hands nor my battered feet, nor the presence of my best friend. My soul screamed without sound, trying to grasp something, trying not to fail . . . and the wretched truth struck me hard—that if I must lose all that I had gained from the past, I *could not* lose Augustin. So I pushed aside all other thoughts and clutched my heart's familiar chains, that fiery hand, that devil's soul, crying a desperate prayer for God's mercy, that He would preserve our bond across the great expanse of time.

And the colors around me grew brighter, a whirling crimson interspersed with images, memories, pictures of

my past in both eras. A burning city . . . a dance in the dark
. . . five magical children . . . a rich man mourning his dead
wife . . . a brilliant woman leaping over clumps of flowers .
. . a smoky dorm room occupied by abusers . . . a devil of
blue fire, his eyes flaming with desperation, his teeth bared,
sweat beading on his dead brow, his hands clinging to me,
to my spirit . . . though I flew so fast . . . *so fast* . . . .

I screamed, shutting my eyes, my love bursting upon
the currents of time, vibrating in my spirit, begging for the
impossible. A wretched moan arose from somewhere
beneath me, its tone wailing along with my own cries as
though it, too, had lost all of its hopes to eternity's bleak
abyss. A corner of my brain wondered vaguely what sort of
creature could produce a noise so desolate . . . and why
would it voice its pleas to time's currents . . . when they
rushed forward without care. But then I heard voices all
around me, whispering, rebuking, females, sirens. And for
the first time, I realized that I could understand them, for
they were speaking Ælte Teutonica, the language of my
heathen ancestors.

*Foolish human witch, what is this audacity that drives
you? He shall not overlook your meddling forever . . . he
shall require your service. Your God shall grant him sway
over you . . . your heart belongs to him, for he directs
Muniche's fate . . . she shall not release you, the one who
travels time lightly. Your mistakes shall cost you your life
. . . eternal damnation. What wisdom shall you purvey to
your peers . . . to your people . . . to the future? What but
the fall of the Teutons . . . the damnation of Muniche, your
beloved home. You have forsaken him . . . he shall not
forgive, and he shall tear his servant from your hands.
Your beloved priest belongs to him, not to you. Your love
shall fail . . . your future shall crumble . . . if you do not
remember . . . if you do not learn . . . if you spurn your
destiny . . . your obligation to the one who guards these
gates . . . to Wuotan . . . to your master.*

Then that horrific laughter reverberated through my
spirit, chastising me, degrading me, mocking my faith in
God when I tampered so freely with the forces of evil.

Wuotan knew me, and he was determined to ruin me, to destroy my future and my city, to sever my connection with Augustin. I sensed it all, every intention, every malicious desire . . . and I wished for a lingering second that I had heeded Hans' advice and never used the Torstein . . . for then I would not face the wrath of this sadistic demon.

But God had conquered Wuotan already. I reminded myself of this as his laughter wracked my spirit. Heaven was open to humans like me due to God's love and grace alone, and no demon could claim my soul or my destiny. *You cannot convince me otherwise.* I hurled the thought outward into the swirling rays and darkness, promising myself all over again to never lose faith in God, to never let go of love, to believe that one day even my cursed husband would realize the truth, though I may never meet him again on this side of eternity . . . .

. . . And my body exploded from the labradorite gates of time, falling onto grass, onto my knees, a cool summer breeze caressing my cheeks as I sank upon the ground. My eyelids remained shut, and my hands trembled, my fists clenched into tight balls. My heart sprinted erratically with a piercing pain, a strange uncertainty, an obscure delusion. I took a deep breath and worked to bring my awareness back to what awaited me on the other side of that maelstrom between eras.

All of the sirens' warnings spun through my head along with Wuotan's awful laughter, and one phrase gripped my pounding heart in a vise of panic: *He shall tear his servant from your hands.* I choked on my breath, sensing the bonds of Muniche yet upon my heart. I could feel the pulsing life of modern München all around me, pervading my spirit. My right fist tightened, and I heard the sound of paper crunching as I pressed my hand upon my chest and gasped out his name, a ghostly whisper, a tearful plea: "*Augustin . . . .*"

About that time I realized that someone was panting in an agonized manner not far from where I knelt upon the grass. A male voice spat out a few curses in Teutonica before rasping out the word, "*Wazzar.*"

I opened my eyes, telling myself firmly that I had to get it together. I was not the only one who had just rushed forward in time. No matter how much I wanted to seek my cursed lover somehow across the expanse, I needed to ensure that my companions had all arrived—and shut the portal behind us. I blinked once, taken aback for a second by the perfection of my vision—contact lenses. I quickly confirmed the presence of three figures at my sides, one to my left and the others to my right. Then I twisted my torso around and raised my left fist in a silent command to the numinous gateway towering behind me. *Should have shut that the second you got here, Swanie,* I rebuked myself. *Wuotan probably wants to suck you back in there so you can moan along with that mysterious voice.*

I watched the portal vanish soundlessly, like it had on the other occasions when I had traveled time. The panting noises to my right had intensified, reaching the point of hyperventilation. I shook myself and turned back around, my gaze passing over Freia, who stood silently gaping at where the portal had disappeared, her eyes glowing gold with her element, her pale hands clutching her bag against her breast. I noticed my own bag plopped upon the ground at my right side—the one I had brought with me to the eleventh century twenty-two years before.

Finally, I raised my eyes to meet Joel's. He stood stiff at my side, clad in the ridiculous tunic and trousers that I had sewn for him before I had any concept of medieval fashion. A touch of madness lurked in his hazel eyes, and his jaw worked in a mechanical fashion. He looked away from me and croaked out the word *water* again in Teutonica, then staggered toward the stream that trickled about a meter from where we all gathered. My cousin Beth had collapsed in a heap just paces away from me, her face screwed up in anguish, wordless sobs spilling from her lips, her arms wrapped tightly around her tawny dress.

Beth died to get back here, and so did Joel, I remembered. *They're probably both reeling from being yanked into time's currents.* I shuffled toward where my cousin cowered, tears streaming down her cheeks. But before I could comfort her and assure her that we were all safe, I heard a thud behind me, followed by a splash and the sound of someone slurping water. Joel had thrown himself at the stream, his bag discarded on the bank.

"Joel, what the heck are you doing? You can't drink that! We're in the city!" I sped to where he crouched, his clean-shaven face drenched with water, and I gave his left arm a not-so-gentle nudge as he raised his hands to his lips to drink some more. The water slipped from his fingers, and he lifted his eyes to mine, confusion the primary sentiment on his face now.

"We're back," I said, switching from Teutonica to English when I saw reason return to his eyes. "I don't know how you died to get here, but we're all back now. And you can't just drink water from the stream in my backyard. If you need some that bad, I'm pretty sure there's a thermos in your bag." I nodded once toward it.

"Huh." Joel sounded dazed, and he looked beyond me to where I heard Beth sobbing. "Wait a minute. Is that *Freia?*"

My faithful friend of the eleventh century had drawn my cousin into a hug. I heard her speaking softly but could not discern the words. *And it's not like Beth got the chance to learn Teutonica. She won't understand a word Freia says to her.* I glanced down at my right hand and saw, to my surprise, that I held a roll of parchment in a devil's grip—an item that I had *not* brought with me to the past, so long ago . . . just over a minute ago. *Prince Otto's song came to the future with me . . . how is this possible?*

"Swanie." Joel's voice pulled me from my jumbled reverie. He had retrieved the thermos from his bag, his expression appearing relieved when he peered at the water inside. "How in the world did you bring Freia to the future? Did you learn some crazy Teutonic magic that we didn't know before? Necromancy maybe?"

"Well . . . ." I could not think of what to say. I looked from Joel's face to the parchment in my right hand. "Freia can tell you. I need to go help Beth." I felt a blush rising in my cheeks as I turned away from him. Joel had been my husband for fifteen years in the eleventh century, and he knew full well that I had never loved him. We had married to protect the secrets of the future; but here in June 2000, he was my cousin's boyfriend of two years.

And my cousin had died a gruesome death just minutes before, according to her internal clock, a victim of a Gypsy's spear. I knew that I needed to soothe her, but I feared what would come once she learned of all that she had missed. Twenty-two years of "adventure" in the Middle Ages, most of them loaded with boredom and pregnancies. But I had certainly uncovered a plethora of information that the history books—even the Teutonic ones—ignored. *And I learned how it feels to love a Teuton priest who treated me like an equal . . . .*

"Freia," I said, my voice breaking on her name as memories of Augustin inundated my mind again. Freia looked up at me from where she sat with one arm wrapped gently around Beth's shoulders. I gritted my teeth and tried to shove my worries aside long enough to get the current situation under control. "Could you . . . go tell Joel what happened right before we got here? And make sure he doesn't drink anything else from the stream. I need to talk to my cousin." I offered her the Prince's song, my fingers hesitant to loose their grip on it. My left hand was still clenched into a tense fist.

"I can," Freia replied, accepting the parchment and rising to her feet. Her eyes had returned to their natural green. "How are your feet?" she asked me, her gaze drifting down to the hem of my red-violet dress.

I shook my head and heard myself chuckle. "As fine as they were when I was twenty years old," I observed, waving Freia away so I could concentrate on Beth. As she departed, I wiggled my toes inside my leather shoes, surprised and relieved at the lack of pain the movement produced. *I'm twenty years old again, but my mind is forty-two . . . and my heart . . . .* Vaguely, I heard Freia unrolling the parchment and telling Joel softly in Teutonica that Prince Otto had granted me the Song of Time just as the Saxons had overrun Muniche.

I knelt down to my cousin's level, working to shove aside the sensation of Muniche's spirit rejoicing within me—for her city triumphed now, its dark days long gone. *Muniche, you need to shut up,* I thought, just in case the spirit of my city was an actual entity that might heed its female representative's wishes. *I'm glad you're alive and well, and it's nice that you found me worthy of taking my mentor's place. But it would have been nicer if you'd let me go while I writhed in the currents of time, to be honest.*

Beth blotted her tears on the square of tawny fabric that she had pinned to her hair in preparation for our journey. Her brown eyes locked with mine, and I felt traces of ice seeping into my blood in response to my anxiety. How could I bring myself to tell her everything? Where could I possibly start?

"Swanie . . . did you get to Joel . . . before those freaks killed him?"

I shut my eyes for a moment, trying to keep myself in the present. Right now, I needed to reassure my cousin. The last thing she had said before she died in the eleventh century was to help Joel; her brain was still processing that experience. "Yeah, Joel and I got away from them," I said, quirking a smile that felt incredibly forced. I reopened my eyes and looked at Beth's hands. She clutched the fabric of her head covering in her lap. I saw that it was damp with tears.

"And then you opened the gateway again and came back, right?" My cousin's question brought my head up. I looked at her, my forehead wrinkling in bewilderment. "And you brought that lady with you because those men were after her, too?"

I wished more than anything that I could agree with her. "Actually . . . ."

"So . . . this isn't going to be one of those moments where we get back and everything's changed, right?" Joel stood behind me now with Freia at his side. She offered me a wavering smile, as if she had not yet fully come to terms with the fact that she had followed me into the future, a land far different from her own.

"I'm pretty sure that doesn't happen with Teutonic time travel," I responded, my gaze shifting back to Beth. Her hands were busy with her head covering, folding it into a neat square. "The Prince never mentioned anything changing, and he used the song three times. I think you really just become 'a part of history' when you use the Torstein or the song, just like the spell says." The Teuton historians should have clarified that. Instead, they had left things open-ended to terrify time travelers.

"Were you worried that you changed something when you killed that one guy?" Beth asked, looking from Joel's face to mine.

I had not realized that Beth had seen me kill the Gypsy who had stabbed her. An odd bubble of laughter spilled from my lips. "That's hardly the worst thing I did in the past," I muttered.

"Swanie, there's someone standing in the trees, watching us," Freia put in, closed out of my dialogue with Beth and Joel due to her ignorance of English. She pointed toward the trail to my father's house, then appended in a low voice, "He probably wonders who I am."

I circled around slowly, my ice cooling my veins afresh when I saw Hans standing rigid at the entrance to the path. His priestly robes swept the ground, his graying hair appearing silver in the moonlight, his stricken expression suggesting that he had heard and understood every word the four of us had spoken since our emergence from the gates. We had been here at the banks of the stream for almost five minutes now, quite likely, and none of us had bothered to acknowledge Hans' presence. The insanity of the moment hit me as my blood pulsed with ice: *I once loved Hans . . . considered his kiss the pinnacle of earthly glory . . . but now . . . .*

Beth climbed to her feet at last, and I stepped forward, gesturing for my three companions to follow. Then I nodded once at Hans and spoke the necessary introductions in Teutonica with all of the propriety I had learned in medieval Muniche. "Hans, allow me to present my best friend of the eleventh century, Lady Freia Denlinger von

Eisenwald. Freia, my father's chief servant—and the Teuton priest whose lessons brought me to your time—Herr Johannes Meissner."

Freia smiled brilliantly at Hans and curtseyed, which prompted Hans to blink, his eyes darkening with black fire when he bowed at her in return. I sensed my cousin's uneasiness; she looked at me with a blank expression, probably still thinking that we were about to return to those tornadic currents. I suddenly remembered that Beth and Joel were scheduled to fly back to Philadelphia at nine a.m. tomorrow. *They need to get some rest, and Freia does, too.*

I addressed Hans again, this time in English, asking him to show my three companions back to the house so I could have some space to think. "Freia can stay in my room. I'll be there eventually." Hans made a sound of acknowledgement and stepped forward to take up two of the bags. Beth narrowed her eyes at me, her right hand clasped in Joel's left. His face looked drawn, his posture implying that he did not particularly wish to be close with his twenty-first century girlfriend. *And I'm leaving him on his own to deal with the fact that he has Teuton blood now, the thing Beth has long desired.*

I felt no sympathy for him.

Beth started prodding Joel with questions as they left me by the gazebo, and I took a deep breath and focused on the cool night air, silently asking it to soothe me, to clear my mind so I could figure out this mess. I heard Freia's voice drifting quietly along the breeze, asking what had become of my bond with Augustin. I shifted my gaze to her, where she stood at my side with her bag tucked beneath her left arm, her expression concerned. "I don't know," I whispered.

After they had all gone, I opened my left fist for the first time since I had burst through the gates—and there, in my palm, lay the Torstein.

To be continued . . . .

Book IV comes out in December 2021
Order now from your preferred platform!

C.L. Carhart would be thrilled if you would leave a review for this book. Reviews help buoy an indie author's career, as well as her spirits. She appreciates your feedback!

Sign up for C.L. Carhart's newsletter for an inside look at her author undertakings, along with information on new releases and the occasional secret deal.
https://sendfox.com/clcarhart1066

Astral Fantasia is available on library platforms! Ask your local library to order it in eBook and paperback so that C.L. can reach more readers.

Follow C.L. on social media:
https://www.facebook.com/CLCarhartAuthor
https://www.instagram.com/c.l.carhart.author
https://www.minds.com/clcarhart/
https://www.bookbub.com/profile/c-l-carhart

Teutonica Translations

Aelte Teutonica – old Teutonica, used in the B.C.E. years
Der Weg Teutonisch – The Teutonic Way
Eihalbe/Eihalbae – singular/plural, fairy of silver oak
Elle – the length of a man's elbow to the tip of his middle
　　finger, a cubit
Gæstelort Troumerae – spiritual dream world
Leitaeri – Prince/Keyholder of a Teuton city
Teutona – female Teuton
Teutonica – old Teuton dialect
Thaler – medieval Teuton currency
Torstein – stone of the gate
Toteheri – dead army
Wazzar – water
Wuotan – demon lord of the Teuton people
Zoubaraera – witch

Medieval Hours of Muniche

Vigils – midnight
Matins – 2 a.m.
Lauds – sunrise
Terce – 9 a.m.
Sext – 12 noon
None – 3 p.m.
Vespers – lighting of lamps/dusk
Compline – before bed (dark)

Pronunciation Guide
(for names and commonly used words)

Abelard – AB-uh-lard
Adeline – Ad-uh-LEE-nuh
Augustin – Au-GUS-tin
Bayerisch – BEYE-rish (eye is pronounced like eyeball)
Bayern – BEYE-urn (eye is pronounced like eyeball)
Dane – DAH-nuh
Der Weg – Dare Veg
Eihalbe – EYE-hahl-buh (eye is pronounced like eyeball)
Fonsi – FON-zee
Freia – FREYE-yuh (eye is pronounced like eyeball)
Ina – EE-nuh
Isar – EE-zahr
Jarvis – YAR-viss
Leitaeri – Leye-TARE-ee (eye is pronounced like eyeball)
Leitalra – Leye-TAHL-rah (eye is pronounced like eyeball)
Muniche – MYOO-nih-khuh
None – Nohn
Swanhilde – Swan-HIL-duh
Thaden – TODD-n
Thaler – TAHL-er
Torstein – TOR-stein (stein is pronounced like a beer
    stein)
Toteheri – TOH-tuh-hare-ee
Traudl – TROW-dool (trow is pronounced like cow)
Teutonica – Too-TAHN-ih-kuh
Wuotan – VOH-tahn

About the Author

C.L. Carhart has been writing since the age of 4, dabbling in everything from children's books, to fantasy, to historical fiction. Eventually, her lifelong interest in European history inspired her to create a paranormal fantasy realm based on the Teutonic people groups. The *His Name Was Augustin* series provides a first glimpse at this other-world—a place rife with ancient mysteries and dark magic.

Born and raised in southern New Jersey, C.L. spends her free time hiking with her husband, enjoying metal music, snuggling her feline familiars, and dreaming of the wonders of Germany.